THE DICTATOR'S
REVENGE

A NOVEL

PAUL SHEMELLA

PAGE PUBLISHING, INC.
Conneaut Lake, PA

First originally published by Page Publishing 2021

ISBN 978-1-6624-4024-3 (pbk)
ISBN 978-1-6624-4026-7 (hc)
ISBN 978-1-6624-4025-0 (digital)

Printed in the United States of America

For Charlie and Tina

CHAPTER 1

August 1993

Oscar Castillo parked in the visitor's lot, turned off the engine, and sat back. He took a deep breath and considered what he was doing at an American prison. The man got out of his Avis rental car and locked it with the key fob. He ran a finger between his double chin and white collar to let in some humid air. He was already sweating. Black pants and shirt simply absorbed the sun. Florida heat was exactly the same as Panama heat. He should have felt at home, but he did not. Father Castillo was a man on a delicate mission.

He was about to hear the confession of Manuel Noriega.

Castillo walked slowly into the waiting room of Miami's Federal Correctional Institution, the low-security facility where the US government had deposited General Noriega more than three years before. Glancing furtively at the men, women, and children waiting patiently for their own prisoner visits, he approached the front desk and took out a letter. As if to ensure that he was actually supposed to be there, Castillo examined the signature. It was his authorization to meet with Noriega, signed by the director of the Federal Bureau of Prisons.

"Good morning, Father, what can we do for you today?" asked the official behind the counter.

"I am here to see General Noriega," replied Castillo in perfect English. "This is the letter that authorizes my visit." He extended the document to the polite middle-aged Latina, along with his picture identification. She tapped her computer and found his name.

"The general will be with you shortly, Father. You will meet with him in the deputy administrator's office," she said, pointing to her left. "Please wait here until someone takes you in."

Castillo moved a few paces away and sat down on a metal chair. He was a large man, not obese but too large for the chair. After a few minutes, he got up and paced the lobby. Moving around was a way to dissipate his nervous energy, but it was also to keep from freezing. It was too cold inside *every* building in Florida. Air-conditioning was a modern curse.

Fifteen minutes later, Castillo was greeted by two armed guards in warden uniforms. Motioning to the door leading further inside, they flanked him as he turned to follow. "This way, Father," said one of the men too seriously. His partner regarded the priest with an eye of caution. Castillo was used to receiving certain deference for his position. He did not get it here.

The guards led Castillo through a metal detector, stamping an ultraviolet ink spot on his hand. The priest carried only a Bible, which the guards did not open. They showed him into the cleanest office the Panamanian had ever seen. No papers lying around. No family pictures were displayed behind the bare wooden desk. Two metal chairs. Cardboard filing boxes were neatly stacked in metal cabinets against the side walls. Opaque shades were drawn, except for one window facing him. A second door at the back of the room. The priest had seen confessionals with more charm.

Castillo sat while the guards left the room. A few minutes later, they returned, escorting a reasonably fit short man with a pock-marked face. Wearing a pressed Panama Defense Forces uniform, the prisoner projected confidence—even here. In almost a hushed tone, one of the guards directed the former general to sit down across from Father Castillo. Manuel Antonio Noriega, Bible in hand, sat at attention and smiled at his old friend Oscar.

"*¿Qué tal, amigo?*" asked Noriega. It was a question the priest had wanted to ask the prisoner.

Castillo replied, "*Así, así.*" Indeed, both men were okay—but not especially happy with their circumstances.

"Cold enough for you?" asked the general, continuing in Spanish with uncharacteristic sarcasm.

Oscar Castillo laughed out loud. "Hell is not fire and brimstone after all. Hell is icy cold!"

"Amen," said Noriega. "You should have brought a sweater!"

Castillo nodded vigorously but nervously, hoping the session would not last too long. Noriega disguised his own fear, a skill he had perfected during a calculated rise to power. He was aware that his "confession" would be tape-recorded by the prison staff and shared with the American agencies that had incarcerated him. He thought they probably had a video camera running as well, but he couldn't see it.

"Thank you for coming all this way, Father. I wanted you to hear my confession so that I can take communion at the Catholic Mass celebrated here at the prison next Sunday." Noriega hesitated long enough for those listening to understand what he had just said. "I have a lot to tell you."

Castillo leaned forward. "But, General, you could have asked any number of priests to hear your confession." He let the statement hang in the air. "Why me?"

"Because I know you," continued Noriega. "We are both Panamanian...and *criollo.*" The priest watched as the general—whom he still considered the legitimate head of the Panamanian state—placed his Bible on the table between them. Noriega had lost his country but not his command voice. Even mixed with friendly banter, he conveyed an intimidating air of authority. "I also wanted to trade Bibles with you. Mine is old and worn. Yours is brand new. I have plenty of time to study scripture."

Castillo struggled to avoid betraying his surprise. Noriega had never been a strict Catholic. In fact, the general had long hedged his spiritual bets by practicing several religions, including *Santería.* But the priest was encouraged by what he heard. Perhaps Manuel

Antonio had undergone an epiphany in prison. The Bible had saved many prisoners on this earth, even those who never made it out of prison. Castillo placed his own Bible on the table.

"I would be honored to take your Bible home with me, Tony." He handed his book to Noriega and accepted his old friend's book in return.

"Thank you, Oscar." Noriega finally relaxed a bit, placing his hands under his chin. "You will note that I have highlighted my favorite verses, especially *Romans 8:31.*"

The prisoner recited the passage that had enabled him to persevere against overwhelming depression.

"If God be for us, who can be against us?"

Oscar Castillo opened Noriega's Bible to the correct page. Inserted inside the book was a thin white envelope with the name "Jorge" scrawled in pen. He quickly closed the Bible. The priest's hands were shaking.

Both men noticed; the prison officials, watching and listening, did not.

Noriega locked eyes with Castillo. "I would like you to thank Jorge for his support... I did not have time when they took me away."

"Of course, I will, Tony... Are you ready to confess your sins?"

"I am."

Castillo withdrew a white satin stole from his pocket and draped it around his neck. "Then let us begin."

Without hesitation, Noriega crossed himself, beginning the dialogue he had learned as a child and never forgotten.

"Bless me, Father, for I have sinned. My last confession was three years, seven months, and eighteen days ago...shortly before I was kidnapped by the war criminal George Bush."

Father Castillo now understood that this would be no ordinary confession.

"And what are your sins?"

Noriega took a deep breath. Castillo secretly wished his chair were more comfortable.

"I cheated on my wife."

"Okay," said the priest, letting the word linger for a long second. "What else?"

"I failed in my leadership responsibilities."

"How is that?"

"I did not anticipate an American invasion. It made no sense for the *gringos* to gang up on Panama. The war they launched on December 20, 1989, was the greatest example of overkill in military history." Noriega drew a quick breath and resumed his confession. "I did nothing wrong, but I was stupid and naive. I allowed the Americans to misunderstand me." The general hesitated then added, "Of course, there were traitors on my own staff feeding me bad information… They collaborated with Bush's people."

Rather than indulging the temptation to soothe his friend's conscience, Castillo pressed on, "And what other sins have you committed?" He almost called Manuel Noriega "my son." That part of the dialogue just didn't fit.

"My failure led to the deaths of Panamanian civilians…lots of them."

The priest thought about this before speaking. *Military commanders must always feel this way.* He wondered how God felt about it. Castillo had no experience with which to evaluate Noriega's admission. Both of them would have to pray for the Lord's forgiveness; the general because he was responsible, and the priest because he was incapable of assigning penance for a sin he did not understand.

"You are *responsible* for their deaths, but you did not kill them."

Noriega smiled in the way that had made it easy for his enemies to call him evil. "*Si, por supuesto*, the Americans actually killed them. They bombed the *Chorillo* neighborhood, Panama City's poorest, and set it on fire." The smile disappeared. "And what do you think God will do about that?"

Castillo groped for a suitable response. Now under pressure, he quickly found one. "God has been judging military commanders since the beginning of civilization, my friend. He will know what to do. I think you can live with your conscience until you meet him."

"And you think I will see God after I die?"

"Yes, Manuel Antonio. Unlike the Americans, God will judge you fairly."

This was a confession way off track, but Castillo now understood perfectly that Noriega's request for confession had more to do with politics than with God. Nevertheless, the priest thought he could provide a useful service after all. Who knew? Perhaps Manuel Antonio would be able to sleep better on his stainless steel bed.

"They accused me of trafficking drugs. I never did that."

"I know," replied the priest. "You had your country's best interests at heart."

"Yes," said the general. "I was always governing with Omar's image in my head. Torrijos wanted to make *Panamá* a more equal society, to reduce the power of the *rabiblancos* and lift up the people who look like us. I realized right after Omar's death that I could not improve the lives of ordinary Panamanians by simply taking money away from the rich White families. Torrijos got us started by negotiating the canal treaties, but that was not enough, soon enough, to bring prosperity. I had to build a stronger economy quickly, and for that, we needed a banking system that would attract capital from throughout the region. I made *Panamá* a great place to do business."

"Omar Torrijos was a gift from God," asserted the priest.

"Yes, he was, Oscar. I was humbled to be the man to begin finishing his social project."

Castillo pulled an image of the Torrijos mausoleum at Fort Amador into his mind. "Omar said he did not want to go into the history books...only into the Canal Zone. He did both."

"Yes," affirmed Noriega with a smile. "Six and a half years from now, Panama will be fully sovereign...but with the wrong people in power."

Castillo wanted to change the subject, to get back to confessing sins rather than mistakes. But he couldn't figure out how to do that, so he just continued the conversation.

"And part of your social project was to make the defense forces stronger, *verdad*?"

"*Si*," replied the general. "The *rabiblancos* had all the real power, and they were still puppets of the Americans. To change the social order, *Panamá* needed a firmer hand. Omar was too nice to everyone, including those who opposed us. He converted the national police into a national guard. I transformed the national guard into a capable defense force. I am very proud of that. We were ready to *work* with the Americans to guarantee the neutrality of the canal. We were not ready to fight a *war* with the United States. They betrayed the trust we had placed in them when we signed the treaties. Starting with Reagan, the American right wing tried to *reverse* the treaties. They wanted the canal back, and I would not let them have it."

Castillo listened with a more-than-sympathetic ear. Long ago, he had been labeled by the Americans as a "radical priest." *They only see things as good or evil. Dualism died a long time ago, but they didn't get the memo.* Oscar Castillo was on the CIA's watch list for his social-ist—even communist—leanings.

"You were right to oppose them."

"I also opposed their wars in Central America. I did not help them kill our Latin brothers. They hated me for that."

The priest nodded to the cadence of injustice and called out, "¡*Exacto*! You did the right thing again…in God's eyes as well."

"I think I've told you enough of my sins, Father. Here I sit as an American prisoner of war, but that is a *political* penance. Please tell me, what is my *spiritual* penance?"

Castillo was happy this would soon be over. But what pen-ance could he give Manuel Noriega that would improve the man's interrupted life? The only sin Oscar recognized was the first one. He knew from long experience that most Latin husbands cheated on their wives. It was still a sin, but not something to send a man to hell.

"Say ten *Our Fathers* and ten *Hail Marys*."

"Is that all?"

"And continue to read your Bible."

"I appreciate you're giving me a new one, Father."

Noriega stood up and walked around the desk to embrace a now-standing Castillo. Oscar wrapped his arms around the dictator as he'd hugged his own father.

"Bless you, Tony, and go with God."

Noriega signaled to the guards he knew were watching from behind. They came at once to escort him back to his tiny quarters, isolated from the main prison population. Castillo turned, left the room, and returned to the front desk to check out.

The priest strode into the Florida heat. After an hour of refrigeration, it almost knocked him down. He walked slowly to the car with a deep sense of dread. Sitting there in the parking lot, with Noriega's Bible in his lap, Father Castillo knew what he would have to do. His return plane ticket to Panama would have to be changed for a ticket to Pasto, Colombia. Outside that city—in a large guarded compound—lived "Jorge" Mena Velasquez, the most ruthless and powerful drug lord in Latin America. Noriega's friend; Castillo's nightmare. Manuel Noriega had given Castillo a letter to deliver; the priest had responded with a solemn promise.

Oscar Castillo prayed for God's protection. He was going to need it.

CHAPTER 2

OSCAR CASTILLO LOOKED down on the city of *San Juan de Pasto*, sprawling in the shadow of the *Las Galeras* volcano. The astonishing beauty of the setting did not ease his mounting anxiety. Castillo was about to carry Noriega's letter to the leader of the richest drug cartel in Latin America. A violent man. A sinful man. A man he had met only once but would never forget. Jorge Mena Velasquez would not remember their encounter in Panama City all those years ago. But that was not the biggest problem the priest would have to deal with. Mena was surrounded by spies and bodyguards, heavily armed and authorized to shoot anyone who might threaten the boss. Oscar would have to *find* the kingpin without becoming one of the bodies piling up under the Colombian sun. As the plane landed hard on Pasto's high-altitude runway, Father Castillo looked to the darkening heavens for guidance on how to pull this off.

God was not in a talkative mood. The priest was on his own.

Still in his white-collared black uniform, Castillo walked slowly across the tarmac toward the terminal, wheeling a small carry-on bag behind him. Manuel Antonio's Bible had not been out of his sight since he'd left the Miami prison earlier in the day. The reluctant messenger stopped to catch his breath and shivered from the cold. He longed for sea level and the Panama heat. Once inside, Castillo fought the urge to book the first flight out of Colombia. But he had no idea when he would be going home. Or *if* he would be going home. The rosary beads in his pocket offered some reassurance on that matter. At the moment, however, he needed a conduit, someone who might know where Mena could be approached safely…and how?

God will protect me…but who will direct me?

The church, of course! Castillo knew that even drug dealers attended Mass (especially if they were acting out a legitimate lifestyle). That's how he'd met Jorge Mena in Panama City. There were many Catholic churches in the Pasto area…too many. Which one served the man he was seeking? As he walked to the rental car desk, Oscar tried to remember the name of a priest he'd worked with at a conference years ago in Managua. *Wasn't that guy from Pasto?* Racking his brains as he sat in the rental, Father Castillo finally came up with the name. Now what he needed was a hotel room and an internet connection.

Oscar found a comfortable room at the finest hotel in Pasto. He'd once been told (as a joke, he thought) that terrorists might blow up the best hotel in town but that the drug barons would probably own it. With a sharp sense of irony, Castillo felt safe here. He took a hot shower and washed off the smell of fear that had permeated his clothes. The hotel's business center offered him a better way to find people than did the phone book in his room. If Father Roberto Santiago still maintained a flock in Pasto, Castillo now had the capability to find him. After a cup of strong Colombian coffee, the priest went downstairs and got to work.

It did not take long. Not all the churches had websites. For those that did, he started in the center of the city and worked his way outward. When he got to *El Sanctuario de Las Lajas*, the name Roberto Santiago jumped off the page under a stunning photo of the Gothic church. Known as a miracle of God in the abyss, the elaborate structure was situated on and over the *Guáitara* River near Ipiales, more than seventy kilometers from his hotel. He inquired at the front desk and was told it would take him around ninety minutes to drive the route. Returning to the computer, he was reminded that the church was a pilgrimage site, visited by fervent believers from all over the world. Castillo had never been there.

It was time to become a pilgrim, albeit for a different reason.

He slept fitfully, jolted awake every hour to gasp for breath in the thin mountain air. On top of that, Castillo worried about what he would learn from Father Santiago. Under no circumstances would Father Castillo explain *why* he needed to meet with the drug lord. Some priests couldn't be trusted. After all, the Papal *Nuncio* had betrayed Manuel Antonio's trust and simply handed him over to the Americans. Oscar was terrified that he might actually *find* the drug lord. If Santiago could lead him to Jorge Mena, Castillo would fulfill his obligation to deliver Noriega's letter. If his colleague could not help him, Oscar would be on the first plane back to Panama. Inside his head, loyalty fought with reason. So far, loyalty was winning.

* * *

Castillo decided to visit the sanctuary without calling ahead (Father Santiago would not remember him without seeing his face). Just after breakfast, wearing a fresh white collar, he was coasting down the Pan-American Highway through rugged but very green terrain. *Las Galeras* sent a white plume of ash into the bluest sky he had ever seen. The broad vistas reminded him of his home province of *Chiriquí*. For the first time since he'd listened to Noriega's confession, Oscar Castillo felt optimism. Indeed, he drew strength from the stunning landscape. God was with him…at least for now.

The church fitted right into the scenery, almost like a Gothic Frank Lloyd Wright house. Castillo found himself thinking that Wright might have been inspired by the design. There was a bridge across the river leading to the front of the edifice. A moat, protecting God's castle. Oscar walked quickly across the bridge. Not a pilgrim. Not a tourist. He went right to the rectory, stopping a random resident priest at the entrance.

"Excuse me, Father, I am Father Oscar Castillo from *Panamá*. Can you tell me where I can find Father Roberto Santiago?"

The Colombian priest smiled and shook Oscar's hand with both of his own. "I am Father Ordóñez… Come with me."

They walked into the residence and down the hall. There at the end of the passageway was an office with an open door. The plaque beside the doorframe bore the name of the man who could perhaps tell Castillo where to find the cartel leader.

Father Ordoñez leaned in to address the older man behind the desk. "*Monsignor*, there is a priest from *Panamá* here to see you."

The senior cleric rose from his chair. "Show him in, Father."

Entering the office, Oscar bowed slightly. "I am Father Oscar Castillo, Your Grace. I wanted to ask for your assistance in locating someone in the greater Pasto community."

Santiago dismissed Ordoñez and motioned for Castillo to sit in the large chair next to the desk. "I think I have seen you before, Father."

"Yes, you have… It was in Managua at the conference of Catholic leadership around four years ago."

"Ah…yes," replied Santiago. "I remember you, and I thought later that year about the pain you must have been going through as a result of the *Yanquí* invasion." He shook his head back and forth. "Such a waste."

"Indeed," Castillo responded. Not wanting to get into a political discussion, he changed the subject. "But I wanted to ask you about this church. It is a pilgrimage site. I am sorry to say I have never been here."

Father Santiago's eyes caught fire. Castillo felt he was in the presence of a true man of God as the elder priest demonstrated his passion for history. "My name preordained me to become fascinated with pilgrimage. Even as a child, I was captivated by the story of Saint James and his journey to *Santiago de Compostela*."

"Another pilgrimage I am embarrassed to say I have never made," interrupted Castillo. "My poverty is not an excuse for failing to visit Spain."

"You must go someday, my friend." Santiago regarded his visitor's bulk. "And you should walk as far along *El Camino de Santiago* as you are able."

"Yes, I promise you, I will do that." Castillo smiled. "Even though I am fat."

Santiago laughed softly then suddenly changed his tone. "So you have come to this sanctuary to seek one of my flock?" He sat straighter at the desk. "And who might that be?"

The Panamanian lowered his voice even though there was nobody else in the room. He thought of this meeting as a form of confession. "Before I tell you that, you must promise me that you will not tell *anyone* the name of the man I am seeking."

"Of course," said Santiago. "I am, after all, a priest."

Castillo signaled his understanding with a nod of the head. "I am looking for Jorge Mena Velasquez."

Not an inkling of surprise crossed the Monsignor's face. Roberto Santiago, thought Castillo, could have been a great poker player.

"And may I ask why you seek him?"

"No, respectfully, you may not," said Castillo without hesitation. "I am bound by the confidentiality of the confessional."

"I see," said Santiago without smiling. "Well, if you're still here on Saturday, you can find him in *San Juan de Pasto*. He will be there dedicating a new hospital for underprivileged children that bears his name."

Oscar Castillo tried not to be shocked. The surge of electricity in his limbs gave way to a pragmatic realization that such a gesture made perfect sense. The brutal drug lord—a prolific murderer, to be sure—*needed* a nonthreatening persona. A popular image to shield him from the judicial reckoning he deserved. Also, a way to launder some of his dirty money. Did he even care about the kids? Perhaps, thought Castillo, but God would judge the drug lord, not the humanitarian alter ego.

"That is wonderful news," said Castillo somberly.

"Do you need a place to stay for a few days, Father?" asked Santiago. "You can sleep here in the rectory if you wish. We have a spare room."

"Yes, thank you," responded the Panamanian. "That would be perfect. I need some time to relax and pray."

Monsignor Roberto Santiago rose and embraced Oscar Castillo. "Welcome to our brotherhood, Father. You will get plenty of relaxation and prayer before Saturday."

Wednesday was half over, but it would be a long wait. Relaxation was out of the question. Prayer would be his mental sanctuary.

* * *

Castillo sat on the uncomfortable bed across from a bare wooden desk. Noriega's Bible called to him. The sealed letter inside teased him. The priest was so tempted to open the good book and read the letter that he had to pray hard for the strength not to do it. Oscar understood that he would be asked by the murderer whether he knew what the letter said. He prayed that the murderer would believe him. But still, he agonized over what was waiting in Noriega's Bible—not just a benign note of thanks, to be sure. The eyes of his childhood friend had told him otherwise. The priest considered just burning the letter and pretending he had not promised Manuel Antonio he would deliver it.

But Oscar Castillo could not do that. He was a loyal friend and a man of God.

For four nights, he had slept (poorly) in the rectory, walking daily through the forest and over the rocks near the sanctuary. On Saturday morning, he drove to Pasto and located the hospital dedication ceremony. It was not difficult. A large crowd had gathered in front of the new building, waiting for *Señor Mena* to arrive and cut the red ribbon strung across the pillared entrance. Castillo parked as close as he could to the sea of poor but clean children and their hopeful parents. He then walked to the back of the crowd. The mayor and his staff were there, representing a grateful government. Signs and flags added to the effect.

A rock star was coming.

A black limousine parted the crowd in front of Castillo. The heavy car stopped at the ribbon. Four large men, all dressed in the same black suits, got out and formed a cordon. Even from his vantage point, Castillo could see that the men were concealing weapons under their jackets. Each bodyguard watched the gathering through dark sunglasses. Jorge Mena Velasquez got out of the car and stood facing the crowd. A cheer went up, and the great man raised his hand.

18

The mayor stepped to the microphone and gave a brief introduction. Then Mena made a short speech about how he had risen from childhood poverty to become a successful businessman. Castillo noted that the kingpin did not mention *which* business. He was actually impressed with Mena's speaking style. The murderer sounded like a caring benefactor, giving back to the community.

Oscar Castillo—deliberately looking very much like a Catholic priest—worked his way through the crowd until he stood at the rope separating the onlookers from the event. *Señor Mena* cut the ribbon, and the ceremony was suddenly over. As the fat man strode quickly back to his limo, Castillo leaned over the rope and clasped his hands under his chin, where Mena's goons could see them.

"Sir, I would like one minute of your time." Castillo's shouted request was so unexpected that Mena's men froze momentarily. They did not know what to do with an inquisitive priest at the head of a jubilant throng. Their boss came to the rescue.

"And who are you?" asked Mena in a threatening tone, hurrying to get in the car. The priest felt a wave of nausea crash over his body as the guards frisked him rather too roughly.

"I am Father Oscar Castillo from *Panamá*, and I have a letter to give you."

Mena shot a quick nod to his bodyguards, and Castillo found himself sitting in the back of the car next to the man he feared so much. Mena turned to him. "Okay, Father, make it quick."

Castillo knew that his next few sentences would determine whether or not he ever made it back to Panama. He would have to say *something* to the drug lord, and it would have to be the truth. Castillo was incapable of lying. He was first of all a priest, but it was more than that. He sweated easily. Whether it was a lingering guilt or some undefined medical syndrome, his face would instantly reveal any deception at all. The tight white collar did not make his condition any easier to conceal.

Castillo opened his Bible and took out the letter. He handed it to Mena and blurted out one sentence. "Manuel Antonio asked me to give you this."

Without saying anything, Mena took the letter and tore it open. He read it as Castillo sat there staring straight ahead. It was a short letter, written carefully in pencil.

> Jorge,
>   I have treated you well over the years, and it is time to pay me back. There is $50M sitting in the National Bank of Grand Cayman (account no. 378948275). Take this money and destroy the Panama Canal. If you are successful, there will be an additional $50M for you in another account (I will give you that number through an intermediary). Executing this operation will be good for your business. Panama's banks and the Darién rainforest will remain available to you. If I cannot have the canal, then nobody can. I do not care anymore.
>
>   Manuel Antonio

When the kingpin was finished, he turned slowly to Castillo. Mena did not have a commanding voice like Noriega, but his frightening eyes cut right through the priest's affected calm.

"Have you read this letter?" asked Mena in a rhetorical tone. "It would have been easy to steam it open and glue it back together."

"No, sir, I have not read the letter." Castillo took a big gulp. "Neither did my friend Tony tell me what was in it." *So far, so good.*

"Have you told anyone else that you were looking for me?"

Castillo swallowed hard again. He had not anticipated this question. "Only *Monsignor Roberto Santiago* at *Las Lajas* sanctuary. That is how I knew you would be here today. I did not tell him why."

"And you told no one else?"

"I swear to you in front of the Lord that I have not."

Jorge Mena Velasquez waved his hand, abruptly dismissing Castillo. The priest could not get away from the man and his bodyguards fast enough. Landing hard behind the wheel of his rental, he drove directly to the airport and flew back to Panama City.

* * *

Oscar Castillo spent the next few weeks doing paperwork, administering to neighborhood parishioners and celebrating Mass. The satanic eyes of Jorge Mena Velasquez still haunted him, but the priest had started to believe that he was out of harm's way. He had stopped looking over his shoulder and was beginning to recover his optimism—until a few days later. Sitting in his quiet office, drinking a cup of robust Panamanian coffee, he was bludgeoned by the front page of *La Prensa*.

Colombian Priest Killed

> The bloody corpse of *Monsignor* Roberto Santiago was found yesterday morning in his quarters at the *Las Lajas Sanctuario* near Pasto, Colombia. The killer entered the church's rectory during the night and shot the priest in his sleep. The murder weapon appears to have been a 9mm automatic pistol, perhaps with a silenced barrel. Police are said to have commented off the record that this gruesome act has all the hallmarks of an organized crime assassination. There is no evidence that Father Santiago, a beloved figure recognized by the Vatican for his service, was involved in any way with criminals in the area. *La Prensa* will continue to update the Panamanian public on this tragedy as new details emerge.

He couldn't breathe! He was sweating profusely. He ran to the bathroom and vomited into the toilet. He cried out in desperation. *Lord…how could you let this happen?* The priest tried to compose himself. Unconsciously, he looked over his shoulder again. So he was not out of danger…not by a long shot. Roberto Santiago had been murdered for merely *knowing* that Castillo was meeting with the drug lord. Mena's *sicarios* would come for him too; there was nothing he could do. Oscar had known all along that he should have read Noriega's letter (he would have destroyed it right away if he had). But that was no way to treat a friend. Oscar Castillo was going to heaven; there was no doubt about that.

Timing was now the issue.

CHAPTER 3

September 1993

FREDDY ALEGRE STOOD at the transom of the pilot boat and watched the lights of the *Hanjin* container ship glide into the Caribbean Sea. He could feel the pressure of the last ten hours leaving his body, replaced by extreme fatigue. Only the pride that comes with a job well done kept him on his feet. In Freddy's case, the job had been to pilot the huge commercial ship through the Panama Canal without a scratch. He was going home to get just enough sleep to do it again the day after tomorrow. The night sky was a thick carpet of stars stretching to the eastern horizon. A balmy evening in paradise. Freddy found himself wondering how life could get any better.

Alegre climbed into the Panama Canal Commission's shuttle bus and began the two-hour ride to his home outside Panama City. Now forty-two years old, Freddy felt he could do this job for another decade or so then retire on a pension large enough to keep his wife and two sons comfortable. As demanding as it was, the pilot's job carried more prestige than Freddy's former life as master of a ship the size of those he now guided through the strategic waterway. He could also watch his kids grow up. The American canal pilots, mentors and friends, had trained him well. In a little more than six years, they would transfer all the canal's operations to professional mariners like Manfredo Alegre Rivas.

Soberanía total.

The small bus pulled out of the *Gatún* Locks security zone and onto the Transisthmian Highway, headed toward the Pacific side. The asphalt and concrete road with potholes the size of small cars; they bounced through jungle darkness at forty miles per hour. The driver had traveled this route—the only genuine road between the seas—thousands of times. Freddy, conditioned by years of sleep deprivation, fell asleep to the uneven rhythm of the pavement and Panama *salsa* on the radio. Merchant seamen, he had always said, could sleep anywhere.

Neither he nor the driver heard the muffled explosion around the next bend in the road.

Suddenly, a massive kapok tree, still bouncing from its fall, lay across the pavement, blocking the bus! The driver skidded to a halt just short of the thick trunk, jolting Freddy out of his deep sleep. The radio, weirdly, continued to play *salsa*. Alegre, shaking with adrenaline, reached out and turned it off. The man behind the wheel sat back and exhaled loudly. *That was close!* Unfastening their seat belts, both men exited the bus and moved into the tangle of branches covering the vehicle.

Then they heard the gunfire.

"Get down!" shouted the driver. Alegre ran instead…into the dark of the jungle. Shots rang out behind him. An agonizing scream followed Freddy into the trees. Not looking back, he could hear thundering footfalls and labored breathing.

"*¡Dios mío!*" shouted Alegre, zigzagging through the underbrush. Running blind, he tripped on a root and dived headlong onto the forest floor. As he scrambled to pick himself up, a strong hand gripped his upper arm. The attacker's other hand slammed the barrel of a pistol into his face.

"Come with me, fool!" The assailant spoke a strange version of Spanish. Aided by night-vision goggles, he pulled the pilot to his feet and marched him back to the road.

A Toyota Land Cruiser waited on the other side of the downed tree. Freddy, barely conscious, tried to focus. Two other men stood in the beam of the Toyota's headlights, cradling assault rifles. The shuttle bus's lights were still on, but there was no movement.

The driver must be dead...why am I alive?

The assailant pushed Freddy through the open door and onto the back seat of the Land Cruiser. The others checked their fields of fire then got into the car on both sides of the captive. The man with the pistol sat down behind the wheel and sped into the night—toward Panama City.

"Where are you taking me?" asked Alegre, still in a stupor and shaking uncontrollably. The pilot was looking straight ahead, his hands now restrained with plastic handcuffs.

"Somewhere far from here," replied the driver. "If you give us trouble, we will kill you, just like your driver. If you cooperate, we will let you live."

Freddy slowly held up his bound hands. "Why are you arresting me?" *Panama does not have police who do* this!

"Be glad we didn't shove a sock in your mouth," said the driver without taking his eyes off the jungle road. "There will be checkpoints... You must appear to be one of us. When we are stopped, you will not talk...*entiende?*"

Alegre nodded vigorously in the dark of the crowded back seat. "Yes, I understand." He lowered his hands to his lap. The goon to his right covered the pilot's cuffed hands with a towel.

The Land Cruiser bounced along past Madden Dam. Freddy knew exactly where they were. Madden lake, created after the original construction of the canal, provided a reserve supply of fresh water to operate the locks at the Pacific end. He could not imagine where they were taking him. Most of all, he couldn't imagine why these men had kidnapped a mere canal pilot. He had very little wealth to go with his prestige. Bandits usually went after rich White people, not mixed-race common folk. He glanced at the heavens and thanked the Lord he was still alive.

Whoever these men are, they want *something from me.*

The man behind the wheel drove carefully through the outskirts of the city and then beyond Tocumen International Airport. Freddy could easily guess where they were headed; there was only one road into the east of the country—the jungles of *Darién*. The Pan-American Highway did not connect Panama with Colombia; the *Darién* was simply impassable. But he knew there were many places to loiter along the way. Lawless places. Dangerous places. Places Freddy had never been…and had not expressed any intention of ever going. Now, it seemed, he was being taken to one of them.

But why?

About sixty minutes past the airport, the driver began to slow the vehicle. A checkpoint lay in their path. Freddy Alegre braced for a confrontation. Sandwiched between thugs, he began to pray. *I am going to be caught in the crossfire!* The Americans had destroyed Panama's military, leaving the country with a family of weak law enforcement institutions. After only three years, the *Fuerza Publica* did not inspire confidence in any of Panama's citizens. The cops were still corrupt. Many were incompetent. Freddy knew he was very close to becoming a statistic.

"Remember," said the driver, turning around. "You are one of us… No talking. If you make us kill the *Policía*, we will kill you next!"

Freddy took a deep breath as the Land Cruiser slowed to a stop.

"*¿A donde van?*" asked the middle-aged traffic cop, bending slightly to address the man at the wheel.

"We are going to my mother's house in Yaviza," replied the driver, however unconvincingly. The three unshaven men in the car looked like thugs. The clean-cut man in the middle looked like something else, especially since he was sporting a black eye. The cynical policeman was used to this.

"Please let me see your identification, *señor*."

The driver reached into his breast pocket and produced a forged *cédula*, bundled with a fifty-dollar bill. The document was close enough. The uniformed young man did not even ask to see identification from the others. The Land Cruiser was waved through.

Back up to speed, the vehicle continued toward Yaviza. The town was famous for two things: being, literally, the end of the road…and being the location from which the Spaniard Balboa, following the salty tide, discovered the Pacific Ocean. Freddy Alegre, now wearing a blindfold, guessed they were headed to somewhere near the fortress left in Yaviza by the Spanish.

Suddenly, the driver turned off the highway at Chepo as the sun came up over the San Blas range. Freddy realized they were not going all the way to Yaviza, but where *were* they taking him? As the Land Cruiser bounced along in the dirt, he could not tell which direction they were headed. But if this was indeed a kidnapping-for-ransom, there would have to be a safe house at the end of the road. That is, if they didn't just kill him.

Then the vehicle stopped. It was already hot. One of the thugs next to Freddy rolled down his window. The humid air did not cool him, but the light breeze brought with it the smell of salt water. The same air that had drawn Balboa to his destiny. Freddy Alegre was a seasoned mariner, and he prepared himself for a boat ride. He did not know how *long* a boat ride, but he thought it would be a lot better than sitting in the back seat of a car on a bad road.

Soon—still without sight—he was stumbling over grass and rocks, led by his captors slightly downhill. He could hear the car door slam shut, followed a few seconds later by the unmistakable sound of a heavy vehicle gathering speed and plunging into the water! Freddy now felt even more isolated and alone. On the verge of tears, he thought about all the storms he had endured in the waters of the Bermuda Triangle, where mountainous seas reminded him that he was not the master of his fate. Manfredo Alegre, a practicing Catholic, raised his head to the sky and asked God to throw him a life ring.

"¡*Terminado*!" shouted the driver as he watched the Toyota disappear into the river, signaling the end of the operation's first leg. But Freddy's ordeal was just beginning. His minders helped him into a boat, now waiting at the shoreline. Assuming a crew of two, Alegre thought there must be at least five men transporting him…somewhere. He figured the boat would have to be more than thirty-five feet long, perhaps capable of navigating along the coast. It was obviously a fishing boat; he almost choked on the stench. One of the men fired up two badly tuned inboard gasoline engines, and they began to move.

Freddy thought about his wife and children. The prospect of his own death was not as frightening as the possibility that his wife and children would end up alone. His boys might be denied a role model, just when they needed it the most. He decided that, whatever his kidnappers wanted from him, he would provide it.

This is no time to be a hero.

As the boat chugged along in the smooth water, Freddy still had no idea what they wanted. The thugs did not talk among themselves. He thought they might be sleeping. He was still blindfolded and handcuffed. He sat on the deck with his knees pulled up to his face and tried to calm himself.

After an hour or so, Freddy began to feel the gentle heaving of the sea. He was in his element, but that did not ease his anxiety. He pleaded with his captors to take off the blindfold. He heard nothing back. He tried again—silence. Manfredo Alegre Rivas had gotten used to being in control while afloat. Indeed, control was his *life*. It was difficult—excruciating—to *not* be in charge. He was thirsty. He was exhausted. He was terrified.

At least he was alive…for now.

CHAPTER 4

CARL MALINOWSKI STOOD at loose attention in front of the deputy commander. Rigid attention was not customary for special operations officers, except when receiving awards for bravery. The lieutenant commander's khaki working uniform was neat but not perfect. Colonel Reginald Stewart, whose green jacket was loaded with shiny silver and brass, talked rapidly. Like a machine gun on full automatic.

"We don't know who kidnapped this guy. It could have been organized crime...or disorganized crime. We *do* know that his canal commission shuttle bus was stopped by a fallen tree on the Transisthmian, coming back from *Gatún* Lock this morning in the dark."

"That's a great place for an ambush," interjected Carl. "Sounds like the bad guys know how to use explosives."

"Yeah...and they don't mind shooting people. The driver is dead." Stewart stood up and motioned his operations officer to the map on the wall. "Here's where they grabbed the pilot," said the colonel, pointing to a point on the road halfway between the Caribbean and the Pacific.

"What are you hearing from the Panamanians?" asked Carl. "A canal pilot doesn't fit the profile for a kidnapping-for-ransom crime."

"Right...not rich enough."

"Does SOCSOUTH have a role to play here, sir?" It was a rhetorical question. The Special Operations Command would, of course, have a role to play. The former "Canal Zone" was still effectively controlled by the Americans.

Stewart looked at his best junior officer with a rare smile, gleaming white teeth momentarily lighting up his black face. "And that, commander, is precisely why you're here."

Carl grinned. As the acting operations officer for the joint command, he would take the lead on whatever the Special Operations Command ended up doing. "Where do we start, Colonel?"

"You're the J3, Carl. I'm gonna need an assessment as soon as you can find out more about what's going on. By the end of the day, I will need three things from you, what you know, what you don't know…and what you think."

"Got it, sir. By the way, how's General Duncan?"

"He's pretty sick, Carl. The boss had to be transferred to Walter Reed. Dengue fever is a tough animal to beat. I'll be acting commander here for at least a few more weeks."

Carl left Stewart's office and walked rapidly down the passageway to his cluttered but private office. He knew that the best information on the kidnapping would come from the Panamanians. Sitting down at his messy desk, Carl called a number he had never dialed from the office.

"*Buenos días.*" The answering machine continued in Spanish. "At the tone, please leave your name, number, and the name of the official with whom you wish to speak. That person will call you back."

Carl was speaking to a recording device at the headquarters of the "Technical and Judicial Police" of the *Fuerza Pública*. Knowing his voice would be kept on file, he chose his words carefully.

"This is Lieutenant Commander Carl Malinowski, the J3 at SOCSOUTH. My number is 586-392. I would like to speak to Major Ana Maria Castaneda." He hung up the phone and waited.

It didn't take long. Thirty minutes later, Major Castaneda called back.

"¿*Carlos…qué tal?*" He could see her smiling in his imagination.

"Fine, Ana, I'm good," said Carl in Spanish. "Can you meet me at the usual spot in one hour?"

"*Es posible*," she said, cautiously.

Carl sensed discomfort in the major's voice. She was a former intelligence officer, having a personal conversation on an unclassified government phone. He also sensed her eagerness to see him.

Carl looked at his Rolex. It was 1015. "Okay, see you there."

* * *

Carl read the Panamanian newspaper accounts of the kidnapping. Then he took a shower. The "usual spot" was Ana Maria's small house in the Bella Vista neighborhood of Panama City. Carl and Ana Maria had a yearslong history of information exchange, often mixed with other benefits. In their on-again, off-again symbiosis, Carl had learned a lot about what the Panamanian police knew. The major's other contribution had nothing to do with intelligence. Ana Maria enjoyed having sex, especially with Carl. She was not the most beautiful woman he had ever made love to, but she was certainly the most talented.

It was time to mix business with pleasure again.

Panama City reminded Carl of Miami…but with more drug money. As he drove to the rendezvous, he marveled at the shiny new condo towers, now growing like a rainforest at the edge of the Pacific. Panama's economy was booming, but Carl found himself nostalgic for the old days…until Noriega had ruined everything. Ana Maria had, in fact, worked for the dictator. She and Carl had met in the classroom at Florida State University, Panama Branch, at the beginning of 1989. Ana Maria had enrolled in a bachelor's degree program, made available to Panamanian students as a means to strengthen ties between the two countries. Carl had gone there to audit a course on Latin American foreign policy. Too busy getting to know each other, they hadn't learned much about Latin America.

Having observed his arrival from the window, she opened the door as he started to knock and swept him into her arms. They had not seen each other in three months, so there was a lot of catching up to do. Two hours later, over coffee, they sat at the kitchen table in various stages of undress. The afternoon rain was due. Ripe mangoes fell onto the tin roof. A romantic mood slowly and reluctantly turned serious. Carl felt a bit guilty about having such a good time while working a crisis for Colonel Stewart. But the intelligence business was all about building (and sustaining) relationships. It was okay to enjoy the process. And she would tell him everything she knew.

Carl switched to English. "Ana, you know I had two reasons to see you. We've taken care of one of them. Now I have to talk to you about the other."

Like most middle-class women in Panama, Ana Maria could be extremely attractive. With black curly hair down, the right clothes, and shiny jewelry, she turned a lot of heads. Her body was so athletic that men hardly noticed the enormous eyes that seemed to jump off her ordinary mestizo face. Carl knew he was not her only lover. He was okay with that...for now.

"Yes," she sighed. "I thought it might have something to do with the kidnapped canal pilot." Her law enforcement side kicked in. "Where do you want me to start?"

Carl sat forward. He did not have a notepad. He didn't need one. Blessed with a near-photographic memory, Carl could soak up information like a sponge, holding it for the exact moment he needed to use it.

"Tell me about the pilot," responded Carl.

"His name is Manfredo Alegre Rivas," she began.

"That's not a Spanish first name," interjected Carl. "He must have an Italian mother...like I do."

Ana Maria replied in perfect English without emotion. "That's right, Carl...you should have been an intelligence agent."

"Sorry for the interruption. Go on."

"Known as 'Freddy,' Captain Alegre spent fifteen years at sea, riding large merchant ships, attaining the status of 'master.' He came ashore to become a pilot. He's been guiding ships through the canal ever since. He is forty-two years old with a wife and two sons. Freddy is five feet nine inches tall and weighs about 160 pounds. You've seen his picture in *La Prensa* today, so you know he has black hair and a rather handsome face."

She took a long breath, poised to continue. Carl had one question.

"Who would kidnap a pilot? He doesn't have a lot of money."

"We don't know who did this, Carl…yet. The kidnapping makes no sense. The canal is what makes Panama run. Pilots are rock stars here. We do not know of any person or group who would want to hurt one."

Like many Panamanians, Ana Maria's command of the English language, honed at Florida State, was superb. Carl did not have to worry about translation issues. They made love in Spanish; they did business in English.

"Okay…no suspects. Tell me about what happened on the Transisthmian."

Ana Maria reengaged her professional voice. It was more than just speaking English. She spoke an octave lower than when, in the bedroom, she cried out for more of him. She was focused and direct. A different person altogether.

"The shuttle bus was stopped by a fallen tree about halfway along the highway. A driver was taking Captain Alegre home from the *Gatún* side. Only the two of them were on the bus…which is not much bigger than a van."

"Did you get a report from the field yet?"

"I went to the scene myself early this morning, Carl. It was pretty easy to see what happened. Someone used explosives to make the tree fall directly across the road…apparently right before the bus got there."

"We call that an *abatis*," interrupted Carl. "A single tree makes a good obstacle for a nonarmored vehicle. The scary part is that the kidnappers knew how to make a tree fall precisely across the road. That speaks to a higher degree of training…perhaps military."

Ana Maria raised her bushy eyebrows. "Thank you, Carl. There's a word I had not heard before." She focused again. "I'll get our people to look for a military connection."

"*De nada*," replied Carl, a broad smile creasing his rugged face.

"The kidnappers had their own vehicle staged on the Pacific side of the *abatis*," continued Ana Maria. "The canal commission employees apparently managed to get out of the bus. The driver froze. Captain Alegre ran into the jungle. The assailants shot the driver dead then chased Alegre into the forest. At least one of them wore night-vision goggles. We know that because a pair was dropped on the road."

Carl sat up straight. "That's another military connection. NVGs are not easy to come by." Ana Maria nodded and took another note. Carl shifted gears. "You say that Alegre bolted…right into the jungle, in the *dark*?"

"Yes, that is what we think."

Carl chuckled. "I'd like to meet this guy. He must have a big set of balls to do that."

"He's going to need those balls now," said Ana Maria dryly. "Wherever he is."

* * *

Carl learned much more in the heat of the afternoon. By the time he left Ana Maria's house, it was getting dark. He drove quickly back to the base and found himself at the door to Stewart's office. It was almost 1900. He knocked twice.

"Come in," said the booming voice. As Carl approached his desk, Stewart frowned at him. "I expected you sooner. This better be good."

Carl responded right away without sitting down. "Yes, sir, I think it is." He went to the map on the wall and began his briefing.

"Here is what we know." Carl took a black marker to the white-board next to the map and started making bullet points. "One, that a canal pilot was stopped in the middle of the night and taken away by unknown assailants. Two, that the driver was shot dead. Three, that a pair of night-vision goggles were found at the scene."

Colonel Stewart sat up straight and interrupted. "That's a new one."

"Yes, sir… You can see there might be a military connection… Also, the use of explosives to make an *abatis* across the road."

"Good catch, Carl… Keep going."

Carl went back to the board. "Fourth, that Captain Alegre is one of the most respected of the canal pilots. He has no history of engaging in anything shady. The Panamanians do not think he has any hidden wealth. Fifth, that Alegre has a wife and two young sons, eleven and thirteen years old."

There was a pause in the briefing while Stewart thought about what Carl had told him. "Is there anything else we know?"

"That the getaway car could only have gone toward Panama City since it was on the Pacific side of the Kapok tree. There was not enough room for a vehicle to get around that obstacle."

"One more thing, sir," said Carl. "The Panamanians don't have the capacity to deal with this. I learned that they plan to ask the US government for help…and that they will keep it from the public. This may happen as soon as tomorrow. The request will come to our embassy, but I can't give you the details of what it will say."

"Okay," said Stewart. "I'll alert the general to standby for a meeting with both governments…somewhere. Now tell me what we *don't* know."

"Sir," began Carl as he went back to the board, "first, we don't know who did this. Second, we don't know where they took the pilot. Third, we don't know what kind of car they drove. And fourth…we don't know *why* they did this."

"That's a lot not to know," responded the colonel. "What do you *think*?"

"I think there's a military connection…but I'm not sure which military. It could be former PDF soldiers. Remember, we taught them these skills at the School of the Americas." Carl hesitated and looked at the floor before continuing. Then he looked up at Stewart. "It could also be some of our own."

"Let's hope not, Carl." Stewart went back to his desk to finish paperwork before going home to his wife. He looked up at Carl. "Where did you get all this great intel in such a short time?"

"I have a source," replied Carl, suppressing a smile.

CHAPTER 5

THE INITIAL MEETING on what to do about the kidnapping was held at the headquarters of the Panama Canal Commission, standing majestically beside the canal, late on the first day of the crisis. In order to avoid calling attention to the purpose of the gathering, only the deputies of appropriate institutions had been summoned. The president of the republic had dispatched his deputy interior minister. The US Embassy's deputy chief of mission and the deputy commander of US Southern Command had also attended. Colonel Stewart, the acting commander of the Special Operations Command, had not received an invitation. Major Castaneda, deputy director of the Technical and Judicial Police, the PTJ, had been in the room.

Carl sat in his small den, reading after dinner. When he was home, he enjoyed fixing a reasonably healthy meal and then catching up on all the books he never had time to read during the day. Television was limited (the only thing he really missed were Red Sox games). Computers were new, mostly used for word processing. Phone calls to the United States were expensive (he had very few friends to call anyway). Carl was an eclectic and random reader. Whatever caught his eye usually ended up on his coffee table pile (he was halfway through a history of the American Civil War and just starting a science fiction classic). He didn't mind living on a US military base in the former "Canal Zone." He was traveling most of the time anyway.

His phone rang just after 2000. It was Colonel Stewart.

"Sorry to bother you at home, Carl, but I got a call just now from the four-star's deputy. I am expected to attend a meeting at 0800 tomorrow at SOUTHCOM headquarters to determine what to do next. I'm taking you with me."

"Got it, sir. I'll be in early." The telephone line was unsecure, so there was nothing else he could say.

"See you at zero-seven, ready to discuss our agenda for the meeting," said Stewart. "Get some rest, Carl… I think you're going to need it."

Ten minutes later, Carl's phone rang again. It was Ana Maria.

"*Carlos*… I need your body and your brain. In that order."

Carl put his book back on the pile with a mixture of excitement and intrigue. So much for getting some rest! "*Me voy rápido*… I'll be there in twenty minutes."

* * *

After finishing in the bedroom, Carl and Ana Maria convened at the kitchen table. Their meeting would be brief, just like their love-making. Ana Maria suspected—or rather hoped—that Carl would soon be busier than he had been since *Just Cause*. She was due at the presidential palace for a midnight meeting. Having worked most of the stress out of her system, she was ready to review the bidding.

"After delivering the situation update, I was able to stay for the whole meeting. I learned some things I would like you to know. I also want to see what you think."

Carl rested his chin on both hands as he tried to shake off the afterglow of their union. "Sounds good, Ana… I'll help you as much as I can." They were now speaking in English.

Ana Maria adjusted her tone. It seemed to Carl that she had shaken off her afterglow more quickly than he. "The Panamanian government has formally requested American assistance in finding the pilot." She paused. "You and I both know that Panama does not have the capability, or the capacity, to deal with this…but we don't want our citizens to know that."

"Yes," responded Carl. "It's true that Panama needs the help… but don't you think your people will catch on when they hear about US military guys running all over the country? You know better than I do… This place runs on rumor."

Ana Maria nodded vigorously. "Yes…and that is why we asked for *spies* to handle this rather than soldiers." She stopped and waited for Carl's reaction.

"Spies? You mean that your government wants the *CIA* to find the pilot?"

"Yes," said Ana Maria quickly. "We think that would give your government, and ours, plausible deniability."

Wow!

Carl Malinowski was a hard person to surprise. But this was an unexpected turn. "And what do you think will happen when your people find out that the hated CIA is running around Panama, looking for this guy?"

"That, we think, would be better than uniformed military doing it." She softened her tone. "What do you think?"

"Still too soon after *Just Cause*," said Carl, nodding. "I get it." He thought about it for a few more seconds then added, "I think you're right. And there would be US troops *everywhere*. We have a saying in the military… If it's worth doing, it's worth *over*doing."

"And the CIA *doesn't* think that way?"

"No…the CIA actually has *other* people do its dirty work for them." Carl was now laughing.

Ana Maria smiled for the first time since they'd gotten out of bed. "So I guess that means you like my idea!"

"Very much, *mi amor*." The problem is that CIA, in this case, would have no foreign government to recruit from… Their only source would be the US."

She thought about what that meant and drew the right conclusion. "Okay, that means CIA could use American soldiers in civilian clothes, right?"

Carl flashed her a wide grin. "Yes, that would work…but they'd have to use the *right* soldiers."

Ana Maria understood immediately what Carl was suggesting.

"Or sailors?"

"Exactly!" he responded with an intensity she rarely saw. "My boss would allow me to do this. I would use just a few men," said Carl, deliberately using the subjunctive. "Have your government request that CIA enlist the support of Special Operations Command South…and I can make this happen."

* * *

The next morning, LCDR Malinowski sat next to Colonel Stewart at the long table in the secure conference room at Quarry Heights. The commander, General Kenneth Wells, had invited only four other people to the meeting: the SOUTHCOM operations officer, the staff intelligence officer, the command's legal officer, and the CIA station chief.

As always, General Wells was the first to speak. "Early this morning, gentlemen, the Panamanian government asked our embassy to begin looking for Captain Alegre, using special operations personnel under CIA command." He looked at every person at the table before continuing. "Normally, a foreign government does not make such a specific request, but I think we all agree that these are unusual circumstances."

Carl—the junior man in the room, by far—had to force himself not to smile.

The four-star looked at the station chief. "What do you think, Frank?"

Francisco de Silva was a CIA veteran of thirty years, dispatched to Panama for his long experience in Latin America. This was his transition job; he and his wife were planning to live in Panama for the rest of their lives. In his five years on the job, de Silva had managed to maintain secrecy regarding his intelligence position, as well as credibility in his cover as a senior political officer in the US Embassy. "I like the idea," said the head spook.

The station chief was a man of few words. Indeed, that had been the key to his success. Reginald Stewart broke the silence, looking back and forth at the four-star and the CIA man. "Sir, SOCSOUTH is ready to support this operation in any way we can."

General Wells turned to his staff. "Okay, now we need a command post that is not tied in any way to this headquarters. I want all of you to establish a working group to elaborate a plan of action… then to set up a watch regime to monitor execution…for as long as it takes."

The station chief jumped in before anyone else could respond. "We can use one of my facilities downtown. We sometimes use it as a classroom, but it's completely secure, and I can have my people install the extra comm's equipment." The others nodded their assent and then looked at Colonel Stewart.

"We'll need only a handful of men," responded Stewart. "LCDR Malinowski here will lead the team." The colonel gestured to Carl. "He and his men have worked undercover before. How soon can you set up the command post? This will take a lot of planning."

De Silva responded directly to Stewart. "We can be up and running by tomorrow night, Reggie." The station chief then looked around the room. "The station and the SOC have maintained close contact for years. We have never seconded Panama-based military personnel before, but that will be an easy transition."

"Any outstanding issues then?" asked General Wells, looking right at his lawyer. The judge advocate was uncharacteristically silent.

De Silva paused for a moment to make sure they were all listening. "Yes, there is one issue."

"Liaison," interjected Stewart. Carl nodded.

"Exactly," responded De Silva. "We'll need a Panamanian liaison officer inside the command post…someone from the PTJ."

"Can you clear that person for access?" asked Wells.

"Yes, sir, we can. I don't normally like to do that, but I can arrange it."

The staff intelligence officer took a note. "I'll ask the PTJ to appoint a liaison officer. As soon as they identify that individual, I will let you all know."

General Wells looked around the table. "And we will grant the LNO access to the isolation facility on base. Any other issues at this point?"

There were many issues with which to wrestle, but none that rose to the four-star level. The meeting was adjourned.

In the car on the way back to SOCSOUTH, Colonel Stewart and LCDR Malinowski started their planning process.

"Carl," Stewart began, "tell me who you need for the team, and I will get them on board."

"Sir, I need three men, all of them SEALs. Senior Chief Jerry Tompkins is working at the naval special warfare unit at Rodman naval station. The other two are back in Virginia Beach, HM1 Jose Rios and EN2 Billy Joe Barnes. With your permission, I'll talk to Commander Fletcher and get his okay to bring in the senior chief. Can you call Virginia to request the others? I'd like to have them down here day after tomorrow."

"Stewart took his eyes off the road long enough to say, "You got it, Carl. Let's meet first thing in the morning to talk about the planning. I'll get started on the intel feed from both CIA and SOUTHCOM. We both have a lot of work to do." The colonel paused for a few seconds. "Whoever your source is out there, try to get as much additional information as you can."

"Thanks, sir. And yes, I'll tap my source again," said Carl with deliberate irony. "I also have some of my own ideas."

"I'm sure you do, Carl!" Stewart was looking at the road, but Carl could see that he was smiling broadly. "I'll let you know as soon as I've talked to the commanding officer in Virginia Beach. I'll tell him it's critical that we have Rios and Barnes."

As soon as they got back to SOC headquarters, Carl called Rodman and set up a meeting with Jordy Fletcher. Then he got his goggles and went to the pool. He needed to think, and his best ideas came to him during long swims. The ideas came, but so did the image of Ana Maria. She was the logical choice as liaison to the CIA command post—the *only* choice. Carl imagined he and Ana Maria would be able to pause their personal relationship long enough to focus on the mission. They were both professionals.

He owed her a lot; she owed him even more.

* * *

Brenda Rios put down the phone and walked into the living room, where her husband was watching a soccer match on TV. It was late afternoon on Sunday in Virginia Beach.

"Come and speak with your commander, Jose," she said timidly. Brenda went to the bar and poured herself a stiff drink.

Jose Rios couldn't suppress a smile as he rocketed off the couch. "Must be important!" he shouted over his shoulder as he hurried to the kitchen.

Jose was always in motion, and it seemed to Brenda that she was always *watching* him move. And that was when he was home! He was gone most of the time, off doing something he couldn't talk about. Brenda was proud of her husband, but she was tired of competing with the Navy for his attention.

Jose came back into the living room to say what Brenda *knew* he would say. "I have to leave in the morning, *querida*." He gave her a reassuring hug, knowing what pain his sudden departure would cause. Petty Officer Rios balanced dedication to resolving conflict abroad with the burden of managing conflict at home. There was no solution to his dilemma.

"Can you at least tell me where you'll be?" She was on automatic. This scene was beyond familiar; it was trite. Brenda was the editor of a local magazine, with a good career and many admiring colleagues. She didn't necessarily blame her loyal and caring husband, but this edition was exceeding its shelf life.

"Panama," replied Jose. "That's all I can tell you."

"I don't know how much longer I can do this, Jose. I love you, but I can't live this way." Tears came as she realized that she was on the verge of losing her composure. "My beautiful *gringa*," he'd always called her. Jose was the most exciting man she'd ever met. He knew a lot about a lot of things, and he could make her laugh suddenly. She had always considered his Colombian heritage a bonus. "Can't you just get out of the Navy and work in a hospital? You could go to medical school... I'll *help* you." She was now pleading with him.

Jose hesitated for a long minute. He knew she was correct to question his priorities. He had no right to make her unhappy. The Navy had rescued him from a life of poverty and petty crime. Becoming a SEAL medic had given him prestige and fulfillment. But Jose would never admit to his wife that it was more than that. He *liked* putting his life at risk for the team. He needed to be part of something larger than himself—a just cause to believe in. Perversely, he *enjoyed* the terror of combat. Only his teammates understood that.

He looked into Brenda's wet blue eyes and put off the final decision one more time. "Let's talk about this when I get back."

But even as he hugged her again, his mind was racing. *What's going on in Panama?* Jose was in love with his wife, but he was a warrior at heart.

* * *

Lorena Barnes stood on the dock at Lynnhaven Bay, waiting for her husband to come back from fishing. It was nearly nine o'clock on a warm September night in Virginia Beach. Hours before, she had received a phone call from Billy Joe's commanding officer with orders for him to get on the first plane to Panama the next day. But Billy Joe had been out of touch since midafternoon. Lucy had almost gotten used to her husband's sudden bursts of patriotic duty, but time was running out for their marriage. Billy Joe had always been wild and crazy—that was one of the things that had attracted her to him. Lately, the combination of his absences and his behavior had become way too much to bear.

Her sunny Latin optimism was gone.

Lori sat down on the creaking boards, just above the smooth surface of the bay. She was tired of being tired. The half-moon illuminated the night just enough to allow a boat to dock without lights. There was resignation on her face when the small skiff finally came into view. Her husband was not alone in the boat. As Billy Joe expertly maneuvered the skiff into its berth, Lucy prepared herself for a confrontation. Billy Joe flashed her the trademark smile she'd always loved.

"Hey, sugar," said Billy Joe in a heavy Southern drawl. Glancing at the girl in the boat, he said sheepishly, "This here's Maggie. She loves to fish!"

Maggie was embarrassed; Billy Joe only a little. Lorena was furious with her husband but felt sorry for his girlfriend. *She probably didn't even know he was married.* This was it for Lori. She was still pretty enough to find someone who didn't lie to her. A man who didn't cheat. Her husband was a fun person to be around—when you could get his attention. Billy Joe was a charmer to everybody he met.

A charmer who had to go.

"You're commanding officer called," said Lori in a monotone. "He's ordering you to fly to Panama tomorrow."

Lori ignored the girl in the boat.

Billy Joe also ignored Maggie. His excitement over the prospect of an important mission overrode any feelings of guilt he might have had at that moment. "Sounds good… I wonder what's going on down there," he replied with professional detachment. "Just let me get the boat tied up…then I'll go home and pack my war bag."

Lorena Barnes could barely contain her fiery temper. "I'll help you pack, and I will drive you to the airport tomorrow." Then she looked into his still-youthful face and said with finality, "But I won't be here when you get back from Panama."

She walked back to her car and drove home to their two-year-old daughter.

CHAPTER 6

BY THE TIME he sat down with Commander Fletcher, Carl was ready to explain why he needed the best noncommissioned officer either of them had ever seen. He was confident that Colonel Stewart had already spoken to the right people in Virginia Beach to get Jose and Billy Joe on a plane to Panama. The team would have to come together quickly, but Carl knew they would not need time to bond. They were combat-tested and ready to go.

"I can't tell you what we'll be doing, Jordy, but you can bet it's important enough to ask for Jerry Tompkins." Carl was sitting in the commanding officer's trailer at the edge of the Panama Canal with the Bridge of the Americas visible through the office window.

"If I were you, *I'd* be asking for Tompkins," said the senior chief's boss. "Despite the negative impact on my command, you can have him for as long as you need him." Fletcher paused for effect. "And you know what a sacrifice that will be."

"Believe me…I know," replied Carl. "Tompkins saved my life in Grenada, carried my water during *Just Cause*, and followed me all over the region after that. He's the best there is."

Fletcher had been around the block a few times himself. "Yeah…I get it, Carl. You need the senior chief more than I do right now. Just make sure you give him back!"

Carl laughed. "I promise, Jordy, I promise. But you should know that once I take him from you, he will disappear from view…

maybe for a few weeks. Colonel Stewart and I do not have enough information yet to be more specific than that."

Fletcher thought for a second then added more options to Carl's toolbox. "And *you* should know that any other resources I have are yours if you need them. That includes the boat unit."

Carl felt the warmth of the brotherhood well up inside him. "Thanks, Jordy… That's why they call this frog family 'the teams.'"

* * *

Carl found Jerry Tompkins out on the firing range, teaching young men to shoot a wide variety of small arms. He stood behind the group, watching the master work his magic with the next generation. The young men would be tested in the crucible of combat… just like he and Jerry had been. Carl was anxious to tell Jerry that the two of them would be tested again…and very soon. Nevertheless, he waited patiently until Jerry was able to break away from his range duties.

"Butkus!" Carl shook the large hand of a man visibly glad to see him.

"Carlos…it's great to see you. I thought those Army guys over at the SOC were holding you hostage!"

"Colonel Stewart sends his respect, Jerry. He and Commander Fletcher gave me permission to borrow you for a while."

Jerry Tompkins was an imposing figure, standing six three in his jungle boots. Carl was a few inches shorter and a lot lighter. Senior Chief Tompkins was a man you could not help looking up to, professionally as well as physically. Carl was completely confident that the man they called Butkus would be there for him this time. Whatever happened.

"Now that's a nice surprise! How long do I get to call you 'Boss' again?"

Carl stood with hands on his hips, an old habit from his college wrestling days. "Too soon to tell, Jerry. I just got tasked to put together a team to do something quickly. You, Jose, and Billy Joe are going to help me do it."

"So the band is getting back together... What's the mission?" asked the big man, clearly delighted.

"Let's go for a slow run, and I'll tell you what I know." Both of them had gotten plenty of exercise earlier in the day. Other men might have proposed taking a walk. Frogmen never did that. "I know just enough to generate lots of questions with no answers," said Carl, leaning toward the road.

"Sounds like old times. Give me thirty minutes," replied Jerry with a grin. "San Juan Hill?"

"I've got my gear in the car... See you at the front gate in half an hour." Carl knew that any run up San Juan Hill would be slow and borderline painful. There were no fun-runs in the teams.

They met at the gate and began by jogging. Jerry, a former fullback, was faster than Carl. But even at thirty-nine years old, Carl could run *farther* than the big man. The air temperature was a bit lower by now, but the daily downpour had pumped up the humidity. The sun was back, and the puddles were disappearing fast. Except for a "dry" season between Christmas and Easter, Panama was insanely hot and humid. Carl and Jerry had long ago gotten used to it. Indeed, they *thrived* in heat.

Looking straight ahead, Carl began his classified briefing. "You've read about the kidnapping of a canal pilot, Jerry. The government of Panama doesn't have the operational capability to find him and get him back. They've requested American assistance...and the SOC has been given the mission."

Jerry responded without looking at Carl. "Okay...that sounds about right. What do we know about the pilot...who took him, where...and why?"

"All good questions. The bottom line is that we have no idea who kidnapped him or where they might have taken him." Carl proceeded to tell Jerry everything he knew about Captain Manfredo Alegre. By the time he was finished, they were off the road and onto a steep and slippery clay trail. Into the rainforest they went. There was no more talking for twenty minutes.

As they came out of the forest, Carl resumed his briefing. "The Panamanians want our operations to be placed under CIA command."

"Wow!" exclaimed Jerry. "That surprises me... The feared CIA making them look weak."

"Yeah...but we think that will actually be better than having us under SOUTHCOM command. If that were to happen, a covert special operation might be turned into a brigade-sized search. Nobody wants that."

"We can do a lot more than a brigade with just the four of us, working undercover," asserted Jerry. "We'll need a civilian vehicle and radio...and a lot more than that."

Carl signaled his agreement and sped up the pace. They raced back to the gate with Jerry ahead by half a stride. The men walked around until they were breathing normally again. "We got a lot of planning to do, Butkus. As soon as Bosco and Tinker get here tomorrow night, I'll give you all some detailed guidance." Carl paused and added, "You put Billy Joe on your couch, just for one night... I'll take Jose. Right now, just get your war bag ready and meet us at my quarters tomorrow at 2200."

* * *

Carl got back in his rusty Land Cruiser and drove home. The Toyota was a perfect vehicle for exploring the back roads of the rainforest while off duty. Carl was a dedicated birdwatcher, something he downplayed around the other men. He'd discovered birds by accident, in the field, sitting still in the jungle with nothing to do but wait for the enemy. Birds—Panama was home to almost a thousand different kinds—were one of Carl's secret weapons. Their behavior told him when it was safe in the jungle and when it was not. They showed him the way to the beach...and the safety of the sea.

Carl's other secret weapon was Ana Maria. For almost four years, she had used him for her own pleasure, as well as keeping tabs on what the Americans were doing. But he had used her too—when he had not been operating somewhere else in Latin America—to find out what the Panamanians were up to. Just before the Americans came for Manuel Noriega, Carl had begun to feel something more than lust. He didn't know if Ana Maria cared as much as he did (being a trained intelligence officer, she was careful not to say how she really felt). Carl was not a spy; he did not tell her the attack was coming. But he made sure she was not in her office when it did.

He had invited her to meet him for a romantic getaway at Coronado Beach, far enough from Panama City, during the time he expected *Operation Just Cause* to launch. She had gone there eagerly, but Carl had stood her up. When the attack came, Ana Maria had been stranded in the hotel. Before she got back to her office three days later, the building had been destroyed by a US Air Force gunship. Having lured his girlfriend away from danger, Carl had executed his own missions with precision. They avoided talking about it, but Ana Maria had never forgotten that she owed Carl her life. Thereafter, their trust had developed into a mutually productive information-exchange relationship—with benefits.

He called Colonel Stewart as soon as he got home. "Sir, I got Tompkins on board. What about the others?"

"They'll be here tomorrow evening on the American Airlines flight, Carl. Meet them at the airport. Put them up for the night. I'm setting up an isolation facility for the four of you to work from after that."

"Will do, sir. Just tell me where, and I'll bring the team there the day after tomorrow. Hopefully by then, we'll know a lot more. Anything else I should know right now?"

"Not yet…still no ransom note," replied Stewart. "You have a great team there, Commander. I'm confident you can do whatever it takes."

* * *

The old fishing boat rode long Pacific swells, thundering loudly on a beach in the distance to his right. The prisoner sat facing aft, back up against a bulkhead. He could tell from the sound of the engines that this was not a rich man's yacht. He knew roughly where they were from the roll and pitch of the vessel, along with a general awareness of time elapsed (the air temperature was at its peak). Captain Alegre was a skilled navigator—even blindfolded—but their approximate position was of little use to him. His captors had taken him east, into the remote *Darién*.

Two of his assailants were seasick. He could *feel* their unease with being at sea. Snippets of conversation he could pick up from the others told him nothing about what was happening. There just wasn't much to listen to. It was clear to Freddy that the men who operated the boat were not friends of the kidnappers. At one point, he heard the slide of an automatic pistol slamming home. He decided the boat had probably been hijacked.

Many hours farther down the coast, Alegre felt the boat turn to port then embrace the soothing rhythm of a following sea. A bit later, he started to feel a slower forward motion without pitch or roll. The pilot imagined that they were plying a flat estuary, almost certainly leading up a river. The cries of seagulls were replaced by the sweet cacophony of jungle birds. It wasn't the birds he was worried about. Like most city kids, Freddy was afraid of the jungle.

They were taking him into the roadless wilderness he knew only from Panama's dramatic history, harrowing contemporary tales, and press accounts of organized crime. The tropical sun set suddenly, and Freddy could see enough at the edge of the blindfold to know that it was growing dark fast. Having been lulled into a bizarre sense of security by the ocean waves, he was now terrified by the prospect of being on unfamiliar turf, under the control of ruthless men who would not hesitate to kill him.

He thought again of his family. *For them, I have to stay alive.*

CHAPTER 7

THE WOODEN BOAT, proceeding slowly, touched mud and ceased forward motion. Freddy had tried to prepare himself for the transition he knew was coming—leaving the relative comfort of the sea for the terror of the jungle. But he wasn't at all ready. He was sick to his stomach, and it was not from the stench of rotten fish. One of his captors suddenly removed the blindfold that had protected Freddy from the ugliness of his new reality. Now he would have to confront the jungle directly. Blind in a different way.

A Coleman lantern illuminated the landing site. As the burly, unshaven men practically lifted him out of the boat, the pilot looked back at the two poor fishermen who had brought them to this spot. Their sad eyes reached out to him. They were brother mariners, saying everything without speaking. Like him, they'd just been doing their jobs. He could not manage to smile at them, but he nodded in grim solidarity. They had his silent prayer.

"*Maria…ayúdales.*" There was nothing else he could do for them.

Two of his captors, both wearing night-vision goggles, dragged Freddy onto a muddy track. In the darkness, he could hear the monkeys in the trees, but he could not see the creatures he knew waited in ambush alongside the trail. He was terrified, to be sure. But the fear of what lay in his path distracted him from the horror of what might happen wherever they were taking him. He thought about running, but he understood that his navigation skills would do him no good in the featureless void.

Two shots rang out!

Freddy flinched before he realized the sound had come from well behind them. The men leading him through the mangrove forest did not flinch. They stopped and waited for a third man to catch up. Guided by one flashlight, the four men hurried into the tall trees. Suddenly, there was dirt underfoot. The night became even darker. Freddy grieved for the fishermen who would never see their families again. *Just like my driver!*

The nightmare, he seemed to know, was just beginning.

* * *

LCDR Malinowski and his men—wearing jeans, untucked shirts, and dirty running shoes—sat at one end of the oblong table in the isolation facility, or "ISOFAC," waiting for their briefers to arrive. The small apartment, situated in a remote hanger at Howard Air Force Base, would serve as their home, their planning cell, and their operating base for however long the crisis lasted. The isolation facility allowed the team to stay focused on planning and execution while intelligence, food, and equipment were delivered to them. The ISOFAC would also preserve operational security. Reginald Stewart had cut his professional teeth as an Army Green Beret. In the new era of joint-service cooperation, Carl's team was quite used to doing business this way.

Petty Officers Rios and Barnes had arrived on schedule at Tocumen International Airport the night before. Carl, wearing a pair of pressed slacks and a white *guayabera*, had met them without fanfare, taking Billy Joe to stay with Jerry Tompkins. Jose had dumped his heavy war bag by the door and slept on Carl's living room couch—in his view, a relatively comfortable way to begin the mission. In the morning, Carl had driven them all to Colonel Stewart's office at the SOC, parking his car in the lot for what he expected would be a long period. No one would ask questions about where Carl had gone. Not at the Special Operations Command. The team had been transported to the ISOFAC in another Land Cruiser without distinguishing marks, driven by an Army sergeant wearing shorts and flip-flops. The driver would stay next door, to be at the beck and call of the team.

There was much nervous anticipation at the table, tamping down the happy talk that normally passed between them. Carl broke the silence.

"Okay, guys, before the briefers get here, I wanted to mention a few things I'd like you to bear in mind as they give us the mission and begin feeding us the intel we need."

He definitely had their attention. All three of them had been with Carl on more than a few missions—some riskier than others. But regardless of the risk, all of them had come back. They trusted him completely. Carl was their leader, but they were more than his followers. Each man brought complementary skill sets to the fight; all of them brought experience and ideas—ideas that Carl always listened to. Four independent thinkers acting together as one. Constantly *reacting* to the unpredictable flow of the situation.

"I can tell you now that we'll be under CIA command for this one." Jose and Billy Joe raised their eyebrows at the same time. "That means civilian clothes and cover stories…the whole shot."

"That's great!" said Billy Joe, almost shouting. "Glad I didn't get a haircut."

"You'll *always* look like a civilian," responded Jerry. "My buzz cut won't fool anyone."

"And I can always be a Colombian tourist," Jose put in cheerily.

"You look like a drug trafficker to me!" joked Billy Joe. "I hope we get to fight with some of those guys."

Carl laughed along with his teammates and then got serious again. "I don't know yet who we're going to fight, if we have to fight at all. But I can tell you that this mission will be different from start to finish. The Panamanians have asked us to find a kidnap victim. They don't have the capability to do it themselves…but they don't want the US military running all over the country. From now on, we'll be undercover without immediate backup."

Two of the three men nodded soberly. "Independent. Just how we like it…right, boss?" Billy Joe had always been the cocky one.

"Not quite, Tinker," replied Carl evenly. "There will be a command center directing our movements." Thinking for a few seconds, he added, "More likely, they'll be listening to what we actually *do* on our own initiative. There's no doctrine or SOPs for this one. I will not let anyone limit our freedom of action in the field…within practical and ethical limits, of course."

"Sounds good to me," said Jose. "As long as we have flexibility out there…wherever we go." The rising pitch in the medic's voice prompted Carl for a response.

"We still don't know anything about where we'll have to go… and I can tell you that our briefers don't know either. As soon as we get the initial presentation, the four of us can start roughing out a concept. Even with the scantiest information, we'll need a plan."

"Okay," said the big man. "Panama's a really big small country… There are lots of remote areas where they could have taken the guy. This could take a while."

"Yogi Berra couldn't have said it better, Butkus. We'll have to prepare ourselves for a long mission." Carl smiled at his team. "I hope you guys are comfortable on your luxury Army cots! I'll try and get us some decent chow… I promise."

Jose chimed in. "Have you figured out a cover-for-status yet, boss?"

"Yeah, Bosco…actually, I have. You guys are gonna learn a lot about Panama birds!"

All three of his men rolled their eyes as a trio of briefers entered the room, led by Colonel Stewart. Carl was not surprised to see Ana Maria among them. She looked at him without expression. He returned the favor.

"Good morning, gentlemen," announced Stewart. "Let me introduce Major Ana Maria Castaneda. She is the deputy director of the Panamanian Technical and Judicial police, the PTJ. Major Castaneda will be our liaison officer to her government. She will also stand watch in the C2 cell…and will advise the rest of us regarding the developing situation."

Carl's team nodded and responded together, "Good morning, ma'am." Carl smiled furtively. He was glad to see her in the fight. She looked great in khaki pants and a stark white short-sleeve blouse.

"You can call me Ana Maria," said the major in native-sounding English that surprised three members of the team. "I'll give you regular updates on the situation, as well as anything you need on Panama and its public forces. You'll also need to know about your potential adversaries." She paused for effect. "We have a lot of bad guys out there."

Still standing, along with the rest of the briefing team, Stewart gestured to his left. "And this is 'Ned' from the three-letter agency in charge of this enterprise. He speaks for the station chief...whom you will never meet."

"Good morning, everybody. We don't use last names where I work. I'll be in charge of the command cell." With wire-framed glasses and a pencil protector in his breast pocket, Ned could have passed for a college professor. He looked too young to be in charge, but the man left no doubt that he was. "As you will learn in a minute or so, we don't have a lot of information to exchange at this time." He gave them a look that convinced Carl that Ned had an operational background, that he would actually understand the team's challenges and needs. "We're working hard to get you more."

Stewart nodded to the older man on his right. "And this is Mr. Pablo Céspedes of the Panama Canal Commission. He and I will be in the C2 cell with the others all the way through."

Céspedes raised one hand and looked at each member of the team, one at a time. His mocha skin reminded Carl just how diverse—and how stratified—the man's country was. White people in Panama inherited privilege and power. The Panama Canal was different. As the economic engine of the country, that vast enterprise valued experience and expertise over heritage. In accented but perfect English, Céspedes spoke from the heart, "I have the biggest personal stake in the outcome of this operation... Anything you need from the commission, just ask me and consider it done."

Three of the briefers sat down at the table, placing unmarked folders in front of them. Ana Maria remained standing and went to a map on the wall. Carl enjoyed watching her move. A momentary lapse of concentration. She turned on the projector and displayed a pleasant Latin face on the white screen. "This is Manfredo Alegre Rivas… He is a very experienced pilot, employed by the Panama Canal Commission. Two nights ago, he was kidnapped by unknown assailants…right here." She pointed to a spot halfway between the seas. "Captain Alegre was the only passenger in a PCC shuttle bus, taking him home to Panama City in the middle of the night. During the ambush, Alegre's driver was shot dead." She filled in some of the other details before pausing for questions.

Jerry Tompkins was the first to respond. "Do we have *any* idea where they might have taken the hostage? Panama's got a lot of places to hide, but we have to start somewhere."

Ana Maria had given this quite a bit of thought. "We think they are still on the Panama City side of the canal. The other side is less populated, and they would have had to cross the Bridge of the Americas to get there. It would have been easier for them to simply disappear into the chaos of the city." She took a deep breath. "After that, we're not sure. There are multiple checkpoints on the road to *Darién* province. As you know, that is the *only* road beyond the air-port, so if the getaway car went that far, they could not have avoided being stopped." She took her eyes off the map and focused on the team. "Our guess is that they're somewhere in the city."

Ana Maria went to the table and sat down. Ned got up and faced the team. "Your mission, gentlemen, is to find Captain Alegre. When you find him, you will perform a rescue in such a way that he is not harmed. Coordinating with Major Castaneda, you are to trans-port Alegre to the proper authorities for questioning…and a prompt return to his family." Ned looked at Carl. "Admittedly, that is not a lot to go on…so far. Questions?"

"Yes," replied Carl, emphatically. "I have a lot of questions… as will my teammates. Let me start by asking you about the rules of engagement. We have strict rules on the DOD side."

"Ours are not so strict," replied the CIA man with a straight face. "We do not want you to kill anyone…unless you are forced to do so."

56

Carl nodded slowly. "We'll do what we have to do in order to bring Alegre back safely…thank you."

"So we're authorized to carry weapons anywhere in Panama?" asked Jerry.

"Yes, you are," replied Ned. "But you'll have to conceal them. We want you to blend into crowds where you encounter them. We also want you to have a plausible explanation for poking around, especially in the bush."

"We can do that," responded Carl. "My team will come up with a cover plan by the end of the day."

"Do any of you speak Spanish?" asked Ned. "If not, we can have Major Castaneda accompany you in the field."

Carl pounced quickly. As much as he'd enjoy having Ana Maria with them, it would cause unit cohesion problems—even though he knew she could keep up with them physically. "Yes," said Carl. "Jose here was born in Colombia, and I myself am quite fluent." He looked at Ana Maria as he added, "With my black hair and Italian features, the two of us can talk our way out of most situations."

That matter settled, they moved on to the next question.

"I'd feel better if we had a 'proof-of-life' video or something," added Jose. "How do we know they haven't just killed the hostage?" This drew a frown from Céspedes.

Billy Joe jumped in. "Do we expect a phone call or something… telling us what the kidnappers want?" He looked at Ana Maria. "It's been more than two days."

"We do expect to hear something from the kidnappers at some point," replied Ana Maria. "They obviously have a solid reason for taking the pilot. Captain Alegre doesn't have a lot of money himself. We think that perhaps these people are hoping to extort the commission." She looked at Pablo Céspedes.

"That's possible," responded the PCC official. "They probably know how much we need Panamanian pilots like Freddy. That gives them leverage. The Americans are training their counterparts all the time, getting ready for the handover, but it's a long process, and we don't have enough pilots ready to go."

After another few rounds of questions, Stewart took back control of the discussion. "If there are no more questions, I will let Ned arrange for his documents people to visit the team this afternoon to begin supporting your mission. You'll need only *shallow* covers, enough to avoid extra scrutiny, especially from the police, but it's important that the people of Panama don't learn who is really behind the rescue effort."

Carl had one more question. "How long do you all think my team will get to plan before we have to move out?"

Stewart let Major Castaneda have the last word. "We think it will be at least a day or so until we have enough additional information. Hopefully, that will include a ransom demand. We want you out tracking the hostage takers as soon as possible. I will keep you abreast of all further developments."

"Thank you, Major." Carl and his men looked at each other and shared the unspoken disappointment of not knowing enough.

CHAPTER 8

CARL AND HIS team stayed at the table after their briefers left the room. They all had many more questions but remained aware that no one had the answers. That made it pointless to ask. They would have to wait.

"Okay, frogs," began Carl, "now we have time to think this whole thing through…just the four of us. Let's take a break and meet back here in ten minutes." He laughed. "It's not as though we can go anywhere! Chow should be here in about an hour, so we can make a good start. This afternoon, we can talk to the documents folks and use the gym…such as it is."

Jose got up to make coffee in the efficiency kitchen. At least they would have a week's supply of his Colombian stash. Carl took his break by touring the ISOFAC. It didn't take long. The cots were set up in a berthing compartment, separate from the work area. The head, doubling as a locker room, connected the dormitory to a home-style gym. As he inspected the cleanliness of the showers and toilets, Carl checked the capacity of the storage lockers. His small team would have more than enough room to store their field gear. Walking into the gym, he was reminded that Army soldiers did not need as much exercise as his SEALs did. There was a pull-up bar, a bench-press, one sit-up board, some dumbbells, and a treadmill, with a few mats scattered around the cluttered room. At least it was clean, he thought. They could not venture outside, so this would have to do.

Reconvening in what Carl had designated "the planning cell," his team got right to work. They did not need the secure telephone and computer sitting on a corner table—at least not yet. With enough time and not enough information, the initial planning session was an exercise in speculation. A marketplace of ideas that would set the stage for developing a detailed plan later on.

Carl went to the wall map and whiteboard. "Okay, you guys, this is the part where Colonel Stewart usually says, 'Tell me what you know, tell me what you *don't* know…then tell me what you think.'"

"Well," began Jerry, "the first part is pretty easy. The second part is going to take a long time. The third part is a real challenge at this point…but we'll be able to do some freethinking, maybe for a day or so."

"Why don't we just bulletize the first two categories on the board?" ventured Jose. "Make two columns. The 'Don't know' column will lead to our request for Essential Elements of Information." He grinned. "That major looks like a good source for most of our EEI. Whoever got *her* into the loop sure knew what he was doing."

"And…she's built like a cheetah!" added Billy Joe with a twinkle. "I bet she can run the pants off all of us…except Bosco, that is!"

"That's enough of that," warned Carl a little too quickly. "Major Castaneda is a professional police officer who may hold the key to our success. Through her, we get to see what the Panamanians can do for us."

After an awkward pause, Carl took a black marker and made Jose's two columns. "All right…what do we know?"

"We know they took the pilot at night on the highway, using a downed tree to stop the bus," said Jerry. "They shot the driver, chased the pilot into the forest, threw him into a vehicle, and drove toward the city." The senior chief took a quick breath and continued his rapid recitation. "We also know that Captain Alegre, I recommend we start calling him 'Freddy,' ran into the forest without hesitation." As the others flashed understanding, Jerry finished the thought.

60

"Knowing what he did in that situation could help us predict what he'll do when we find him."

Carl was writing on the board almost as fast as Jerry spoke.

"We know the rounds that killed the driver came from an AK-47," added Billy Joe. "Also, that they used explosives to take down the tree… I'd say the kidnappers have some military experience."

Carl stopped writing. "Good catch, Tinker. What the major *failed* to say this morning was that the kidnappers were using night-vision goggles."

"How do you know *that*, boss?" asked Jose with a surprised look. "It makes sense, of course, since they were able to find him in *la selva* in the dark.

"I saw the initial report from the crime scene," replied Carl. "The police found a pair of NVGs on the ground next to the tire tracks. It looks like the assailants just dropped it."

Jerry asked what they were all thinking. "So why did Major Castaneda not tell us that in her brief?"

Carl tread delicately. "I think she probably didn't want to imply that our soldiers may have taken the pilot…because that is a distinct possibility. She was being diplomatic. She knew I'd seen the report and that I would pass it on to you guys."

"Sounds like you *know* her!" Billy Joe blurted out.

Carl thought quickly about his options. He could simply deny that he knew Ana Maria…or he could just tell his men and get it over with. The first option would put him at risk of eventually losing their trust (since they would find out anyway). The second option would expose the fact that he had a secret back channel to Panamanian police. Both options were bad, but the second was less bad than the first.

"Yes, I do… Major Castaneda and I have known each other for almost four years."

Knowing looks spread around the table. "Wow, man, good for you!" said Jose with what sounded like admiration. "You're running her as a source?"

"Not exactly, Bosco… She and I share information once in a while. It's all unclassified, of course."

Each of his men asked themselves what other things Carl and the long-legged major had been sharing. But they were professional enough not to ask him. They let Carl bury the issue with one more statement.

"Ana Maria Castaneda is a thirty-six-year-old former intelligence officer, now deputy director of the PTJ. She's a graduate of Florida State University, a friend of the United States, and smart as a whip." He could not prevent a broad grin from spanning his face. "And yeah…she's sexy as hell. You guys busted me…for being a man!" Carl immediately felt better. "And none of that goes beyond this room… Are we clear?"

They all nodded…more seriously than he had expected. "Now, frogs…what do we *not* know?" He turned back to the board.

"We don't know anything about the getaway car, and we have no idea where they took the hostage," offered Jerry. "One of the first EEI requests should be whether the tire tracks can be traced to a particular make of car."

"What else?" Carl asked the team, scribbling with the marker again.

"We don't know *why* they did this," said Jose. "That seems to be the most important thing right now." He sighed. "We don't even know who *they* are!" He grew more serious. "I just hope they're not Americans."

Carl stopped writing and assumed his trademark hands-on-hips posture. He looked back at the team. "So what do we *think* at this point?"

After a brief silence, Jerry was again the first to speak. "If they really *are* in the city, we can use some lessons we learned from the *Guzmán* caper last year in Lima. What do you think, Carlos?"

"I was thinking that too, Butkus. It's almost a perfect analogy." Carl and Jerry, working as advisers, had assisted Peruvian forces in capturing the fearsome leader of the terrorist group, *Sendero Luminoso*. Following standard procedure, they had concealed their own role and made sure the Peruvians got all the credit.

"Yeah…that bastard made himself vulnerable when he left the mountains for the city," added Jerry.

Jose sat back in his chair and tossed his pencil on the table. "I don't think they're *in* the city." He waited until the others were ready to hear his reasoning. "If they *are* on the Panama City side of the canal, that means they're also on the *Darién* side. Assuming they had a plan for getting that far, we have to consider the possibility that our quarry is now somewhere deep in the rainforest. And you guys know just how deep *that* is."

"That would certainly make it more difficult," admitted Carl. "Anyone else?"

"I'm the boat guy," Billy Joe put in. "To avoid the roadblocks, they probably used a boat from somewhere in or near the city, taking him down the coast toward the Colombian border. If that's the case, we could probably locate where they picked him up...but I don't know if we could *ever* find where they're holding him now."

After a pause to consider the implications of what had just been said, Carl felt obliged to add, "Then we'll continue to plan for each possible scenario...and hope for a ransom demand."

* * *

The soldier in flip-flops delivered lunch to the team: a box of "Meals, Ready-to-Eat." The sergeant, dispatched by Colonel Stewart, apologized to the men, explaining that the SOC had not had time yet to mobilize the base kitchen. The MREs would have to do for today.

During the meal, they discussed cover stories. Carl knew what would work best. He *lived* in Panama. He'd been there longer than the others. He was also the boss. "Okay...I realize you guys know almost nothing about birds." He remained serious as the others laughed quietly. "But it's the best cover plan I can think of. I know a lot about Panama's birds, and a group tour will explain why we're out looking around the country." The chuckling stopped. "While in the city, we're just another bunch of tourists taking pictures and buying *molas*."

"So what if someone asks me about birds, only to find out I know next to nothing?" asked Billy Joe.

"I've got two words for you, Tinker," said Carl with a grin. "Harpy Eagle."

Three men laughed...politely.

Carl persisted. "If you roughnecks are ever lucky enough to watch a Harpy Eagle grab a monkey out of a tree without slowing down, you'll be hooked... Trust me!"

"I used to *shoot* birds in the Everglades," countered Billy Joe. "But I guess I should leave this one alone."

Jose's brown face lit up. "Good idea, Tinker. You're the best climber we have, but you look too much like a monkey!"

Carl tried not to laugh. "Hey...you don't need to know about *all* the birds... Shit, there are a thousand species, just in Panama. If you tell nosy people you came here to see Harpy Eagles, they'll be predisposed to believe you. The Harpy Eagle, found only in Panama, is an iconic bird that verges on the mythical. If they ask about other birds, you can just say you're a novice and tell them to talk to me. I'll play the guide."

"Boss...that's actually a good cover," said Jerry seriously. "I think we can all learn enough to play these roles."

Not long after they finished their field rations, the sergeant came back with a young man and an older woman.

"Gentlemen...this is your documents team, Iris and Aaron. Just let me know when they're done, and I'll take them back downtown."

All the men stood up and shook hands with the Agency people. Like the morning briefers, Iris and Aaron carried unmarked folders. Carl motioned everyone to the table, where the pair sat opposite the team.

"Okay," said Carl in a friendly tone. "What do you need from us?"

Iris, apparently the senior and more experienced of the two, spoke first, "We need to see your wallets."

Carl and his men reached into their pockets.

"And your passports...please." Iris smiled at the men, but she was all business. Aaron looked on, obviously *learning* the business.

They had their passports at the ready and promptly handed them over. Iris and Aaron poured over every piece of paper and plastic in each of the wallets as their owners became bored.

Then the documents team looked at the passports.

"You guys certainly travel a lot," remarked Aaron, still paging through the thick booklets. "I see that most of your travel is within Latin America…but there are some visas here for countries in Africa and the Middle East."

Iris interrupted, "What do you want to use as a cover-for-status?"

Carl took that one. "We want to appear to be tourists from Virginia…visiting Panama to see tropical birds. I will be the leader of the group. The cover story doesn't have to stand up to more than casual scrutiny."

"Even so," responded Iris, "these passports will just not be credible. Too many different destinations, and some of them give you away as military people. Iraq, for instance, for Mr. Barnes in 1990. Israel for Mr. Malinowski, and so on. Also, we'll need to create Virginia Beach addresses for Malinowski and Tompkins." Iris continued, "We'll need to make false passports for each of you. Your military ID cards can't be in your wallets when you go in the field… but you'll need them to get back on the base."

"And how do you propose we do *that*?" asked Jerry.

Iris had a ready answer. "We'll leave the ID cards in a locked mailbox as close to the base as possible. You'll have twenty-four-hour access, coming in and going out."

All the men nodded their approval.

Iris continued, "Any other incriminating items will be kept in our office safe until this is over." She paused to make sure they were listening. "I think we should *add* something to your wallets as well."

"Business cards," said Jose. "I'm a medic… I can talk all day about working at a hospital back home."

"Okay," said Iris. "That's good… What about the rest of you?"

"I know everything about boats," offered Billy Joe. "You can make me a jack-of-all-trades at a fictional marina…call it 'Lynnhaven Marina' in Virginia Beach."

Carl looked at Jerry, who deferred to him. "I could be a free-lance writer… It'll be easy for me to play that part if I have to."

Jerry finished the auditions. "I can be a fitness trainer at a Virginia Beach gym." Everyone smiled at that. Jerry was a poster child for the job.

"We need an explanation of how you all came to be friends," said Iris, adding dryly, "You don't exactly look like Audubon people."

Jerry jumped on that one. "You could make the other guys membership cards for the fitness center where I work. That would bring us together in the story."

"It would also explain why you guys are so incredibly fit," added Aaron. "There's nothing you can do to hide that."

Carl sat up. "Let's make the big guy here an executive. Call it 'Jerry's Gym.' I'll be taking 'my friends from the gym' down to Panama to tour the canal and the city…and to see Harpy Eagles in the jungle."

"Done," said Iris. "Now let's take your passport photos…then we'll get out of your hair for today."

When Iris and Aaron were gone, Carl and his men spent two hours using the Army's gym. After showers and gear maintenance, they enjoyed another MRE for dinner. Jose brewed more of his strong coffee, and they wrestled with contingency planning for most of the night.

CHAPTER 9

THE MAN AT the tiller looked like just another peasant. He motored his wooden *piragua* along the jungle river faster than any man could walk. But no man could walk in this place. The boat had been fashioned from one enormous tree. The outboard was an adaptation of a lawn mower engine, fitted astern, and biting just below the surface of the coffee-colored froth. The man was alone. He carried no cocaine or weapons (except for his own automatic pistol). He had enough food for the six-hour journey, almost all of it in darkness. He was not worried about being stopped by the police. There *were* no police on this river. Although he had much to hide, police presence would have definitely made him feel safer. The river ran through a section of the forest known to provide sanctuary for drug traffickers, FARC guerrillas, human traffickers, and assorted bandits.

The local wildlife was not very friendly either.

The sun was rising, low on the horizon beyond the trees. The town of Yaviza, the end of the *Carretera Interamericana*, was also a riverport with a post office. That was all he needed this time. At the confluence of the *Chico*, Fort San Geronimo came into view. He smiled through rotten teeth (what teeth he still had) upon seeing the ruin. The *conquistadores* had built the fortress to protect their gold from people like him. A bit farther upriver, the coxswain maneuvered his *piragua* into the dense rainforest and stepped onto a muddy bank. He concealed his craft in the foliage and began to walk the final leg of his journey. He carried with him a letter to the Panama Canal Commission, detailing what the pilot's kidnappers wanted and how they planned to get it. The return address on the envelope could not be traced to anyone currently alive.

The indigenous messenger carried his precious cargo into the office. Even in sleepy Panama, he knew the letter would take only two days to arrive. More than enough time to prepare for the exchange, even if the government moved quickly. As he handed the envelope to the postal official, he felt a sense of accomplishment (in a criminal sort of way). This was the easiest courier mission he had ever completed. Now all he had to do was get back to the rendezvous downriver with the man in the fast boat who would pay him the rest of the money. Before men or snakes—with more malicious intent than his own—could find him. They would kill him before they knew what he was doing there.

Jungle rules, as always, were in effect.

* * *

Carl and his team slept later than usual. After a real breakfast—and a lot of strong coffee—they got back to work. Even if they did not receive new intelligence today, there was plenty to do. Carl went back to the whiteboard and read the written bullets.

Scenario one: Panama City. Scenario two: Other side of the canal. Scenario three: Mountains outside the city. Scenario four: Darién rainforest.

Carl raised his mug to the men around the table. "Any other possibilities?"

"No...I think we've got the first part right," said Jerry. "I thought about it all night, check that...all morning. These are the four."

"I wouldn't rule out one of the islands in the Gulf of Panama," Billy Joe suggested in his laziest Southern drawl. "If I was a kidnapper, that's where I'd go...there's lots o' rocks out there with nobody on 'em."

A blinding flash of the obvious came to all of them. "Of course," said Carl, chagrined he hadn't thought about it himself. "That makes sense… We appreciate your criminal mind, Tinker. We might need to find a boat big enough to get us out there." And they added the island option to their list.

"Now comes the hard part," said Jose, a growing urgency in his voice. "I know we talked and walked through all this last night… but without more intel, it'll be tough to translate that thinking into practical courses of action."

"Then we'd better get started," replied Carl emphatically, turning back to the board. He wrote the words Panama City, and they began again.

Three hours later, they had a rough course of action for each scenario, along with EEI requests. Every "what-if?" had a preliminary answer and a list of equipment they might need. The rest of the day was consumed with exercise, the cleaning of weapons, the sharpening of knives, the repacking of rucksacks, the rigging of civilian clothes for covert snooping around, and a lot more thought about what might happen in the next few days. They worked independently…but also collectively. Four warriors with one vision. Each knew instinctively what the others were doing, and why. Hardly any conversation was needed; only body language and long experience.

One team, one fight.

Carl watched his men prepare for war. Well, not exactly war. *Then what?* They didn't have law enforcement authority, but that didn't seem to matter. Unless the kidnappers turned out to be Americans. He didn't know exactly what they would be called upon to do, but he was confident they could do it. Anything at all. Any time, any place. These were the best men he had ever led.

Jerry Tompkins had grown up on a cattle ranch far out on Wyoming's high plains. He'd excelled at sports but also done reasonably well as a young student. It was assumed that he would just take over his uncle's ranch, but Jerry dreamed of a larger stage on which to live his life. He had been a high school hero. He wanted to be a real hero. Before accepting a football scholarship to the University of Wyoming, Jerry had enlisted in the Navy. He did not have to seek out the SEALs; they had come to him. The blond-haired, blue-eyed mountain of a kid was just what they needed. In the field, his teammates called him "Butkus" for his size and strength. Jerry had always appreciated the football reference. In his prime at thirty-five, Senior Chief Gunner's Mate Tompkins was Carl's right arm. The ultimate expression of the SEAL Ethos.

I am *that man.*

Jose was just as important to the team. Fleeing the violence in Colombia, his mother had taken him to New York City when he was three. The violence in Queens had taken place on asphalt instead of dirt, but it was the same violence. Gang war there had even been conducted in the same language. Maybe not as much blood but still a dangerous place to be a kid. In his late teens, Jose had come to a crossroads; he could make a living on the street, or he could get out. With no father to guide him, the would-be punk found himself in church, asking for advice. The priest, a Vietnam veteran, convinced him to join the Navy. After a year in the fleet, Jose needed more action. The SEAL command had been looking for Latino operators. Jose quickly found his calling: killing bad people and saving good ones. His nickname became his field name. Jose's mother had called him "Bosco" after his love for chocolate milk. She'd thought it was cute. Jose was stuck with it.

Billy Joe was a piece of work. A smart but reckless young sailor who had grown up in rural Southwest Florida, fixing and operating his fisherman father's boats. The man they called "Tinker," steeped in movies and books about the sea, had dreamed of being a pirate. Two hundred years too late, he'd decided to become a SEAL instead. He'd brought with him a bias for action and a penchant for getting in trouble. Rescued by Carl from a court-martial early in his sputtering career, Billy Joe Barnes had become a good sailor and a loyal follower. Carl had done more than save Billy Joe's career; he'd saved the young man's life during the fiasco in Grenada. Petty Officer Barnes was absolutely fearless under fire. He was the man you wanted next to you in a firefight. But he was always eager for a bar fight. With wing-men like Bosco and Butkus, Tinker had managed to stay focused on the most important fights.

Late in the afternoon, Carl picked up the secure phone and called the Special Operations Command.

"Stewart."

"Good afternoon, sir. I just wanted to check in."

"I was just about to call you, Carl." Stewart's voice was grim. "We have nothing at all to report."

"Not anything?" came the astonished reply. "Not even from the major?"

Stewart sighed into the phone, something he almost *never* did. "No, I'm afraid all of us are in a holding pattern until we get something from the hostage takers."

Carl absorbed the news without emotion. A blank slate complicated the challenge, but it also gave him some ideas. "Okay, sir, we're continuing to plan for five possible scenarios. The EEIs are piling up. When can we expect another briefing?"

"I've suggested command cell come back tomorrow after lunch…say 1300. Can you be ready to brief all of us on what you have so far?"

"Yes, sir, we can. I hope the others have some answers to our many questions." Carl paused for effect. "I'm used to planning with inadequate information, but we're groping in the dark on this one."

"Got it, Carl. See you tomorrow. Out here."

The team again worked late into the night, preparing to brief the briefers. That arrangement was backwards, of course. The command cell was telling the team that, basically, "your guess is as good as mine."

* * *

Next morning, the team assembled a list of items they might need to execute whatever courses of action might be required. Jerry went to the sergeant's studio apartment, adjacent to the ISOFAC.

"Mornin', Joe. Here's the list. The commander would like to have all this stuff by the end of the day."

The sergeant looked over the list:

> Four M-21 rifles with standard scopes and magazines

Two AN/PVS-4 night-vision scopes (with water-proof cases)
Four SIG Sauer P226 pistols
Four Walther PPK pistols
Four pairs jungle fatigues without insignia
Two civilian backpacks for Rios and Barnes
Three pairs of 8×42 binoculars
Three copies of *The Birds of Panama* by Robert Ridgely
Four pairs of civilian sunglasses (all different; anything but Oakleys)
Two cans of 5.56 ammo
Two cans of 7.62 ammo
Two boxes of 9mm ammo (one of them down-loaded rounds)
One box of .380 PPK ammo
Four silencers for SIG Sauer P226 pistols
One box of MK13 day/night flares
Four ankle holsters for SIGs and PPKs
Four shoulder holsters for SIGs and PPKs

"Okay, Senior Chief," said the sergeant, still in flip-flops. "I'll get on it. How's the chow?"

"Not bad, but the confinement is killing me. Can't wait to get outa this place!"

Jerry went back to his team on the other side of the wall. SEAL boredom was setting in. They needed a real mission.

At precisely 1300, the briefers came to their door. They were armed again with unmarked folders. Carl wondered (almost aloud) if there was anything new in the folders. He led the briefers through a "brief back" on all five possible scenarios, laying out the questions in the form of essential elements of information. The list of equipment was discussed with no controversy. Carl's bottom line came last.

"We've told you what we know…and what we don't know. Now here's what we think."

The briefers all nodded. Carl noticed the corners of Ana Maria's lips turn up, ever so slightly. She had heard him do this before.

"The fact that we haven't heard anything from the kidnappers tells us that they may have taken Captain Alegre to a remote location. We don't think they're in the city. If that were the case, it would've been no problem for them to communicate with us. We don't think they're on the other side of the canal—too rural…and it's almost a *cul-de-sac* in tactical terms. If they're in the mountains near the city, the road network would've made it relatively easy to send us a ransom note by now." Carl stopped to see if the visitors were following his logic.

"And what about the remaining scenarios?" asked Ned, speaking for the others.

"We think the kidnappers took their hostage into the *Darién*, way off the grid. That would explain why we haven't heard anything yet. As we say, 'Amateurs think about strategy. Professionals think about logistics.' If that is where they are, this is a logistics nightmare for them, but it may help *us*." Carl looked right and left to his men then focused on the briefers. Confident but not cocky.

"We're pretty comfortable operating way off the grid."

* * *

Father Oscar Castillo sat down to breakfast in the rectory. The window shades were down. He had not ventured into the city since his return from Pasto. The sister had brought him the paper as she always did. There on the front page was the account of Freddy Alegre's kidnapping. The priest had not heard about this, not even in rumor-driven Panama City. He was sweating again. Manfredo Alegre Rivas belonged to his parish! Father Castillo had an obligation to console the pilot's family. To pray with them. But he was in hiding, fearing that the drug lord Mena's *sicarios* would kill him. He was sure they had killed Father Santiago…whose only sin had been to direct Castillo to the kingpin. Castillo's sin was far greater. He had carried the letter to Mena…without proof that he had not read it. *Qué dilema*! He was required to reach out to the Alegre family. How could he do that without exposing himself to Mena's retribution?

I am a dead man walking…like Jesus.

Father Castillo then had his own epiphany. *Just do it*! He had always tried to live the purest Christian life he could. If the worst happened, it would be the holiest way to finish his earthbound story.

CHAPTER 10

THE PHONE CALL came in the middle of the second night, not long after the team had gone to sleep. Carl leapt off his cot like a shot.

"Three nine three seven...may I help you?"

"Carl...this is Colonel Stewart. Get ready for a visit from the command cell principals."

"Got it, Colonel. They must have something specific to tell us now."

"They do. See you in one hour."

"Yes, sir, out here."

Carl put down the secure phone and got the team ready for a real briefing.

Exactly one hour later, Colonel Stewart led the briefing team back into what Carl's men had begun calling "the cage." Jose poured coffee, and they took the same seats at the table.

Stewart was the first to speak. "The Panama Canal Commission received a letter late this afternoon. I'll let Mr. Céspedes explain."

"First, my apologies for taking so long to get this to you. The commission is a bureaucracy. The letter was not addressed to a single individual. I only got my hands on it two hours ago." Pablo Céspedes took a wrinkled piece of paper from his unmarked folder and began to read. The letter was in Spanish, and he translated it sentence by sentence for Jerry and Billy Joe.

To the American Canal Commission,

We have your pilot. We will kill him if you do not bring us $1 million in $50 and $20 bills at the time and place listed below. There will be no negotiation about this—and not one *policeman*! Find a bagman and have him deliver the money to this location: latitude 8°4'31" N; longitude 78°46'3" W. We will be there with the pilot at 2:00 a.m. on the morning of the twenty-third. If we receive the money, you will receive Alegre— still breathing. Then this thing will be over.

You do not need to know who we are.

Billy Joe was already standing at the map on the wall. His pulse was racing. They all waited for him to announce the location of the proposed exchange. It took less than a minute.

"It's an island in the Gulf of Panama," said Billy Joe triumphantly. "It's really small...doesn't even have a name."

"There are no police out there...that's for sure," added Ana Maria. "Nothing for me to deconflict."

Carl looked across the table at Ned. "Can your folks get us some high-resolution imagery of this?"

Ned did not hesitate. "Sure...we can have the photos in a few hours," said the CIA man. "I assume you want both high altitude and low."

"Yeah," replied the team leader. "Strategically, we'll need to know where the island sits in the Gulf, relative to Panama City...and to wherever the kidnappers may be hiding out. Those pictures will supplement the nautical chart."

Jerry burst in, "And tactically, we'll need to see what the island itself looks like up close in order to work out a plan for the exchange."

"The bad guys didn't say how they intend to deliver the hostage to us," added Jose, looking at Colonel Stewart. "I think it would be really hard for them to use a helicopter...wherever they're coming from." He shifted his focus to Billy Joe. "Once we get those images, I think we'll find there's no place flat enough, or long enough, to land a fixed-wing aircraft."

"Yeah, I think they'll come by boat," said Billy Joe, again studying the map.

"We could fast-rope in," said Carl. "That's much easier than going in by boat, but it's a military capability, and it would give us away as Americans." He looked at Jerry. "I think Billy Joe is right. We're in for a long boat ride."

Ana Maria spoke up again. "I will make sure the maritime service doesn't try to intercept your boat at sea." She stopped talking and then continued in a lower voice. "That will be easy to do since Panama has only a handful of patrol boats..." She shot an ironic smile at Carl.

Ana Maria had been analyzing the ransom note, now in her hands. "I don't think this was written by a Panamanian." She held up the paper. "Most of my countrymen, especially the criminals, would refer to the police as *tongo* rather than *policía*. Also, they would use the word *vaina* instead of *cosa* to mean 'thing.'"

"And the relabeling of the Panama Canal Commission is also suspect," added Pablo Céspedes. Even though, technically, the Panama Canal is still owned by the United States, no Panamanian would refer to the PCC as an *American* institution. The name is a point of pride here."

"The twenty-third is the day after tomorrow," Stewart put in. "But 0200 makes it the middle of the night on the twenty-second. We're going to have to hustle to get this done."

Carl continued Stewart's point. "Yeah...we'll have the whole day today and then tomorrow...but only up until the time we have to leave to make the rendezvous." Carl looked at Billy Joe. "How long a transit will this be?" Then he turned to Ana Maria. "And where do we get a civilian boat capable of making the trip?"

She did not have a ready answer.

Tinker quickly estimated the distance. "A little more than one hundred nautical miles." He thought a few seconds. "At twenty knots, that would be around five hours but fifteen knots is more realistic, given the Pacific swell and the wind chop. That would make it about seven and a half hours."

Jerry broke in, "I know just the boat to meet that mission profile," added Jerry. "We'll need to build in some extra time to make sure we get there early. Best departure time might be around 1700."

"That's before sundown," cautioned Jose. "If we're going to use the boat Jerry has in mind, there's an OPSEC issue."

"We can leave the dock in a Zodiac…and rendezvous with the *Luisa* in a remote location on the way out," said Carl. "We'll call it a training exercise. No one will see the connection."

Ned, who as a CIA officer was supposed to know everything that happened in Panama, cocked his head. "What, exactly, is the *Luisa*?"

Carl hesitated to make sure he got the explanation right. He and Colonel Stewart had convinced General Wells to let some officials within the Panamanian public forces know about the sportfishing boat. Ana Maria had been on the short disclosure list. The CIA station chief had not.

"It's a fishing yacht we inherited from Panama after *Just Cause*," Carl began.

Ned gave him a frustrated look. "And why were we not told?"

Stewart rescued Carl from the question that sounded more like an accusation. "You can chalk that one up to bureaucratic turf politics, Ned. DoD didn't want CIA to try to take the boat for its own use. We actually got it from the US Marshal's Service. They had confiscated the boat from Panama before the invasion. The SOC seized Noriega's other two pleasure boats, but we had to give those back. So…we ended up with one really good covert surface platform."

Ned did not like to look clueless, but he did. "Okay…so how do you cover and operate the boat?"

Carl jumped in. "The vessel is moored in various places around the canal and manned 24-7 by sailors from Commander Fletcher's boat unit over at Rodman." Sensing Ned's acquiescence, Carl went on, "We repainted and reconfigured the boat to be unrecognizable to the locals. The crew is specially chosen for their ability to blend in with the Panama fishing crowd…an international set of part-time residents. These sailors are native speakers of Spanish and longtime Panama residents. They support our training exercises on a regular basis, but this type of operation is the real reason we have the platform."

Ned frowned at Stewart. "You're right, Reggie, CIA would have opposed this." Then he smiled. "But right now, I'm glad you have the boat. We can talk about institutional roles and missions later."

Stewart nodded. He'd known this would happen at some point. CIA was understandably protective of its covert operations role. But he strongly believed that DoD also needed a limited covert capability…especially here.

Jose raised his hand. "What about the money? What does it weigh, and how big a satchel will we need to carry it?"

Pablo Céspedes had been doing some back-of-the-envelope calculations. "At the Commission, we handle a lot of cash. I can tell you that a single bill weighs about one gram. That means a million dollars in one-dollar notes would weigh about one metric ton. We can extrapolate from that to figure out what a bag of $20s and $50s would weigh."

There was silence in the room as everyone tried to do the math. Ana Maria beat them all to the punch. "If we put half in twenties and half in fifties, the bag will weigh about ninety pounds."

"I can carry that in a large civilian backpack," said Jerry. Everyone except Carl nodded approval.

"You could do that, Senior Chief, but it would turn you into a mule. I think it would be better to split the load into at least two parts. That way, all of us can defend ourselves and move with agility at the objective." He looked at Stewart. "Colonel, let us work this out in a way that balances all our tactical concerns."

"You have my permission to handle the cash in any tactically feasible way you choose," replied Stewart. He turned to Pablo Céspedes, who nodded in agreement.

Jose shifted his attention back to Céspedes. "Can you get the cash that quickly? And do you have a few leather bags we can put it in?"

The PCC official responded right away. "Yes, we can do that. Accompanied by armed guards, I will bring it to you here first thing in the morning." He turned to Carl. "You'll have to sign for it, of course."

Carl took a furtive gulp. "Got it, sir. We'll take good care of your money." He looked at Ned again. "Do you have a locator beacon we could borrow…one that could be monitored in the command cell?"

After a momentary pause, Ned nodded. "You want to be able to track the kidnappers after they hand over Captain Alegre," said Ned with a rising pitch in his voice.

Carl gave Ned his Dirty Harry imitation. "Yeah…we do. And if they *don't* hand over the hostage, we want to be able to hunt them down."

"I can get you that, Commander," said the CIA man. "You'll have it by the end of the day."

There were no more questions. The briefing team left the room. The colonel stayed to speak with Carl and his men. Stewart focused his leadership aura directly on the team.

"You guys feel okay about this?"

All four of the men nodded at once, restraining themselves from showing the elation they felt.

Carl answered for the team, "We got it, sir. When do you want to take our briefing?"

Stewart did not smile, but each of them understood they had his full confidence. They respected him as a leader. He would not second-guess them. He would make sure the command cell gave them the flexibility they needed to respond to the evolving situation they were about to face in the field.

"I'll bring the command cell back to listen to your plan tomorrow at 0900. That'll give you time to jock up on schedule."

It was happening. They felt the thrill of what they knew was coming, along with the fear of what they did *not* know.

* * *

The kidnappers arrived at their base camp in the middle of the night. They bound Freddy's feet and kept him isolated in a broiling tent all the next day, only dragging him out deep in the night. The pilot had become robotic, paralyzed by the unrelenting fear of the last forty-eight hours. He smelled of stale sweat. Hunger pangs had given way to a general feeling of weariness. His captors had counted on exhaustion and fear to weaken his resistance to their questioning. They guessed the jungle darkness would make him even more pliant. As soon as they sat him down in the mud, the interrogation began.

"Tell us what you do for the canal commission." The voice was soft, nonthreatening. An educated Spanish. Freddy was surprised. He answered humbly, in simple sentences, hoping they would not beat him.

"I am a senior pilot. I guide ships through the canal."

The soft voice responded right away. "So you know how the canal works." It was a statement.

"Yes. I *have* to know that," replied the pilot.

"So…how *does* it work?"

Freddy was so tired he did not think about the implications of what he had just been asked. He was proud of his role in facilitating the flow of world commerce. The canal was a miracle of straightforward engineering…easy to explain.

"It's really very simple," said the hostage, now feeling more like a guest in the jungle camp. He was still terrified, but relaxing a bit had reminded him of his thirst. "Before I explain, sir, could I have some water?"

The silent partner brought him a cup of tepid water, drawn from the river.

Freddy drank the water and continued his lecture. He wanted to sleep but understood that, as long as he was talking, they would not kill him.

"Yes…the French had tried to build a sea-level canal across the isthmus in the last decade of the nineteenth century. But this attempt was doomed to fail for two reasons. First, the geology of Panama and, second, the prevalence of yellow fever and malaria. The French effort resulted in about twenty thousand deaths…and they never found the angle of repose."

"What is the angle of repose?" asked the soft voice.

"That is where the slope of the bank becomes shallow enough not to produce regular landslides into the trench. Panama's soil is very plastic, almost like lava flowing down a mountain slope."

"So what happened after the French abandoned the project?"

"The Americans supported Panama Province's separation from Colombia, and the new country allowed the United States to build the canal."

The soft voice became louder. "*Por supuesto…*the *gringos* are the criminals who took Colombia's patrimony. Of course, it is always the Americans."

Freddy went on, puzzled as to why even a criminal from his country would take Colombia's side. Now that Panama was going to get full control of the canal, such sentiments sounded odd.

The voice returned to its soft timbre. "So how did the Americans design the canal? As a pilot, do you think it is a good piece of engineering?"

Two things were holding Freddy together at this point: his family and his professional pride. He had vowed not to say anything about his wife and children; he quickly returned to expressing his pride.

"The Panama Canal was a marvel of engineering a hundred years ago, and it is still a marvel of engineering today," he began. "The locking system functions on fresh water and gravity. Rainfall is captured in two lakes, and those reservoirs drain into the locks on each coast, raising and then lowering the ships to sea level. The builders dug through the continental divide but had to settle for an eighty-five-foot rise of the water level between the seas."

"So the lakes are the key to working the locks?" asked the soft voice.

"Yes…very much so," replied the pilot. "Without the lakes, the locks would not work at all." He thought for a few seconds and then added, "Of course, without the locks, the canal would be just a long ditch with no ships."

And Captain Alegre talked on…far into the early morning hours of September 22.

CHAPTER 11

CARL AND HIS men briefed the command cell at 0900 the next day, laying out the concept of the operation and time line. They presented an "execution checklist" by which a series of scripted transmissions would be passed to Ned's team by high-frequency radio signal, indicating milestones in the team's mission. There was no other way for the command cell to track their progress. Actions to be executed at the objective were kept vague owing to the lack of specific information available to the team. Carl and his men would have to sort out the situation on the ground. It was agreed that Ana Maria would brief the Panamanian government in general terms about the operation. She would also ask the *Servicio Maritimo* to avoid intercepting the Americans within a prohibited zone bounded by written coordinates.

As soon as the others had given their approval, Pablo Céspedes bent down and, one at a time, lifted two heavy leather satchels onto the table. He then presented a one-page document to Carl.

"Sign here, Commander."

Carl signed for the money and looked up at Pablo. "Do you want the bags back?"

"Keep the bags," replied the PCC official. "Just bring back my pilot."

The crew of the *Luisa* was waiting at the door as the command cell briefers left the ISOFAC. Carl brought them into the planning cell and sat them down across from his men. The sailors did not look like sailors. They were living the cover of big-game fishermen in their late thirties. Posing as a couple of early retirees from Venezuela, they spoke only Spanish to the locals. They were also man and wife.

"You already know Senior Chief Tompkins," said Carl to the couple, "I don't think you know Petty Officers Rios and Barnes." He turned to Jose and Billy Joe. "Meet Juan and Rosa."

They all shook hands and got to work. Bonds of trust, so essential in small-unit operations, would materialize quickly. Carl's men understood perfectly that Juan and Rosa were just as important to the successful accomplishment of this mission as they were.

"From here on, I will refer to my men by their field names… Butkus, Bosco, and Tinker." Each raised his hand on cue. "We'll just call you Juan and Rosa if that's okay."

The couple nodded approval.

"My name is Carlos."

The yacht's crew left an hour later, ready to execute a mission profile for which they had long prepared.

* * *

The combat rubber raiding craft, loaded down with four men and their equipment, motored slowly out the southern end of the Panama Canal. Past the dock at Balboa where, four years before, they had come from underwater to sink two of Panama's most capable patrol boats. Passing the site of that attack, they glided under the Bridge of the Americas, the only pavement linking the two halves of a country cleaved by the great canal. To all those who saw the black Zodiac glide by, the men in green fatigues were assumed to be engaged in a training exercise—just like so many times before. Indeed, the pattern had been set long ago to conceal what was now happening. The sun was dropping fast toward the horizon—but not fast enough! Their rendezvous with the *Luisa* would take place thirty minutes before the sun sank into the ocean. They were on a tight schedule.

There was a hostage to recover.

As the Zodiac cleared the causeway, Billy Joe adjusted course toward *Taboga*, the closest inhabited island in the *Perlas* chain, ten miles south of the canal entrance. About halfway to the island, he adjusted course again, a bit west of south. Just in front of them loomed a small islet they had often used for training. The chart did not show a name for the barren outcrop, so the sailors had named it "Flat Top Rock." As the Zodiac rounded the rock, the yacht *Luisa* came into view. The backside of Flat Top was their best chance to remain undetected during the transfer. Billy Joe closed with the modest sport fisherman then cut the outboard engine as the rubber craft bounced against *Luisa's* hull. Jerry and Jose jumped into the cockpit, helped up by Juan and Rosa. Carl and Billy Joe started handing weapons and field gear into four pairs of outstretched arms.

Five minutes later, the Zodiac was landing at the gravel beach cove, and *Luisa's* anchor was aweigh. Carl and Billy Joe dragged the rubber boat beyond the high-water line—a long pull due to the extreme Pacific tides. They stowed the engine inside and covered the craft with an olive-drab tarpaulin. After anchoring the corners of the tarp with heavy rocks, they ran to the water's edge and swam back to the mothercraft, waiting just seventy-five yards off the beach. The sun was momentarily resting on the surface of the sea beyond *Taboga*. It would be dark in a few minutes. Carl and his men always felt more comfortable in the dark. They had accomplished the daytime linkup without being seen (as far as they knew). The team was now relatively safe in *Luisa*.

At least for the next seven hours.

Rosa, navigating from the flying bridge, short brown hair wild in the wind, picked up the HF radio handset and transmitted a code word to the command cell in Panama City.

"Arcturus, I say again, Arcturus."

"Roger, out," replied Colonel Stewart.

Juan, emerging from his undercover life, joined Carl and his team in the long cockpit of the forty-three-foot vessel. Designed for groups of up to six fishermen hunting Pacific Sailfish, the deck had been stripped of its fighting chair and live-bait tanks. Juan and Rosa had lashed the tandem sea kayaks to both gunwales, leaving plenty of room on the deck to prepare gear for the mission. All of them confronted a combination of knowns and unknowns for which to prepare. Carl did not need to direct the men; they knew what to do.

"Let's take the next hour to get jocked up. Then we can talk about the 'what-ifs' and decision points." The men nodded at the boss and donned LED headlamps to light the encroaching darkness.

Carl and Jose replaced their jungle fatigues with loose-fitting hiker's clothes and well-worn civilian high-top boots. With their Latin faces and colloquial Spanish, they could easily pass for Panamanian bagmen, recruited by the Canal Commission. They would conceal their 9mm pistols in ankle holsters, but there was a limit to the amount of gear they could take to the exchange site. They were not even sure where the transaction would take place although overhead imagery suggested the islet's only beach as the most likely spot. Jose wore his medical kit, as always, like an appendage. Both of them would need squad radios, red-lens flashlights, and day-night flares. They had settled on wearing fanny packs rather than rucksacks, a balance between fooling the kidnappers and being ready to fight their way out. With each man lugging a forty-five-pound bag of money—and only secondary weapons—they would require backup.

And backup they would have. Jerry and Billy Joe remained in their military fatigues and prepared to swim ashore. Their gear included fins, UDT life jackets, K-bar knives, day-night flares, M-21 rifles, and night-vision scopes with waterproof cases. No ruses—military all the way. They also carried Ned's homing beacon, along with an industrial-strength staple gun. Captain Alegre and his recovery team would have the protection of two trained snipers, unseen by the kidnappers. Jerry had to assume the hostage takers would come by boat. The chart, amplified by imagery, told them to expect a small craft capable of beaching itself in the lee of the point. Whoever showed up to take the ransom would be prepared to make a quick getaway. Jerry guessed there'd be at least four targets, two men for the drop and perhaps two others to operate the boat. Instinct and creativity would be just as important as firepower.

Carl glanced up from his own tasks every few minutes to watch the men work. When all of them were ready, he began the final briefing.

"I don't need to remind you guys that this one will be tricky." Dim light from four headlamps moved up and down. Juan sat in the same circle as the others, waiting to review for the team *Luisa's* part of the plan. It was like a good marriage. SEALs in Panama never went anywhere without boats; boats never went anywhere without SEALs.

Carl continued, "This is where all that training pays off, frogs. We have the confidence to get this done…but we don't have the full picture. This is pickup basketball. We'll need to maintain situational awareness and react quickly to changing circumstances we encounter on the ground."

"And in the water," added Jerry, looking at Juan. "What can we expect in terms of wave action and surf tonight?"

"Rosa and I have never been to this island," began the skipper. "But we've seen lots of others in the *Perlas* with beaches facing the same direction. There will be a windward and a lee on either side of the point." Juan placed a forefinger on the satellite photo, laid out in the middle of the circle. "Judging from the swell we're riding at the moment, the surf on the windward side should be about chest high. The leeward side will probably be flat or close to flat." Juan thought for a few seconds. "And the wind chop has gone away since the sun went down. You should have a smooth surface for the approach."

Jerry nodded. "That's both good and bad." He looked up at the moon, now shining almost full. "When is moonset?"

"Should be down before we get there, Butkus, but not by much. The tide will be around plus nine, so you guys'll have lots of water to wallow in." Juan then added the best news, "And the current will be about one knot…running toward the point."

"At least the tide and current gods are with us," responded the big man. "Tinker and I will be pretty easy to spot out there…that is if the bad guys are paying attention."

"They'll be focused on the *Luisa* and the hostage exchange," Billy Joe put in. "Good tactical swimming should get us around the point quick enough to set up."

For another hour, Carl and his men brainstormed all the what-ifs and reviewed the probable decision points. Then they rested as best they could on the deck of their mothercraft.

* * *

Ahead of schedule (according to the SATNAV), Rosa had slowed *Luisa's* speed of advance over the last leg of the transit so as to arrive at the site precisely thirty minutes before rendezvous time. One hour out, the islet came into view on radar, and all hands got ready to go. Rosa moved quickly from the exposed flying bridge to the pilothouse helm, promptly slowing *Luisa* to bare steerageway. Juan and Carl unlashed the sea kayaks and lowered them to float on either side of the yacht. The dull-green plastic boats rode easily in the smooth sea. Carl and Jose sat on the gunwales and fended the kayaks off with their feet while Jerry and Billy Joe performed final equipment checks. Slowly, Rosa increased *Luisa's* speed to seven knots.

Trolling speed for Tuna.

The mothercraft began a clockwise circumnavigation of the island, a reconnaissance, to assess the situation before committing the team. Also, to pose for the kidnappers.

We are here...not a threat to you...ready to recover the hostage.

As expected, a sleek speedboat lay partially beached on the leeward side of the point. The stern of the ocean racer was still in the water. With moonlight fading fast, Billy Joe found the *Steiner* binoculars and confirmed that the lower units of all three enormous outboards were in the water and running in neutral. In the boat were five heads, one of which *had* to belong to Captain Alegre. Billy Joe smiled with approval at Jerry in the dim light of the cockpit, white teeth in sharp contrast to his blackened face.

Jerry turned his game face to Carl. "Ready, boss."

First, Billy Joe, then Jerry, lowered themselves carefully onto the portside kayak and into the water. The transition took precious time (Juan had assessed this maneuver to be the riskiest part of the launch). Rosa maintained a constant speed on a steady course, her starboard side facing the beach. Once Jerry and Billy Joe were safely hanging on the outside of the kayak, Carl and Jose handed down the sniper weapons, magazines in place, locked and loaded. The weapons rested temporarily in the forward and after cockpits of the kayak, their owners clutching them with spare hands as they rode to the drop-off point. The kidnappers would never know Jerry and Billy Joe were in the water.

At least that was the plan.

As *Luisa* passed 250 yards astern of the kidnappers, the frogmen simply let go of the kayak, waited for their forward motion to bleed off, and then slung the weapons around their shoulders. Six feet apart, they began a slow, stealthy swim toward the back of the racing craft. *Luisa* continued at seven knots until taking station on the other side of the point, precisely 150 yards off the north side of the small beach. Carl and Jose did final equipment checks and shoulder slaps. Paddles in hand, they climbed slowly into separate kayaks, still floating high against *Luisa's* hull. As rehearsed, they sat down in the rear wells and signaled okay. Juan lowered the heavy hard-plastic containers into the empty forward well of each boat. The money did not destabilize the kayaks; it steadied them.

Carl and Jose began the dangerous trip into the beach, aware that the kidnappers would be observing them, probably with binoculars. In fact, they *counted* on being observed. Dressed for the part—but ready for anything—the kayaking bagmen paddled side by side.

Two targets instead of one.

On Juan's signal, Rosa repositioned the *Luisa* a few hundred yards farther from the beach. A precaution. If a firefight erupted at the exchange site, they could easily—if not safely—bring the boat closer in for an emergency extraction.

Rosa put down her binoculars and reached for the radio handset. "Betelgeuse. I say again, Betelgeuse."

Stewart's voice came back without hesitation. "Roger, out."

And they waited.

Jerry and Billy Joe swam silently north toward the getaway boat. Carl and Jose paddled south, getting ready to beach their kayaks without dumping the cargo. It was now clear to every member of the team that the exchange would take place on the sand in front of them. It sounded simple: trade the money for the hostage…everyone back to their boats and clear the area. But Carl had learned a big lesson in his long tactical life.

Nothing is simple.

CHAPTER 12

JERRY AND BILLY Joe breaststroked toward what they now recognized as a "go-fast" boat, notorious for delivering large drug cargoes at high speed over long distances. The moon was finally down, but the surface of the water was smooth enough to reflect starlight. A long look from the enemy would reveal the tops of two human heads covered with olive-drab cloth. The men glided silently closer. Especially with fins, they were at home in the water. An effective defense under these circumstances, however, would be nearly impossible. The swimmers were now at their maximum point of vulnerability, but the kidnappers were not searching for them. Jerry could see that four of the heads in the boat were watching Carl and Jose paddle through the low surf at the opposite side of the beach. *Poor situational awareness!* The fifth head in the boat was hanging down. A sign of exhaustion.

The pilot!

The getaway boat's engines idled louder.

Thirty yards out, Billy Joe passed his rifle to Jerry and reached into the rucksack, now hanging from his chest. Momentarily treading water, he withdrew the beacon and staple gun. With Jerry holding a covering position, Billy Joe swam the tag to the starboard quarter of the go-fast. Crouching in the shallow water, he stapled the device to the fiberglass hull. The device would be difficult to see, he reckoned, broadcasting from just above the boat's soft chine. Billy Joe could not hear the kidnappers. In the rumble of the engines, they would not hear him either, but he was close enough to smell their cigarette breath. He sank below the surface and stroked underwater all the way back to Jerry…and his own weapon.

With rifles at arm's length and fingers on trigger guards, Jerry and Billy Joe sidestroked laterally around the point. Toward the waves rolling onto the windward side of the beach. Riding the current, they reached their sniper/observer position in under ten minutes. It took them another few minutes to take the night-vision scopes out of the waterproof containers and fix them to each rifle. The starlight was just right. Their targets would be no more than one hundred meters away.

Carl and Jose began to stumble out of their kayaks in four-foot surf. Water rushed into the rear cockpits, threatening to capsize the flimsy boats and dump their cargoes into the surge. As they struggled to beach the kayaks, Carl thought quickly about how difficult it would be to launch them again. A black inflatable with a flat bottom and a spray tube was what they *really* needed. They were making do with nonmilitary boats, not designed for riding waves or carrying large amounts of cash. Jose managed to get his boat on the beach, followed a few seconds later by Carl. They dragged their kayaks past the high-water line, each resting on one knee, scanning the sandy objective. The mystery boat was still idling on the opposite beach, but none of the crew had budged.

Carlos and Bosco would have to go first.

Butkus and Tinker set up in prone positions on the gentle slope of the windward beach. They had a panorama to divide into two fields of fire, from three o'clock on the right to nine o'clock on the left. Every human being on the island was in sight—and in range. They themselves were in the open, but it would have taken a sharp eye to pick them out of the gravely sand, washed by a steady rhythm of sprawling waves.

Jerry broke squelch on the squad radio to tell Carl that he and Billy Joe were ready.

As they helped each other lift the square boxes from the kayak wells, Jose glanced at the plastic boats and whispered, "*Valió la pena, Carlos.*" Carl agreed that all the effort to this point had been worth it.

They unsnapped the boxes and removed the leather satchels. Jose laid his money on the sand then took one strap of Carl's satchel in his left hand. Together, they took the first steps toward the market-place, one bag between them. The hundred-meter walk to the center of the beach felt more like a klick. It wasn't so much the weight of the money; it was the heavy burden of responsibility. Getting this wrong was not an option.

They were about to buy a human life.

The pair stopped at the geometric center of the beach. They stood tall in place as three figures got out of the ocean racer, formed a line abreast, and began a slow walk toward them. The night sky was so brilliant they could watch the figure in the middle being half-dragged across the sand. A few minutes later, Carl and Jose were face-to-face with two large unkempt men in camouflage, wearing night-vision goggles. Each used one hand to prop up the hostage and held an AK-47 in the other.

Freddy Alegre, whose outline was just visible to Carl and Jose, appeared to be taking his last few breaths. They could hear him wheezing. His eyes were cast to the sand they knew he could not see. His knees buckled as he leaned on one captor then the other. It was clear to Jose that the man would need his medical skills—assuming he and Carl managed to get him back to the *Luisa*.

"*¿El dinero?*" shouted one of the men, identifying himself as the negotiator.

"This is half the money," replied Jose in gutter Spanish as he and Carl dropped the bag with a thud. "The other half is back there." He pointed at the beached kayaks. "The bags are too heavy for one person."

The kidnappers dumped their captive on the sand like a sack of coffee beans. "Go get it!" ordered the negotiator. "This guy stays here!" He pointed his weapon at Carl.

"Can you give me a hand?" asked Jose. "You'll get it more quickly that way."

The kidnapper didn't hesitate. "No! If you are too weak to carry it, then *drag* it back here…but make it quick."

Jose turned and walked slowly toward the kayaks. Halfway there, he heard another shout. "Hurry up…or we will shoot the prisoner right here!"

Suddenly, Freddy sprang off the sand and scrambled away from his surprised captors. Lunging past Carl, he ran madly toward Jose!

One shot rang out, followed immediately by two more shots, thudding into human flesh almost simultaneously.

Alegre lurched forward, fell in his tracks, and started screaming.

Both Freddy's captors crumpled to the sand as Carl went to one knee and drew his pistol from its ankle holster.

Without waiting for instructions, Jose ran to Freddy, writhing in pain but alive. Carl checked the negotiator and his partner for signs of life. There *were* no signs of life. Jerry and Billy Joe had drilled each of them in the head.

Two more shots—this time directed away from Carl. Then the roar of three powerful outboard engines. The boat's operators, saved by the sound of the kill shots, cowered below the dashboard as they backed the go-fast into deeper water. Banking the boat like an aircraft, the driver pushed his throttles all the way forward. Within seconds, they were speeding away from the island at close to fifty knots. Jerry and Billy Joe took four more shots at the ocean racer, but the target was moving too fast…and at the wrong angle.

Carl bristled with energy. He needed to shout at *somebody* in the dark. "Butkus! Tinker! Fall in on me!" He knew they couldn't hear him at that distance.

His teammates were already running in his direction.

Carl stood his ground until they got to him. "You guys wait here… I'm going back to check with Bosco." And he was gone in an invisible cloud of sand.

Jerry and Billy Joe rolled the bodies clear and picked up the leather satchel. "Looks like we get to take the money back," said Billy Joe, grinning.

"Now all we need is to take the *pilot* back," replied Jerry sternly.

Billy Joe responded with reduced enthusiasm. "Right, Butkus, but he's in good hands right now."

"Yeah…if anyone can patch him up, it's Bosco."

Jose worked fast. By the time Carl got there, the medic had torn off the patient's pant leg. Jose was wearing a headlamp and probing the pilot's wound with his hands. Carl could see a river of blood coming from the pilot's right hamstring. Jose didn't take his eyes off the patient but spoke to Carl.

"I can save him, boss, but we have to extract *now!* Femur's not broken. The wound is low enough to give me room to apply a tourniquet, but we have to get him back to the boat!" Jose applied more pressure to the wound and looked quickly up at Carl. "Luckily, the bullet missed the artery. I can put a hasty patch on the femoral vein once we stretch him out on the flat deck." With his free hand, Jose took a cloth bandana from the fanny pack. He wrapped it around Freddy's leg and used his flashlight to twist it tight.

The bleeding stopped.

Freddy Alegre was in shock. He was moaning like a wounded animal. "Carlos, there's a morphine syrette in my medical kit. Hit him in the other thigh."

Carl took the syrette and injected the drug into the pilot's leg. "Good," said the medic. "Now unwrap a battle dressing and hand it to me." Jose tied the bandage tightly around the man's leg. *So far, so good.*

"I'll be right back!" shouted Carl, leaning toward the center of the beach.

"*¡Rápido!*" responded the medic, holding the flashlight and the pressure dressing. The hostage's blood stained the sand where he lay. Jose figured they had about ten minutes to get him through the surf and onto *Luisa's* deck.

Carl rocketed back to Jerry and Billy Joe's position. As he arrived, his teammates were preparing to carry the corpses to the kayaks. Carl changed the plan on the spot.

"Drop the bodies and take the money!" He pulled them toward the kayaks with his voice. "Follow me!"

Jerry and Billy Joe, rifles slung, fell in behind Carl. Jerry had the leather satchel under his arm like a high school kid carrying books. The three of them sprinted up to Jose and saw right away the problem to be solved.

Survival is a long series of problems. Solve them all, one at a time. When you're done doing that, you get to go home.

Carl had drilled that maxim into his men for years. Now they were living it real world.

"Butkus, you're the strongest swimmer. I want you to chest-carry the hostage through the surf back to the boat." He pointed at the big man. "Get your fins back on."

"Got it, boss."

"Tinker, give your fins to Bosco so he can stay with his patient while Butkus tows him out. He'll need to keep the tourniquet tight as they go."

Jose nodded as he donned the fins.

"Okay, Tinker, you and I are going to paddle the boats, the weapons, and the money bags back through the surf."

Everyone was moving as Carl called the audibles. Pickup basketball. Every team member cross-trained with every other, except that Bosco was the only one with field surgical training.

As Jose clung to his patient, the others quickly donned their headlamps.

Butkus had one more question, shouting as he sat down hard to pull the fins over his jungle boots. "What about the bodies, Carlos?"

Carl decided without having to think. "Leave 'em! The hostage is the priority. Right now, I don't care who these guys were. We can come back later if we need to get 'em…that is if the vultures don't get 'em first."

"That's the right call, boss." Jerry stood up abruptly then bent down to help Jose carry the groggy patient into the water. Fins forced them to walk backwards, but once in the water, they'd be glad to have them. The big man took off his own life jacket and secured the horse collar around Freddy's neck. He blew air into the bladder and gave Jose a thumbs-up.

Carl and Billy Joe pushed the kayaks down the beach and dragged the bow ends around to face seaward. They hurried back to get the weapons and the money. Five minutes later, they were pulling the loaded boats into the surf.

Jerry sidestroked with one hand and chest-carried Freddy with the other. Jose kicked as hard as he could while squeezing the pilot's bandage with both hands. Jerry dug hard with his fins, pulling both of them through the waves, directly toward the mothercraft.

Monitoring through binoculars, Juan and Rosa had already moved *Luisa* as close to the beach as possible.

Carl and Billy Joe struggled to get the boats through the surf… then paddled fast onto the rolling surface of the smooth sea.

Jerry and Jose got to the boat first. Juan and Rosa reached down and hauled Freddy aboard like a trophy Sailfish. They laid him gently on the deck as Jose, fingers gripping the port gunwale, simply vaulted himself into the boat. Jerry came up next, to find Jose already digging into his war bag for the extra kit he needed.

Carl and Billy Joe reached Juan and Rosa's outstretched hands a couple of minutes later. As Jose and Jerry prepared the patient for field surgery, the other four unloaded the kayaks and left them tied off to each gunwale.

Rosa took the wheel and pointed *Luisa* toward deeper water. Jose would need a steady deck for the next hour and, proceeding slowly to the leeward side of the island, she gave it to him.

Juan took the handset and broadcast the code word.

"Capella, I say again, Capella."

Stewart's voice came back. "Roger, out."

All hands stood ready to help as Jose found an IV bag and began unwinding the hose. Into Freddy's arm went the needle. They took turns holding up the bag while Jose reached back into the wound. Juan laid a blanket over Freddy's now-shivering body.

There was nothing else the rest of them could do but pray for Jose and his patient.

* * *

One hour in the lee of the island was all Jose needed. He managed to patch the tear in Freddy's femoral vein. He was able to release some pressure on the tourniquet…but not much. The patient would need a proper operation as soon as they could get him to a hospital.

Given where they were, that would not be soon. Carl rigged another IV bag. Jose got the precious fluid flowing into Freddy's arm.

Jose finally looked up at the others. "I've done everything I can do… Now we need to get him a real doctor."

Carl knelt next to Jose and Freddy on the deck. He looked around the group in the dim light. "I think we're stuck with a long ride back to Flat Top."

Jose spoke first, "By the time we get him into the Zodiac, the patient will be in pretty bad shape, Carlos. He can't tolerate a medevac at sea…but we could frag a helo to meet us at Flat Top."

Carlos turned to Jerry. "What do *you* think, Butkus?"

Jerry thought for a few seconds. "I think the helo at Flat Top is our best option here." He glanced at his watch. "It's almost four in the morning… We could be ready to transfer the patient around 1100." The big man looked at Jose. "Can he make it that long?"

"Yeah… I say he can, but it'll be pretty tight." Jose rummaged through his war bag. "I've got two more IV bags…and the bleeding has stopped." He paused. "At least for now."

Carl took back control. "Okay…that's the plan." He turned to Juan. "We've told the command cell we have the pilot. Now we need to tell them he's wounded and that we need a helo on standby."

Juan picked up the handset and spoke the appropriate code word.

"Supernova, I say again, supernova. Details to follow."

CHAPTER 13

THE SUN CAME up quickly over the *Darién* rainforest. Carl had always been struck by the suddenness of day and night at low latitude. In fact, he realized, suddenness was fast becoming the central theme of this operation. Now they faced the sudden and unexpected mission of saving a life the team had meant to protect. Rosa was at the wheel on the flying bridge again. The tandem kayaks were lashed to the gunwales as before, and the weapons were stored below. Jose had been kneeling all night, monitoring his patient's vital signs. Jerry and Billy Joe were sitting against the salon bulkhead, facing aft, dozing, but ready to assist Jose if needed. Juan and Carl stood at the transom, watching the sun climb through low cumulus clouds into the clear tropical sky.

Luisa had been making the best available speed for three hours. Flat Top Rock was still three hours out. Carl, hands on hips, turned to the undercover sailor and spoke over the low roar of the inboard diesels. "I think it's time… Go ahead and send the rendezvous details to the command cell."

Juan climbed to the bridge, grabbed the HF handset, and began to transmit—in the clear—the instructions they had cowritten after Jose's field surgery.

"*Mercado… Pescador. El pez está listo.*" The fish was ready to deliver to market.

"*Pescador… Mercado. Estámos listos también.*"

Juan continued in precise Spanish. "We are three hours out from Flat Top. Request helo medevac at 10:00 a.m. Two pax. Bring blood for Freddy. Will mark LZ with smoke when ready for pickup."

Jose would be leaving with his patient, whether or not there was a doctor on the bird, whether or not he jeopardized operational security. Carl could not have stopped him anyway, and he trusted Jose to protect the team's cover.

"Roger…wilco." Ana Maria's voice was five-by-five. Carl felt a wave of pleasure wash over him. They were now teammates as well as lovers and soul mates.

Just as suddenly, Carl's mind was back where it belonged.

Luisa cut through the sea, throwing the biggest wake she had ever made. Rosa did not reduce speed even though, pushed by the current, they were ahead of the time line. Carl wanted to be early in order to allow plenty of time to transport Freddy ashore. Earlier, he had learned, was always better.

As they approached the rendezvous point, Jose started a new round of worry about his patient. Vital signs were stable, but he had lost a lot of blood and could not afford to be jostled too much on the transfer. Jose's vascular patch was holding, but he didn't know for how long. He looked up at Carl.

"Now…if we just had a Stokes litter, getting the patient to the beach would be pretty straightforward." The medic exhaled to reduce stress. "But we don't."

Carl ducked into the main cabin and examined the wooden components of the boat's storage lockers and bunks. Nothing long enough…that is without some major saw work. And there was no large saw on board. He left the cabin, stepped carefully around the patient, ascended to the flying bridge, and spoke to Juan.

"Do you and Rosa have anything we could use as a stretcher for Freddy?"

Juan didn't have to think too long. "There's a surfboard in the forward berthing compartment."

"It's part of our cover-for-status," Rosa added defensively.

Carl gave her a supportive look. "Seems to be working." He continued with urgency in his voice, "We could knock off the fins. What do you think?"

Juan was already moving.

"Perfect. Bring it out then get me a hammer."

With the assistance of Jerry and Billy Joe, Juan and Carl lifted the patient onto their makeshift stretcher. Jerry fished a handful of bungee cords out of his war bag, and Billy Joe found a couple of more. In just a few minutes, they had the patient tied onto the board, ready to transport.

Rosa slowed *Luisa* on the backside of Flat Top, and Juan went up to get the anchor. Soon the fishing boat was riding the hook, less than one hundred yards from the landing zone. Jerry and Billy Joe scrambled onto the gunwales and dived into the water. They swam quickly to the pebble beach and retrieved the stashed Zodiac. Five minutes later, they were motoring back to the mothercraft.

As the Zodiac bounced against Luisa's hull, Jerry handed the sea painter to Juan and stood by to receive the stretcher. Billy Joe remained at the tiller while Carl jumped into the rubber boat. Jose and Juan lifted the makeshift Stokes litter over the transom and into the hands of Jerry and Carl. They lowered the patient onto the solid aluminum deck as Jose jumped in next to them. Juan untied the Zodiac and watched Billy Joe coax the boat into the beach. As soon as the boat touched gravel, Carl, Jerry, and Jose carefully lifted the surfboard and carried the patient to the flat top of the islet to wait for the helicopter. It was 0945.

Carl took a day-night flare from Jerry's K-bar knife sheath and activated the red smoke end, holding it high over his head. Almost right away, they all heard the chopper coming in from the direction of Panama City. Carl recognized the sound of the blades. It was a "Huey" utility helicopter, certainly Panamanian, not a US Army Blackhawk, as he had expected. Even for the medevac, Ana Maria and Ned had chosen to continue the facade that this was a Panamanian operation. That was good. He wanted Panama to get the credit for recovering their pilot. Wounded but alive and expected to stay that way.

A win-win situation.

The helicopter flared, sending dust high into the air. Carl and his men carried Freddy to the open port side of the aircraft, blades still turning. Carl was not surprised to see Major Castaneda, sitting in the middle of the bench seat. She saluted not just Carl but also the whole team. Jose climbed into the bird and sat next to her, looking over his patient at the pilot. On his signal, the chopper lifted off in a whirl of dust. Carl watched as the medic donned a pair of headphones and started briefing the third passenger. This, he knew, was the handoff to Panama's better-than-average hospital system. Jose would find a way to catch up with Carl and the others later.

Billy Joe guided the Zodiac back to the *Luisa*, still at anchor. Juan and Rosa helped off-load the team's gear into the rubber boat. The leather satchels were handed down last. Before leaving, there was something important Carl wanted to tell the crew. He stood up.

"I know how long you two have waited for a real-world operation. Now I think you agree that it was worth the wait. We could not have done this without you. Don't let your guard down. I gotta strange feeling this thing isn't over yet." He paused as Juan and Rosa nodded firmly. Carl sat down on the main tube as Billy Joe engaged the outboard engine. Still looking at Juan and Rosa, he added, "I'll make sure you're invited to attend the after-action review. We need your input."

"Aye, aye, sir. You call, we haul," replied a beaming Rosa.

Carl turned to Jerry and Billy Joe. They looked as weary as he felt, coming down off the high of a risky mission. Bone-tired but in a good way.

"Time to give Commander Fletcher back his Zodiac."

* * *

Carl and his men returned the Zodiac, piled their gear into Fletcher's command vehicle, and got a ride back to the ISOFAC. It was late afternoon. Carl called Colonel Stewart to check in and learned the after-action review would be conducted at 0900 the next day. After cleaning weapons and checking their equipment, the team fell onto their canvas cots and slept for a long time. This was the rigid sequence spliced into their genetic code. Get back from the field, get ready to go out again, then rest.

Jose was in the kitchen brewing coffee when the others woke up.

"How's Freddy?" asked Carl, shuffling out of the berthing space.

"He'll be okay," replied the medic. "The Panamanian doctors are good, and the hospital is clean." Jose had not been to sleep since before *Luisa's* arrival at the hostage exchange site.

"Good job out there, Bosco. I don't need to say that you saved his life…but I will." Carl smiled groggily at the medic. "How did you explain to the hospital how you ended up with Captain Alegre as a patient?"

Jose laughed. "Major Castaneda did all the talking. She explained to them that I had been fishing with friends aboard a private yacht when we stumbled on the wounded pilot just lying on the beach. She called it a *milagro.*"

"The real miracle is that they bought that bullshit," said Carl. "I guess she also told them you're a Colombian doctor here on vacation."

"How did you know that, boss?"

"Because that's what *I* would have told them. Good to have you back."

Carl called the team together in the planning cell. It was six o'clock in the morning. Time enough to linger over bad food and good coffee. Time to prepare for the after-action review.

"I think we did the best we could," began Carl. He looked at Jerry. "You and Tinker took down the kidnappers just like we planned. We did *not* plan on the hostage suddenly running away from them." Carl paused again. "I should have anticipated that."

Jose broke in, "Carlos, there was no way to predict that. We both thought Freddy was semiconscious. Neither of us realized he was putting on an act."

"You're right, Bosco. I really thought we could wait for the head-shots then just pick up the hostage and walk him back to the boats. We were right to assume the kidnappers were planning to execute the hostage anyway just as soon as they had the money."

"We'd have taken them out before that," said Jerry firmly.

"And what'd you guys make o' the go-fast?" asked Billy Joe. "That's a beautiful boat if *ah evah* seen one! It looks like one of Reggie Fountain's boats."

Jerry jumped in, "Drug traffickers, no doubt... Now *there's* a mystery."

"That beacon could help us solve it," Billy Joe put in. "Why would druggie thugs kidnap a pilot?"

"I hope we get to find out," replied Carl. He then repeated what he'd said to Juan and Rosa. "I gotta a strange feeling this thing isn't over yet."

All nodded. They and their field gear were ready to go—any time, any place.

* * *

The command cell arrived at exactly 0900. Pablo Céspedes didn't sit down until he'd shaken the hands of Carl and his whole team, including Juan and Rosa.

"Thank you, all. You have the utmost gratitude of every member of the Panama Canal Commission. I've just come from the hospital. Freddy Alegre is going to be all right."

After they all sat down, Carl and Jerry hoisted heavy leather satchels onto the table.

"I told you I didn't need the bags back," replied Céspedes, grinning.

Carl smiled. "Look inside, sir. It's all there. We just never got around to handing it over."

Ana Maria covered her mouth to hide a look of unprofessional amusement. ¡*Bien hecho*!

Carl became serious again. "I'm very sorry we could not prevent the kidnappers from injuring Captain Alegre, sir. Most hostages give up and accept their fate. We did not understand going in just how brave a man your pilot is."

"He would love to hear you say that."

"I will visit him as soon as I can," promised Carl.

The discussion, focusing on lessons learned, lasted more than an hour.

After the other briefers left, Colonel Stewart stayed.

"I just wanted to say, more personally, how proud I am of you men. No one really knew where this was going, but you dealt with the uncertainty admirably well. You also made the SOC look good in front of two other US agencies, as well as another government. Well done, or as you say in the Navy, 'Bravo Zulu.'"

"No higher honor, Colonel," responded Carl. They all shook hands.

Carl and his men began packing their gear. Jose and Billy Joe would spend one more night in the ISOFAC before departing for Virginia Beach. Carl and Jerry would just return to their quarters on base and resume a normal life.

At least that was the plan.

* * *

Carl and Ana Maria did not wait very long. By midafternoon, they were making mad love as huge drops of Panama rain pelted Ana's metal roof. They did not want to waste the opportunity to let passion burn through the curtain of uncertainty that had shrouded them for days. Sometime in the early evening, they sat at the kitchen table, savoring their coffee. Afterglow gave way to another side of Ana Maria that Carl enjoyed almost as much as the sex—a stream-of-consciousness exchange of ideas about things that matter, English or Spanish, whatever came to mind.

"You guys did a great job out there, Carl," Ana Maria began. "I had a really bad feeling about this one."

Carl studied her disheveled face. A strand of black hair hung over one eye. She did not toss it back behind her ear…but let him do it. She kissed an index finger and placed it gently on his lips.

"You were just as much a part of this as we were," said Carl, recovering his train of thought. "The tactical stuff was pretty straightforward. You made it work politically."

Ana Maria cast her gaze to the coffee cup in her hands. "I have a knack for politics, Carlos. What I don't understand is how to *lead* people." She took a deep breath as if what she was about to say would be difficult. "For the first time, I have seen you with your men. I want to learn to lead like you do…to inspire my subordinates. I want to get the most out of them…not just once but again and again."

Carl thought about how to answer her. Ana Maria was a natural leader; she just didn't know it yet. "It's all about culture." That was a good place to start. "You have to create an organizational culture that makes everyone want to succeed."

"Tell me more."

"The *first* thing you should do is to avoid making them feel like subordinates."

Ana Maria was taking mental notes. "So you have created a culture within your unit that encourages subordinates to feel as important as the leaders?"

"Exactly."

"I noticed that you let them all give their opinions…even in public meetings."

"Sure. They have significant contributions to make."

"But what if those contributions are inconsistent with what *you* want?"

"Usually," said Carl, "they already know what I want."

"Panama has a real problem with corruption," she said with pleading in her voice. "How do I crack that one?"

"Pay people what they think they're worth. It's much better to have the government pay them than the criminals. That's expensive in the short run, but it's a lot cheaper in the long run. If you want professionals, you have to pay them as such."

Ana Maria thought another few seconds. "I was also amazed at how your team worked together without any hesitation."

"Training is the key," Carl continued, enjoying the moment. "Well before we go in the field, I know—we *all* know—who can do what and where our limitations lie."

"And then you learn lessons, adjust the training, and prepare for the next operation."

"Yes," responded Carl. "We just learned a lot at the after-action review. Now we'll apply those lessons."

Ana Maria leaned across the table. "I want to establish a program to bring your people into more frequent contact with mine… and you in particular." She stood up and walked around behind him.

"That's a great idea, Ana. Let's work up a proposal for both governments."

Ana Maria started massaging Carl's neck. "Absolutely, *cariño*… Now I have another proposal for you."

Carl got up and chased her back into the bedroom. She was a fast runner.

"Please stay the night," she implored him when they were settled in.

"Your lead, *cariña*."

Ana Maria took the phone off the hook, and the bedroom was filled again with the sweet sounds of stress reduction.

CHAPTER 14

ANA MARIA'S PAGER went off just after midnight. She reached for the device and made it stop. Carl rolled over and tried not to pay attention. The major got out of bed, turned on the night table lamp, and went to the telephone. She dialed a number, and Carl heard her actively listening to the PTJ duty officer.

"Okay…when? Where? Do we have an ID on this person?" She took a pencil and paper out of the drawer and began scribbling notes. After hanging up, she stood in front of the bed, hastily donning her uniform. Carl was fully awake and sitting up.

"Bad timing…but I have to go." She had flipped a switch in her head. The lover was suddenly a policewoman. Ana Maria bent down and kissed him on the forehead. Carl—of all people—understood her transformation.

"Can you tell me anything?"

She hesitated then decided to disclose the nature of the phone call. Unprofessional, to be sure, but Carl was more than just a lover.

And he would have more than a passing interest.

"A priest was murdered on the street tonight…right near the hospital where Captain Alegre is now a patient."

Carl was even more surprised than Ana Maria had been. "Was he driving a car or walking?"

"He was driving a car. That's what makes this different." Ana finished buttoning her dark blue shirt. "The murder took place at eight thirty this evening, but it took the office this long to notify me." She exhaled in frustration. "Now I have *two* mysteries to solve."

Carl had never heard of a murder like this in Panama City. There had been plenty of murders during his five years in the country. Mostly armed robbery...but not something like this.

"Sounds like a professional hit job," said Carl, sitting up in bed.

"Yes, it does," replied Ana Maria. "At first glance, it looks like Father Castillo was ambushed leaving the hospital."

"*Chuleta!*" Carl felt a knot in his stomach. *Holy shit!* "Who would want to murder a priest?"

"That's what I intend to find out," replied the investigator. I won't be back for a while. You can stay here if you want."

And she was out the door.

Carl stayed in Ana Maria's bed until her scent dissolved into the sultry night air.

* * *

It was still dark when he left Ana Maria's house. She had not come home, and he did not expect to see her anytime soon. Carl had learned during their intermittent affair that she was just as tenacious as he was. Relentless was a better description. Carl was sure that she would find out what had happened—whatever it took. He didn't have a theory, but something in the back of his mind told him to stand by for yet another sudden development.

As soon as he finished a quick breakfast in his quarters, he called Colonel Stewart. True to form, the acting commander was in his office before dawn.

"Good morning, sir. Sorry to bother you so early, but I'd like to come and see you." Carl took a deep breath. "There's something I need to tell you...and something I need to ask you."

Stewart sounded like he'd been up all night. Carl assumed the colonel had been working on other issues. The Special Operations Command had responsibilities all over Latin America. Carl's operation was not even the most important.

"Okay, Carl, can you come over now?"

"Yes, sir, on my way."

Fifteen minutes later, Carl was sitting in Stewart's office, nursing a cup of coffee. He came right to the point.

"Sir, there was a murder in the city last night."

"Yeah," replied Stewart. "I know, but how did *you* find out about it so early? The papers aren't even out yet."

Carl shifted in his seat a little too visibly. "I have a source."

Stewart frowned. "You've told me that before, but you haven't told me who it is. Now might be a good time."

Carl took a furtive gulp. "Yes, sir, now would be a good time to tell you that I've been sleeping with Major Castaneda off and on for a few years."

Stewart's eyebrows went up. He actually smiled. "Wow, I did not see that coming!"

"I wasn't really hiding it, sir. I'm just a very private person as you know." The line between professional secrecy and personal privacy was not an easy one to draw. Carl had been bracing for an ass-chewing. It did not come.

"Well, if you're going to have a source," said the colonel, "it doesn't get any better than Ana Maria Castaneda! What else did she tell you about the murder?"

"Not much, except that the victim was a priest and that he was shot while driving a car."

"It looks like a professional hit," added Stewart.

"I thought the same thing, sir. But who would want to kill a priest?"

"I don't know," said the colonel evenly.

"That's what Major Castaneda said." Carl looked Stewart right in the eye. "She did say she'd find out, sir...and I have no doubt that she will."

Stewart changed the subject, or so he thought. "And what did you want to *ask* me, Carl?"

"I have a voice in the back of my head, sir, telling me that the murder of the priest is somehow related to the kidnapping of Captain Alegre."

"I have the same feeling," responded Stewart. "Do you have any evidence…other than proximity to the hospital?"

"No, sir. It's just a feeling at this point. But I'd like to ask you to keep Rios and Barnes in Panama for a few more days…just in case we need them."

Stewart did not have to think about that one. "I'll call Virginia Beach. You tell Bosco and Tinker to stay put."

* * *

Carl put down the phone and drove rapidly to the ISOFAC. Jose and Billy Joe would be in the final stages of packing for the flight back to Virginia. He wanted to stop them before they got into the SOC command vehicle. As he drove up to the building, he could see that he was just in time (although he would have ambushed them at the airport if necessary). Carl rolled down the window and leaned out.

"Bosco! Tinker!" The men were dressed for travel and loading the van. Carl exited the Land Cruiser and took a few steps. "Change of plans. Let's talk inside."

Both Jose and Billy Joe were visibly relieved as they lifted their luggage from the van. Carl knew they would be excited about the prospect of further combat action. He did not know that, for different reasons, each of them wanted to stay in Panama as long as they could.

Walking into the planning cell, Carl explained the situation. They were not going back into formal isolation, but Jose and Billy Joe would live at the ISOFAC until there was more information available. Jose pulled out the last of his Colombian coffee and brewed them a pot.

"Major Castaneda is on the case," said Carl without emotion. "She will get the information we need."

"I guess she *will*," Billy Joe blurted out.

Jose was thinking backward and forward at the same time. "When can we go see my patient, Carlos?" Before Carl could answer, the medic added, "He almost certainly has information we might need."

"Visiting hours begin at 1100, Bosco…just you and me, though. And I still want to hide our participation in his rescue from the authorities."

"Got it, boss. Remember, I'm a Colombian doctor on vacation!"

"And I'll be here cleaning guns and sharpening knives," announced Billy Joe. "Let me know what Freddy says…then maybe we can get back in the field."

"Let's hope so," said Carl firmly. He felt an elation that ordinary men would not have understood. It wasn't the prospect of killing bad men; it was the thrill of surviving the ordeal.

* * *

Carl gave Jerry a quick call, directing him to return to the ISOFAC as soon as possible. Then he called Jordy Fletcher and asked for an afternoon meeting at Rodman.

Jerry arrived at the ISOFAC twenty minutes later. "Sorry I couldn't be here sooner, boss."

Carl just smiled.

Where do we get such men?

"No problem, Butkus. I'll make this quick." He glanced at Jose and Billy Joe then looked back at the big man. "A priest was murdered in his car last night. The colonel and I think it might be related to Captain Alegre's kidnapping. No evidence yet, but our instincts have driven us to keep Bosco and Tinker here for at least a few more days."

Jerry nodded and grinned. "Sounds great to me, Carlos. What do you want us to do for the rest of today?"

"Nothing yet. Just catch up on your rest and wait for additional information. I'll be meeting with Commander Fletcher later today to inform him that I'll need you indefinitely." That made Jerry smile. "Bosco and I are on our way to see Freddy. He might have something else to tell us." Carl glanced back at Billy Joe. "Tinker will stay here with you. We'll be back in an hour or so."

"Got it, boss. See you then."

Carl and Jose drove to the hospital and found Freddy Alegre's room. Though still drugged and supine, the pilot was fully awake.

The whole interview was in Spanish. Jose went first. "Captain Alegre, you might not remember me. I am Jose, your caregiver from the rescue team. You look a lot better than you did the other night."

"I feel pretty good, sir. I don't remember much, but I do know how close I came to death. You and God saved my life."

"I think God had more to do with it than I did, Captain," replied Jose. "That bullet just missed your femoral artery. I'm just glad I could help."

Carl seized the moment. "Captain, we do this for a living, and I can tell you that we've never seen a hostage as brave as you were."

Freddy Alegre smiled broadly. "But I should not have tried to run away from them."

"¡*Exacto*!" said Carl playfully. "That surprised us too. We would not have let them execute you, but you did not know that." Carl paused, more serious now. "My name is Carlos, by the way. Jose and I are trying to find out who killed Father Castillo after he visited you last night."

"He was my *priest*! Who would do that?"

"That's what we are trying to find out. We think it might be related to your kidnapping."

"That's what the lady policeman said...the one with the long legs."

Carl should not have been surprised that Ana Maria had beaten them to the pilot's bedside. But he was. "Yes, we are working with her as well."

Alegre tried to sit up. Discovering that he was too weak, the pilot lay back down with pain on his face. "The major also asked me what Father Castillo said to me. I didn't have much to tell her, except that he heard my confession." The pilot suddenly remembered something else. "The *padre* also told me that he had been meaning to visit my wife and children...but that he did not feel safe driving around in the city."

Carl and Jose raised their eyebrows at the same time. "Did he say why?" asked Jose.

"No," replied Alegre. "But he seemed distracted…as if there was something bothering him. I have known Father Castillo a long time… since I was a boy. I have never seen him nervous, about anything."

"And he did not tell you what that was?" asked Carl.

"No…he did not," replied Alegre.

Carl pressed for more linkages. "Captain, can you tell us a little about your captivity? I know you don't remember much after you were shot, but what about before that?"

Alegre put his hand on his forehead. "Most of it was very bad… but some of it was not so bad."

"How do you mean that?" asked Jose.

"I mean that the *matónes* who kidnapped me, shot my driver, and then the two fishermen, they are thugs…murderers."

Carl was surprised again. "Tell us more about the fishermen."

"My captors blindfolded me…then we drove to the junction of a rough road and a narrow river. It was there they transferred me to a fishing boat. I did not actually see the fishermen until right before they were shot. That happened after their boat took us down the river into the Gulf of Panama then south and east."

"How do you know it was the Gulf of Panama?" asked Jose.

"Because there was no way for them to get to the Caribbean side due to their own roadblock. And we did not cross the Bridge of the Americas. So our route had to be through the city and east from there, along the *Carretera Interamericana*."

"How do you know they did not cross the bridge?" asked Carl. "You were blindfolded."

"Yes, but I would have felt the roadbed of the bridge. It is famously rough. The bridge also rises and falls quite steeply." He took a deep breath. "And I know we went through the city…just by the traffic noise, even at night."

"How do you know they took you down the *Interamericana*?" asked Jose.

"We passed through a roadblock."

"Just one?" asked Carl.

The pilot nodded vigorously. "Yes, I remember that because they removed my blindfold and ordered my silence as they bribed the *tongo* to let us pass."

"And about how long was the drive?" asked Carl, excitement welling up inside him.

The pilot did not hesitate. "About ninety minutes, total."

"That's pretty impressive," remarked Carl. "Your senses are keen, Captain."

"I am a mariner, sir. I have a good feel for where I am…all the time."

The sudden burst of pride seemed to use up most of the pilot's energy. His eyes were getting heavy. Jose wanted to ask Alegre about the part of his captivity he'd told them was "not so bad." A quick glance at Carl told him they should wait.

"It's time we let this hero get some more sleep, boss. He's in good medical hands here." Jose reached down to gently tap the man's shoulder. Carl gave the pilot a thumbs-up. Freddy was asleep before they could turn around and head for the door.

Carl and Jose walked quickly back to the Land Cruiser. Once inside the vehicle, they felt safe talking shop.

"I can't wait to find out what the lady policeman with long legs found out," said Jose with a straight face.

"Neither can I," said Carl, grinning.

After dropping Jose off at the ISOFAC, Carl went home and called Stewart. "Sir, Jose and I just talked to Alegre in the hospital. We have some new information."

"That's good," said the colonel. "Ned has called a meeting for all of us this afternoon. Be in my office at 1630."

"Got it, sir. Out here."

Carl had some lunch, did a little reading, and then went to see Jordy Fletcher about hanging on to Senior Chief Tompkins for a while. He also thanked the commander for lending him the *Luisa*. After praising the performance of Juan and Rosa, Carl told his friend he might need them again soon.

CHAPTER 15

Carl sat down in Colonel Stewart's office. He was early, as usual. He wanted to see the others file in…and to judge the looks on their faces. Carl had been trained to always go into a meeting more prepared than anyone else. *Think about what you will say, to whom, and why.* He needed to get as much information as he could this afternoon. He was hoping to get the rest of it from Ana Maria later.

One on one…without stress.

Ned walked into the office first, followed by Pablo Céspedes and Major Castaneda. The three of them found chairs around the small table in front of Stewart's desk. The colonel sat down and turned to Ned.

"Okay, Ned, this is your lead. I think we all have information to share." Stewart looked around the table without smiling.

"Thanks, Reggie. I'll go first and then go around the table to see what everyone has to contribute. Hopefully, we can put this puzzle together enough to come up with an effective course of action."

All of them nodded and waited. Ned laid a large nautical chart on the table.

"We have been monitoring the locator beacon your men placed on the hull of the mystery boat." He looked up at Carl. "That beacon is telling us a story."

Ned pointed to the islet where Carl and his men had recovered the hostage. "Here is where you fixed the beacon to the boat."

Leaning forward, Carl inspected the red line, drawn in pencil, leading from the islet to mainland Panama in a southeasterly direction.

Ned traced the red line with his finger, stopping at a point on the *Darién* coast. "The boat went straight to *Bahía de Santa Cruz*… then up a narrow river into the thick rainforest." He pointed to a break in the riverbank. "This is where they stayed until the next day."

Everyone had the same question. Carl spoke first. "And where did they go the next day, Ned?"

Tracing the coast with his finger, Ned led the others north to a wide bay at the entrance to a meandering river. Colonel Stewart got out of his chair and walked around the desk to get a better look.

"At last light, the boat raced up the coast to *Golfo de San Miguel* and then into the mouth of the *Tuira*. That's the river that runs down from Yaviza. As you know, Yaviza is the last town on the highway before the *Darién* gap. The boat stopped at *La Palma*, just after dark, then crossed the river and stopped at *Puerto Quimba*. It stayed for less than one hour in both places then returned to *Bahía de Santa Cruz* before dawn." Ned looked up. "This is indeed a go-fast boat."

"I grew up in Yaviza," said Ana Maria. "I know that area very well. If I were a drug trafficker, I would find it a great place to transship cocaine." The major could see she had their attention, especially Carl (to whom she had never said where she came from). "There's a sleepy airport at *La Palma*…and a small dock at *Quimba* that connects by road to the *Interamericana*."

Ned looked back at Ana Maria. "Well…that's very helpful, Major. Assuming this is what you suggest, can anyone tell me why drug traffickers would need a million dollars badly enough to risk kidnapping a canal pilot?"

Pablo Céspedes had no answer. Neither did anyone else.

"That's a puzzle," said Carl. "But…at least it's not a mystery. Puzzles have solutions. Mysteries don't. We just need more information."

"I talked to Captain Alegre at the hospital," Ana Maria put in. "He did not have any idea why someone would want to kidnap him. He has no financial resources to speak of…and those who took him could not just assume the commission would pay that kind of ransom."

"They didn't know how much we value our pilots," interjected Pablo Céspedes. "Especially Freddy Alegre."

"Maybe it wasn't really about money," said Carl thoughtfully. "What if the traffickers just wanted to *talk* to the hostage." He could see that no one had considered that possibility.

"Then why would they even demand a ransom?" countered Ned.

"The money would have made a nice *propina*...perhaps for underpaid security thugs. They could have felt entitled to a little extra for taking the risk."

Ana Maria added some information to the mix. "Captain Alegre told me that his captivity was very bad...but not *all* bad."

Carl jumped in. "He told me the same thing." Ana Maria shot him a surprised look. "But Jose and I had to leave before he could explain what he meant."

She continued, "He told me that one of his captors was actually *nice* to him...that he spent a whole night just talking about his job."

"In response to questions?" asked Carl.

"Yes...that's what he told me," replied Ana Maria.

Carl almost jumped out of his seat! "That's an interrogation, pure and simple. Bad guys and then good guys."

"Yes, Commander... Good cop, bad cop," said the major. "Only, in this case, they scared him out of his mind first...then calmed him down. The pilot must have been very tired by then."

"They just wanted him to feel relieved...so he could tell them about his personal life," suggested Carl. "Instead of the bad cop after that, they were just going to shoot him dead. We stopped two of them from doing that. The other two sped away in the boat."

"For *Bahía de Santa Cruz*," said Ned, pointing again to the chart.

"So it was just the details of his personal life they wanted?" asked Céspedes. "That's not worth a million dollars."

Uncharacteristically, Reginald Stewart had been listening in silence. Perhaps because of that, he was struck by a stab of insight—like a bolt of lightning.

"What if they wanted detailed knowledge about how the canal works? That might have been worth a lot more than a million dollars."

Stewart looked around the table. His eyes fell upon Carl.

"You're a trained saboteur, Commander. What would that knowledge be worth to you?"

Carl bent over the chart again before answering. *The kidnapping was just the opening act!* He had many questions. They would need much more information.

"A lot," said Carl somberly. "If that is what they wanted…they got it." He looked around the room. "And we have a real problem."

* * *

"Whatever happened to 'business before pleasure?'" Carl was lying next to Ana Maria, listening to his own racing heart as night fell around them. Tropical fragrances drifted into her bedroom through the open window. He rolled to rest his head on Ana Maria's chest, gently rising and falling, to find her heart racing just as fast as his.

"Business can wait… Pleasure could not." Ana Maria drew him closer, and he could feel her body relaxing. No more stress…at least for now.

Carl propped himself up on one arm and looked into her dark eyes in the waning light. Almond eyes. Alive with pleasure, like Carl himself. At that moment, a vision of Ana Maria in a wedding dress flashed into his mind. He felt joy and fear at the same time.

First, Ana Maria and then Carl fell asleep to the sounds of the city in the distance. One hour later, he was awakened by kitchen sounds. Pulling on a pair of pants, he followed the aroma and found Ana Maria cooking *arroz con pollo*. She offered him a glass of Chilean white wine. They toasted to pleasure-before-business then sat down to a nice Panamanian meal. He was pleasantly surprised; she was actually a good cook. *She never does this!*

They ate like two people who, for days, had been too busy to eat. Professional tenacity had its drawbacks, but getting fat was not one of them. They devoured Ana Maria's food and then lingered over multiple glasses of wine. Their personal relationship had always been mostly about sex. Now, Carl noticed, they were talking about themselves, their hopes, and dreams. Things that really mattered in the long term. They also found that the more they talked, the more they wanted to say. Carl wanted to find out why his longtime girlfriend was so circumspect, so careful. Ana Maria wanted to find out what was in Carl's soul.

"Carl...I've been wondering why you enjoy your work so much. I think you know why I enjoy mine. Helping people as a police officer is much more satisfying than being a soldier, defending them against an imagined threat like the United States."

"I love being in the jungle, Ana...and the water." Carl rarely articulated this sentiment, but he was grateful to her for asking him to do it now. "It's certainly the tactical challenge. I've been trained to do certain things...and I do them pretty well, especially with other men similarly trained. It's all about the team. Without Jerry, Jose, and Billy Joe, I'd be in trouble." He was on the intimacy train and could not stop it in time. "We have a bond stronger than love."

"I would like to get to know them better."

"If we can get them to work with your people on a regular basis, you'll get to know them quite well."

"I'm curious to know," she began haltingly, "how you deal with death. By that I mean two things. First, the risk to you and your team, and second, how you process the reality that your job involves killing people."

Carl took another sip of wine. "Two very good questions, for which I may not have adequate answers. Regarding risk to the team, I think it's a matter of training. If you have trained to perform all the tasks, under the expected conditions and to the necessary standards, then you go into a situation with the confidence that you can prevail...and survive.

"You aren't worried about your safety?"

"Knowing what your teammates are going to do before they do it. That…and sound operational procedures…keeps you safe. The ability to succeed and survive comes from repetitive team training."

Ana Maria nodded slightly. "I think that is good advice for me and my team. We could use better training, but the resources are simply not there."

We can show you ways to do more with less, Ana. The most important element is leadership…and you *have* that. You're a natural leader."

Ana Maria smiled and sipped more wine. "You flatter me, Carl. Are you trying to get into my pants?" She winked at him.

"I've already *been* in your pants!" joked Carl. "Seriously, there's a lot you can do with leadership. Without it, you can do nothing."

"Then I look forward to lessons in leadership."

"Count on it, *cariña*. Now for your second question." Carl's smile vanished. "I don't like killing other men, Ana. I do it when I have to…but it's just sometimes a part of getting the mission done."

"Do you think about it afterward? Even though I'm a competitive target shooter, I've never had to kill anyone. My profession is finding things out, not using deadly force."

Carl took a longer sip of wine. "There's a difference between fighting and killing. When we kill guys who are trying to kill *us*, that is fighting. When we use deadly force against people who do not threaten us, prisoners or innocent bystanders, then we are killing."

"I see the difference," said Ana Maria. "You're a fighter and not a killer."

"That's how I see myself, Ana, but it's a bit different in the jungle. There, the rules break down. If my adversaries play by the jungle's rules, I have to be prepared to do the same. That doesn't mean I go around killing people who don't threaten me, but I may have to bend the rules from time to time."

"It's complicated…yes."

Carl sat back and raised his glass. "If I've learned one thing so far, it is that *nothing* is simple. If someone tells you otherwise…run like hell."

They drank to that.

It might have been the wine. Ana Maria took a deep breath and made a surprising announcement. "I will never make love to another man again, *Carlitos*. You have made me a faithful and dedicated lover." She was smiling in a way that Carl had not seen before—like a cat sitting in the sun.

"I love it when you call me that, Ana. You may not believe this, but I haven't been with another woman for a long time."

"Now we have something else in common." Ana Maria pointed her wine glass at Carl. "To fidelity then."

"To fidelity."

"I am flattered that you have no other loves but the Navy…and me," said Ana Maria with a twinkle in her eye.

Carl took the comment as another good sign. "I'll have to leave the Navy someday, Ana. Then it'll be just you and me."

Ana Maria was shocked. "Are you *proposing* to me, Carl?"

"Not yet, *mi amor*…but that may be where we're headed. I think you know that I love you."

Ana Maria beamed. "You've never said that to me before… wow!"

"I didn't have time to say it…and you didn't have time to listen."

"I do think it's too soon to talk about marriage, *cariño*. After we solve this puzzle, perhaps we could try living together. I suddenly feel very close to you."

"Suddenly…after all these years?"

She faked a frown. "*Es muy complicado.*"

They finished the meal and retired to Ana Maria's living room couch with Irish coffee. They switched to English. It was time for business.

"I wanted to tell you that I learned something else from my inquiries yesterday into Father Castillo's murder," began Ana Maria. "I did not want to say this in front of the others. There is—as of yet—no firm connection between the pilot's kidnapping and the death of the priest. It would have been a distraction. Also, I wanted to talk it over with you first."

Carl sat forward. "So let's talk."

"I went to Father Castillo's room at the church and searched through his possessions…also his papers."

"And you found something useful."

"Yes…I think so, but you tell *me*."

"Okay…shoot."

"The priest flew to Miami recently…then to Pasto, Colombia. I found the ticket stubs with his luggage."

Carl stood up and paced around the room.

"There's more," Ana Maria went on. "I called around to different rental car companies at Miami Airport until I got someone at Avis to verify his reservation. The account says that he drove only 60 miles and turned in the car on the same day."

"And you want to know what that could mean," said Carl evenly.

"Yes…where could Father Castillo have gone for one day, thirty miles from the airport?"

They both blurted it out at the same time.

"Noriega!"

CHAPTER 16

CARL STAYED THE night with Ana Maria. They couldn't sleep. They couldn't even make love. The realization that Manuel Noriega might have had something to do with Father Castillo's murder kept Carl and Ana talking far into the wee hours. By the time the sun came up, they had a plan.

Carl went home, showered, and then called Colonel Stewart. "Sir, I had an epiphany last night. We need to talk about it."

"I've never heard you use that word, Carl. To hear you borrow from religion is an epiphany in itself. Please come over right away." Reginald Stewart, who took his religion very seriously, smiled to himself and waited for his J3.

Carl jumped into the rusty Toyota and drove directly to SOC headquarters. He jumped out and strode quickly into Stewart's office. Looking at his Rolex on the way in, he saw that it was only 0710. He had the rest of the day to convince Stewart and the others to send his team back into the field.

"Okay, frogman, sit down and tell me about your epiphany," began Stewart.

Carl took a seat, forgetting about the customary cup of coffee. He found it difficult to stay in his chair as he started the conversation.

"I said yesterday that what we are dealing with is a puzzle and not a mystery, that more information will get us to the solution. I have more information…along with some speculation."

Stewart tried not to grin at Carl. He failed. "I guess you and Ana Maria have already talked about it…right?"

Carl came as close as he ever had to blushing. "Well…yes. We put our heads together last night."

"Two heads are better than one. Let's try for three, shall we?"

"Yes, sir." Carl went to the map on the wall. Stewart got up and followed him. Carl pointed to *Bahía de Santa Cruz.* "Here is where Ned told us the go-fast went after we recovered the hostage." Carl traced the same lines Ned had shown them the day before. "And here is where the boat went the next night. Major Castaneda suggested it might be transshipping cocaine at these points…here, and here." Carl pointed to *La Palma* and *Puerto Quimba.*

"Okay, Carl, that is what we know. What else do we know?"

"We know that Father Castillo was murdered in his car while leaving the hospital after visiting Captain Alegre."

"A murder that looked like the work of a Colombian *sicario.*"

"Yes…a professional hit, normally associated with drug cartels," replied Carl. "And here's something else we know." Carl paused to make it more dramatic. "Father Castillo had recently flown to Miami. Major Castaneda, who found a ticket stub in the priest's luggage, thinks he visited Manuel Noriega."

"Wow! I assume she's checking that this morning."

"Yes, sir…she is. We'll know for sure in about two hours."

Stewart looked back at the map. "So what do we *not* know at this point?"

"We don't know why the priest also had a ticket stub for Pasto, Colombia, in his luggage."

"And what else?" asked Stewart. The city of Pasto made no sense to either of them.

"We don't know what Noriega might have told Father Castillo… and we don't know why the priest was murdered on the street." Carl went further. "And…we don't know what the go-fast boat is *really* doing down there." He pointed to the map again.

"Okay," said Stewart. "What do you *think*?"

Carl drew a deep breath. "I think Noriega is the link between Alegre's kidnapping and the priest's murder." Carl wound up and delivered his best pitch. "And I think we need to find out what is really happening along the *Darién* coast. There's a lot we still don't know, but I think we're onto something."

Colonel Stewart admired LCDR Malinowski's strategic thinking as much as his tactical performance. Successful special operations required both—that was, indeed, why they were called "special operations." Not better—just different. Operations that could be performed by no other soldier, sailor, or airman. Operations with high strategic value. The colonel had gone out on a limb for Carl before. He was about to do it again.

"We need to get your team down to *Bahía de Santa Cruz*, Carl. The sooner, the better."

"That's what I was about to recommend, sir. How soon can we get the command cell together?"

"This afternoon," said Stewart, already reaching for the phone. "Be back here at 1500." He waved Carl out of his office, then called out as the younger man got to the door, "And have a concept of operations, ready to brief!"

"Got it, boss. Good to go." The SEAL equivalent of *Yes, sir.*

* * *

"The go-fast is underway again," said the CIA man. Ned went to the map and traced a line due west, and then northwest, from *Bahía de Santa Cruz*. "The boat is a bit more than forty miles out in the Pacific, running along the coast."

Stewart, who had never ridden a fast, open boat on the choppy sea, was the first to comment. "That sounds like a pretty uncomfortable drug run."

"Uncomfortable is not the right word," added Carl. "A kidney belt is part of the kit. If you have to stand, and you fall to your knees, it's almost impossible to get back on your feet."

"Actually, it fits the mission profile quite well," responded Ned. "We don't know where they're going to stop, but we've seen go-fasts run for twenty-four hours at fifty knots without refueling."

"They carry extra fuel in addition to the drugs," Ana Maria put in. Our maritime service tracks them, but our patrol boats are nowhere near fast enough to catch them."

"They got underway at 2100 last night. If it runs for twenty-four hours, the boat could make it all the way to Nicaragua tonight," Ed continued. "We'll report to all of you when and where it stops."

Pablo Céspedes did not know why he was still a member of the command cell. Freddy Alegre had been recovered. The commission had even gotten its money back. Pablo was happy to be in the room, but he did not see any connection between the go-fast boat and the Panama Canal. "They would never attempt to transit the canal," he said. "We have customs inspections and a great deal of security."

"Still, you would be wise to issue an alert," suggested Ana Maria. "Some of the pleasure boats we see along the canal could double as drug carriers."

Céspedes was happy to be of some use to the group. "We will do that, Major. *Muchas gracias.*"

Carl listened to all this as he considered the implications for his proposal. Colonel Stewart had instructed him to have a concept for finding the base camp from which the go-fast was operating. If the boat was not in *Darién*, he and his men would just have to wait until it came back. At the moment, there was no way to determine when that would be. The destination—and the purpose—of the boat's voyage was a puzzle within the larger puzzle they were trying to solve.

Ana Maria rose and went to the map. "Gentlemen, we've been looking for a connection between the kidnapping of Captain Alegre and the murder of Father Oscar Castillo. The priest was ambushed by what we think was a professional hit man while leaving the hospital." The major looked around the table before continuing. Carl gave her a reassuring smile. "I found a possible connection."

She focused her attention on Ned's eyes. They looked like dinner plates. *Ojos como platos.*

"During a search of Father Castillo's residence, we found evidence that he flew to Miami last month. I checked the mileage on his rental car receipt and guessed he might have visited Manuel Noriega in prison. I called the prison this morning, and they confirmed that Castillo did indeed visit Noriega."

She watched everyone's reaction to this. Ana Maria was aware that Carl had already told Colonel Stewart. The others were visibly shocked.

"And do you know what they said to each other?" asked Ned, sitting a bit straighter.

"I thought we'd gotten rid of this *ladrón* for good." Pablo Céspedes shook his head slowly back and forth. "Just the name of that criminal gives me chills."

"We don't know what they talked about," replied Ana Maria. "That's what I intend to find out when I interview Noriega."

"And how soon will you be able to do that?" asked Céspedes.

"I filed a request with the US Bureau of Prisons right before I came over here. It will take them a few days. I will fly to Miami as soon as the request is granted. You and I are the only people in Panama who know this." She waved one hand across the room. "And I wish to keep it that way."

Silence in the room. No body language. The secret was safe… for now.

* * *

Carl and Ana Maria had decided not to spend every night together; this was one of the off nights. He had been trying to relax by reading some good science fiction. Relaxation had been impossible; he'd just stared at the pages. He was fully dressed, waiting for the call. The phone rang, and he leapt off the couch. He was about to find out where the mystery boat had finished its punishing ocean transit.

"Carl, it's me. I just got a call on the secure phone. Come to my office now."

Carl was in Stewart's office fifteen minutes later. "Sir, what did you find out?"

"The boat is dead in the water…right in the middle of the Gulf of Fonseca."

"Yikes!" exclaimed Carl. "The puzzle just got harder to solve."

"Why would they go *there*?" asked Stewart, addressing the question to both of them.

Carl thought for a few seconds. "That's a good question, Colonel. As you well know, I've been in that very spot quite a few times in the last couple of years. It makes no sense...but, then again, it makes a lot of sense."

"What do you mean by that, Carl?"

"Depends on the motive," said Carl. "If the boat is carrying a load of drugs, then Fonseca is a good spot to off-load it. I spent a lot of time in El Salvador during the Civil War...until last year. We were helping their navy interdict the arms being smuggled across Fonseca from Nicaragua. If that boat's in the middle of the gulf, it would be in a position to avoid the authorities of three countries, El Salvador, Honduras, and Nicaragua. The Gulf is where their territorial waters all come together."

"And how do you assess the level of cooperation among the three governments?" asked Stewart.

"Very poor," answered Carl without hesitation. "Especially at night, the Gulf of Fonseca is an ungoverned space. That's why we had so much trouble with it during the war. The Salvadorans found arms and other contraband all the time. It's a great place to transship cocaine."

"Then why did you say it also makes *no* sense?" Stewart enjoyed the back-and-forth, playing catch with ideas until everything made sense.

Carl had explained the second possible motive first to give himself a few more seconds to think about the first. He wondered why the go-fast would make a drug run all the way to El Salvador when the traffickers seemed to have such an easy setup in *Darién*.

"Okay, if the motive was *not* drugs, and we have to assume that is a possibility, then we'd have to find another reason for them to make a rendezvous at sea, at night, at the confluence of maritime borders for three uncooperative nations." Carl stopped long enough for Stewart to weigh in.

"Perhaps it was a transshipment of prisoners. Maybe the kidnappers who took Captain Alegre took other hostages we never heard about."

"That's certainly feasible," said Carl. "It could also be a pickup rather than a delivery...or a swap."

Stewart nodded. "Yes, we have to consider that a possibility. Any of those three countries would be vulnerable to organized kidnapping-for-ransom. Wealthy people, lots of political turmoil...and a tremendous amount of corruption. My god, those places make Panama look like the first world!"

"The boat could have delivered cocaine *and* taken possession of one or more hostages," suggested Carl.

The conversation was interrupted by a loud ring from the secure phone on Stewart's desk.

"The boat is moving again, Reggie."

"Thanks, Ned. Can you tell me what direction it's headed?"

"Back toward Panama." Carl tried to read Stewart's face but came up short.

"Okay, Ned, let us know when and where it arrives...thanks. Out here."

Stewart looked up at Carl. "It's coming back. We have a little more than twenty-four hours to plan for your reinsertion into the OPAREA. We need to find out what that boat is *really* doing."

"Got it, sir. I'll be ready to brief the command cell tomorrow night...or whenever."

* * *

Carl decided not to call Ana Maria. It was past midnight. She would find out from Ned in the morning anyway. Carl also thought she needed the sleep (they were both pretty tired from the night before). He picked up the phone and called Jerry at the other end of the base. Carl then got Jose and Billy Joe out of bed. Finally, he contacted Juan, aboard the *Luisa* somewhere nearby, on the secure UHF radio.

Less than an hour later, all the players met at the ISOFAC. The group spent the rest of the night working out a viable concept for discovering what the mystery men in *Darién* were actually doing. The real reason for the Alegre kidnapping…and the Noriega connection (if there was one), waited for them in one of the most challenging tactical environments on earth. By dawn, they had a rough tactical plan, ready for more information to make it smoother. The team had the rest of the day to prepare their gear and rest. Juan and Rosa left to gas up the *Luisa* and rig for sea.

Carl called Ana Maria's pager just after dinner. She called him back right away. He knew they would both be too busy to meet, but he wanted to hear her voice. He did but not for long.

"The authorization for my visit came through, Carl," said Ana Maria, speaking carefully on the unsecured phone. "Now I just have to be patient."

English, not Spanish. Business. Ana Maria would have to stand watch in the command cell while Carl was downrange. When he returned from the field, she would go to Miami. Only after that, thought Carl, could the puzzle be solved. "Okay…see you tomorrow, Ana."

"Get some rest, *cariño. Hasta mañana.*"

Carl put down the phone and waited for Stewart's call.

Sitting at his desk, Reginald Stewart waited for Ned's call. The secure phone rang just after 2300.

"The boat is back at *Bahía de Santa Cruz*, but it didn't go straight there. The crew stopped near *La Palma* for about an hour before returning to where they started."

"Is 0800 a good time for the briefing?" asked Stewart. "If they're going back to the field tomorrow, the team will need to get an early start."

"Yes." Ned was a man of few words, even on a secure phone.

Stewart called Carl back, and they met briefly at the SOC. Stewart gave him a green light in advance of formal authorization. Carl would present a *pro forma* briefing to the command cell then get his operation rolling before noon. Launching in the light of day was not Carl's preferred option, but there was no time to lose. They would have to melt into the *Darién* jungle in time to conduct surveillance on the target through the night and into the next day. The mystery boat was the key—but it was not the target.

Carl and his men would have to find the crew and get to know them personally.

CHAPTER 17

JUAN AND ROSA met them on the back side of Flat Top. As before, Jerry and Billy Joe left the black Zodiac under a tarpaulin and swam back to the *Luisa*. Carl surveyed the thirty-or-so ships lying in the roadstead, waiting to transit the canal, trying to determine whether any of them had noticed. *Luisa*, he concluded, was too far away from the ships to be seen taking Carl's team aboard. He also noted that there were no small craft in the vicinity of the rock to watch them either. They all felt sure the daylight launch had not been compromised. Rosa set a course for *Darién*. The rest of the team performed final checks on their equipment and tried to get some rest.

It was going to be a long afternoon and a longer night.

A storm far out at sea was stirring up the Gulf of Panama, adding transit time they didn't have. A local rain squall further slowed their progress. *Luisa* pitched and rolled through cresting whitecaps and rising swells, headed generally southeast. Juan had to tie extra lashes on the kayak brackets to prevent the plastic boats from breaking loose. Carl had always told his men to think of rest as a weapon. They all tried to relax, but rest was elusive on the heavy sea. Passing the lee shore of *Isla del Rey*, the seas flattened for a while. As soon as she could, Rosa put the *Luisa* on a southerly course. There was something important to do before they arrived at *Bahía de Santa Cruz*, and it had to be done before dark.

Luisa finished the first leg of their journey just in time. The sun hung on the horizon as Juan anchored the boat seventy-five yards east of the unnamed islet where they had recovered Freddy Alegre.

"Ah…Treasure Island!" announced Billy Joe. Jose laughed at him. "You're a pirate after all, Tinker! I was thinking we should call it Fantasy Island." The laugh was short-lived. There was serious work to do.

They wore "shorty" wet suits and inflatable life vests. Each had a SIG Sauer in a shoulder holster. Without fins, they jumped in the water. Five minutes later, they were all standing on the beach. Rosa had come down off the flying bridge and perched herself on the transom. The former Navy rifle champion sighted in her M-21 with daylight scope and signaled with a hand gesture. Once they were covered, Carl led his men carefully across the beach.

The bodies were still there. Carl scanned the sky and found no vultures. Pelagic species, mostly terns and frigate birds, feasted on small fish, chased to the surface by larger fish. Vultures, he thought, would find plenty of bodies in the mainland jungle. The men Carl's team had killed, still clad in generic camouflage, lay rotting in the disappearing sun. Thankfully, night-vision goggles had protected their eyes from the crabs. Jerry and Billy Joe unfolded the body bags. Carl and Jose helped them place the bodies into the bags and zip them up. The stench was overwhelming, but they worked through it, determined to find out who these men had been.

The fact that the bodies were there at all told Carl something about the survivors who sped away from the scene. *They left KIAs on the battlefield.* But that was not enough. He needed to take at least one of them alive. He realized there was no guarantee they would find anyone at the base camp upstream from *Bahía de Santa Cruz.* If there was a base camp at all. Dead men in their hands were worth less than live ones in the bush, but that was better than nothing. They carried the KIAs, one at a time, to the water's edge. They swam the plastic bags back to the mothercraft, to be stored in the forward lazarette. A medical examiner would inspect—and perhaps dissect—the decaying corpses in order to discover anything at all about their identity. Then the bags would be dumped into a lime-filled pit.

It was now dark but with the rising moon a couple of fists above the horizon. Time to find the base camp. Juan called the command cell on the HF.

"Arcturas, I say again, Arcturas."

Ned's voice came right back, "The rocket is stationary, four hours to get back, over."

Juan replied, "Roger, out." The mystery boat was doing business—somewhere—four hours at maximum speed from the presumed base camp.

Luisa charged south and east into the night, Juan now at the wheel. Fifty miles to go. Almost three hours with moderate seas on the starboard quarter. Carl and his men did final preparations, rigging for surveillance and possible combat. There was no way to know exactly what they would find ashore. Another polaroid, developing before their eyes. Improvisation would be the key to getting the job done. They were good at improvisation.

As the *Darién* coast painted just five miles out on radar, Carl and Jose started unlashing the port side tandem kayak. Juan gave Rosa the wheel and got ready to anchor inside the point. Rosa slowed *Luisa* to bare steerageway as they rounded the headland and moved into shallower water. Carl and Jose turned their green plastic boat upright and lowered it into the water stern-first. Tying it to a cleat, they began to load themselves, along with all their kit, into the fore and aft wells. Juan went forward to drop the anchor as Jerry and Billy Joe got their own kayak into the water on the starboard side. Ten minutes later, both crews were ready to paddle.

Jose carried the heavy radio on his back (each member of the team carried a small squad radio on his vest). Rosa broke squelch to test the UHF connection and gave Jose a thumbs-up in the dim light of the cockpit. Beyond the execution checklist, they would not need the UHF radio. There was no air support or fire support; they were on their own. An emergency extraction would not be easy in *Bahía de Santa Cruz*. Carl wanted Juan and Rosa to be ready if he and his men were forced to swim all the way out. The inflatable life jackets would allow them to swim all night if necessary. Flotation might also be needed for wounded teammates. As usual, the sea would be the only escape route.

Luisa would be their only ride home.

The two crews pushed off and stroked out together, paddles sheathed in cloth to prevent flashing in the moonlight. The men wore solid green jungle fatigues without insignia, Vietnam-era uniforms no longer used by American forces. Green and black camouflage covered their faces. Camouflage flop hats concealed hair and prepared them for inevitable rain the next day. Ammunition pouches, knives, and canteens hung from web gear. Small jungle-green backpacks carried medical supplies, ponchos, energy food, and assorted other field items. Their old jungle boots, still best for moving and sitting in the mud, were already wet.

Around their necks and secured behind them were slung H&K MP-5 9mm submachine guns. SIG Sauer P-226 pistols were secured in thigh holsters in case they needed secondary weapons. All carried night-vision goggles in dry bags, stashed under blouses, splash-proof but not waterproof. With full military kit, especially in the dark, there would be no attempt to pass for adventurous civilians. Close inspection (if they were dead) would uncover the swim fins strapped to their backs, marking them as something different from ordinary soldiers. Mostly, they resembled what they were.

Armed men, looking for trouble in a rainforest full of armed men.

They paddled in rapid rhythm on a compass course, Carl's boat in the lead. He could hear the pounding surf to his right and his left. The plunging waves became louder and more threatening as they stroked for the sandy beach. Moonlight glinted off the foam left in the wake of breakers. Kayaks rose and fell with the Pacific swell then slipped quickly through the narrow passage. Suddenly, they found themselves in a glassy smooth gap between dense clusters of tall trees. Another unnamed jungle river. Jose broke squelch on the UHF, and Juan made a call to the command cell.

"Betelgeuse, I say again, Betelgeuse.

Ned's voice replied, "Roger, out."

The men paddled into the rainforest, more slowly now and completely without noise. Kayaks were one of Carl's favorite insertion platforms, but there would be no defense if they were attacked while still inside the boats. A landing needed to be found. And fast.

But not too fast.

In the moon's shadow, they held water next to the left bank of the river. As rehearsed, the men donned their night-vision goggles. They scanned for somewhere to hide the kayaks…and a trail to where they thought the base camp might be. None of these things had been visible on the satellite image. Back to the basics of jungle warfare—just like the hungry jaguars they knew were hunting in the blackness ahead.

Paddling very slowly along the bank, the men looked left and right. Left for a landing; right for evidence of river traffic. They expected the mystery speedboat to come back to this very spot sometime before daybreak. There was no guarantee of that, but it fit the pattern. If the boat were to come back early—even right now—the team had an emergency plan: dart into the overhang of the trees and hope they were not seen…or hope they could scramble for solid ground from which to fight.

But hope was not a good plan.

They needed solid ground…and time. They drifted soundlessly with the weak countercurrent along the tree line. Carl and Jerry inspected the riverbank for a way in while Jose and Billy Joe continued to watch the river. They kept their own silence, but the jungle was alive with the cacophony of a billion species…all competing for resources in the pitch-black arena. Survival of the fittest. A cautionary tale for Carl, the amateur naturalist. He and his men would be more fit than their competitors; the survival part was open to question.

Suddenly, through his goggles, Carl spotted a ghoulish-green object that did not belong to the jungle. Nature, he knew, did not draw straight lines. He thought it might be a structure, jutting into the shallow channel along which they paddled. As the kayak got closer, a shape started to form in front of them. Boards, not perfectly straight but still unnatural. A dock! And the time to get set up. Maybe enough time to recon the area for a base camp.

They would have to hide the kayaks far enough from the dock to avoid detection…but near enough to recover them in a hurry. As quietly as possible, they turned the boats around and backtracked until they found a flat grassy shelf next to the river. Carl and Jose nosed into the bank and got out to look around. The clear patch was surrounded by thick underbrush, lying between the river and the rainforest. No trails led in or out. The green boats would be almost impossible to spot here, thought Carl. *Perfect.*

They would have to swim about a hundred yards to the dock in full gear and swim out later. Taking a prisoner or two would complicate matters, but there was a plan for that. They would put the captives in life jackets and tow them all the way back to *Luisa*. The men helped each other get the kayaks onto the grassy shelf then submerged themselves in the river. There was no need to use fins for such a short swim. With the survival advantage of night vision, they breaststroked carefully in a line along the riverbank, Carl in the lead and Billy Joe at the back. Carl was always in the lead. The others trusted him to get them where they needed to go.

Ready to fight.

Still in the water, the four men gathered side by side at the edge of the wooden dock. It was not a large dock. From the end of the structure, Carl could rest his foot on the riverbank. They hung under the boards for thirty minutes, listening to the night and watching the path into the jungle. Each man had unslung his MP-5 and kept it ready to aim. Nothing with two legs came down the path. No predators, animal or human. From this point on, Carl and his men would themselves be the predators, looking for information. Perhaps they'd find more than that. Jerry reached up and laid his weapon on the dock. He pulled himself up and tested the strength of the boards. Satisfied, he turned around and lifted the others. The team assembled at the trailhead, checked equipment, and formed a column.

Carl led them into the jungle as each man held a field of fire. Billy Joe kept watching behind as he listened for the returning mystery boat. Slowly, they crept along the muddy path into the darkest void on the surface of the planet. Triple canopy jungle. Night-vision goggles hung around their chests. Without starlight, it was too dark, but there would suddenly be too *much* light if they came upon a base camp. The path twisted and turned for another two hundred meters or so (amphibious sailors switched easily from yards at sea to meters ashore). They navigated by the *feel* of the forest. Hearing rather than seeing.

Then a light, glowing dimly through the trees.

Bingo!

The mission was materializing before their eyes...but not one of them yet knew what it would be. Surveillance, for sure. Capture, the main objective. Killing...if necessary. Hostage rescue? A possibility. They had no idea how many were in the camp or what threat they posed. They would have to identify the bad guys then see if there were any good guys among them. They'd have to sort them all out... and deal with each one accordingly.

The expected return of the boat and its crew added more uncertainty. What—or whom—were they trafficking? The deeper into the jungle they patrolled, the brighter the light. Then two more lights. Then two more. Carl took out his 8x42 birding binoculars and focused on the source of the lights. He observed a cluster of makeshift wooden huts, topped with thatched roofs, situated in a circular tree line. The primitive structures surrounded an open area of grass and dirt. The dirt would be muddy in this, the rainy season. The light came from an array of Coleman lanterns, strung between huts. A pile of rocks suggested the clearing was used for cooking. Carl peeked under the black tape that covered the luminous dial of his Rolex. It was 0130. He was not surprised by the lack of movement in the camp. The number of buildings (four) and the size of the layout (about fifty meters across) did surprise him.

What is *this place?*

Carl turned to his men and gathered them into a penguin huddle. In a low whisper, he conducted a very short briefing. Each man gave him a squeeze on the arm to signify understanding. Then Jerry and Billy Joe slid into the forest to Carl's right, off the trail and toward the river. Carl and Jose moved slowly left to the other side of the camp as Carl plugged his squad radio into one ear. Both pairs melted into the trees about ten meters and began a surveillance routine. They would sit back to back in these positions for the rest of the night or until the boat came back.

The mission so far had been limited to gathering information. As always, however, they expected the unexpected. Less than an hour later, they got it. Billy Joe heard the sound of high-performance outboard engines in the distance. He reached for Jerry's arm to signal him. Then the big man heard it too. The go-fast boat was coming back way early. *Shit*! Jerry took the squad radio from its pouch and whispered to Carl.

"The boat is back, boss."

CHAPTER 18

"Sɪᴛ ᴛɪɢʜᴛ, Bᴜᴛᴋᴜs. We have time to get this right." Carl could now hear the boat coming upriver. He checked his watch again: 0230. Much earlier than they'd expected to see the boat. *Ned's report must have been wrong!* There had been absolutely no movement inside the camp so far, but that was about to change. Carl and his men would be watching, waiting…and deciding. They needed information, then action.

The camp was suddenly active. There was enough lantern light to see some detail as men began coming out of the rickety wooden structures. Carl trained his binoculars on individuals as he and Jose waited for the boat's crew to join them. He counted five people in the open. Two of them wore camouflage uniforms. The other three were dressed in khaki pants and long-sleeve shirts. They were all swatting mosquitos as they moved quickly through the humid night air. Even in the dim light, Carl could see that all the men were Latin. The three in civvies were noticeably overweight and did not seem to have weapons; the two in cammies, looking fairly fit, carrying AK-47s in one hand, muzzles pointed at the ground.

Soldiers?

Jerry trained his binoculars on the camp from the opposite direction. Like Carl, he saw that five men were preparing to receive the boat crew…and whatever cargo it brought. He noticed a firepit as the camouflaged men slung their AKs and brought dry wood from one of the buildings. He monitored the four buildings as firelight began to illuminate the compound. Billy Joe concentrated on the path leading from the dock. He and Jerry were only ten meters off the trail, but they both felt comfortable in the thick vegetation. Commotion and rapid voices added to the jungle din. All the Americans had to do was stay motionless in the mud and the mosquitos. The mud was, by far, the easier to deal with.

The engines in the distance stopped abruptly, creating enough of a lull to hear some of the voices in the camp. Jose listened intently to the chatter.

"Those guys don't sound Panamanian, Carlos," he whispered into the boss's ear. "They look and sound more like Colombians… my people. They're physically bigger, and they move faster."

Carl nodded ever so slightly and slowly leaned into Jose's ear. "Especially those guys in cammies," added Carl. "And most Panamanians wouldn't be caught dead in this place."

"Yeah, we got Freddy out of here alive. Now we just need to get our *own* asses out." Long years of whispering had left Jose with the ability to express emotion without elevating the volume. If Carl could have seen Jose's worried face, he would not have been concerned. Bosco always wore that look in the field, but he never lost his sense of humor.

Five minutes later, there were voices coming down the trail. Jerry counted three men, all carrying bundles wrapped in plastic. Heavy bundles, it seemed. He got on the squad radio.

"Three guys coming your way, Carlos. Heavy loads. No idea if anyone is still with the boat."

"Got it, Butkus," responded Carl. "We'll need to count heads at both ends."

"Yeah…," said Jerry. "As soon as the show is over, Tinker and I can take a slow walk down to the boat."

Carl smiled to himself. "Agree… Bosco and I will find a way to get inside those huts. Meanwhile, we wait until the decisive moment."

"When is that?"

"I'll know it when I see it," said Carl, straining to see across the compound. "Here they come… Let's see what they do."

The mule train came to a stop at the door of the second hut. The bundles thudded to the forest floor, whereupon the three men, not in the best shape, turned and walked quickly back toward the dock. Carl noticed.

"Butkus…they're coming back your way. If they're going back and forth, they could be the only guys in the crew."

"Okay, Carlos, I'll let you know when they head back your way."

Ten minutes later, Carl got another call from his number two. "Coming back now with three more bundles."

"Okay, Butkus, let's see how long they can keep this up."

Carl recounted five men clustered in front of the second hut—two with weapons and three without—setting up a long table, made of freshly hewn tropical hardwood. A meal was materializing before Carl's eyes. He turned to Jose and whispered, "I see five, plus three… what about you?"

"That makes eight of them versus four of us, Carlos." Carl could almost *hear* Jose smiling in the dark. "Pretty good odds, I think."

"So far, Bosco, so far."

The bearers made one more trip then stayed in the compound to eat with the others. An all-night high-speed run, thought Carl, would make anyone hungry. He'd seen nine bundles go into the second hut. He did not know what else was in there. He and Jose needed to find out.

"Butkus, you and Tinker can take that walk now. Let me know what you see."

"Will do, Carlos. Talk to you at the other end."

Jerry and Billy Joe rose from the jungle floor and took their MP-5s in both hands. They moved very slowly to the trail as Jerry watched the camp, now to his right, with one eye. Billy Joe led Jerry to the edge of the forest, and they began their walk to the river. There were lots of footprints in the mud, but they couldn't see them. Night-vision goggles would not help them here. Like other jungle creatures, they relied on their remaining senses. Down the trail they went… until Billy Joe saw the star-studded sky ahead through a narrow break in the trees.

The river!

The go-fast boat was tied to the dock, riding high in the water. Billy Joe quickened the pace. Jerry could almost *feel* the younger man's excitement building. His own adrenaline rush was not far behind. Jerry walked as fast as he could, covering a field of fire behind them.

Billy Joe stopped at the dock and waited for Jerry to catch up. He looked lovingly at the outboard engines in the starlight then stepped onto the boat. Jerry covered the whole compass as Billy Joe stood inside the ocean racer. The boat rocked away the extra weight as he looked out at the river.

Suddenly, an invisible figure came at him from out of the dark! Taken completely off guard, Billy Joe felt himself going down—hard. *Can't breathe*! The attacker wrestled him to the wet deck and quickly put him in a sleeper choke, cutting the blood supply to his brain, attempting to break his neck.

You bastard!

Jerry heard the commotion and ran to the side of the boat, ready to shoot. The big man hesitated for one full second. With the last of his strength, Billy Joe had managed to roll his opponent over, denying Jerry anything close to a clear shot in the dark. And without a silenced weapon, he was sure any gunfire would be heard in the camp. There was no time to alert Carl. Others would come running down the trail. In the dark. Some with AKs. He couldn't afford to make a loud noise.

"Tinker, let him roll on top of you!" Jerry drew the K-bar knife from his waist-level sheath and jumped onto the boat. Billy Joe had apparently heard him and was now pinned underneath his attacker. Jerry plunged his knife into the man's back all the way to the hilt.

That stopped the fight.

As Billy Joe gulped air, Jerry withdrew his K-bar and slid it back into the sheath. He rolled the dead man off his teammate and onto the deck. There would be blood—lots of blood. No way to cover up the killing. Once Jerry was sure Billy Joe would be okay, he called Carl.

"Carlos, we just had a fight down here at the boat. Tinker was surprised by a crewman who'd been sleeping on the bow cushions. I couldn't afford to shoot and alert the others. I had to stab the guy."

Carl took the news in stride. "Butkus, you did the right thing. Stay put for now. Back to you soon."

Carl turned to Jose. "Butkus and Tinker are on the boat…with one dead crewman. This is the decisive moment, Bosco, we have to move fast."

Jose whispered back, "They're all sitting at the table…now or never."

Carl got on the radio. "Butkus, you and Tinker get back here now! We have them clustered. We're going to try and take them all prisoner. You guys cover the escape to the dock."

Carl and Jose crouched in the jungle blackness and crept toward the makeshift dining table. The cooking fire lit up the middle of the compound. They knew from long experience that the night vision of those looking toward the edge of the clearing would be almost zero. The diners were not exactly convivial, but there was some conversation to mute Carl and Jose's approach. For once, Carl appreciated soggy ground underfoot; it made less noise. He could see that the military campers sat on opposite sides of the table, AK-47s next to them on the benches.

Side by side, MP-5s at the ready, Carl and Jose burst into the clearing.

"You take left!" shouted Carl on the run.

Jose shouldered his submachine gun, stopped running, and aimed at one of the military faces. Carl did the same for the other one.

"¡*Manos encima de la mesa*!" All but two of the surprised diners put their hands on the table. The men in camouflage reached for their weapons. Carl and Jose gunned them down with short bursts of 9mm to the chest. The others simply cowered…but kept their hands on the table.

Carl covered Jose as the medic ran to the left bench, and then the right, to drag the bleeding bodies away from the others. He picked up the men's weapons and carried them over to Carl. Without saying a word, Carl directed Jose to stack the bodies next to the fire and the two AK-47s at his feet. At that moment, Jerry and Billy Joe ran into the clearing.

"Butkus, you and Tinker search all the buildings. Bosco and I will secure the prisoners."

A head nod from Jerry, and the team executed their emerging plan.

Jose wriggled out of his rucksack and turned around. He reached inside and produced three pairs of plastic handcuffs. With Carl holding the table at gunpoint, Jose began cuffing the prisoners with their hands behind their backs.

The wooden buildings were arranged in a semicircle at the edge of the clearing. Jerry and Billy Joe shouldered their weapons on the move. Jerry kicked down the flimsy door of the first hut and followed Billy Joe in. The relatively small space was filled with five large wooden barrels, tools, cookware, dry wood, a can of gasoline, and assorted spare parts.

Jose continued to secure the prisoners. Carl, the veteran chess player, was thinking two or three moves ahead. Jerry kicked down the second door and again followed Billy Joe inside.

Inside the second hut were stacks of bundles. Wrapped in clear plastic and tied with manila cord, Jerry counted the packages he could see. There were at least twenty-seven bundles in the hut. The Americans had just witnessed nine of them being carried in from the dock. Jerry estimated they were about twenty kilos apiece, each one packed with a white substance.

"This is not a sugar mill," commented Jerry.

"Jackpot!" shouted Billy Joe. "Let's see what else these guys are hiding."

The third hut was a makeshift barracks...now empty. Bigger than the others, filled with cots and mosquito nets, this seemed to be where all the inhabitants of the base camp slept. Nobody home. They could conduct a more thorough search later.

Jose was binding the wrists of the third prisoner.

Carl was trying to decide what to do with all the prisoners.

Jerry kicked down the last door and burst into the hut behind Billy Joe.

"*Holy shit!*" The fourth hut contained two prisoners in handcuffs. The men were sitting on wooden boxes, topped with cushions, wrists bound in front of them. *Cushions?* The men were dark-skinned but looked quite different from their captors. Serene and polite. Skinny and bearded.

"Are you hostages?" asked Jerry, taking one knee in front of the men.

"In a manner of speaking," replied one of the men in educated but heavily accented English.

Jerry and Billy Joe came out of the fourth hut and ran to the center of the compound. Jose was finished cuffing three of the surviving inhabitants.

"Carlos, we got two more in hut number four." Jerry was shaking his head in disbelief. "They're handcuffed but comfortable. They speak English. I have no idea where they came from."

"That *is* a surprise," replied Carl with a bad feeling in his gut. "Let's get them out here." He turned to Billy Joe. "You got some more flex cuffs, Tinker?"

"Yeah, boss." He dug into his pack, came up with the three more sets of cuffs. He handed them to Carl. "I got some duct tape too if you need it."

Carl gave the cuffs to Jose and turned his attention to the bearded strangers. He could see that they were not quite hostages… and not quite guests. The two men looked Middle Eastern. While Jose handcuffed the three bundle bearers, Billy Joe decuffed the English speakers and bound their hands behind them with tape. Carl sat them down on the bench next to the Latins. It was time to find out who all these people were, starting with the men in khakis.

Carl nodded to Jose, now standing in front of the table. Jose began in rapid but proper Spanish. Schoolbook language.

"Who are you…and what are you doing here?" He swept his hand in an arc.

Nothing. Six expressionless men, staring into the dimly lit space. Jose tried again.

"You are *narcotraficantes*! Tell us who you work for."

Nothing. Jose tried Colombian colloquial.

"Okay, I think you guys are Colombian. I myself am Colombian. Tell me the truth, and we will treat you well."

Nothing. Jose continued in his Medellín accent.

"Who were those men in camouflage? Soldiers?" Bosco pointed at the bodies. "We did not want to kill them."

Nothing. Jose turned to Carl and switched to English. "We're going to have to use some coercion to get them to talk, boss."

Carl nodded, looked at Jerry, then hesitated a few seconds. "Not here, Bosco." Then, in loud Spanish, he added, "We will take them to a place where I know they will tell us everything! Get ready to move."

Carl turned to the two English speakers, sitting calmly on the bench. "And just who are *you* guys?"

Only serene smiles. Carl tried again, a little more forcefully.

"Let me try this one more time… Who *are* you guys?"

"Guests," said one of the men. He said nothing else.

Carl looked at his watch: 0325. "Butkus, did you and Tinker find a water supply in any of those buildings? Also, any gasoline?"

"I think they store water in those barrels we found in the first hut," said the big man.

"You and Tinker go verify that and then tell me if you can roll one of the barrels down to the pier…also confirm the gasoline."

Jerry gave Carl a surprised look then took Billy Joe back to hut number one. Carl and Jose prepared the eight prisoners for movement.

Jerry came back a few minutes later. "Yeah, boss, there's water in the barrels. I can carry one on my shoulder—oh, and there's a can of gasoline in there, probably to start fires."

"Good. Give Tinker all your excess gear and follow the crowd." Carl went over and picked up the AK-47s. He checked the curved magazines. Each was full, with thirty rounds. He slung both rifles around his shoulders and adjusted the rest of his gear.

Carl gave his men a hasty briefing. "Bosco, you and Tinker lead this column down to the dock. Butkus will be right behind you. I'll walk rear security."

All his men were curious, but Billy Joe was the first to ask.

"So, where're we goin' with the prisoners, Carlos?"

"Treasure Island," replied Carl with a grin. "Get ready to drive that boat."

CHAPTER 19

JOSE AND BILLY Joe led the parade of prisoners to the dock as Carl conferred with Jerry at the back of the pack. Even though the big man was struggling with a heavy barrel of water, he talked as he walked. Events were unfolding faster than they wanted, but that was how field operations worked. Once you began executing a plan, complexity took you for a wild ride. Improvisation was essential. *Anticipate… then react with whatever resources you have.* Carl's intent was to relocate the prisoners to the island where they'd recovered Freddy Alegre just a few days ago. Now he wanted to know Jerry's view.

"So, Butkus, my improvised plan is to put all the prisoners on the go-fast and take them over to the island. I think we can learn more about them out there…without the fear of discovery. What do *you* think?"

Jerry's torso was bent to the right about ten degrees. He didn't know how much the barrel weighed, but it felt like a 110-pound dumbbell. The water sloshed back and forth, making it harder to handle. But Jerry had become accustomed to being a bearer of heavy objects. In addition to weapons and underwater operations, strength was part of the skill set he brought to Carl's team.

"It's brilliant," said Jerry emphatically. "The only thing that worries me is that all these guys will see the *Luisa*…and blow its cover. I mean, you can't fit them all in an open boat for that long a run."

"That's something I hadn't considered," said Carl honestly. "We could just blindfold them before we leave the dock. We could then hand some of them off to Juan and Rosa and take the rest in the go-fast."

"That works," replied Jerry. "We should follow the *Luisa* out to the island then transfer everyone ashore in the go-fast. The bad guys beached the bow end of that thing pretty effectively before Tinker attached the beacon."

"A good thing, that was. The beacon brought us this far. Otherwise, we'd have just patted ourselves on the back for a successful hostage rescue."

"And sent Bosco and Tinker home," added Jerry. "But I have one more question, Carlos. What are we going to do with the prisoners when we get back to Panama City?"

Carl smiled at his teammate in the darkness. "We're *not* taking them back with us, Butkus. We're gonna leave 'em on the island. Why do you think you're carrying that heavy barrel of water?"

The light came on for Jerry. "So…you're gonna let the Panamanians deal with them later." It was a statement. "They'll be pretty hungry by the time that happens…but at least they won't die of thirst."

"Yeah, but I want them to *think* we're leaving them there forever. We'll make sure they know there's no escape from that place… and that no one will find them. Maybe they'll be more interested in talking to us before we leave. I still want to figure out who all these people are."

Jerry managed to turn his head toward Carl. "Got it, boss. The island variant of the Captain Bligh scenario."

"Yes, hopefully, they haven't seen the movie. Bligh made it back…and so will they."

"To Panamanian custody," affirmed Jerry. "And we let them take credit. Like I said, Carlos, it's brilliant."

They were about halfway to the dock. Carl had one more thing to do. "Butkus, there's something I need to do back at the camp. You keep going. I'll catch up. Tell Bosco and Tinker to leave them all in flex-cuffs and cut some cloth to blindfold everyone." He took an

LED headlamp out of this leg pocket. "Tell Tinker to get the boat ready. He'll have to get rid of everything that takes up space in order to fit the prisoners on the deck. We'll have to leave the kayaks on the riverbank."

Jerry nodded and kept walking. Carl turned and jogged back to the base camp. Still carrying the AKs, he walked through the empty doorframe of the first building and found the jerry can. He ran to the second hut and poured gasoline on the mountain of cocaine bundles, emptying the rest of the can as he toured the camp. Surveying the scene one more time, he turned back and tossed a signal flare onto the pile of drugs.

That felt good.

Carl ran away from the erupting flames and did not stop until he got to the dock. The fire rose above the tallest trees, visible, he thought, for miles at sea.

Billy Joe needed to off-load five fifty-five-gallon drums full of fuel. Jerry handed him the barrel of water and reached for the first drum. It was much heavier than the water, but he horsed it onto the dock. Five minutes later, there was still one fuel drum in the boat. And there it would stay. Jerry moved the body of the man he'd stabbed to death behind the fuel drums on the pier. Someone would find it—and the two bodies in the base camp—if they ever stumbled on this place.

Unlikely. The jungle would heal quickly.

Jose's UHF radio came to life just as Carl rejoined the group. "Bosco, this is *Madre*. Our radar just picked up a fast-moving boat coming into the bay."

"*Madre*, this is Bosco. Roger that." *Holy shit!* Before he passed that word to Carl, Jose had to find out two more things. "Can you see what direction the boat came from…and what's the range to the river mouth?"

"Bosco, *Madre*, the boat came from the south. It's still five miles out but moving fast. Over."

"*Madre*, Bosco, thanks, wait, out."

Jose put the headset back in its bracket and ran to Carl as he approached the dock. "Carlos, we have a big problem. There's another boat coming our way. I just got a call from Juan. The boat is coming from the south…five miles out and closing at high speed."

Carl thought about what he'd just heard. It did not take him long to decide. "Bosco, we've got to assume the two boats are part of the same operation. We have to get out of here before the second one arrives. Whoever is in that boat, wherever they came from, have probably seen the fire by now. They'll be focused on what's happening at the camp. That'll give us some running room."

The prisoners were sitting uncomfortably on the dock in a line, facing the river. Billy Joe had already cut eight pieces of cloth for blindfolding them. The two "guests" were now officially prisoners… and just as uncomfortable. He covered the group with his MP-5 and leaned toward the others, forming a tight circle around Carl.

Carl glanced at his watch again: 0410. Another two hours until sunrise.

Only a few minutes until the second boat would be in the river!

Carl talked rapidly in the lingering moonlight, patting each man on the shoulder as he told them what to do. He briefed Jose last.

"Bosco, tell Juan we'll close his position as soon as we deal with the second boat. He should be ready to accept four prisoners with blindfolds for the run to Treasure Island. Tell him we will transfer one person from our team with the prisoners."

"Got it, boss." Jose moved a few steps away and made the call.

"Everybody okay with this plan?"

The team was ready.

They pushed the prisoners onto Billy Joe's boat and sat them down on every horizontal surface available. The trio of three-hundred-HP outboard engines were already running at idle. Carl and Jerry cast off the lines, and Billy Joe put the go-fast in gear. He steered the boat slowly out of the narrow niche in the bank and onto the river. Turning into the current, he increased speed just enough to avoid making a wake. Billy Joe, the most experienced coxswain Carl had ever seen, guided the overloaded boat into the shadow of the first bend in the river. A place they could loiter, out of the current. Tinker shut down the engines, and they waited for the second boat.

Jerry and Jose used the blindfold material to gag each of the prisoners. For the moment, sound was a bigger threat to the team than sight. The moon dropped into a cloudbank just above the horizon. With his binoculars, Carl still had a decent view of the niche in the riverbank. He could see the second boat slowing down at the mouth of the river, and he followed its progress upstream. He was relatively sure that Billy Joe's boat could not be seen, especially by men trying to figure out what had happened to their base camp… and to the men they had expected to be there. He was sure that many of the arriving crew would run toward the fire, still raging out of control.

Sow maximum confusion…take maximum advantage.

Fire was always a good way to sow confusion. They were now in a solid position to take advantage. For the next few minutes, stealth would allow them to retain that advantage. No shouting. No light sources. Blend into the stillness. Get ready to move downstream at the decisive moment.

The second boat slowed then veered into the niche on the riverbank. Carl watched it disappear into the trees. The flames at the base camp were still burning above the jungle canopy. He timed five minutes on his watch. Billy Joe's boat was holding steady; his hands were on the throttles. Jerry took Jose's MP-5 and covered the prisoners with two weapons. Jose took the radio off his back and put on his fins. Carl gave his weapon to Billy Joe and sat down to put on his own fins. He nodded to the coxswain when the five minutes were up.

Billy Joe started the engines and gently pushed the throttles forward. He eased the boat out of its holding position and into the current. He kept the boat right in the middle of the river, only thirty yards from the niche. Taking it out of gear, he floated toward the mouth of the river at walking speed. Carl and Jose climbed over the port gunwale and lowered themselves into the water, hanging there. Billy Joe had one hand on the wheel and the other on his submachine gun, training it at the riverbank. As the boat drifted past the niche, Jerry reached down and tapped his boss on the head. Carl and Jose let go of the gunwale and let the boat drift past them. They kicked stealthily toward the dock, muddy water up to their eyes.

It didn't take them long to reach the second boat, now dockside. Carl didn't see anyone as he cut the aft mooring line with his K-bar. Jose cut the forward mooring line and glided around to the back of the boat. Both men pushed against the outboard lower units and kicked hard until the boat started moving. After they were clear of the dock, Jose drew his knife again and gripped it in his right hand. He pulled himself up far enough to see into the boat.

There was no one in the boat.

In the dim light, Jose could see a large cargo of plastic bundles. He lowered himself back into the water and put his knife back in its sheath. The pair continued slowly pushing the boat away from the bank and into the current. Gathering momentum, the ocean racer started pulling them toward the bay. They muscled up and jumped into the boat. Looking back at the dock, Carl did not see anyone coming to get them. The enemy was still confused. They hadn't yet noticed that they were marooned in an extremely remote patch of jungle.

Improvising all the way, Carlos and Bosco worked out what to do with their new boat. A quick inspection found the key still in the ignition. Carl would not have to set the boat ablaze in the middle of the river after all. He and Jose would not have to swim to Billy Joe's boat. Jose sat on the bow cushions, facing aft, as Carl started the engines. They counted the bundles lying on the deck. Twenty kilos times ten. Two hundred kilos of cocaine...and eight unidentified prisoners.

Headed for Treasure Island.

Billy Joe waited for the second boat to catch up. He maneuvered his craft alongside Carl's and began transferring prisoners. Once they had balanced their loads, Billy Joe led the patrol into the bay. Back toward the mothercraft at moderate speed. About halfway out, Carl decided to modify the plan again. After huddling with Jose, he briefed Jerry on the squad radio. Jerry immediately fired up the UHF.

"*Madre*, this is Butkus. We now have two go-fast boats. New plan. Lead us to the island. We will not transfer anyone to your vessel. Stay far enough ahead, and out of sight, until we finish our business ashore. Will contact you when we are ready to re-embark. How copy, over?"

Rosa's voice came back five-by-five. "Butkus, this is *Madre*, roger all that. Out."

Both go-fast boats proceeded toward the island with the *Luisa* far enough ahead to avoid being seen by the prisoners, still hand-cuffed and gagged. With long Pacific swells and a light wind on the port beam, Carl estimated they would make the island in about three hours. He looked at his watch again: 0545.

They would have all day to get to know everybody.

CHAPTER 20

THE TWO GO-FAST boats idled seventy-five yards off the beach in the lee of the point. The *Luisa* was riding at anchor, well to the north. Out of sight and, for a while, out of Carl's mind. He had enough to think about with eight prisoners, two high-performance racing craft, and (literally) a boatload of cocaine. The sun had been up for only two hours, but the heat was already spiking.

Billy Joe went first, putting the bow of his boat on the sand. There was no surge on the lee side, and he ran the hull far enough onto the beach to offload the prisoners feet-dry. Jerry jumped off the boat and helped each of them, still handcuffed, onto the sand. There was nowhere to run. The four men, tired and thirsty, stood staring at the barrel of Jerry's MP-5. Billy Joe backed off the beach and anchored his boat. He dived into the Gulf of Panama and swam quickly to the island.

After Billy Joe's boat was riding the hook, Carl beached his boat in the same cusp on the beach Billy Joe had used. Jose helped the prisoners off the boat, where they mingled with the other four. The team was aware that eight men, cooperating with each other, could give them trouble, even in handcuffs. They had to be guarded. That task fell to Jose. Jerry and Billy Joe off-loaded the cocaine bundles, and Carl steadied his boat. When they were finished, Carl anchored next to Billy Joe's boat and swam in to join his men.

Eight prisoners and one large pile of cocaine, now sitting on a tropical beach in the blazing sun. Carl gathered his team in a huddle out of earshot. He spoke in low tones.

"Okay, guys, here's where it gets tricky. We want to find out who these people are. We have the rest of the day to do that. I have some ideas about how, but first, I'd like to hear yours."

Billy Joe was the first to speak up. A broad grin lit up his weathered face. "I say we just shoot 'em one at a time. It pro'lly wouldn't take long till we got some answers." The wannabe pirate took a quick breath. "Better yet, we should feed 'em their own cocaine. They can watch what it does to innocent people."

Carl tried not to reveal how much he hated that proposal. *Seriously?* He turned to Jerry.

"Butkus, what do *you* think we should do?"

The big man did not smile. "I think that just because they're criminals, we can't murder them in cold blood. These guys don't threaten our lives. It would be better to interrogate them. The hotter the sun…and the thirstier they get…the more they'll want to talk to us."

"I think we should cool them off in the surf," added Jose. A couple of hours—even in eighty-degree water—should loosen their tongues." He laughed. "That always did it for *me* back in training!"

"Yeah, but the water on the Silver Strand is a lot colder than this," Jerry put in. "I think we should start by just asking them again and again who they are…and what they're doing."

Carl thought another twenty seconds before speaking. He looked at the bunch of bedraggled prisoners, sitting slumped over, then at his own men.

"Murder is out of the question, period. Interrogation is the way to go…but I need to remind you that we're not really trained to do it." He made sure they were all with him before continuing. Even Billy Joe nodded. "Butkus is right. There's no shade on this beach… and as the sun gets higher, they're gonna feel like barbecue."

"Bad for us too," said Jose, looking at the sky. "At least we have flop hats…and these." He produced a pair of Oakley sunglasses and put them on.

"You wanna give 'em some water now, Carlos?" Jerry put in. "I stashed the barrel over there." He pointed to a spot just above the high-water line.

"Yeah, I think we should try the good-guy, bad-guy routine. We each have two canteens… Let's donate four of them to the prisoners."

They unhooked the canteens from their web gear and handed them to Jerry.

"We'll organize it this way," Carl continued. "Jose and I will start with one of the Latins. Then we'll interrogate one of the English speakers. I'm really curious about those guys. We'll set up over there." He pointed to a spot on the wet sand roughly twenty meters from the group. "Each prisoner will get a drink of water right before we talk to him. The others will have to wait their turn. If they want water, they'll have to talk to us. Butkus, you and Tinker keep the group under control. You can start by taking off their gags. Rehandcuff them in front and keep the group sitting down. I don't want them to talk to each other. Your Spanish is good enough to tell them that if they talk, you'll put the gags back on. Questions?"

There were no questions.

Carl and Jose walked to the interrogation spot on the wet sand. They discussed quickly how they wanted to manage the interview. When they were ready, Jerry brought the first of the Latins to them. Carl handed the man a canteen and waited until he had taken a long drink with both hands. Jose, whose Spanish was only slightly better than Carl's, took the lead.

"Give me your wallet."

"I have no wallet."

"Empty your pockets."

The man thrust both hands into his pockets. He came up with some pocket litter, but not anything to indicate nationality or specific activities. Jose read all the scraps of paper and handed them back.

"So… *mi hermano*… who are you?"

"I am not your brother."

"Do you have a brother?"

"I have a brother and a sister."

"Where do they live?"

"I will not tell you that." The prisoner managed a wry smile. "You think I am stupid, do you not?"

"No, I do not think you are stupid. I think you are stuck here on this beach with no food, only a little water, and no way home." It was Jose's turn to smile. "How can we send you home if we do not know where your home is?"

The man in khaki thought about what Jose had just told him. He looked back at the group, then at the go-fast boats, then at Carl. The weakness of his position seemed to suddenly dawn on him. There would be no escape from this place. He would die here. The group would run out of water in less than two days. He did not want to think about what would happen after that. The man looked at the sky and wondered how long it would take the vultures to find his body. He realized that his only hope of ever getting off the island would be to *talk* his way off.

"Okay…I was born in Colombia."

"That is better," said Jose. "I was also born in Colombia…in Medellín." A true statement. Jose's tone became threatening, his face menacing. "I think we are in the same business."

"And what business is that?" asked the prisoner.

Jose's face brightened. "Judging from all the cocaine we took from you, I think the answer is obvious…do you not agree?"

"You think we are trafficking drugs." It was not a question. "Yes, of course, we are. That is the only way I can support my family."

"And what organization do you work for?"

"You expect me to tell you that?"

"Yes, you are going to tell me that, or you will never see your family again!"

The man in khakis thought again about his own death. The vultures would be bad enough, but his family would never know what had happened to him. His wife, his two daughters, his son—sadness and despair. He could not let that happen. Even if he survived this ordeal, the cartel would have him killed. But at least his family would know how he died. They might even get his body to bury in a Pasto cemetery.

"I work for the Mena cartel... You are from the Medellín cartel, no?"

Jose tried on another menacing smile. "Yes, I work for the Medellín cartel. These *gringos*," he pointed at Carl, "are American collaborators. All they want is money... That is the way all those Americans are, you know."

Carl rubbed his hands together on cue. A perfect cover story... improvised on the fly. "And who were those guys in camouflage back there?"

The man in khakis, having already opened up a bit, saw no reason to hide the identity of the others. "They are FARC."

"FARC? What are they doing in Panama?"

Carl shot a look at Jose. "Let this guy sit down."

The prisoner sat down hard. He was surprisingly candid. "They are here to help us with security. We are businessmen. They are soldiers just like you."

"They *were* soldiers," quipped Carl. "And we are not soldiers!"

The prisoner was now engaged in a semiconversation with Carl and Jose. "But you are dressed and equipped like soldiers."

"Yes, we are. And perhaps if your security guards had been better soldiers, they would be the ones asking the questions now!" Carl went on. "We did not *plan* to kill them, but now that you have told us who they were, I am glad we did."

The Alegre kidnapping rushed into Carl's mind. Now the tactics made sense. But even if FARC soldiers had kidnapped the pilot, Carl still could not figure out why.

"Tell us about the second boat... Where did it come from?"

"I do not know about the other boat. They do not tell me anything. I just do my job and keep my mouth shut."

"Fine. Now," asked Carl with a wildish stare, "what should we do with you and your fellow businessmen?"

"You are Medellín. We are Pasto. I expect you will kill us."

Carl shouted to Jerry, and the big man came to haul the prisoner back to the group. Billy Joe brought Carl and Jose one of the English speakers. Carl gave him the canteen and waited. The man drank a lot of water.

"Okay, so who are you, and what are you doing here?"

The bearded man with the heavy accent sat mute on the wet sand. He was obviously trying to decide how much to reveal to save his own life. Carl and Jose had been surprised to find him and his companion among those trafficking drugs. Were they part of the cocaine operation…or were they connected in some other way?

"I am a guest of the people who run the boats," replied the man tentatively.

Carl stayed calm. It took some effort. "You already told me that, mister—do you have a name?"

"My name is Munir."

"And what kind of name is that?"

"I am from Pakistan. I am trying to get to the United States to join my brother and his family."

"And you were just hitching a ride with drug traffickers?"

The man smiled for the first time. "Yes, that is what I have done."

"Then why did they handcuff you?" interjected Jose.

"They wanted to keep me safe, not to wander out into the jungle."

"Is your companion also from Pakistan?" asked Carl.

"Yes, he is my cousin."

"How much did you pay these fine gentlemen?" asked Jose.

"I paid them fifty thousand dollars."

Carl and Jose were surprised again. Fifty thousand was a lot of money for a man who simply wanted to join his family. *Where did he get that kind of money?*

Carl was finished with this line of questioning. There was nothing he could do, legally or illegally. He'd have to let the Panamanians sort this out. "And now you're going to spend a lot of time with them on this remote island. These guys owe you a refund, but it doesn't matter because nobody is coming to get you."

The Pakistani man simply bowed his head. "*Inshallah.*"

Jose looked at him coldly. "God has not willed this at all. You and your cousin made a bad bet."

Carl glanced at his watch. The day was almost half over. The run back to Flat Top would take about six hours. If they left now, the *Luisa* could get them there just after dark. The mission was effectively over. The team needed a detailed debrief—and further orders—immediately after their return to the ISOFAC. He also needed to make a longer radio transmission as soon as they got back to *Luisa*.

Carl turned to Jose. "What do you think, Bosco? I think we're done here."

Jose had already figured it out. "Yeah, we need to get out of this place." Let's get the prisoners back in a cluster, leave them some water…and then get away in the boats. They can have the cocaine. It's a drop in the bucket compared to the tons of the shit our guys move every year."

Carl laughed out loud. "Yeah, maybe they can snort some of it to relieve the boredom of being marooned on this god-forsaken island!"

Munir looked at Carl and Jose in horror. "You're just going to leave us here with all these criminals and nothing to eat?"

"That's right," affirmed Jose. "With luck, the Panamanian maritime service will find and rescue you."

The bearded man who called himself Munir stared at them with controlled anger. No, it was more than that, thought Jose. It was blind hatred. He could understand why the man would be angry; he did not understand the hatred. What they were doing was just business. As far as the man knew, they were about to leave him to die with the *narcotraficantes*. Here was an enigma within the larger puzzle. Munir was not just a desperate immigrant, trying to join his family. He was something else…but neither Jose nor Carl knew what that was.

And they didn't have time to find out.

An hour later, Carl and his men were aboard the *Luisa*. While his teammates were reshuffling gear and refueling the go-fast boats, Carl went into the pilothouse and reached for the HF handset.

"This is Carlos. Supernova, I say again, Supernova." Code, in this case, for "the mission didn't quite go as planned, and we will need assistance."

Colonel Stewart's booming voice came back quickly. "We are ready to listen to a longer transmission. Go ahead, over."

"This is a long story. Best told right after we get back to your position. For now, let me just say that we are all okay…and beginning our return to Flat Top. I would like to speak directly to the major if she is there."

"I'm here, Carlos." Ana Maria's voice sounded as if she already knew what Carl would say. She didn't. He almost asked her if she was sitting down.

"This is an urgent request for search and rescue…not for us but for a group of eight foreigners now marooned on the island where we recovered Freddy. With them is a large pile of white powder bundles. They have no food and only enough water for a day or two. Request you send one of your patrol boats to pick them up. Can you make that happen tomorrow?"

There was silence on the line. After a minute or so, Ana Maria came back with her answer. She would not have time to talk to her boss—or the president of the republic.

"Roger that, Carlos. We will rescue the castaways tomorrow before dark."

Carl's men were in the drug boats. He gave Juan a thumbs-up as he finished the transmission. "One more thing, major. My team has two fast boats and two body bags for you to pick up at Flat Top on your way back. I will anchor the boats on the backside. *Madre* will look after them until you get there. How copy, over?"

Ana Maria's voice betrayed a sense of disbelief. *Really?* "Got it, Carlos. Will do ASAP. Out."

Carl got thumbs-up from both Billy Joe and Jose, now loitering their boats, fueled and ready for sea, behind *Luisa*. It was one o'clock in the afternoon. He called up to Rosa on the bridge.

"Full speed for Flat Top!"

CHAPTER 21

CARL AND HIS men swam into the gravel beach at Flat Top, still dressed in full military kit. It was almost eight o'clock in the evening, but the moon gave them enough light to work. The transit along the *Perlas* chain had passed without incident with Billy Joe and Jose patiently following in *Luisa's* wake. They had anchored the boats close to the beach, saluting Juan and Rosa before diving into the refreshing salt water. The men were tired, but the exhilaration of a good tactical outcome kept them going. Now all they had to do was ride the Zodiac into Rodman and hitch a ride back to the ISOFAC.

Carl had called ahead to propose the debriefing be conducted right after they got back. He still had a strong feeling they were in the middle of something, not at the end. Stewart, who shared Carl's feeling, had called back to tell him the command cell would gather at the ISOFAC for a midnight session. Carl was anxious to tell the complicated story while it was still fresh. He also wanted to hear Ana Maria confirm that the Panamanians would pick up his prisoners the next day. He did not want the prisoners to die on Treasure Island; he wanted them to live so they could tell Major Castaneda everything they knew.

Back at the ISOFAC, the four men cleaned their weapons and other gear, getting ready to return to the field quickly if called upon. Only then could they relax. After showers and a feast of MREs, there was barely enough time to write down some notes from which to explain the details of what had happened. At precisely twelve o'clock, the command cell principals filed into the room and sat around the table. Jose poured them coffee, and Carl got up to begin the debrief.

"Thank you all for coming over in the middle of the night." He looked at Ana Maria and was surprised to see her smiling. "A lot has happened in the last two days, and the team wanted to get you the details without delay." He paused to take a deep breath. "And there are a lot of details."

The group sat at rapt attention. Carl glanced at Colonel Stewart, who signaled to proceed.

"Let me start at the end," Carl began. "The outcome of this mission was both better, and worse, than we expected. Earlier this evening, I informed Major Castaneda that we marooned eight prisoners on the small island where we had recovered Captain Alegre. She agreed to get the maritime service to 'rescue' them expeditiously." Carl used air quotes to indicate that the maritime service would be taking the prisoners into custody. "They are still handcuffed in front. There's some forest on the island, so they'll be able to get out of the sun. We left them with enough water to survive the next two days, assuming they don't manage to kill each other." Carl took another breath. "Oh…and we left about two hundred kilos of cocaine on the beach with the prisoners."

This was news to Ned and Pablo Céspedes. Colonel Stewart pretended to be surprised. Ana Maria responded.

"I want to thank LCDR Malinowski for letting us make the collar…and take the credit. As soon as the patrol boat picks them up, my government will begin interviewing the prisoners. I will provide each of you with a full report."

Carl continued, "My team also captured two high-performance ocean racers, one of them the boat you've been tracking by beacon." He paused to let that sink in. "These guys apparently discovered the beacon and left it ashore to fool us into thinking the boat wasn't moving." Carl hesitated again. "They succeeded. We were surprised when the go-fast came back to the base camp early."

Carl smiled then went on. "The second boat came into our possession through a series of events I'll describe in a few minutes.

We drove the boats back and anchored them on the far side of Flat Top. The *Luisa* is watching them until Major Castaneda's people pick up the boats…and the two body bags inside. *Luisa* will back off just before the maritime service arrives. We saw no reason to compromise the asset."

"Body bags?" Ned's emotions were caught between admiration and outrage. Admiration for the sheer boldness of Carl's actions; outrage at the independence he had not expected from a military man. "Whose bodies?"

Carl read Ned's expression and continued with professional calm. "We recovered the two men we'd been forced to kill during the hostage exchange. Their bodies had been lying in the sun for a couple of days. The bags don't smell very good." Carl gave Ana Maria an apologetic look. "Our rationale for bringing them back was the hope that Panama's government might be able to positively identify who they were and to find out what they were *really* doing in *Darién* with AK-47s and night-vision goggles."

Ana Maria burst into the conversation again. "The identification might also give us leverage in dealing with the Colombian government. If FARC is using Panama as a sanctuary, and it appears that they are, then the Colombians will have to help us root them out."

Ned turned to Ana Maria. "Are you getting ready to go out and collect all the commander's presents?"

"Yes, we are. The patrol boat *Chiriquí* will be leaving Panama City in a few hours."

Ned nodded approval. His admiration seemed to be stronger than his outrage. He looked at Carl, now standing at the wall map. "Okay, Commander, proceed."

Carl presented a summary of the operation then gave the floor to Jerry. The big man filled in some of the details then yielded to Jose. The medic added what he could and gave the floor to Billy Joe. The team's boat expert provided the details his teammates had left specifically for him. There were only a few questions; the principals were simply stunned by the blow-by-blow description of all that had taken place.

"That's a lot of action for just two days…especially for a reconnaissance," remarked Ned sarcastically. "What do you guys plan to do for an encore?"

Carl regarded the CIA man grimly. "That's the right question, sir. It's clear to the tactical team that we're in the middle of a play here. We're just not sure what the next act will be."

"So what do you *think*?" asked Ned.

Carl responded by smiling furtively at Stewart. "First, I'll tell you what we know with high confidence. Then I'll say what we don't know. Then I'll tell you what we think."

"Fair enough, Commander. Continue." Ned was beginning to show signs of discomfort. Reginald Stewart had never been prouder of his *protégé*.

Carl took a black marker and began scribbling on the whiteboard. He divided the board into three columns.

"We know that six of the prisoners are Colombians who say they work for the Mena drug cartel. We know that they've been transshipping cocaine, using the go-fast boats we captured. We're pretty sure the men we killed were soldiers from the Revolutionary Armed Forces of Colombia, or FARC, said to be providing security for the operation. The English-speaking prisoners told us they are Pakistani citizens, trying to get into the United States. We know that the base camp at *Bahía de Santa Cruz* is a node in the trafficking network. They use more than one boat, running drugs between Colombia, Panama, and Central America." Carl paused then brought the audience back to the beginning. "And, of course, we know that the Colombians kidnapped Captain Alegre."

"Okay, what do you *not* know?" Carl could see that Ned appreciated the logic in his approach.

"We don't know for certain which Colombian port they use for loading the cocaine onto the boats. We don't know why the Colombians, admitted drug traffickers, are bringing Pakistani citizens into their distribution network. And, finally, we have yet to find out why they kidnapped a Panama Canal pilot."

Ned nodded again. "Okay, now what do you think?"

Carl stood with his hands on his hips then paced back and forth in front of the map. "We think the Mena cartel is trafficking more than drugs. The two Pakistanis are very likely not who they say they are. My sense is that there are a lot of dangerous people being trafficked through *Darién* province."

Ana Maria interrupted him, "Just to be clear, there's a difference between human trafficking and human smuggling. Trafficking is when people are transported against their will. Smuggling is when people *want* to be transported. We'll do what we can to find out why the Pakistanis really wish to travel north to the United States."

Carl continued, "Thank you, Major. We'll be just as anxious as you are." He shifted his attention back to Ned. "We think they're using Tumaco as the point of debarkation for trafficking drugs north. It's the logical starting point, given that it's the closest port to Pasto."

"And what is the significance of Pasto?" asked Pablo Céspedes.

"Pasto is the city closest to Jorge Mena Velasquez's villa. 'The Pasto Cartel,' another name for his organization, has cornered the market for production and distribution of cocaine coming out of *Nariño* State."

"How did you get them to admit they work for Mena?" asked Ned.

Carl could not suppress a smile. "We convinced them no one was coming to their rescue. That seemed to be enough incentive. They were disappointed when we left them on the island—desperate is a better word. We told them we worked for the Medellín cartel. They were surprised we didn't just kill them." Carl was no longer smiling. "I thought of it as a deathbed confession."

"And when we take them into custody, they will be grateful enough to tell us more," added Ana Maria. "Well played, Commander."

Carl continued, "Also, I still think there's a connection between Captain Alegre's kidnapping and the murder of Father Oscar Castillo. We'll need more help from Major Castaneda to figure that one out."

Colonel Stewart reminded them of what Carl believed was the elephant in the room. "And there is a possibility that whoever ordered the kidnapping of the pilot could have the intent to attack the Panama Canal. Remember how they got Alegre to talk about how the canal works."

"Who would want to damage the canal?" asked Céspedes, almost to himself. "We have always believed that the canal's neutrality is indeed its defense. Every country on earth benefits from the flow of trade through Panama."

Carl nodded. "That's what *we* have always thought. I've called this a puzzle. We need more information to solve it. I said at the beginning of the debrief that the outcome was both good and bad. Good because we learned a lot. Bad because we realized we have a lot left to learn."

"*Esta vaina no se acabó*," said Pablo Céspedes somberly.

"No, this thing is not over," responded Carl. "Not by a long shot."

Carl and Ana Maria had agreed to conceal from the group their theory that Manuel Noriega was the link to all that was happening. She would interview Noriega then present her findings to the command cell—whatever she found out. Maybe then the puzzle could be solved. It was late, and there were no more questions. Ned looked around the room.

"If no one has anything to add, I'd like to adjourn and let you all get some sleep. We will stay in contact and meet again when we have more information."

Everyone left the room, except Colonel Stewart and Carl's team.

"What should we do with Petty Officers Rios and Barnes?" asked the Colonel. Carl interpreted this as a rhetorical question.

"I think they should stay here until we figure this out, sir."

Jose and Billy Joe nodded in unison. "Yes, sir. We should stay."

"Done," said Stewart. "I'll call Virginia Beach in the morning. The ISOFAC will be available to all of you until this is over…whenever that is."

* * *

Carl followed her home. Ana Maria opened the door and wrapped her long arms around him. She rested her head on Carl's shoulder as he carried her directly into the bedroom. It was almost three o'clock in the morning. Carl hadn't slept in two full days, but that did not matter. Ana Maria kept him going for another two hours. Afterward, they slept deeply until almost noon. Later, over coffee, they tried to avoid talking about the operation. That, it seemed, was impossible.

"For the first time, *Carlitos*, I worried about your safety." She took his hand across the table.

Taken off guard, he fumbled with a response. "Well…it wasn't that dangerous, really. Our training is good, and my team works together as one."

Ana Maria was fascinated by Carl's ability to live in two completely different worlds, seemingly at the same time. She knew he had killed people in the field, but she had seen how gentle he could be at home. A ruthless jungle warrior one day, a model citizen the next. Ana Maria found herself loving both men.

"But there are men out there trying to kill you… That sounds pretty dangerous to me." She drew a breath. "And tell me more about your training. I mean, how does one go about learning to kill another human being…even bad human beings? I carry a gun, and I'm a very good shot, but I've never had to kill anyone."

Carl looked directly at her as he formulated a response. He had thought a lot about what he would say if ever asked this question. He and his teammates had an unspoken rule not to talk about killing. It was just something you did. To survive. To complete the mission. But Carl knew it was more than that.

"As I've said before, Ana, I don't enjoy killing. Anyone who does enjoy it should never be given a weapon. When you're out there in contact with the enemy, there's no time to think about it. You just react to the situation. The men we killed at the *Darién* camp…we didn't go in there with the intent to kill them. But we had to do it to protect the mission. We killed the kidnappers on the island to protect Freddy Alegre. Then there are the times when you have to *plan* to kill the enemy. Those are the tough ones."

"Like when there's a guard in the way?" she suggested. "But how do you prepare for that?"

"You have to develop the ability to suspend empathy."

She understood right away. "That makes a lot of sense. You can't think about the human story behind the gun."

"Absolutely right, Ana. That's where you rely on your training. Killing becomes a mechanical procedure, a tactic, rather than an act of passion."

"I don't know if I could get that far into the training."

"I'm not sure I'd *want* you to. Call me sexist, but I don't think women should be asked to kill deliberately. If you have to use your gun for police duties, that would be different."

"I wouldn't call that sexist at all, Carl. I would call it a natural extension of our biological roles, set in motion before recorded history."

Carl agreed. "It all goes back to the Stone Age, doesn't it? I'd be out there with my teammates, taking down a Woolly Mammoth. You'd be picking berries and talking about children."

She laughed out loud. "Yes, but some of us women have evolved beyond that!"

"I don't know too many men who've outgrown the Woolly Mammoth hunt," said Carl with a grin.

"The next time you go out, and that may be very soon, I will struggle to avoid worrying." She reached for his hand. "Our relationship is different now."

Carl was touched that she would even care about his coming back. Perhaps, he thought, she would stay with him this time after all. "Over and above the training, Ana, I keep two rules in my head all the time. Speed without haste… Anger without rage. These words bring me success, and success brings me home."

She flashed him the electric eyes that made his knees weak. "I didn't doubt your ability to survive the operation… I guess it's more that I just missed you." She extended her other hand and brushed his cheek.

He thought about what she meant… It made him feel even better than he already did. Carl wanted to be wanted for something besides his body. To be appreciated as a teammate and a companion. This was a new development. "I missed you too, Ana…a *lot*."

She giggled like a young girl. Carl had never heard that sound coming from Ana Maria's lips. He enjoyed it immensely.

"I'm sure you didn't have time to think about *me* out there."

He smiled at her, shaking his head. "Oh yes, I did. It's not all action, you know." He held her gaze. "There were long periods of waiting, especially on the *Luisa*. I was very glad to have you in my thoughts during those times."

"I hope I didn't interfere with your activities!" she added with widened eyes.

"Not at all, *cariña*... I have a switch in my head that I can turn on and off. I call it the warrior switch. You stayed on the boat when I went over the side. I love being in the field...especially when the danger is greatest." He paused and took both her hands in his. "But I felt better than ever because I knew you'd be here when I got back."

Ana Maria was visibly pleased to hear this. "I have never meant that much to a man, Carl. I don't know what to say."

"Say you'll keep caring about me."

"I will, *cariño*... I will."

CHAPTER 22

THE PATROL BOAT *Chiriquí* appeared off the leeward side of the point just before sunset. The prisoners had been sheltering in the shade but came running to the water's edge as soon as they saw the boat. Their drinking water was gone. Still in handcuffs and very weak, the men had passed the day peacefully, quietly accepting their fate. Some had prayed. Others had simply gone to sleep. The Pakistanis, who had isolated themselves from the Colombians, were often prostrate, facing Mecca. Now it seemed they would all be saved—or killed. At this point, they almost didn't care which. The slow death they had expected was worse than anything.

The Panamanian sailors ferried the prisoners off the beach in a black Zodiac. All the men could think about was a long drink of water and something to eat. Where they were going was not an issue. Once all the prisoners were aboard, the crew hauled the bundles of cocaine onto the boat and stored them in the forward berthing compartment. At that point, water was distributed to the men sitting on deck, and food was promised. The patrol boat weighed anchor and got underway. It would take them most of the night to reach Flat Top Rock.

Approaching Flat Top before dawn, the boat's radar painted two small surface craft, stationary off the islet's only beach. The radar picture also showed a somewhat larger contact, slowly moving away toward the island of Taboga. With the aid of a searchlight, the Panamanians found the go-fast boats and dispatched four of their crew to take possession, body bags and all. By the time the sun was peeking over the central *cordillera*, a formation of three *Servicio Maritimo* craft were seen approaching the Pacific entrance to the Panama Canal.

It was the morning after Carl and Ana Maria's "down day" (they'd spent the afternoon looking for jungle birds in the rainforest near the city). It was time to resume solving the puzzle. Carl went to the ISOFAC and spent the day with his men. They did physical training and performed gear maintenance, waiting for further instructions. Ana Maria got her people started interviewing the prisoners, now in a temporary holding facility. She had produced two lists of questions for the experts to present—one to the Colombians, the other to the Pakistanis. Ana Maria herself would be tied up all day, finding out what she needed to know. Carl could not be involved in the interview process, but he would learn what *he* needed to know later that evening.

Late in the afternoon, there was still one more thing on Ana Maria's schedule. She hated giving press conferences, but that was part of her expanding portfolio at the Technical and Judicial Police department. If Panama was to take credit for the arrest of eight *narcotraficantes* and the seizure of two hundred kilos of cocaine, then Major Castaneda would be the one to announce it to the country. She appeared before the cameras of *La Prensa* and other Panamanian media outlets at six o'clock in the evening—after the last editions but prior to the late-news broadcasts. Having discharged her most distasteful duty, Ana Maria drove a few minutes to the sanctuary of her home. After a soothing shower, she put on a silk robe and waited for Carl.

* * *

Carl finished his day at the ISOFAC and made a call on Colonel Stewart. They sat in Stewart's office as the sunlight faded outside. There were a few things both of them wanted to add to the information shared with the whole command cell.

"I'm very proud of you and your men, Carl. None of us expected such a favorable outcome."

"Neither did we," replied Carl candidly. "I have to admit, there was an element of luck, but we adjusted to exploit the situation on the ground. I couldn't ask for a better group of sailors to lead."

"You may get to do it again."

"Yes, sir, and that's what I think we should talk about."

Stewart looked tired. It must be, thought Carl, all those other situations he was responsible for managing. Carl had often wondered why any good military man (or woman) would want to be in command at a high level. Too far from the field and too little direct contact with the people who *are* in the field. Carl understood that Stewart was different, a too-rare exception. The colonel had always paid attention to Carl and his men. He was a caring leader who understood them. Carl trusted Stewart to keep his team from getting in over their heads.

Boldness was a weakness as well as a strength. Carl was aware of that, but he needed to be reminded from time to time.

"So where do you think this thing is going?" asked the colonel.

"I think, sir, that we're seeing just the tip of an iceberg. I can't see beneath the surface, but something is definitely there. We got the feeling downrange that the Mena cartel is trafficking more than just drugs. The Pakistanis have a good cover story, but I don't buy it. If we could look deeper, we'd be able to fill in the picture a bit more."

"Are you asking me if your team can go down there again?"

"Yes, sir. I would like to observe the network for a prolonged period to prove they're running guns and people, as well as cocaine."

"You mean the part of the network you haven't already rolled up, right?"

"As I said, sir, we got lucky. The beaconed go-fast came back early. Then the second boat came in unexpectedly, just as we were in a good position to take it away from them."

"What about the fire?"

"I wanted to burn the cocaine and most of the camp anyway. By coincidence, the fire was really well-timed. The second crew just abandoned their boat at the dock and rushed to the scene." Carl sighed. "Sometimes confusion is your friend."

"So what do you think happened to the crew of the second boat?"

"I expect they're still at what's left of the base camp. At least they have fresh water."

Stewart smiled. "I guess that's even worse than being grilled by Major Castaneda downtown."

It was Carl's turn to smile. "Oh, I don't know about that, sir… She can be pretty brutal."

Stewart laughed out loud. "Okay, enough about your personal life. I think it would be hard to get you guys back into the bush now that the hostage situation has been resolved and you've busted part of Mena's network. I like your enthusiasm, though. Let's see what the major learns from the prisoners."

Carl wore a look of disappointment. "I understand, sir, but the operator in me knows that there's much more going on down there. The Panamanians—God bless 'em—aren't ready for what may be coming."

* * *

Carl went home and took a shower before driving to Ana Maria's for the night. Their relationship had quickly evolved from lust into something much more. She was in freefall. He could feel it, hear it, and see it as they made love. Ana Maria had packed a small suitcase into which she'd put her dress uniform. Today's interviews had been hard for her. The Noriega interview, he expected, would be more interesting.

Now totally relaxed, they sat across from each other at the kitchen table, talking late into the night. It was a dress rehearsal for the debrief she would give the command cell after getting back from Miami. It was also another wonderful dangling conversation.

"I wanted to thank you again, *Carlitos*, for giving us all those presents…the prisoners, the drug seizure, the boats. It means a lot to my government…and to me." She sighed. "I just wish I hadn't been obligated to brief the press this evening… I *hate* that!"

"Giving you the presents was my pleasure," said Carl. "The whole idea was to hide our role and give you credit. Sorry about the press conference… I could *never* do that."

Ana Maria thought about the natural tendency of individuals and institutions to take credit for their actions (or steal it from others). Carl had willingly *given* it to others. "It must be hard to work in the shadows…not getting the credit you so richly deserve."

Carl had thought about this for his whole adult life. "It's not hard at all, *cariña*. My accomplishments, and those of my men, are reward enough. We don't need others to praise us…or even to know what we've done. *We* know, and that's all that counts."

"I think you really believe that, and I am starting to think that way as well. I hope that someday I can give you the credit for something *I* do."

Carl leaned across the table and kissed her on the cheek. "I'm sure you'll find an opportunity to do that, *mi amor*."

Ana Maria was fascinated by Carl's self-assurance. No toxic *machismo* to go with it. Confident but not cocky. Her male colleagues and subordinates spent too much time trying to impress other people (mostly women) but not enough time training themselves and their people. Leadership, she was learning, was not merely intuitive. It required practice. Her people had a lot to learn, and she looked forward to having Carl and his men teach them.

She took another sip of Chilean wine. Ana Maria's inhibitions had already been shattered. She charged further into his soul. "We've talked about where this puzzle may be taking you and me, *Carlitos*, but what are we going to do after it's solved?" Ana Maria rested her chin on both hands. "What do you want to do with the rest of your life?"

Carl should have been nervous about the question, but he wasn't. He was surprised by that. "My life has been episodic…up to now," he began. "That has made it more exciting, but at some point, I think I'll want to settle into a lifestyle with fewer surprises."

She sat up straight. "How many episodes have you had so far? It sounds like you're writing a book."

"In a way, I guess I am," he replied. "I'm nowhere near the end of the story, but it's time to think about how many chapters I want to write."

"What chapters are in your story so far? If you don't mind... I don't mean to pry." Ana Maria, having lots of her own baggage to keep private, had been reluctant to ask him personal questions. Events of the last week had swept away her reticence.

Carl tried to give her a short answer. "I grew up in Boston... You know some of the stories. My father was a fisherman. We were not poor but not by any means well to do. That was the first chapter."

"And you went into the Navy after high school."

"Yes...I suppose that would be chapter two. I struck for Gunner's Mate as a fleet sailor then applied for SEAL training, the notorious BUD/S course. Then I got married way too young. I spent four years as an enlisted operator. That's when my marriage fell apart. I was never home."

"No one should get married before age thirty," she asserted.

"Yeah, you're right about that, Ana. It wasn't really her fault... Just poor judgment on my part."

"So that was chapter three?"

"Yes, I think so. Then the Navy sent me to college. I got my degree at Old Dominion in three years then received a commission."

"Which chapter are we on now?"

"I think college would be chapter four. It widened my perspective. School gave me lifelong habits I couldn't get from the Navy... like reading." He thought for a few seconds. "Chapter five would be my second watch in Virginia Beach, learning how to lead SEALs. That's harder than it sounds. I mean, they're *all* leaders—that's what we recruit for—so they don't necessarily think they need to be led. I wish I had a nickel for every time a young sailor told me he had a better way to do something."

"Did he?"

"Yes, in many cases, he did. In fact, I learned that to lead a bunch of natural leaders you need to let them take on informal leadership roles. You have to listen to them and give them a long leash."

"So you need to develop trust."

"Exactly, but the trust has to go both ways."

She nodded enthusiastically. "So what was the next chapter?"

"Coming down here. That would be chapter six."

"Right before you met me."

"Yes…and being with you, even off and on, has made this chapter the most enjoyable part of the book."

She beamed. "That's nice to hear, *cariño*. I'm glad you didn't give up on me."

"I should be the one saying that, Ana. I was gone most of the time…enjoying the other parts of the chapter."

"Operations…saving the world."

"Yes…being in the jungle and the water. Direct action and indirect action. I do love it."

"Indirect action?"

"That's when we help other countries build capacity to confront their own security challenges. For instance, we've worked for the last three years with the Colombian Marine Corps, setting up riverine interdiction units all over the country."

"Do you think you could ever give it up?"

Carl did not hesitate. "Yes, I could…under the right circumstances. Maybe not right away, but sooner than I thought just a few weeks ago." He smiled into her big eyes and leaned across the table. "If you know a woman who'd like to help me live out the next chapter, please let me know."

"Would that be the last chapter?"

"Probably not, Ana, but I really want someone who will commit to helping me finish the book."

Ana Maria suddenly realized she'd taken the conversation too far. Her confidence had been growing all night; now it was fading. Carl had spoken to her from his heart. Though her chest was pounding, she was still speaking from her head. She had baggage to unload but now was not the time. She rose from her chair and moved quickly around the table. Carl took her in his arms, and they held each other until Ana Maria's voice came back.

"Let's get some sleep, *cariño*… I'm on a plane in the morning."

* * *

Early the following day, Carl drove Ana Maria to Tocumen Airport and dropped her off at the curb. She would be gone for one night and the better part of two days. As he left the parking lot on his way back to the city, Carl was already sorry he hadn't gone with her—not to the interview but just to be along for the ride. He knew, however, that for Ana Maria, this one would be personal; she had worked in Noriega's Intelligence section as a young officer. Carl knew when his advice was not wanted. Ana Maria was focused and tough. He trusted her to get whatever information she could from the monster Carl had helped send to prison.

CHAPTER 23

JORGE MENA VELASQUEZ brooded over the day's copy of *La Prensa*. His business empire had a lot of money tied up in Panama's banks, and he needed to keep abreast of events there. It was only in the paper that he'd found out what had happened at *Bahía de Santa Cruz*. The kingpin hated to be surprised. He hated it so much that he would have to find someone to punish for letting six of his employees—and those difficult Pakistanis—be captured by Panamanian "Public Forces." It was embarrassing enough to have his people busted by Colombian police...but *Panamá*? The quintessential banana republic. He had a lot of issues with his own government, but at least Colombia was a real country.

Panama's Maritime Service Arrests Colombian Narcotraffickers

> The Technical and Judicial Police (PTJ) announced last evening the Panamanian government's arrest of eight Colombian drug traffickers and the seizure of some two hundred kilograms of cocaine. The arrests were made at a remote base camp in the Darién rainforest by maritime service sailors. The specific circumstances of the operation including the location of the base camp were not disclosed. The sus-

pects, who have already told the police they are members of the "Pasto Cartel," reputedly led by Jorge Mena Velasquez, were turned over to the PTJ for detailed interviews over the next few days. According to Major Ana Maria Castaneda, deputy director and spokesperson for the PTJ, the Colombians appear to be using Panama as the key node in an extensive regional trafficking network. Major Castaneda said that additional information will be made available as soon as her department has completed its investigation. She took no questions.

Mena put the paper down and paced the room alone. The trashing of his good name in a Panama press account was more than he could take. He picked up the phone and dialed a number in Panama City.

* * *

Bypassing baggage claim, Ana Maria strode quickly to her rental car. She was in a hurry to get settled into a hotel room. It would take all evening to steel herself for the confrontation with Manuel Noriega in the morning. She was ready for the interview but not so much for the distasteful encounter. The afternoon was hot and humid, but darkening cumulus clouds offered the promise of a thunderstorm. Ana Maria checked into a Marriott near the airport, about thirty minutes' drive from the Miami Federal Correctional Institution.

After a short nap on the very comfortable bed, Ana Maria pulled on her running shoes and went to the hotel's fitness room. She was pleasantly surprised to find an assortment of dumbbells on a rack against the wall in addition to the treadmill and elliptical trainer. For the next hour, she put her lithe body through an aerobic workout for the first time since the crisis began. Ana Maria enjoyed immensely the stress relief she got from making love to Carl. But it was not enough. She needed the cardioversion of a heart pump, along with the strengthening of long and short muscles.

Back in the room, she stood in front of the mirror, sweating. Ana Maria liked to sweat, especially with Carl. Training runs in the jungle and jungle sex in the bedroom. She stripped off the workout gear and examined her glistening reflection. Long legs (men always noticed that first), small breasts, tight stomach, and shoulder-length curly jet-black hair. Her cappuccino skin suggested a typical mixed heritage: Spanish and indigenous with a touch of Africa. Ana Maria did not consider herself beautiful, but she could see why Carl was attracted to her. He was always looking into her eyes—that is when he wasn't admiring her legs. She jumped into the shower and let it stream onto her face, like the cooling waterfall of her childhood near Yaviza.

At precisely nine o'clock the next morning, Major Ana Maria Castaneda, in dress uniform, marched into the prison visitors' waiting room. She went to the front desk and checked in.

"*Buenos días, señora…* I am Major Castaneda. I have a nine o'clock with General Noriega."

The older Latina responded with professional polish. "Please sit down for a few minutes while we get him, *mi Mayor*." Ana Maria retreated a few steps and took a seat. Although she could not know, it was the same chair in which Father Castillo had waited for the prisoner. She didn't have to wait for long.

"Please come with me." The uniformed guard gestured to Ana Maria. She followed him through a heavy glass door to the security checkpoint. After placing her purse on the conveyor belt, the major was scanned and cleared. She was led into a bare office with one desk and two chairs. As she sat at attention, the back door opened. There stood General Manuel Noriega, Ana Maria's former boss. He carried a book at his side, like a pistol.

"*Buenas*, Ana Maria." A menacing tone for such an informal greeting. The voice came from a past she did not want to remember. Ana Maria tried to utter a response as Noriega stepped forward to take the seat across from her. He placed the book in his lap. Wearing a starched khaki uniform with medals, polished brass, and shined shoes, Manuel Noriega looked exactly the same as when she had last seen him. That occasion had been shortly before the invasion, October 1989. Ana Maria had attended a ceremony at the *Comandancia*, celebrating Noriega's victory over the hated Americans. The general had beaten back a coup attempt, engineered (he said) by the CIA. He was on a collision course with the United States. In fact, he had just declared war on the Americans. The image of Noriega brandishing a sword in front of the cheering crowd was still in her head.

Ana Maria also remembered her secret meeting with Carl Malinowski later that night.

"*Buenos días, General.*" That was all she could manage…for now.

Continuing in what passes for Spanish in Panama, Noriega took control of the meeting. "I have followed your career since my departure. I see that you are now the deputy director of the PTJ. Pretty impressive at age thirty-six, if I do say so." His crooked smile accentuated the pockmarks on his face. "Why, after all these years, did you want to see me?"

Ana Maria had been breathing evenly through the initial barrage. She was ready for the conversation they needed to have.

"I did not *want* to see you."

Noriega feigned disappointment. "That is a surprise, of course. When you worked for me at the Intelligence Directorate, you were always glad to see me… Perhaps it was because you wanted to be promoted. I remember you as a very ambitious young woman."

"I was never glad to see you."

Noriega's eyebrows went up. "That is not what I remember. You had a lot of potential, girl… If you had played your cards right, you could have eventually become the G2."

"That was never my objective." Ana Maria was now in a working rhythm. Dancing with the devil. "I wanted to serve my country."

Noriega laughed out loud. "Not really, my dear. You wanted to serve your own interests."

"I have never served my own interests."

"Then how do you explain your affair with General Torrijos?"

Here we go.

"I was very young. Omar Torrijos, our great leader, seduced me. I gave him my virginity. How could I serve my country any more than that?"

"You were a whore then...and you are *still* a whore!"

"Omar made love to me... You tried to *rape* me!"

"I did not think it was possible to rape a whore. You spread for Torrijos...and you should have spread willingly for me. That's what female subordinates do...especially those with reputations like yours."

"I loved General Torrijos...and you killed him!"

"There is no evidence that I placed a bomb on that airplane."

"But you did... I know you did!"

"If you really think that, then why did you stay in the G2? Why did you not just become an American?"

"I think you already know why I stayed."

"Yes...I do. I have learned since then that you became a spy for the Americans. That makes you a traitor as well as a whore."

"Whatever you think I did, it was in the service of *Panamá*."

Noriega wanted to change the subject, not because he felt guilty...or because Ana Maria's accusation had made a dent in his delusion, but he was simply tired of this woman. This traitor. This whore. And she had only been in his presence for ten minutes.

"So what did you really want to say to me?" Noriega looked like a general, but he was still a criminal, incarcerated in a prison.

Ana Maria composed herself and came to the real reason for her visit. Sitting up a little straighter in the chair, she began her police agenda.

"We know that you were visited here by Father Oscar Castillo last month. We want to know why...what he said to you, and what you said to him."

Noriega tried to hide his agitation. He could not. "Oscar Castillo is a childhood friend of mine! I asked him to hear my confession so I could receive the sacrament of communion."

"But surely there are many priests available around here. If confession was all you needed, it would be very unusual for Father Castillo to come here all the way from Panama."

"I also wanted to see my old friend."

"So he heard your confession. What else did he hear from you?"

Noriega shifted ever so slightly in his seat. "He brought me a new Bible. My old one was worn from all the studying I have done since coming here."

Sure *you have*…

Ana Maria noticed the prisoner getting nervous. She had been trained to notice. "Okay…so why did you not just order a new Bible from the prison? I am sure they would have given you one."

"Because I wanted Oscar to sign it for me." Noriega took the book from his lap and shoved it across the table. "See for yourself."

Ana Maria opened the Bible and read the dedication. She knew that Castillo and Noriega had grown up together. It made sense for the general to summon his friend for this transaction. But that did not allay her suspicion.

"Father Castillo was murdered on the street just a few days ago."

Noriega expressed surprise. "I did not know that. God rest his soul."

"We think he was killed by a Colombian hit man…a *sicario* on a motorcycle. The murder remains unsolved."

"That may be, Ana Maria. There are many bad people in the city. I always preferred living in the interior."

She knew why the prisoner continued to use her first name and in a condescending tone, at that, as if she were an insignificant actor, coming from backstage for one line in his larger-than-life play, as if she were his servant…or his mistress. Major Castaneda was determined not to let it get to her.

"Father Castillo was killed right after leaving the hospital where Captain Manfredo Alegre was recovering from a gunshot wound. Alegre is a Panama Canal pilot, who had been kidnapped by Colombian drug traffickers. He was freed by our heroes from the *Servicio Maritimo*."

Noriega tossed his head back. "That is not a real military outfit."

Ana Maria smiled for the first time. "I can see that you have been out of the country for a long time, sir."

Noriega said nothing.

"We know that Father Castillo traveled to *San Juan de Pasto* immediately after leaving here. We think he went there to speak with Jorge Mena Velasquez."

The prisoner looked puzzled. "Oscar did not tell me about that. Perhaps he went there to visit the *Las Lajas Sanctuario*. Many Latin American priests make that pilgrimage…as do Catholics from around the world."

"We think Father Castillo was murdered by the kingpin Mena because of something the priest did for you…a favor perhaps."

"I know nothing about that."

"We think Father Castillo went to Pasto to meet with Mena at your behest. We are not sure exactly what he said."

"It could be that Oscar went there to visit the sanctuary…and then to attend the ribbon-cutting ceremony for the new hospital."

"How did you know about that?"

"I read all the newspapers I can get my hands on. And yes, the city fathers in Pasto named the hospital for Jorge."

"Your friend, Jorge?"

"He was not my friend, but I knew him well."

"You let him traffic drugs through Panama…and you let him launder the money through Panamanian banks."

"That is not true! He is simply a good businessman. I courted people like him to make investments in Panama. If he had been doing anything illegal, I would have been the first to know about it."

Ana Maria laughed. "Do you think I am stupid enough to believe that?"

Noriega chuckled to himself. "Yes…I do."

"So you deny that Father Castillo met with Jorge Mena in Pasto?"

"I know nothing about that," repeated Noriega.

"And you deny that you asked Jorge Mena Velasquez for a favor, using your friend as a messenger?"

"Yes, I would never do that."

"Then we're done here," said Ana Maria, lapsing into English. She stood up and turned toward the door behind her.

Manuel Noriega, still seated at the desk, called to her, "And tell that American you fuck that I had nothing to do with all this. I am just a prisoner here…thanks, in part, to him!"

Now that's a surprise.

Ana Maria thought she'd gotten through the interview with only minor bruises. She had learned nothing, but her early suspicions had been strengthened. Noriega had asked his friend Mena for a favor. Mena's people had kidnapped a canal pilot. She still did not know why. None of her colleagues had a solid theory. But now there was a new question hanging in the air.

How in the hell does he know I'm sleeping with Carl…and when did he first find out?

CHAPTER 24

ANA MARIA KEPT walking. She dropped her visitor's badge on the front desk without slowing down. Once in the rental car, she drove directly to the airport and flew back to Panama City. Carl was there to pick her up. As far as her office knew, she was on two days' leave. She'd paid for the trip to Miami from her own funds.

He leaned over and kissed her after they got into the Land Cruiser. "So, how did it go?"

Ana Maria was obviously distracted. She stared straight ahead as Carl drove out of the parking lot. At the former *Omar Torrijos International Airport*, for god's sake! She did not know what to say to him. If she kept it all to herself, it would haunt her forever. If she told Carl the whole story, he might simply walk away.

¡*Mierda*!

"I learned nothing new…except that our suspicions are likely correct. Noriega did use Father Castillo to send a message to the kingpin Mena. Now Castillo has been murdered, by Mena's assassin! We still don't know why they grabbed the pilot."

Carl merged into Panama's chaotic traffic, headed for Ana Maria's neighborhood. "I think they wanted the pilot to teach them about the canal. It wasn't about the ransom at all."

Ana Maria nodded slowly. "Okay, then why did they want to know more about the canal?"

"I think Noriega asked Mena to do something to the canal. You say he thought Mena owed him a lot for making Panama's jungles and banks available to transship drugs and launder the cartel's money."

"I did say that."

"So what would you do if you were Manuel Noriega in prison with a secret bank account and nothing left to lose?"

"You mean how would I get revenge on the Americans?"

"Don't forget the Panamanians. He always held a grudge against the elite of this society."

"So he gets back at the United States *and* Panama's *rabiblancos* by interfering with ship traffic on the canal?"

Carl shot a glance at Ana Maria in the deepening twilight. "Colonel Stewart was right… I'm a trained saboteur. I think Noriega wants to *destroy* the canal."

Ana Maria gasped. "Why would he want that…the canal is our biggest economic driver? All our citizens, even those of us who are *not* lily white, depend on the canal's revenue. Noriega's people…my people."

"I know it doesn't make sense, Ana, but dictators don't see it that way. You know what they say about absolute power."

"Yes, that it corrupts absolutely."

"It's not just Noriega. I've worked in many other countries where dictators have destroyed the economy…simply to satisfy their own egos."

"You're right, Carl… Look at Guatemala and Nicaragua." She thought another few seconds. "Or Argentina!"

Temporarily silent, Carl was doing three things at once. Driving the car was one. Figuring out what Noriega had in mind was another. The third thing was to watch behind the car, just to make sure they were not being followed.

Old habits.

It was effectively dark by now. The traffic was jammed up as usual through San Miguelito. Jobless young men were crawling all over the Toyota, trying to wash Carl's windows. He quickly rolled down the window and gave them money to go away. As the young men vanished into a sea of belching cars and two-cylinder motor-bikes, Carl inched forward on the pavement. It was then that he noticed something out of place in his rearview mirror.

A real motorcycle. The rider wore a black leather jacket and a helmet. *In this heat? Panamanians don't wear helmets!* The bike was closing on the Land Cruiser as Carl continued to roll through the bottleneck.

Carl glanced at Ana Maria. She read his expression. "What's wrong?"

"Hang on," said Carl in a calm voice. "I think we're being followed."

Carl floored the accelerator and wove through the traffic. The motorcycle, nimbler than the Land Cruiser, wove after them. The rider still had both hands on the handlebars.

"Ana, listen to me. There's a motorcycle behind us, ridden by a man in a leather jacket. This is what happened to Father Castillo. Slide down in the seat!"

Ana Maria slumped until she could not see over the dashboard. "Carl, tell me this is a nightmare!"

"It's not a nightmare. Stay where you are but be ready to get out and run."

"Run where?" She was still in her police uniform.

"Into a crowd…surround yourself with as many people as you can."

"When?"

"Wait for my signal. Unfasten your seat belt *now!*"

"What about you?" She fumbled for the belt.

"I'll come back for you. Just stay close to where I let you out!"

Carl continued to weave through heavy traffic, speeding up and slowing down as necessary. The motorcycle stayed right with him, lane-splitting to catch up. The vehicles were dancing in the glare of a hundred sets of headlights. Carl understood that if he stopped the Land Cruiser on the main road, the motorcycle would pull up next to him. If the rider had a gun under his jacket, Carl and Ana Maria would be dead. The *sicario* would be after *her*, he reckoned, but the shots would come from Carl's side of the car. Probably through his head.

"Get ready to jump!"

The motorcycle surged aside the left rear bumper of the Toyota. Carl glimpsed the side mirror as the rider reached into his jacket and pulled out a machine pistol with his right hand. Carl's brain flashed an UZI or MAC-10 warning. Technical differences didn't matter. The biker was about to fire a fusillade of .45 ACP rounds without slowing down.

Not good!

Carl accelerated to open the distance, pulling up to the back end of a luxury sedan. The assassin was gripping the bike's handlebar with one hand and his weapon with the other. Carl waited for half a second then slammed on the brakes. The motorcycle shot past him on the left. Carl made a ninety-degree turn to the right and careened onto a side street.

"Now!"

Ana Maria opened the door and jumped out. She lost her balance and rolled onto the dirt shoulder of the narrow street. Carl watched in what seemed like slow motion as Ana Maria got up and sprinted into a crowd of ordinary citizens, walking along the main road. She was a gifted athlete. If the killer managed to exit the highway in pursuit of his target, he would lose her in the maze of houses behind the street. Carl was no longer worried about Ana Maria.

Now he could deal with the *sicario* one on one. *Mano a mano.*

Carl bounced around the block and got back on the shoulder of the main road. Driving recklessly across the centerline, he pointed the Land Cruiser back toward the airport. He stood on the accelerator then slowed down so he could watch for the motorcycle coming back. Sure enough, there it was, gaining on him again!

Fuck!

The good news was that the assassin was no longer after Ana Maria. Carl could only assume she had been the target. No one could have known that he was going to be at the airport. For the moment, at least, she was safe. The bad news: now *he* was the target!

Carl drove as fast as he could, threading through the slower traffic headed east. He shot a quick glance in the rearview. The motorcycle was right behind him! He could not see the rider's hands, but he knew that one of them held the machine pistol, lowered at arm's length. Ready to aim.

Do something unexpected!

Carl veered sharply to the left…right into the oncoming traffic! The Land Cruiser crossed the single lane, oncoming cars braking and banking to avoid him. He immediately jolted the Toyota back to the right without slowing down. He was now on the dirt shoulder of the road, driving recklessly against the cars coming from the airport. Cars that were now racing along between Carl and the motorcycle! The rider put his weapon back in the jacket and grabbed the handlebars with both hands. Carl looked ahead and saw nothing but headlights, mere inches away on his right. Pedestrians were bailing out to his left. He glanced behind him and saw the motorcycle starting to cross through the oncoming lane.

Then he heard a loud crash and turned all the way around in time to see sparks flying. He jammed on the brakes and skidded to a halt. Carl got his pistol out of the glove compartment and exited the Land Cruiser, dodging headlights in both lanes to get back to the scene. As he approached the broken motorcycle, the assassin was lying on the side of the road, cars going around him without stopping. He was bleeding but moving. His helmet had come off, and the machine pistol was on the pavement several yards in front of him. The killer saw Carl coming and crawled faster toward the weapon.

Carl ran faster than the killer could crawl. The man's neck was exposed. Carl jumped on it and heard a loud crack.

Plausible denial.

No police at the scene yet. He wasn't worried about witnesses (Panamanians preferred to see dead bodies lying on the front page of their newspaper). Carl picked up the machine pistol, released the magazine, and emptied the chamber. He scattered the ammunition into the bushes then tossed the magazine. At least the weapon would not be fired—at the police or anyone else. He ran back to the Toyota. Throwing his own gun on the passenger seat, Carl made a U-turn to the left and merged quickly into the traffic, heading back toward Panama City. Five minutes later, he spotted Ana Maria standing on the side of the road. She was still in a crowd, well off the road. She saw Carl as he skidded to a stop. He opened the door, and she jumped in. Carl spun the tires, kicking up dirt as he got back on the highway.

"Where's the killer now, Carl?"

"In hell…where he belongs." No further details. Ana Maria was smart enough not to ask.

She shifted in her seat then held Carl's pistol out to him. "Here's your weapon."

"Just put it back in the glove compartment, Ana… Are you okay?"

Ana Maria slid over next to him on the bench seat. She took a deep breath and exhaled forcefully. "I'm okay, *Carlos*. Let's go home."

"My home, not yours," said Carl abruptly, thinking that Ana Maria was tougher than he thought. "This guy was after you, not me. There may be another assassin out there, looking for you. We can't take the chance that he knows where you live."

"So you want me to stay at your quarters on the base?"

"That's the safest place…for now. If there's another killer out there, he won't find you…and you already have a visitor's pass to get on base."

Ana Maria looked up at him. "You saved my life, *Carlos*… again."

"It was my duty and a pleasure, Ana." He smiled down at her. "Now you can live with me…at least for a while."

"That sounds really nice, *cariño*." Ana Maria rested her head on Carl's shoulder all the way to the naval base.

* * *

After getting Ana Maria set up in his quarters (since she had little baggage, it did not take long), Carl called Stewart at the SOC. The colonel, as usual, was working late.

"Colonel…LCDR Malinowski here. Major Castaneda and I have a lot to say to the command cell. How soon can you get them together?"

Stewart did not take long to respond. "I can have them all at the ISOFAC at 0800 tomorrow, Carl. How's that?"

"Perfect, sir. We are unraveling the puzzle. See you in the AM."

Carl handed Ana Maria a towel, and she headed for the shower. Then he called Jerry Tompkins.

"Butkus, I need you to come with me to the ISOFAC in the morning. Call Bosco and Tinker. The command cell will be there at zero-eight. I want the whole team to hear what Major Castaneda and I have to report."

"Got it, boss. Good to go."

Carl poured two glasses of Jamaican rum, straight up, and waited for her in the living room. She emerged a few minutes later, wearing the towel around her waist. Her hair was still wet. She looked like a coffee-colored mermaid. After what they had just been through, Carl thought she was remarkably composed. She sat next to him, and he handed her a glass.

"Take this and drink it all down. It'll settle your nerves."

Ana Maria raised the glass to her lips. "My nerves are fine now, *cariño*, but this should help me sleep."

"This is the first time you've slept at my place."

She drained the glass and looked into his eyes. "It feels good, *Carlitos*… It feels good."

* * *

"Good morning, everyone," began Reginald Stewart. LCDR Malinowski and Major Castaneda have some new information to share with all of us." He gestured to his J3. "Commander?"

Carl went to the map. Ana Maria sat at attention in the same civilian clothes she'd worn on the front end of the Miami trip (since her dress uniform was now stained with San Miguelito dirt). "By now, you may have heard about the accident on the *Interamericana* near Tocumen Airport last night." He surveyed the group and saw every head nod. "That was no accident."

Ned raised his eyebrows. "Tell us more, please... The only thing we know is that a motorcyclist was killed in a road accident...and that police are investigating."

Ana Maria interrupted. "Yes, we are, Ned. It's early days yet."

Ned turned to Carl. "So tell us why you think it was not an accident."

"Because I was there," said Carl evenly.

There was total silence in the room—not even Colonel Stewart had known.

"Major Castaneda asked me to pick her up from the airport. She had made a personal trip to Miami and did not want her office to know about it just yet."

Ned pressed. "So you were driving her back from the airport last night...right where this motorcyclist was killed on the road?"

"Yes...Major Castaneda was the target."

Silence again. Every person in the room looked at Ana Maria, including each of Carl's men.

"Tell us more," responded Ned.

"We were slugging through the traffic in San Miguelito. I noticed a powerful motorcycle behind us, ridden by a man in a leather jacket and wearing a helmet. As I tried to open the distance between vehicles, it was clear that he was following us."

Carl looked over at Ana Maria. She was nodding her head, unfazed by the memory.

"Suddenly, we were trying to outrun a motorcycle in heavy traffic. I knew we would lose. I also knew that Colombian *sicarios* assassinate people this way. That's how Father Castillo was murdered near the hospital. Then I saw the machine pistol come out of the guy's jacket."

"How did you know that Major Castaneda was the target?"

Ana Maria spoke up, "My theory is that the Mena cartel was attempting to punish the Panamanian government for destroying their *Darién* base camp and capturing six of their people. Remember, you gave us the credit, and I took it to the press conference."

Carl interjected a thought he'd been mulling over all night. "I think that's right. The cartel, and their agents in Panama, would have seen Major Castaneda on TV and in the newspapers."

Ana Maria managed to smile. Turning to Carl, she spoke to everyone in the room, "I want to thank you again for letting Panama take the credit for this… The assassination attempt changes nothing."

"So how did you escape from the killer, Commander?" Ned took up the conversation thread again.

"I waited until the bike started to pass me on the left. As soon as the rider aimed his weapon, I jammed on the brakes, and he sailed past us. I turned onto a side street and let Major Castaneda jump from the vehicle. She ran into a crowd. I drove onto the highway, headed back toward the airport."

"What happened next?"

"The only thing I could do to get away from the bike was to veer into the oncoming traffic." Carl sensed that everyone in the room except Ana Maria was having trouble believing what he was saying.

"And *then*?"

"I was running on the dirt shoulder, against the traffic, as fast as I could. The killer tried to follow me onto the wrong side of the road."

"So did he make it across?"

"No…he didn't make it. The Land Cruiser is a lot more visible than a motorcycle in the dark. I made it because all the drivers could see me. One of the drivers failed to see the bike and knocked it off the road. The rider was thrown about thirty feet to the pavement. The machine was a smoking wreck."

"Was the rider killed in the crash?"

Carl had anticipated this question. He realized he was on shaky legal ground, even under CIA rules of engagement. "Yes…I went back to the scene just to make sure."

"So then you just left the scene, assuming the Panamanian police could figure it out."

"Yes, I had to recover Major Castaneda and get her to safety. We thought there might be another assassin out there, looking for her. I unloaded the assassin's weapon and threw the empty magazine and .45 rounds into the bushes."

"That was so nobody in the crowd could use it against the police," said Ned as Carl nodded.

Colonel Stewart spoke for the first time. "You did the right thing, Commander. Where is the major going to stay now?"

"In a safe house," replied Carl with a furtive smile.

Ana Maria got up to give her story. Not about the crash but her visit to Miami. Once the major had everyone's attention, she threw a verbal hand grenade on the table.

"I believe that Manuel Noriega has paid the Mena cartel to destroy, or seriously disable, the Panama Canal…in order to take revenge against the governments of Panama and the United States."

CHAPTER 25

THE COMMAND CELL convened the following morning to discuss the possibility that the canal might be sabotaged. During the previous meeting, Pablo Céspedes, more than the others, had been shaken by Major Castaneda's statement—especially since she had just been in the presence of the reviled dictator. Carl had endorsed Ana Maria's thesis to the group, stating that—even if they were wrong—they had no choice but to plan for the worst-case scenario. Before they'd left the ISOFAC, he'd promised to lead them through an analysis of the canal's vulnerabilities…from the perspective of a saboteur. Ana Maria had agreed to reinterview Freddy Alegre later that day for additional clues regarding the intent of the cartel. Carl and his men had spent the rest of the day preparing for the risk assessment exercise…and, more importantly, what *they* could do to preempt the worst case.

Ned began the meeting by asking Ana Maria to brief the group regarding her second interview with Captain Alegre. She rose and stood by the map on the wall.

"Let me start by telling you that Captain Alegre is doing well. The hospital expects to release him the day after tomorrow. He wanted me to express his gratitude to the men who brought him back… He thinks you guys are a mercenary unit of some kind, hired by Panama to free him."

Ana Maria looked right at Carl and then at his men.

"He's not too far off," said Carl cheerily.

199

"The pilot told me that his captors had hijacked a fishing boat in order to transport him to the *Darién*. He guessed the pickup location to be somewhere not too far east of the airport because they only had to go through one checkpoint. He said that when they got near the camp, the kidnappers shot the fishermen. Even though blindfolded, he was very sure about that…and scared to death. They marched him through the jungle for the better part of a night and one full day, probably a 'back door' to the camp where our team captured the *narcotraficantes*. Once there, his kidnappers turned him over to another man…who actually treated him well. Alegre told me they spent all night talking about his profession and how the Panama Canal works. Captain Alegre, by that time, was very tired. He did not realize he was being interrogated…but, in fact, he was."

"What specifically did he tell them?" asked Pablo Céspedes.

"He explained why he loves his work…and that his passion is driven partly by the sheer engineering elegance of the canal. I think we can assume that the cartel now knows almost as much about the canal as does Captain Alegre."

"There's a scary thought!" Reginald Stewart almost shouted. "We'd better figure out what they plan to do with that knowledge… and fast."

Stewart gestured to Ned. "Anything else we need to say before Carl here gets us into the target analysis drill?"

Neither Ned nor anyone else spoke up.

"Okay," said Stewart, turning to Carl. "Let's get started."

Carl got up and went to the board. "We call this analysis tool CARVES," began the tactical commander. He drew a matrix on the whiteboard, scribbling the assessment criteria across the top:

"C" for Criticality. "A" for Accessibility. "R" for Resilience. "V" for Vulnerability. "E" for Effects. "S" for Symbolism.

"Okay, does everyone understand the criteria I've listed?"

"What's the difference between accessibility and vulnerability?" asked Pablo Céspedes.

Carl reverted to teaching mode. "Accessibility is the degree to which a saboteur can gain access to the critical node in a system. Vulnerability is a measure of how difficult it is to destroy that particular component once access is gained. Take, for example, the Norwegian operation to sabotage the German heavy water plant at *Vemork* in 1943. That facility was almost impossible to get into, being situated on the edge of a deep canyon. But once the attackers managed to get in, they had no trouble destroying the plant's capacity to produce the deuterium the Nazis needed to make an atomic bomb."

"Thank you," said Céspedes grimly. "The canal, you will find, is accessible but not particularly vulnerable."

"I hope you're right," responded Carl. "Let's see if we can test that theory."

Céspedes interjected one more thing before Carl could continue. "We have always believed that the canal's defense is its very neutrality. All nations benefit from using it. No nation has an incentive to destroy it, so what's different now?"

"The difference," replied Carl, "is that we are evaluating the canal's attractiveness as a target for a nonstate actor. The Mena cartel transports its drugs via fast boats or airplanes west and north, along both coasts. They don't need the canal. It could be that Noriega's revenge would make it *easier* for Mena's cartel, not harder. Political chaos in Panama might be good for their business."

"I agree with that," Ned put in.

"So do I," said Reginald Stewart.

"That is the value of getting an outside opinion," said Pablo Céspedes soberly. "Thank you."

Ana Maria spoke to everyone, "I am afraid that all of you are right. We have a real threat on our hands."

Carl jumped right in, "So how do we best prepare ourselves for that threat?" He nodded to Jerry, Jose, and Billy Joe. "This method is an adaptation of the Army Special Forces model we use for sabotaging enemy industrial facilities." He shot a glance at Colonel Stewart. His boss was beaming. "Today we have to think like the bad guys."

Sounding again like a teacher, Carl continued the introduction. "Threats and risks are not the same thing. A threat can be reduced or mitigated by the defender's anticipatory actions. We'll look at each threat to the canal…then assess its potential to cause harm, to the system and to the people who operate it. In other words, we'll come out with a prioritized list of risks, based on the experience and expertise in this room. At that point, Panama will be able to distribute its scarce defensive resources in the most effective ways."

Ned turned to Reginald Stewart. "If the major's theory is correct, will Panama have the resources to do this? The United States is committed to defending the canal. Can't we just use the Army?"

Ana Maria took the question. "Technically, no. By treaty, the United States is committed only to ensuring the canal's neutrality. That's not the same thing as defending it. When Omar Torrijos was negotiating the treaty with President Carter, he never considered the threat from nonstate actors."

"Since we're not sure about the threats, or the risks associated with those threats, I recommend we keep this *entre nous* for the time being," cautioned Ned. "If we were to deploy the US Army along the banks of the canal for the next month, the citizens of Panama would freak out."

Ana Maria nodded vigorously in agreement.

Colonel Stewart finished the thought. "Yes, that's exactly what we wish to avoid. I think this command cell is the way to go, at least for now. Commander Malinowski will continue working with Major Castaneda to leverage Panama's capacities. With a sound target analysis, it's possible that we can protect the canal without using American troops."

Carl took the marker in his fingers again and pointed to the left side of the matrix. "Okay...let's list the threats to specific components of the canal here...in any order. We'll determine the priority later, based on the data we generate for the matrix."

Three hours later, they had a prioritized list of eight risks. First on that list was the *Miraflores* lock on the Pacific side. Second was the three-tiered *Gatún* lock on the Caribbean side. The third highest priority was given to the *Culebra* Cut, the narrowest stretch of the canal, where the American builders had literally burrowed through the Continental Divide. Now they would have to decide what to do with the list.

"Okay," began Ned, after they had all taken a break. "Where do we go from here?"

Colonel Stewart was the first to respond. "I think we need to send Carl and his team out to each of the sites to do some *tactical* analysis…putting themselves more deeply into the imagination of a potential attacker."

"That's a good idea," replied Ned. "How do we ensure that none of these men get arrested for looking like actual attackers?"

"My office gives them a get-out-of-jail-free card," said Ana Maria helpfully.

"Our cover works perfectly for this," Carl put in. "As tourists looking for tropical birds, we can explain the binoculars. If we get rolled up, we can say we're just dumb Americans with no idea we'd gotten too close to the canal."

"And our people will refer any infraction to me personally," added Ana Maria. "Also, I will use the next two days to collate the results of the interviews my officers have been conducting with each of the prisoners. I am particularly curious about the Pakistanis… We still don't have the truth about what they are up to."

"Good," concluded Ned. "Now we have a plan for the near term. I suggest we take this hour by hour. We can meet back here the day after tomorrow unless we find evidence that Major Castaneda's theory is correct. Then I will call you back here right away. Please respond to your pagers as quickly as you can. None of us wants to be surprised going forward."

"I will brief the president of the republic," Ana Maria responded.

"And I'll brief General Wells," added Stewart. "He has already directed me not to move on this until we have some substantiating evidence." The colonel paused for effect. "We have to exercise strategic patience, but be ready to act tactically at any time."

Carl answered for the team. "Got it, sir. We're good to go."

* * *

Carl loaded his team into the rusty Land Cruiser and drove them across the isthmus to the *Gatún* locks. The set of three basins was designed to lift ships of up to 110 feet in width 85 feet to the level of the massive *Gatún* Lake. Ships transiting south stayed at that elevation until being lowered again in two stages: *Pedro Miguel*, then *Miraflores*, nearest the Pacific entrance. They sat in the Toyota, as Carl drove slowly over the canal toward Fort Sherman.

"I agree with Pablo," said Jose. "This thing is easy to get to, but it would be very hard to destroy, not without a lot of explosive, that is."

"Yeah," added Billy Joe. "The locks work on simple mechanics and gravity. I don't see how they could sabotage them."

Jerry was looking for a critical node within the locking system. "I can't find an obvious point of vulnerability. We should drive along the lake and see it from another angle."

Carl drove over the dam, along the northern shore of Lake *Gatún*. "Tell me again what you guys think about the dam as a target? If they were to breach that, this whole lake would drain away into the Caribbean. It would take the commission years to get the canal back in operation."

"Yeah, we talked about that in the analysis," Jerry put in. The dam is so strong. I don't see how they could take it down."

"I agree, man," added Jose. "See the shape of the thing... It's curved to have more strength against the pressure of the lake."

Carl nodded. "Yeah, I think it would be very tough for a couple of amateurs without something really big."

"Like a missile!" Billy Joe said with a mischievous grin. "That would be pretty cool!"

Carl frowned at Billy Joe, dismissing the remark as youthful exuberance. "Okay, let's go see the other potential targets." He turned around and drove back over *Gatún* lock. Soon they were speeding along the Transisthmian, headed for the Pacific side. The road took them through a thick jungle with large trees growing right next to the highway. Somewhere along the way, they passed the site of Freddy Alegre's kidnapping. A little further down the highway, they stopped at Madden Dam, another potential target. The team got out of the Land Cruiser with binoculars and bird books. Carl knew the site well.

"The dam does three things," he lectured. "First, it holds a reserve of fresh water to keep the canal operating through the dry season. Second, the dam provides hydroelectric power to the whole region. And third, the lake behind the dam supplies Panama City with drinking water."

"Accessible but not vulnerable," affirmed Jerry, quoting Pablo Céspedes.

"Except to an aircraft," Billy Joe put in. "Did you guys see the movie *Dam Busters*? British pilots skimmed 'bouncing bombs' off the water into dams in Nazi Germany."

"Yeah, we all saw it," Jose snickered. "I don't think the cartel has a fleet of torpedo bombers."

Jerry brought them back to basics. "It would take a lot of demo to bring this thing down. I do think we should recommend the Panamanians put more security up here even though it's off the beaten path."

"Absolutely," said Carl. "Given all that it does, the police should have a much bigger presence around the dam anyway."

They walked around some and then got back in the vehicle. Just thirty minutes down the road, Carl pulled into the parking lot at *Miraflores* lock.

"Time to take the tour, gentlemen," announced Carl. The four American tourists went to the back of the line, taking in the big picture as they waited. When the team finally got access to the museum and a superficial tour of the lock, their patience was rewarded. Massive steel gates regulated the flow of water through the lock chamber. Outer "guard gates" protected the main "mitre gates" from allision by ships on either side.

Could an organized crime syndicate really blow the doors off this beast?

After the *Miraflores* tour, Carl's team piled back into the Land Cruiser and headed further along the canal to the port of Balboa. Driving over the Bridge of the Americas, Carl pointed out why they had put the structure at such a low priority on their list of risks.

"Okay, so this bridge is the only way to get over the canal on the Pacific side. If someone were to drop the bridge into the canal, the wreckage would disrupt ship traffic for only a few days," continued Carl. "The canal commission has tremendous salvage capacity."

PAUL SHEMELLA

"That's if the cartel has the ton of explosives it would take to put the bridge on the bottom" added Jerry. "And if they had that amount of demo, how would they lay the charges on the bridge abutments without being seen?"

Looking down at the water, Jose nodded. "You're right, man… They would have to use a boat that everyone would notice…even at night."

The Toyota came down off the steep bridge roadway and turned right, following the other side of the canal. Carl stopped the car when they got to Contractors Hill. They all got out and stood at the railing.

"This is the best place to surveil the *Culebra* Cut," lectured Carl. "If you look left and right, you can scan the narrowest part of the canal."

Billy Joe pushed himself up on the railing, leaning dangerously forward. "Wow! My first time up here… It's awesome!"

"You can see how steep the sides are here. They never found the angle of repose…that being the slope at which the land doesn't keep sliding into the canal." Carl went on. "So they have to keep dredging, or the canal will just fill with dirt."

"That's why the commission has such a robust salvage operation," added Jerry. "They can also quickly clean out a ship that sinks in the cut, accidentally or not."

"That's true," said Carl. "But all their dredging resources would be challenged by a massive landslide, though I'm not sure the cartel could trigger one." His voice trailed off.

"I think they could," Billy Joe responded. "There's roads on both sides they could use to approach with a truck full of demo. The tactical problem would be to bury the charge deep enough to cause the earth to move. That could be done, but it'd be pretty labor-intensive."

The visual reconnaissance was over. They drove back to the ISOFAC as the sun was going down. Carl dropped Jose and Billy Joe off then took Jerry home. After that, he went home and waited for Ana Maria.

* * *

She drove up to Carl's quarters just before eight. It had been a long day for both of them, and there was much to share. As he'd advised, Ana Maria had not gone to her house for extra clothes and toiletries. He had asked for a list so he could purchase essential items for her in the Navy Exchange. They'd agreed to keep her away from danger for as long as possible.

After serving her a late supper, they caught up on the case… then with each other. "I have to admit," said Ana Maria, relaxing on the couch with a glass of wine, "this is pretty nice. I've lived alone for so long I really didn't know how good it feels to have someone to come home to."

Carl considered himself a warrior. He had just demonstrated once again that he could be a lethal force in the field—not unfeeling but with a keen sense of justice. Now he was softening again under Ana Maria's spell. He had long experience being a warrior and a lover; he didn't know if he could be both a warrior and a husband.

"I have to tell you, Ana, that I really enjoy having you here in my home. I've been alone for a long time too. It's great to have someone to share everything with…and I mean everything."

She took another sip of wine and put down her glass. "I love being here for you, Carl. The last few weeks have changed me…the way I think about us. It used to be friends with benefits… Now it's more like partners. The passion is still there, hotter than ever for me, but there's a level of comfort to fall back on. I needed some stability in my life, and you're giving me that. I hope I can give you what you need."

"I need you to be my wife, Ana."

Ana Maria had loved a man once, but she had never felt *loved* by a man. She wanted Carl to feel loved by *her*. But it was too soon to say it out loud. With a wavering voice, she managed to tell him that.

"I still need some time, Carl. Let's see how we feel when this is all over."

CHAPTER 26

THE SMALL FREIGHTER lay at anchor in the Gulf of Fonseca. Other vessels passing in daylight hours would see the Panamanian flag flying over the stern, just above the name: *Sixaola*. The cargo ship, manned and loaded but waiting for sailing directions from its Greek owner, had been in the Gulf for one week. The ship's position put it in Nicaraguan waters, several miles offshore, sheltering in the lee of *Cosigüina* volcano. To call it inconspicuous would be to exaggerate its visibility, especially in the middle of the night.

The *Sixaola* was just what they had been looking for.

The pirates motored slowly to the starboard quarter of the mini-bulk carrier in a black Zodiac. The six men wore dark clothing, black bandanas over their faces, with green T-shirts, tied in the back, covering their heads. The rubber boat bounced gently against the barnacled steel hull. One of the men stood on the main tube and, with two others holding his thighs, reached as high as he could for the main deck. With only six feet of freeboard to negotiate, this would be an easy boarding, even for inexperienced hijackers. One by one, five of them helped each other assemble on the dimly lit deck. The last man up tied a sea painter to one of the cleats while the coxswain idled the Zodiac alongside.

The five moved quickly to the ladder leading to the bridge. Knowing that most of the mixed Nicaraguan and Philippine crew would be asleep, they expected a watch section of three sailors. The watch would be performing such anchorage duties as monitoring the ship's position, sounding all liquid tanks, and keeping at least a minimum degree of vigilance. The intruders quietly ascended the ladder, each armed with an AK-47. The lead gunman did not stop at the watertight door. He pushed the handle aside and burst in. The others, bunched behind, fanned out to the four corners of the enclosed bridge, waving their weapons and shouting in heavily accented Spanish.

"All of you get down on the deck...now!"

The three crewmen complied immediately, falling to the steel under them, faces down.

"Hands on the backs of your heads!"

The seamen, almost before they were told, obeyed the black-clad figures under the subdued red light of the ship's nerve center. The pirates were not on the bridge to kill anyone; they wanted the ship—with its crew—intact. The *Sixaola*, at 118 meters long and just over ten thousand tons was the perfect size for what they intended to do. Their research had revealed that the bulker's four holds were loaded with Mexican grain. There was much work to be done in swapping out the cargo in the forward hold.

Then would come the mixing.

But first, they would have to move the ship into port. That meant navigating the vessel out of the Gulf and down the coast to Corinto. The leader shouted at the only Nicaraguan prisoner. "Get the ship's master up here...now!"

The man was allowed to sit up. "I cannot reach the phone from this position."

The hijacker picked up the receiver and stared at the sound-powered phone. "This is not a telephone!" He used his rifle to order the Nicaraguan to his feet and handed him the device. "Get him up here!"

The prisoner toggled the selector switch and cranked the phone to ring in the master's stateroom. He spoke into the receiver. "Sir, we have a situation on the bridge. You need to come up here now."

The master of the *Sixaola* hurried to the bridge, thinking the worst. The reality was worse than that. He was also Nicaraguan—

and much younger—looking like a dazed college student next to his crewmen. "I am Captain Ernesto Sandoval. Who are you, and what are you doing on my ship?"

"It is now *our* ship," announced the leader, leveling his weapon at Sandoval. "And you are going to take this old tub to Corinto. There, you will off-load the cargo in one of your holds and replace it with what we need."

The master was disheveled and confused. He couldn't comprehend exactly what these bearded men were telling him. *Who* are *these people?* He fumbled for a response. "We are waiting here to find out where to take the grain...somewhere in the Caribbean, I think." The master stared at his crewmen on the deck, their cheeks rubbing on non-skid. "In Corinto, dock workers can off-load the grain. What do you want them to load into the empty hold?"

"That...we will tell you when we get there."

"And where will you be taking my ship after that?"

"You do not need to know that at this moment. We are in control here."

* * *

Carl and Ana Maria began the day with a jungle run along Pipeline Road, famous for its astonishing variety of tropical birds. It was a Sunday, and neither of them was expected to be anywhere. As always, Ana Maria ran with a pager in case she needed to contact her office on the unmarked police car's radio, parked at the trailhead. Carl ran with a Walther PPK tucked into a small holster, nestled in the small of his back. It would be difficult to kill somebody with such a small pistol, but he wanted to have at least some protection for Ana Maria. He'd given Jerry the number for the major's pager. The big man would come running (literally) if Carl needed him.

Ana Maria was three inches shorter than Carl, but her stride was exactly the same as his. They ran slowly over the uneven terrain, looking side to side for birds, snakes, and other creatures of the rainforest—not least Colombian *sicarios*. It was a conversational pace.

"I love this place!" shouted Carl to the trees. As he did so, a Keel-billed Toucan leapt from a branch not far from Ana Maria's head.

"Look at that!" responded Ana Maria, watching the toucan disappear into the thick jungle. "I spent my childhood running through the rainforest, Carl, but this is really special."

"You can say that again. I have three of the four things I value the most…right here." Carl scanned the canopy then turned to Ana Maria. "Violent exercise, tropical birds, and you." With a broad grin, he completed the thought. "Not necessarily in that order!"

"And what is the fourth thing?" she asked rhetorically. "Wait… let me guess." She looked at him without slowing down. "Fieldwork."

Carl laughed out loud. "Exactly, but you don't know how that stacks up against the other three!"

"No, I don't," said Ana Maria breezily. "And I don't even *want* to know!"

They ran all the way to where the trail had been bisected by a torrent of rainwater, rushing toward *Gatún* Lake. Standing for a moment to contemplate the raging current, Carl and Ana Maria momentarily pushed all other thoughts to the margins of consciousness. The Colombians, the Pakistanis, Mena's trafficking network, and the potential threat to the canal. Ana Maria even forgot, for a few minutes, about Manuel Noriega.

The run back to the car was more of a race. For Carl, trail-running in jungle boots was good tactical training, surging up and down over the often-muddy terrain. For Ana Maria, it was a chance to show him her speed. At the end of the five-mile dirt road, each of them was satisfied. It had been a contest neither needed to win. Breathing hard and sweating, with hands on hips, Carl walked back and forth until he found his voice.

"You made me *work*, Ana!"

She walked up to him and wrapped her steaming bare arms around his waist. "I'm just getting started, *cariño!*"

They drove home as fast as they could and made love for the rest of the afternoon. As the light faded, the prospect of cooking did not thrill either of them. They were still in bed, savoring the feeling. Carl had a solution.

"What do you say I take you to the Officer's Club?"

Carl was propped up on one elbow. Ana Maria rolled over and looked up at him. "You would do that?"

"Sure! You deserve a nice dinner out."

Ana Maria understood, probably better than Carl, that the invitation was an inflection point in their relationship. Up to now, as a couple, they had avoided public scrutiny. Now the couple would be on display. His willingness to be seen escorting her in full view of his teammates was indeed something new. Ana Maria only wished she'd brought some jewelry with her.

"I can be ready in ten minutes." She felt an elation she could not explain. Actually, she *could* explain it, but the emotion scared her.

"Okay, *cariña*… I'll put on some real clothes and meet you by the front door."

They drove to the club and parked the Toyota. Carl knew most of the officers at the bar as they walked into the dining room. Some of them nodded; most didn't even *look* at Carl. Ana Maria, even without jewelry, moved with a stunning grace he wanted to believe was reserved just for him. He found himself falling in love all over again.

"I hope those guys approve of your Panamanian girlfriend, *Carlos*. I wanted to make a good impression."

"You did… Trust me." Then he added something he had not said before. "I am very proud to show you off, Ana Maria Castaneda."

"I love it when you call me that."

"A beautiful name for a beautiful woman."

They ordered wine and then dinner. They talked nonstop like they'd just met. There *was* something different; they could both feel it. Carl seized the moment.

"Ana Maria Castaneda, let me say it again. I want you to be my wife. We could have a wonderful life together…here in *Panamá*."

Ana Maria's face lit up. Carl thought she was going to tell him she had decided to spend the rest of her life with him. Then she became serious, and his heart sank.

"*Carlitos…mi amor.* There are two things that might cause you to change your mind about me. I have to tell you now… Then you can decide if you want to be my husband."

Carl sat forward. "Go on, *cariña*… I don't think there's anything you can say to make that happen."

Ana Maria sat up straighter. She took a sip of wine. "*Cariño…* you know how much I need my professional life. I think you could handle that, especially if you have a satisfying second career down here. But I am thirty-six. My biological clock is ticking. I would have to choose between becoming the director of PTJ…or having a child. I'm not ready to be a housewife yet…and by the time I am, it will be too late to have children."

Carl smiled serenely. "Is that all? I don't need a housewife, Ana. If we want children, we can adopt them whenever you're ready to settle down. That's not an obstacle for me at all."

Ana Maria reached for his hand. "You would do that for me?"

"Absolutely," affirmed Carl. "I just want *you*. I'm ready to be your husband, but I'm not sure about being a father just yet."

One down, one to go.

"Okay…now comes the real issue," said Ana Maria evenly. She told herself to just blurt it out. Her dreams were about to come crashing down around her.

"Years ago, *Carlos*, Manuel Noriega tried to rape me. I fought him off in time, but he touched me in that spot!" She started to cry. He reached across the table and wiped the tears away from her frightened eyes.

Carl was surprised but not shocked. Ana Maria had worked directly for Noriega before *Just Cause*. She had, in fact, started telling Carl about the dictator's secrets several weeks before the operation. Now it all made sense! Her willingness to leak information was not simply because she'd lost faith in Noriega's leadership. It was more than that. It was personal.

"That is not an issue, Ana. I knew that you'd had a falling out with the general and that you fed me information to help bring him down. I was vain enough to think it was partly because you liked *me*. Now I know it was because you hated *him*. I have no problem with this at all. In fact, I respect you more than ever because of what you did."

She was visibly relieved. "Oh, *Carlos*...I should have told you back then, but I was too ashamed. I have never been able to wash off the filth from his attack."

"You just did," replied Carl. "No more needs to be said." He let go of her hands as their food arrived. "Let's have a nice dinner and talk about our future together."

"That's a wonderful idea, *Carlitos*."

Ana Maria decided there and then that Carl really loved her. She also decided to keep Omar Torrijos in her memory bank for safekeeping.

* * *

The CASA 212 aircraft swept onto the runway at Bluefields Airport. If the landing had taken place during daylight hours, thousands of English-speaking Nicaraguans would have talked about it. Not trusting the central government in Managua, the residents of the aptly named "Mosquito Coast" would have suspected it was a shipment of weapons.

They would have been right.

The unmarked light plane taxied to the far corner of the long airstrip and stopped in front of a windowless concrete building. Two crew members got out as the tail ramp went down. Three men, none of them Latin, had been waiting in the shadow of the building to help unload the cargo. Working together, they carried nine long boxes inside and placed them on wooden pallets. There was absolutely no conversation. In just under ten minutes, the CASA was rolling down the runway again, headed for Colombia.

The three men on the ground watched the plane rise into the dark sky...but not for very long. There was still a lot of work to do. The boxes were in temporary storage, but they were not at all secure. Others had access to the building, and it would be two days until the boats arrived. They set about stacking heavy boxes on top of the weapons containers. The pile of assorted boxes would not arouse attention unless there had been a leak within the community. In this sleepy backwater, that was unlikely. Nonetheless, one of the figures melted into the blackness beneath the trees to watch the building.

The other two men walked back down the muddy access road toward the lagoon. There were a few dilapidated wooden huts along the shoreline, a half mile from the main town. This was not a "safe house" in the strict sense of the word, but the shack would provide them with a place to wait for the boats. There would be plenty of time for them to pray. The transfer of the boxes could be managed without anyone seeing. The problem would be to get the boxes from the airport to the shoreline. They expected the headlights of the ancient pickup truck to be visible to anyone near the access road in the middle of the night. But that promised to be a risk worth taking. Victory would be theirs.

Inshallah.

* * *

Carl and Ana Maria went to work on Monday. He needed to spend the day with his men; she needed to organize the information from her department's interviews of the Colombian and Pakistani prisoners (she would also need to explain the dead motorcyclist… and the empty Uzi). Carl was leaning forward on tactical planning, anticipating (hopefully) a return to the field. Ana Maria would have to prepare a briefing for the command cell, scheduled for 1900 at the ISOFAC.

Ana Maria drove her generic vehicle out the back gate. Carl called Jerry, who gave him a ride between bases to the ISOFAC… continuing to assume the cartel had identified his beat-up Land Cruiser. He and Ana Maria felt relatively safe from attack on the road. They assumed the cartel could not get onto the naval base.

Carl and his men convened in the ISOFAC to discuss possible courses of action for a wide variety of scenarios. They had verified Pablo's assessment that the canal's critical nodes were largely invulnerable to small teams of saboteurs with weapons and explosives they could carry in. The canal system was too simple in its design and too solid in its construction. Even plans for merely interrupting service along the waterway—more likely than imposing catastrophic damage—would require some creative thinking. Stopping it would require more creative thinking.

Ana Maria got to work and immediately found herself in front of the cameras again. The Panamanian press was notoriously aggressive, especially when the news involved dead bodies that could be featured prominently on their front pages. They wanted to know who the motorcyclist was and what he was doing with an Israeli machine gun.

"The deceased was a Colombian assassin," said Major Castaneda from behind the podium.

There was an audible hush from the cluster of congenitally talkative reporters, all wielding microphones and scribbling in notepads. Ana Maria waited for the disclosure to sink in.

"The gunman was killed when he veered into oncoming traffic...and we could not interview him."

The excitement in the press gaggle was palpable. *A Colombian sicario? In Panamá?*

She continued with her scripted remarks. "We think that this Colombian was paid by the Mena cartel to kill a Panamanian police official. That official was riding in a car on the *Interamericana*. The motorcycle crash, *gracias a dios*, prevented the killer from shooting his victim."

The *La Prensa* reporter shouted it out. "Can you tell us the name of the police official who was targeted...and why?"

Major Castaneda looked right at the reporter and paused for a full second. "That would be me... The gunman was chasing me. We think it was retaliation for the capture of eight *narcotraficantes* earlier in the week by our *Servicio Maritimo*."

Another wave of silence rolled through the gathering. It was followed by a frenzy of questions. Ana Maria was not about to answer any of them.

"The cartel prisoners are being interviewed at this time. We will conduct another press briefing as soon as we have more information. To conclude, I can say that Panama's full sovereignty—that which we have all struggled so long to obtain—has been placed at risk. Colombian drug traffickers have been discovered using the deep jungle of *Darién* province for organized crime purposes. This government will not tolerate any such activities."

With that statement, Ana Maria turned and left the stage. She had things to do. Like figuring out how the Colombians were operating their networks…and what the Pakistanis were doing in the jungle at all.

CHAPTER 27

THE *SIXALOA* LEFT anchorage at first light and steamed down the Nicaraguan coast to Corinto. Propelled by two four-stroke diesel engines, the ship covered the distance in just five hours. A pilot, dispatched by the port authority, climbed aboard to guide the ship into its assigned berth. A gang of longshoremen boarded the vessel, opened the hatch cover closest to the bow, and began discharging grain from the forward hold into a shoreside bagging facility. All but one of the hijackers, fearing their foreign appearance might arouse suspicion, guarded the crew in the ship's mess. The leader, still bearing his AK, positioned himself in the back corner of the bridge, daring Captain Sandoval to alert the authorities. Sandoval was shocked to realize that those authorities appeared to be cooperating with whatever was going on.

What was going on became apparent when the grain had been off-loaded. As the master watched from the bridge at the aft end of the ship, longshoremen began carrying large bags of fertilizer from a warehouse and stacking them pierside on wooden pallets. He counted the first thirty bags but stopped counting as the piles grew. The soft voice behind his back told him to begin loading the pallets into the now-empty hold with the ship's onboard crane. The master called down to the mess and directed his deck seamen to spread the bags on the flat surface of the hold's bottom and to avoid stacking them. The hijackers followed the crewmen to their duty stations, watching them from inside the ship. Once the bags formed a sort-of mosaic, the voice told his hostage to have the crew cut into them and dump the fertilizer on the bottom of the hold.

The master complied and so did the crew.

Fertilizer from two hundred fifty-pound bags covered the bottom of the hold, more or less uniformly, to a depth of twenty-four inches. The crew was then ordered to spray diesel fuel on top of the Ammonium Nitrate layer. Twenty minutes later, the longshoremen handed the crew wooden paddles with which to mix the diesel into the fertilizer then form it into a haystack. The laborious process took them almost two hours, after which stood a broad pile of mixture, twice as high as a man's head. The longshoremen took the paddles back and helped the crew reposition the hold's cover. Not one of them questioned what they had seen. Such mystery was normal in Nicaragua. Those on the pier, as well as local officials, had been paid to look the other way. The master thought a pile of fertilizer mixed with diesel fuel in his forward hold made no sense.

To the hijackers, it made *perfect* sense.

After dark, the *Sixaola* got underway and headed south at fourteen knots. In forty-eight hours, the ship would be approaching the Pacific entrance to the Panama Canal.

* * *

The command cell convened in the ISOFAC at seven o'clock in the evening. First on the agenda was Major Castaneda's report on the results of prisoner interviews. Ana Maria had driven alone to the meeting from Carl's quarters. Carl had been at the ISOFAC all day. She got up and went to the map.

"We have finished the interviews of prisoners captured at the base camp in *Darién*. As you are undoubtedly aware, I told the Panamanian press this morning that the Colombians confessed to being members of the Mena cartel. We learned that, beyond this affiliation, they were involved in the operation of a trafficking network, moving drugs, small arms, and people from Colombia to the *Darién* camp. From there, traffic was transshipped by sea, air, and land to various cities in Central and North America. We are work-ing with all relevant law enforcement agencies to map this network. US authorities will be launching operations designed to roll up the northern end, in full coordination with the governments of Panama, Honduras, El Salvador, Guatemala, Mexico…and Colombia."

Ana Maria paused to let the summary information sink in. She was happy to take questions.

"I realize that you don't have a complete network diagram yet, but can you tell us what other critical nodes you've found so far?" asked Reginald Stewart.

"The nodes we know of include, as expected, *La Palma* and *Puerto Quimba*. Based upon Ned's beacon signals, we know they use the Gulf of Fonseca. The Gulf gives the network access to nodes in three different countries, and the governments of those countries do not always work together. Nicaragua has recently elected a president who respects democracy, but she has a lot of work to do in cleaning up after the Sandinista regime."

Jerry Tompkins spoke up, "What about the bodies in camou-flage we left for you at Flat Top? Could your people verify who they were?"

"The medical examiner found tattoos on their forearms asso-ciated with Cuban revolutionaries, *Socialismo o Muerte*. We think the deceased were indeed from the Revolutionary Armed Forces of Colombia." She paused, and Carl noticed her eyebrows go up. "I would like to add that the medical examiner had some unkind words for you guys." She pointed at Carl, who feigned surprise.

"Did you find out where they got the night-vision goggles?" asked Jose.

"We think they took them off dead Colombian soldiers on the battlefield. The goggles were manufactured in the United States."

"What about the Pakistanis?" asked Ned. "You seem to think they're being smuggled. Where do you think they're going?"

"The Pakistanis were the most difficult to interview. They stuck to the story they gave Commander Malinowski's team, that their rel-atives are waiting for them in the United States."

"But you don't buy that, do you," said Carl. It was a statement.

Ana Maria forced herself not to smile at him. "No…we don't. We think the Pakistanis are not just illegal immigrants. They are very religious, not that there's anything wrong with that, but some of the things they said to us indicate they *hate* the United States. Actually," she continued, "they didn't say much at all. Their behavior suggests they are fundamentalists, but our guess is that they are more than that. They are extremists."

"We thought the same thing," responded Carl. "One of them kept mumbling Arabic words while staring into space. We couldn't tell whether he even heard us."

"He is probably what they call a *Hafez*," Ned put in. "These are very gifted individuals who have memorized the Koran at an early age and keep reciting it from memory… They command great respect in Arab culture."

"But these are Pakistanis," said Pablo Céspedes.

"Yes," continued Ned, "but Arabic is the language of the Koran. Almost all Muslims pray in Arabic."

Ana Maria took back control of the briefing. "We think the Pakistanis are trying to get to the United States in order to foment Muslim-American resistance to the government. There's also a possibility they intend to join sleeper cells and plan terrorist attacks against targets in the United States. We have already been in touch with US authorities on this. The FBI will be sending a team to Panama tomorrow to conduct more detailed interviews."

Carl changed the direction of the questioning. "Did you confirm that the network uses Tumaco to launch go-fast boats headed to Panama?"

Ana Maria nodded. "Yes, we did. Their boats can make that run—it's about four hundred miles—in roughly ten hours…though I would not want to go along for the ride."

"No, you wouldn't," said Carl without emotion. "And the run to Honduras would be even worse…but they have a strong profit motive in moving cocaine. I bet they get paid a lot also for smuggling the Pakistanis…and whoever else they move along the coast."

"How does this information relate to our suspicion about possible attacks on the canal?" asked Colonel Stewart.

"We think these details are tangential," responded Ana Maria. "Manuel Noriega may have requested it, but we found nothing to indicate that the Mena network has the capability, or the desire, to damage the canal." She looked at Carl. "I should let the commander brief you on the results of his team's visual reconnaissance."

Carl stood up as Ana Maria took her seat. He looked at each of his men before speaking just to make sure everyone understood he was speaking for them. "We visited potential targets at the top of the list you helped us develop earlier in the week. To summarize, let me say that Mr. Céspedes is right… The canal is accessible but largely invulnerable. In our view, neither of the locks we listed could be destroyed, or significantly damaged, by a small team."

"That's good to hear," said the PCC official.

"Not to blow a hole in your confidence," Billy Joe interjected, "but the eastern bank of the *Culebra* Cut is at risk from a man-made landslide."

"The Commission has a fast and high-capacity dredging and salvage operation," responded Céspedes. "We dredge the cut continually."

"Yes, sir," replied Billy Joe. "But if it were me…I'd drive a truck loaded with high explosive to the top of the ridge and light it off. That might be enough to fill the cut with a lot of dirt."

Céspedes thought for a few seconds. "I see your point, Petty Officer Barnes… Even *our* dredges might take months to clear the channel."

"Whatever you do, sir… I would put security people with lots of guns on that ridge."

Céspedes nodded. "We will…and thank you for calling this to our attention."

"Just thinkin' like the enemy," said Billy Joe. "The trick for them would be to bring that much demo into Panama. You got plenty o' checkpoints for them to get through."

Both Pablo and Ana Maria nodded.

"Are you saying the *Culebra* Cut is the only risk?" asked Ned, turning to Carl.

"No...that is not what we're saying. There are still lots of threats...but not so much from a commando squad. I think if the commission were to increase its overall security posture, such an attempt would be unlikely." Carl paused before delivering the remaining caveat. "Beyond that, I would put more security on both dams. If our hypothetical attackers can get a truck full of explosives through all those checkpoints, they might decide to detonate it somewhere besides the Cut."

"We are prepared to raise the threat level," affirmed Pablo Céspedes. "I would like to suggest that Southern Command also raise the threat level for US forces stationed here."

Stewart nodded. "Yes...I can brief General Wells on that. It should be possible to do it without freaking out the Panamanians. There would be no US soldiers standing shoulder to shoulder along the canal or anything like that."

"Good," said Ned. "I'll brief the station chief."

"And I will brief the president of the republic," said Ana Maria with evident pride.

Carl got the last word. "I'll have my team keep searching for components of the canal system where vulnerability meets accessibility. We will maintain the tactical perspective, keeping all of you informed so you can feed it into your decision-making process."

* * *

After the command cell briefing, Ana Maria drove to the officers' quarters at Rodman. Carl followed Colonel Stewart back to the SOC. He wanted to explain in greater detail the events of the previous night on the way back from the airport. He wanted to assure Stewart that he had not broken any laws and that Major Castaneda was still in danger. He was worried that the colonel might object to his actions.

"She's *living* with you?"

"Yes, sir...but it's for her own protection. You can certainly understand that she can't go home yet."

Reginald Stewart grinned from ear to ear and shook his head from side to side. "Carl...I've never seen anyone better than you are at resolving multiple issues with one bold move."

Carl permitted himself to smile. "I learned that from playing chess, sir. I just wanted to make sure that using my quarters as a temporary refuge for the major is okay with you."

"Oh yes...it's okay. I would call it brilliant."

"Thank you, sir."

"So...while you're in a candid mood, would you like to tell me what *really* happened out there on the road?"

Carl told Colonel Stewart almost everything. He was sure that even the medical examiner would conclude that the assassin's neck had been broken in the crash. Carl withheld that detail from Stewart to protect himself...but he was also protecting the colonel.

* * *

Carl and Ana Maria traveled to work in the morning exactly as they had the previous day—almost exactly. Carl had been trained not to set patterns. Being unpredictable had saved his life before. Unpredictability had become a *way* of life. Ana Maria understood without being told that she would have to take a different route to the office each day. Carl wished he could go with her. She needed a bodyguard. But he had other business to attend to...and he trusted her to be unpredictable.

Carl's other business was to continue the visual reconnaissance of the Panama Canal. The system was fifty-one miles long. There were a lot of possibilities to examine. He and his men spent the whole day driving up and down the waterway, also taking time to walk around with binoculars and pretend to be watching birds. He made it back to his quarters just in time to pour Ana Maria a drink. She came through the door tired, dirty, and thirsty. She knocked back the rum while standing up.

"Let's save some fresh water for the Panama Canal," she shouted over her shoulder, headed for the bathroom.

Carl laughed all the way to the shower. There was just enough room for both of them.

Later, after a quick dinner they'd cooked together, Carl and Ana Maria sat on the couch in the living room, relaxing with glasses of sweet wine.

"I could get used to this," said Ana Maria with an audible sigh. They were now speaking Spanish.

"I like the sound of that, *cariña*. You're welcome to stay as long as you like."

"I need to get some things out of the house."

Carl had not forgotten. A visit to Ana Maria's house would be necessary, not just to get clothes and assorted personal effects but to also look for evidence that another hit man had been there, looking for her. Carl didn't think an assassin would be foolish enough to ambush her at home, but he wasn't 100 percent sure. They would have to be careful.

"First thing tomorrow, Ana, I will follow you out there in the Land Cruiser. We can look for any sign that you are still being targeted. You can go from there to the office. I will bring your things home with me."

She nodded and moved to hug him again. "I feel so safe with you, *Carlitos*. I don't know what I would do without you."

"I'm not going anywhere," said Carl. "Your safety is not just another mission for me… I want you around for a long time."

Ana Maria hesitated before responding to what sounded like another proposal. Inside, she was thrilled to hear him say this. Outwardly, she fought to suppress the feeling, just a little.

"I would like that very much, *Carl*os…but I have to ask you something."

He knew what was coming, and he was ready for it. "Go on."

"Are you ever really going to give up something you love?"

He gave her a surprised look. "You mean fighting bad guys in the jungle?"

"Yes…that is what I mean. I work long and hard, but most of that work is right here in Panama. Your job site is apt to be anywhere in *America Latina*. That was fine when we were just having fun…

but a long-term commitment would make it an issue." She took his hand. "I want you for the long term…but I would ask you to make it a true partnership."

"For you, Ana Maria, I would get out of the Navy and settle down right here in *Panamá*. You people have the perfect word for retirement."

"*Jubilación*." She actually giggled.

"That's it! I would really enjoy that."

She should not have been surprised to hear this, but she was. "You would do that for me? Stay in Panama?" What would you do all day?"

"Be your husband. Support you in every way I can."

"That would not be enough for you, *Carlos*…and you know it!"

He looked at the floor and then back up at her wet face. "I love Panama, Ana. I feel more at home *here* than I do in Virginia. The people, the music, the food, the water, the jungle…all that. You and your people have taught me what's important…and it's not money. I could easily stay here for the rest of my life."

"What would you do for work?"

"Don't forget the 994 species of tropical birds! I would set up a guide business, taking people into the rainforest to see them."

Ana Maria's eyes filled with tears. It took her a few seconds to find her voice. "I'm going to make you so happy!"

CHAPTER 28

THE THREE MEN waited and prayed in the shack on Bluefields lagoon. They did not expect the fast boats from Barranquilla until the next day, and there wasn't much to do. But for a pious Muslim, that did not matter. It mattered even less for an extremist bent on the violent expression of the faith. The weather was hot here, but not as hot as Riyadh. More humid, perhaps, but nothing to detract from reading the Koran, praying five times a day, and planning the attack.

The only real inconveniences had been dressing in Western clothes and eating non-*halal* food. These were exceptional circumstances, and certain accommodations had been required. It was not a sin to pretend to be something other than what they were: holy warriors plotting to rock the world. The *sin* would be to ignore mounting threats to the righteous path of the Prophet Muhammad—*peace be upon him*—and to exonerate those who would compromise Islamic principles for modern lifestyles. This target audience would be Christian, but Muslim apostates carried even more of the blame. Other holy warriors would deal with those traitors.

The leader of the team was Saudi, but the others had been radicalized in the tribal provinces of Pakistan. All shared a set of motives that started with revenge against the Americans. The bearded men in Bluefields had been *Mujahadeen*, fighting against the Soviets in Afghanistan. It was true that the Americans had supported them with weapons to destroy the armored helicopters that killed their Muslim brothers in large numbers. But the Americans had used them as cannon fodder against the hated Soviets. Osama bin Laden had been their inspiration. After they'd driven the Russians out in 1989, bin Laden and his followers had formed an extremist group with a name only a few in the West had yet to hear of: The Base.

Al Qaeda.

The Americans were still in Saudi Arabia, desecrating the soil of the Prophet. It was true they had driven Saddam Hussein out of Kuwait...but only so they could control the Middle East and its oil. American culture was vulgar and sinful. And it was everywhere. Infecting youth, poisoning minds, denying—indeed obstructing—the submission required of the faithful. There was only one way to stop the unrelenting advance of these modern Crusaders. Violence. The more extreme, the better. Attacking every human being who tried to resist a return to the Prophet's perfect world. To erase every symbol of Western power meant to humiliate Muslim believers. To make them know suffering.

We are the holy warriors who will rescue Islam...and the world.

* * *

Carl followed Ana Maria to her house just before dawn. She parked down the street, making sure she had a clear path to the main road. Carl parked in front of the house and walked slowly to the front door—on patrol. He checked for signs of attempted or forced entry. There were none. He walked around the house and did not notice anything unusual. No footprints. No broken windows. Everything looked clean and secure. He walked back to Ana Maria's car and took her by the hand as she got out. Carl had brought the SIG Sauer in a shoulder holster, the 9mm rounds waiting for anyone who threatened Ana Maria. He led her to the house, and she opened the door. Carl watched the street while Ana Maria went inside and turned on a light. So far, so good.

No one had been inside the house. Ana Maria quickly gathered clothes and toiletries, in addition to some books and papers. Together, they carried her things to the car, just as the sun rose at the edge of the city. He walked her back to the police car, kissed her on the cheek, and stood at the curb as she left for work. He got back in the Land Cruiser and drove back to the base. After putting Ana Maria's stuff in his living room, Carl went to the ISOFAC to help his men prepare for the operation they were convinced (and hoped) would come.

But first, they had to work out. An hour with the weights was followed by a group run around the empty field behind the warehouses. As usual, it turned into a footrace. As usual, Jose won easily. After showering, they were ready to brainstorm.

"So we've all been thinking about the canal," began Carl after they were settled around the table. Tinker here's been *dreaming* about it." Carl inclined his head toward Billy Joe and smiled. "Let's start again with what we know, what don't we know, and what we think. Let's consider those categories again separately."

Jerry was first up. "We know that the canal is accessible but largely invulnerable to a small group of attackers...especially drug traffickers. They are essentially businessmen. They don't like to get their hands dirty."

"But what if the traffickers can find someone to do their dirty work for them?" asked Jose rhetorically. "To whom could they contract a commando operation?"

"You mean other than us?" joked Billy Joe. "We could do their dirty work better than anyone, don't you guys think?"

"Brilliant!" shouted Carl. "Let's analyze this from the perspective of what *we* would do, the four of us, to disrupt or damage the canal system. Our sabotage skills are pretty damned good."

"I already told Céspedes what *I* would do," said Billy Joe. "That truck at the top of the cliff would work well...no permanent damage but a big mess in the short term."

"So where else could a truck, loaded with high explosive, get close to the canal?" asked Jose.

Carl went back to the map, pointing to the locks at *Gatún* and *Miraflores*. "Here, and here, there are parking lots for visitors. The lot at *Miraflores* is pretty large. If someone could drive a truck that far, and it was carrying enough explosive weight, they could maybe damage the locks enough to take them down for a while."

"There would be a big-ass crater in the parking lot, man," Jose put in.

"There's pretty good security on those lots most of the time," responded Carl. "And now Pablo says the commission will increase its security condition overall. I think it would be hard for someone to get a truck that close."

Jerry sat forward. "Unless it was a suicide bomber…driving fast toward the lock. But who in his right mind would sacrifice his life for an ambiguous operational result…like *maybe* damaging the canal?"

The light came on in Carl's head. "Terrorists…that's who!"

"But would the cartel contract an operation like that to terrorists?" asked the big man. "The FARC sometimes resorts to terrorism in Colombia…but in Panama?"

"Not FARC," responded Carl. "Think globally." He looked around the table.

"Muslim terrorists?" asked Jerry. "Do you really think they would be involved in an attack on the canal?"

"They wanna take down the West," said Jose. "That would be a great way to do it, man."

"They'd be taking down the whole world," said Carl, almost to himself. "Okay…what do we *not* know?"

"We don't know if Noriega actually contracted Jorge Mena to damage the canal," said Jose. "We *think* he did, but we don't know for sure."

Jerry added to the list. "And we don't know that, even if Mena got the contract, whether he could somehow get Muslim terrorists to take down the canal *for* him."

"We don't know if there's a connection between these hypothetical terrorists and the cartel," stated Jose. "How would they communicate…and where would the explosives come from?"

The light came on again for Carl. "We don't know who the Pakistanis are…or where they were really headed. What if they were part of a terrorist network with close ties to the criminal syndicate that got them into position?"

"You mean there is strategic, maybe even tactical, cooperation between the cartel and the extremists?"

"Yes, Jerry, I think that's it. Or at least part of it," responded Carl. "Organized crime and terrorism have different motives. Criminals do what they do for money. Terrorists do what they do for a political cause. But they've been known to maintain marriages of convenience. Tactical alliances, if you will."

"Yeah, boss, that makes sense," said Jerry with rising excitement. "The terrorists get a foothold near the target and all the tools they need. The criminals use their terrorist allies to disrupt and confuse the governments they're trying to manipulate."

"I agree with all that," said Billy Joe. "But would the terrorists establish a base camp here in Panama? Even in *Darién*, that would be hard for them. Besides FARC soldiers, hiding from the Colombian government, these guys would have no local support. They would stick out like sore thumbs."

"So where?" asked Jose. "And how would they get to the target anyway? Even if they established a base camp in Panama, and built a bomb, they wouldn't get near the canal with all the checkpoints and close-in security."

"Somewhere north of here where they might receive government support," Jerry shot back. "A place just as remote as, say, *Darién*, but easier to work out of."

"The Pakistanis were headed north," Billy Joe pointed out. "We thought they were trying to get into the US." He swallowed hard. "What if they weren't? What if terrorists have established a presence somewhere between here and Arizona?"

Carl didn't want to interrupt the brainstorming session their meeting had become. But he was anxious to arrive at a conclusion they could plan around. "So let's concentrate on the 'What do we think?' question...starting with Butkus."

Jerry cleared his throat. "I think Noriega *did* contract a hit on the canal to his favorite cartel boss, Mena...and that Mena subcontracted the job to some of the Muslim terrorists his organization has been smuggling north toward the US."

Jose was up next. "I think Jerry's right about all that. I also think these guys operate out of a base somewhere near the Gulf of Fonseca. Remember where the go-fast boat went with Ned's locator beacon?"

Billy Joe cracked the biggest smile any of them had ever seen on his weathered face. "And I think the terrorists are planning to use a ship for a weapon. That's the only way they could get close enough to the locks, at either end of the canal." He wiped off the smile and leveled with the others. "If the ship is big enough, with all that momentum, these guys could do tremendous damage, even without explosives."

"Holy shit!" They all said it at once.

* * *

Carl got home before Ana Maria again. He poured himself a shot of rum, knocked it back, and then poured another one for each of them. They were going to need it. Thirty minutes later, she drove up. Her clothes and toiletries were still laid out neatly on the couch.

"¡*Salud*!" They drank the fiery rum then sat down at Carl's kitchen table.

"How was your day, *cariña*?"

Ana Maria gave him a tired smile. "Busy, of course, but no press conferences. I'll take it!"

"Another drink?" asked Carl, raising the bottle.

"Sure, but this one could put me away for the night!"

Carl refilled her shot glass. "After you hear what I have to say, it may be tough to sleep," he said soberly.

She gulped down the alcohol. "Uh-oh, what now?"

"My team spent most of the day brainstorming the tactical options available to the cartel. We think they've contracted the canal sabotage to Muslim terrorists."

"¡*Chuleta*!" shouted Ana Maria, suddenly agitated. She got up from the couch. "¡*Voy por fuera*!"

Carl stood and placed his hands gently on her shoulders. "Not now, *cariña*… It's just a theory at the moment. Don't go rushing out of here with your hair on fire. We need more intelligence before we can plan around that scenario. I've already asked Colonel Stewart to bring the command cell together tomorrow morning. I think you should get some sleep. If our theory turns out to be correct, it may be the last sleep you get for a while."

"You're right, of course." Carl could tell she was feeling the rum. "Just hold me and tell me everything will be okay."

"Everything's going to be okay, Ana. Let's get a good night's sleep."

He hadn't even told her yet about Billy Joe's suicide ship scenario.

* * *

They drove to the ISOFAC in Ana Maria's unmarked car. She had slept well in his arms. He had not slept at all, going through all possible courses of action—for both sides—as he lay there listening to Ana Maria breathe. He'd fixed her breakfast and explained further what the team thought. A worst-case scenario, but that was how they'd been trained. *Get ready for the worst case... If you can handle that, you can handle anything else.*

"Do you really think they could use a ship to ram into the locks?"

"We do," said Carl simply. "If that is what they're planning, the challenge will be to find the ship before they can use it as a weapon."

"And we have to identify the target… 'The canal' is not specific enough," she added.

"*Exactamente*," said Carl. There were a lot of questions hanging in the air.

Ana Maria parked, and they both walked in to find everyone waiting for them. Carl's men exchanged knowing looks; the others, sifting through papers, hardly noticed the couple. Reginald Stewart called the meeting to order, passing the floor to Ned.

"Commander, Colonel Stewart tells me you have a theory and some questions." Ned looked at Carl as if to say, "This better be good."

"Yes, Ned, my team got together yesterday to brainstorm the tactical possibilities. We have a worst-case scenario I think you will all find pretty scary. It's a theory at this point…but highly plausible in our view." Carl looked at everyone around the table.

Ned looked at his watch and nodded for Carl to continue. "Let's hear it then."

"We think Manuel Noriega paid Jorge Mena to destroy the canal as revenge for *Operation Just Cause*. As we've discussed here before, Mena's men, with critical assistance from FARC soldiers, kidnapped the pilot as a means to learn how the canal works…and how it can be disrupted or destroyed." Carl paused to breathe.

"Yes…yes," said Ned impatiently. "We've talked about this… although there is no proof."

"Here's what we *haven't* talked about yet," responded Carl without emotion. "The cartel may have contracted the canal attack to Muslim terrorists. We think the only way they can damage the canal substantially would be to ram a ship into one of the seaward-facing locks."

Carl had finally gotten Ned's full attention. Pablo Céspedes went pale.

"Well," said Ned carefully, "that would be a real problem, wouldn't it?" He turned to Céspedes.

"Absolutely," responded Pablo. "The commission has not considered this a possibility before." Céspedes looked back at Carl. "Do you think they could really do that, Commander?"

"Yes, they could," replied Carl without hesitation. "Muslim terrorists would be willing to launch suicide attacks on the canal if given the right tools and the right training." Carl paused for effect. "The tools and training could be—could have *already* been—provided to them by the cartel. I am a serious student of terrorism. I can tell you they have motivation sufficient to ram a ship into the lock. Even without explosives, that would be catastrophic…would it not?"

Céspedes did not wait until Carl had finished. "Oh my god! Do you think they could load a ship with enough explosive to destroy the lock?"

"You tell *me*, sir. I am merely saying they would attempt to do that if they could. The Islamists have an ax to grind with the United

States and Panama that is far heavier than Noriega's. Terrorism is theater...and there is no bigger stage than the Panama Canal."

There was total silence in the room. A sense of foreboding. A palpable feeling that Carl was right. Reginald Stewart looked right at Carl and broke the silence.

"We *think* they may do this...but what do we really know?"

"I think a better question at this point, sir, is what we *don't* know."

Ned picked up the thread. "Okay...what do we *need* to know in order to prevent this from happening?"

Carl sprang from his seat and went to the whiteboard. "Here are some questions my team thinks we have to answer in the next twenty-four hours." He pulled a bedsheet off the whiteboard to reveal seven written questions.

1. Where could Islamists get a ship big enough to damage the locks?
2. Are the locks even vulnerable to this kind of attack?
3. Which end of the canal would make the better terrorist target?
4. What kind of ship would best serve this purpose?
5. Where and how could they get the logistics support they would need—especially explosives?
6. How much explosive would it take to ensure the lock could be damaged or destroyed?
7. What can the Panama Canal Commission do to protect the locks...and mitigate damage from such an attack?

Everyone was copying furiously as Carl read out loud. "And perhaps the most important question of all..." When they had copied the seven questions, Carl took the marker and dramatically wrote one more question on the board.

8. How do we find the ship before it gets here?

Ned finished writing and looked up. "There's one *more* question, Commander. If we *do* find the ship before it gets here, how can we stop it?"

Carl put down his black marker and faced the table. "My team is trained to take care of that. After you've had time to consider these questions, we'll take you through the mission profile so you're comfortable with our tactics. I recommend that all of you do the necessary research today and tonight. Can we all meet back here first thing in the morning?"

Ned nodded grimly. "Yes…back here at 0800 tomorrow." The CIA man started for the door and then turned around. "Let's just hope they don't hit us before then."

Pablo Céspedes, rising slowly from his chair, was still in shock. "The Panama Canal Commission will assume that such an attack can come at any time. If we see anything that raises suspicion from this moment forward, I will report it to all of you immediately. Let's just hope that our planning is a step ahead of theirs."

Carl was the last to speak. "Hope is not a strategy." Everyone stopped in their tracks and looked at him. "This is what, in my business, we call 'the maximum threat.' We have to assume it's coming. Hope is not involved."

CHAPTER 29

THE COMMAND CELL convened the next morning. Carl could sense considerable tension in the room as each of the members prepared to present the results of their research. Carl's questions were still on the whiteboard, begging for answers. Twenty-four hours was not a lot of time, Carl conceded to himself, but if his theory proved to be true, they didn't *have* a lot of time. Ned took charge of the review.

"I will yield to Pablo on the size of ship necessary to damage the locks…and to the second question of whether the locks are even vulnerable to this kind of attack."

Céspedes's face had still not returned to its natural color. He began, uncharacteristically, in a shaky voice. "Let me take the second question first, Ned. The answer is yes, the locks at both ends of the canal are vulnerable to a ramming attack by a large ship. The locks have what we call 'guard gates' that protect the seventy-ton doors that enclose the basins where the ships are lifted and lowered. But these were designed to guard against accidental allisions."

Ned interrupted him, "Allisions?"

"My apologies," responded Céspedes. "An allision is when a ship collides with a stationary object…like one of the locks. The builders did not design the canal with terrorism in mind."

"Go on," said the CIA man, nodding. "This is all very important background."

"The attacking ship would not have to be 'Panamax' size to do major damage. We have engineers working the numbers, but even a ten-thousand-ton ship, steaming at moderate speed, would probably blow through both sets of gates. If it got into the lock chamber, and kept going, it might take down the canal-side gates as well. If that were to happen, water draining from the lake would quickly scour the ship basin. We could not simply repair it. We would have to rebuild it from scratch."

No one spoke for a full minute. Ned looked around the room, trying to read behind the shocked faces. Colonel Stewart broke the silence.

"Well, all of us will just have to make sure that doesn't happen." That comment didn't seem to help.

"What if the ship is loaded with explosives?" asked Carl.

Céspedes responded with a grim expression, "That would certainly make the worst-case scenario more likely."

Carl turned and looked at his team, sitting together along the back wall. "We did some quick calculations yesterday. The easiest way to get a large explosive charge into a ship's hold would be to use a pile of fertilizer, mixed with fuel oil. Common fertilizer is mostly ammonium nitrate, the same explosive we use in our demolition work to move large amounts of rock and dirt. If a ship could be loaded with just a thousand pounds of this mixture, and rigged to explode on impact, the detonation, combined with the ship's momentum, would be catastrophic."

Céspedes's face turned a whiter shade of pale.

Ana Maria spoke up, "Which end of the canal would be the more attractive target for them?"

"The Pacific end, I would think," responded Carl. "If publicity is what they want, proximity to Panama City, and the international press, would give them a bonanza."

Ned took back the floor. "That answers question number three. What about number four?"

Carl turned around and looked at Billy Joe. "Petty Officer Barnes can take that one, sir."

Billy Joe got up and stood next to a flip chart that hadn't been there the day before. "The most likely ship would be a bulk carrier." He peeled the blank cover page off the chart. "This is a mini-bulk carrier, about five thousand metric tons." He pointed at the ship's deck. "You can see that it's got two holds, both with steel covers. These ships carry loose cargo, normally grain, coal, or scrap metal." He paused for about one second. "Or fertilizer."

"And how many of these types of ships are sailing around between here and the Gulf of Fonseca?" asked Ned with mounting concern.

Pablo Céspedes answered for Billy Joe. "There are many of them. We see them come through the canal every day." The others sat at rapt attention. "And most of them are much bigger than the one in Petty Officer Barnes' picture."

"Do you inspect them before they enter the canal?" asked Ned.

"Yes, we do," replied Céspedes. "But thoroughly enough to distinguish between ordinary fertilizer and the mixture Commander Malinowski described? I am not so sure. The master must certify his cargo to us, but that certification can be forged."

No one knew what to say. The worst-case scenario was getting worse by the minute.

It was Reginald Stewart's turn to speak. "What we've just heard convinces me that the best way to stop this would be to focus on logistics. We need to find out where this putative terrorist cell could get the ship and the fertilizer in the first place. We speculated that a terrorist cell is working out of a country bordering the Gulf of Fonseca. Which one?"

Ned had consulted with the CIA station chiefs in Panama, El Salvador, and Honduras in the hours before coming to the ISOFAC. He had some ideas. "My guess would be Nicaragua."

Carl had an immediate addendum. "That makes perfect sense to me. The Sandinistas are still pissed at us for supporting the Contras in the eighties. Ned's organization actually mined the ports of Corinto, Puerto Sandino, and El Bluff in 1984. Even though they're out of power, Ortega and his cronies pull most of the strings."

"Nicaragua was the consensus view of CIA station chiefs on our conference call early this morning," added Ned. "And it gets better—worse, actually—there is a small Arab community in Managua, suspected of harboring extremist elements. On top of that, Nicaragua carries the resentment of having been passed over by Teddy Roosevelt as the host country for the canal."

"That was almost a century ago," said Ana Maria. "Do you think they really care about it anymore?"

Ned smiled for the first time. "Yes, I think they do. There is a strong lobby in Managua for building an alternative to the Panama Canal through Nicaragua. It's very unlikely, of course, but if your canal were to be severely damaged, Nicaragua could appeal to the Chinese for building the project. Indeed, the Chinese would jump at the chance."

"China is flooding Panama with its citizens and its money," said Ana Maria. "They clearly have a strategic interest in this region."

"The evidence is mounting up," said Carl. "We've answered number six, but I have to say that a half ton of fertilizer would be a small load. Even a mini-bulk carrier could take on more than a few tons of the stuff." Carl stood up and walked quickly to the front of the room. By the time he got there, Billy Joe had uncovered a picture of the ruined Murrah Federal Building. Carl said it as calmly as he could. "Timothy McVeigh's Oklahoma City bomb was less than three tons—of fertilizer."

Carl's dramatic presentation had the desired effect.

Ned broke the silence, turning to Pablo Céspedes. "What about question number seven, Pablo? What can you do to protect the locks?"

"The Commission has already increased the security condition along the length of the canal. We have brought in more armed guards and vehicles to conduct roving patrols." He looked at Billy Joe. "We have stationed more guards along both dams and the *Culebra* Cut." Céspedes needed another breath. "But we can't keep both gates of the seaward locks closed without shutting down the canal."

"That brings us to the last question," said Ned. "Assuming there is a ship ready to ram into the *Miraflores* lock…how do we find the thing before it gets close to its target?"

"We monitor all incoming ships and stage them in the road-stead," responded Pablo. "They come into the canal in the order they arrive, but they anchor offshore, waiting to get in."

"How do you communicate with them?" asked Stewart. "And how do you identify each ship…so you can control what, and who, gets into the canal?"

"We use a UHF radio on a dedicated channel. We also have inspector visits…and there is the pilot boat. A pilot is assigned to each vessel before it gets into the canal entrance. Each ship in the roadstead is drawn into the canal transit process as quickly as possible. We are, after all, a business trying to make money. We have to balance security and commerce every day."

"But what about a ship that doesn't *stop* in the roadstead?" asked Carl. "What if the ship just keeps steaming at top speed until it hits the locks?"

Céspedes had no answer for that. "We would not be able to stop it. That's the short answer."

"So you'd have to identify the ship as far from the canal as possible," added Ned. "Can you do that?"

"The answer is 'yes' and 'no'," replied Céspedes. "The canal is participating in the development of a global network called the 'Automatic Identification System,' or AIS. Ships over three hundred metric tons are being fitted with transceivers they can turn on to let us know who they are and where they are located. The Panama Canal is getting one of the first complete AIS systems…for the very same reason we are gathered here today."

"Well…that should help," asserted Ned. "Can you just extend the security perimeter using that tool?"

"It's not that simple," responded Céspedes. "A ship intending to ram into the canal would simply turn off the AIS. It would sail without notification and without broadcasting to the satellite." Right now, at least, AIS is an honor system."

"Great!" shouted Ned. "So what do we do *now*?"

"We can identify all the ships that *do* use AIS. That would narrow the search for our rogue ship."

Stewart jumped in. "Now we're getting somewhere, gentlemen." He turned to Ned. "Can we get the National Reconnaissance Office to provide us with satellite imagery of all ships transiting between Nicaragua and Panama on both coasts...then match it with AIS signals?"

"Yes," began Ned, "we could do that. All the ships that do not broadcast their AIS transceivers could be assumed to be threats."

"How soon could we get that imagery?"

Ned looked at all the anxious faces in the room. "Given the stakes, I think the station chief could get it from the NRO by tomorrow morning. Then we could synch it with Pablo's AIS readout. Maybe then we'd be able to find a ship to take down underway." Ned cast his eyes on Carl. "Could your team do that?"

Carl did not have to look behind him. He and his men had practiced underway boarding for the last three years. Just in case. Now all that training would pay off. "Yes, sir, we can do that. You just give us the coordinates...and a way to track the ship as we approach."

"What else would you need?" asked Stewart.

"I'd ask for one of Major Castaneda's go-fast boats." He glanced quickly at Ana Maria. "Also, I would request you put a Blackhawk on strip alert."

Stewart looked at Ana Maria. She gave him a thumbs-up. "Okay, the major will give you the boat. I'll give you the Blackhawk."

Carl nodded to Stewart and then to Ana Maria. Then he looked around the room. "My team will lean forward as far as we can...but we can't go anywhere until you find us a ship."

* * *

Carl stayed with his men at the ISOFAC most of the day. He had scheduled a clandestine meeting with Jordy Fletcher in the afternoon. They met on a trail at the back of the naval base. Hiding in plain sight. Two SEAL friends out for a run in the hottest part of a Panama day. Crazy...but normal.

"I wanted to thank you again, Jordy, for lending me the *Luisa* last week."

"No problem, Carl. I hope you got it done…whatever *it* was."

Carl set the pace slow enough to actually have a meeting. "We were successful… Someday I'll be able to tell you about it. Juan and Rosa fit right into our team."

"When do I get Senior Chief Tompkins back?"

"Not sure yet," replied Carl. "The operation is not over."

"I don't need to ask you how he's working out."

"No…you don't. He's the best there is." Carl took a couple of deep breaths. "But Juan and Rosa were just as vital to our mission. I'd like to ask you for their services again."

"Starting when?" asked Fletcher.

"Right about now," responded Carl. "I wish I could lay the whole thing out for you…but I can't."

Commander Jordan Fletcher did not look at Carl as he considered the request. "Understood, brother…but I expect a full debriefing soonest. Tell Tompkins he has my permission to stay on. I'll tell Juan or Rosa to contact you as soon as we get back to the unit."

"Thanks, Jordy. I'll get all three of them back to you as soon as I can. You'll probably read about what we're doing soon enough in the press. Success or failure…it'll be front-page news."

* * *

The men inside the shack on Bluefields lagoon prayed and slept all day. As the sun set, they prepared themselves to receive the three fast boats. First, they would have to fetch the long boxes from the storage building at the airport. The old pickup truck, parked under a tree outside the shack, had been made available to them by a mysterious Nicaraguan calling himself *El Comandante*. The man had told them about his role in the Sandinista revolution, encouraging the foreigners to be brave. He did not know what they were planning to do—and he didn't *want* to know. He only knew that the shoulder-fired anti-tank rockets would allow them to unleash extreme violence.

Somewhere.

Two of the bearded men moved the truck slowly up the muddy road toward the storage building. The third man stood watch on the lagoon, making sure that the array of red and white lights illuminated the smooth surface of the water. The lights would guide their fast boats to the shoreline just outside the shack. Indeed, the boats would be theirs. They could do whatever they wanted with them. The Colombians would teach them to race them across the sea. They would drop off the instructors at the Caribbean island of San Andrés. From there, the three attackers would ride triumphantly to martyrdom.

The Colombians had no interest in killing themselves. Having been well paid, they would enjoy the resort for a few days. Traveling back to Pasto, they would take their chances with the murderous and unpredictable kingpin.

Jorge Mena Velasquez.

The driver backed the pickup to within a few feet of the building. He used the key given to him by *El Comandante* to open the door. Instead of turning on the lights inside, he used a flashlight to find the random pile of boxes. Quietly, the men set to work dragging and carrying the long boxes from beneath the pile and into the bed of the truck. After thirty minutes of backbreaking effort, the nine boxes lay stacked in the back of the vehicle. The driver closed the tailgate and took his position at the wheel. Driving the boat, he thought, would be a lot better than bouncing along in this old truck. He was anxious to get it over with and join his brothers in paradise.

Allahu Akbar! God is most great.

CHAPTER 30

CARL WAITED FOR Ana Maria with a glass of rum on the coffee table and dinner in the oven. She was late, but that was expected. Her position was more important than his—at least for now. But that would soon change. He thought about the lookouts in the fire towers atop the western mountains. The smoke Carl had discovered on the horizon, he suspected, was about to develop into a raging wildfire. He would have to put it out.

If it wasn't already too late.

She hurried through the door and held him for a long minute. He could feel the stress leaving her body, and he wished they could just go to bed.

"I can't stay long, *Carlos*. The command cell is working downtown, and they expect me to rejoin them after I eat dinner." It was clear from her tone that this was not Ana Maria's first choice for evening entertainment.

"I hoped you'd been working with them all day. Yeah, we need to get you back there quickly." He placed both hands on her shoulders. "Why don't you take a shower while I finish cooking?"

Ana Maria sighed deeply and gave him a broad grin. "Good idea. Too bad you have to cook!"

"Hey, I have a vested interest in what you find out downtown," Major Castaneda. "Otherwise, I would hold you hostage for a long time!"

"Seriously, *cariño*, I can tell you that we're getting closer to reducing the number of potential threat ships."

Carl could not hide his excitement. "Great news! When do you think they'll be ready to brief my team?"

"Get ready for an early morning phone call. I'll probably be downtown all night... Sorry."

Carl gave her a quick hug. "That's your job, *cariña*. After you're done, then maybe *I* can get to work."

"The drug traffickers' boat is ready for pickup, Carl. We're keeping it at the maritime base down on the waterfront. You can send one of your sailors to drive it away anytime you wish."

"Thanks, Ana. I've got someone assigned to do that."

"I hope you can give that boat back to me... Personally, I mean...after this is over."

Carl saw tears forming in her enormous eyes. Then he noticed that his own vision was becoming blurred. "I'll be back, Ana. Our training is good, and my team is ready."

They met back at the dinner table to eat Carl's *corvina con ajo*. The fish was not as good as hers, but it was the thought that counted. They both passed on the rum and the wine. There was almost no talk; they were both thinking about their jobs. Then it was time to go.

"I'll call you if I can, *Carlos*, though it will probably be Colonel Stewart who wakes you up early."

She was out the door. Carl cleaned up and went to bed right away.

* * *

Carl's phone rang just after 0400. It was Colonel Stewart.

"Carl, get your ass down here to Ned's facility. The clock starts ticking now."

Carl threw on some tourist clothes, made himself a cup of instant coffee, and practically ran to the Land Cruiser. He was no longer worried about the cartel taking him out on the street; he was thinking about intercepting Mena's suicide contractors, now on the high seas. If Carl was right, a floating bomb was plowing through the sea, headed their way.

He was about to find out.

He parked a few blocks away and walked to the CIA's command center. It took a couple of minutes to negotiate security at the bullet-proof glass window just inside the door. As Carl entered the room, all eyes turned to the tactical commander.

"We have something to show you," Ned began. Carl joined Colonel Stewart, Pablo Céspedes, and Ana Maria, huddled around a nautical chart on the center table. Three young computer technicians stood behind the group. There were two ship's positions plotted on the chart; satellite photos were arrayed in an orderly fashion around the edges of the table.

"We have compared the AIS data to the satellite imagery. There are two candidates headed this way on the Pacific side." Ned pointed to their positions, annotated with the course and speed of each vessel. "There are no candidates on the Caribbean side."

Carl rubbed his chin and stared at the chart as Ned continued. One of the ships was located just off the *Azuero* Peninsula. The second ship was about six hours behind the first, approximating the same track.

"So you're saying that both vessels are running without broadcasting who they are or where they're going and we don't know which of them might have hostile intent?"

"That's right," replied Ned. "The closest contact is about 150 nautical miles from the Pacific entrance on a course of almost due west at fifteen knots. The farther ship is headed west-southwest at fourteen knots. We think the first ship is making the turn into the Gulf of Panama. We'll be able to verify that in about an hour, using updated satellite imagery promised by NRO." Ned looked up from the chart. "I have to say that Washington's response to our urgent request has been very fast."

Carl spoke without moving his eyes from the chart. "That gives us less than ten hours to intercept the first vessel."

Pablo Céspedes jumped in. "So how do we know which vessel to intercept?"

"We'll have to take down each of them in sequence," responded Carl. "Can't afford to choose one…and then be wrong."

"Makes sense," said Ned. "How do you plan to do that?"

Pablo Céspedes volunteered his own strategy. "Can't we just blow the ships out of the water? The helicopters can be fitted with rockets, can they not?"

Both Ned and Reginald Stewart frowned at the PCC official. Stewart spoke first. "Pablo, I understand your position, to be sure. But we can't destroy vessels and kill their crews just because we *think* they might be on the attack. We have no proof. Like it or not, we're going to have to do this the hard way."

Carl, who'd been ignoring Stewart's lecture, looked up from the chart. "Major Castaneda has lent us one of the ocean racers my team captured in *Darién* last week. We will use that boat to intercept the first ship, maybe fifty miles from the entrance…provided we can get a fix on the vessel and track it as we approach for the boarding."

Carl then addressed Pablo Céspedes directly. "Is there a way you can do that for us? Can the commission vector our assault boat into the wake of the ship?"

Céspedes shot him a grim expression. "No, I don't see how we could do that so far out."

Carl shot him a grim expression back. "Please be ready to shut down canal operations if we can't stop the ship in time…okay? The *Miraflores* lock will have to be buttoned up tight."

"Yes," replied Céspedes. "I will get the commissioner, and the president of the republic, to approve that."

Carl turned to Ana Maria. "Major, do you have any patrol boats that could get close to this thing in the next six hours? We'll need a good radar on the scene."

"I'll have to make a quick call, Commander… Be right back." Ana Maria practically ran to the phone at the opposite wall. The line was not secure, but she decided to talk around the subject. All she needed from the *Servicio Maritimo* was the name of a patrol boat, the radio frequency, and the response time.

Carl bent down over the chart again. "We can stage out of Flat Top again. If the first ship is benign, we can wait there to prepare for the second intercept." He looked up at Colonel Stewart. "You promised us a Blackhawk, sir. Can you put it overhead in a high orbit? We'll need a communications link with the command cell, the patrol boat, and the assault craft. Also, we're gonna need some eyes and ears up there."

"Yes, Carl, the Blackhawk can orbit high enough to avoid detection from the ship while relaying your UHF transmissions. With Ned's permission, I'll ride on the bird."

Ned responded right away. "Not a problem, Reggie. That's your bird anyway. I'm still nominally in command…but Commander Malinowski will call the shots at the objective."

Carl turned to the colonel. "Thank you, sir. I'll need a name and number for the aircraft commander. There's some equipment we'll want to give him before we take off in the boat."

Reginald Stewart had been around long enough to know that Carl and his team were not specialists in ship assault underway, a very demanding set of tasks.

"Carl," he began in an almost fatherly tone, "I just want to make sure that you're comfortable doing this. I say that as a friend as well as your commander."

There was no hesitation. Carl locked eyes with the senior officer he respected more than any other. "Yes, sir… We're ready to do this. It's a tough mission profile, especially without multiple rehearsals. But there's really no choice. Either we go in right now, or the canal takes a big hit. Trust me, sir… We have the right people, the right training, and the right equipment."

Stewart smiled approval. "I trust you, Carl… Believe me. You understand that I had to ask."

"I know…and I'm glad you did," responded Carl. "We don't have enough information…but we never do. My guys are really good at improvising."

Stewart smiled and shook Carl's hand. Then he called General Wells to fill him in. The SOUTHCOM commander would brief the Chairman of the Joint Chiefs of Staff.

Carl took another phone and called Jerry Tompkins. It was six o'clock in the morning. They would have to take down the first ship in broad daylight.

"Tompkins."

"Jerry, it's me. I need you and the others standing tall in the ISOFAC in one hour. Got that?"

"Got it, boss. We'll be there, waiting for your warning order."

"We don't have time for that, Butkus. This will be the *patrol* order...and we'll have to be moving by 1000."

"Okay, Carlos...out here."

Carl's next call was to Juan at the number Jordy Fletcher had given him. "Juan, this is Carlos. I need you and Rosa at the ISOFAC in one hour. We won't need your boat...just the two of you. I have another boat to give you, and I think you'll like it."

Juan responded with professional calm, tinged with anticipation. "Got it, sir. We'll be there, ready to roll."

Ana Maria came back to where Carl was standing. "Okay, we have a patrol boat, currently loitering off Contadora Island. That puts it well within the operational radius needed to respond. The boat has a long-range *Furuno* radar they can use to vector you to the target vessel...assuming they can find it."

"Perfect, Major. I'll need the radio frequency and the name of the patrol boat."

"No problem... They are already standing by. You can perform a radio check anytime." Ana Maria had one more thing to propose. "And this is still a Panamanian operation, Carl. I'd like to be on the Blackhawk with Colonel Stewart." She said it loud enough for the others to hear.

Carl looked at Stewart, just putting down the phone. "She's right, sir. We're still supporting the Panamanian government here... and the major can talk to the patrol boat. Also, as the airborne relay, you'll need to know what both surface platforms are saying to each other...in Panama's rapid Spanish."

Stewart didn't have to think about it. "Okay, the major will join me on the Blackhawk. Your MH-60 will be sitting on the runway at Howard, manned and ready within two hours, Carl. Your men can take their gear over there any time after 0800. We'll be ready for take-off at 1000, but I'll wait until you give me the green light."

Ana Maria nodded. "I'll be there before 0900, Colonel." She looked at Carl and then back at Stewart. "And thank you… Panama thanks you."

Carl did not smile. "Roger on all that, Colonel. I'll send our guys over there at exactly eight o'clock. You'll be glad to have Major Castaneda in the air with you." He added a comment that was unnecessary but felt good. "I also feel better with her up there."

Stewart pivoted tactfully. "Sorry we don't have any 'Little Birds' in country. If we did, you could use one of them to get onto the ship."

Carl nodded back. "Yes, sir, I wish we didn't have to use the boat in broad daylight, but it's all we have."

"What sort of gear will you be staging on the chopper?"

"Four M-21s with scopes…and fast ropes. If we have to go after the second ship, it will be in the dark. I wanna have an air option for that one."

Carl was leaving nothing to chance. He moved quickly through the door and jogged to the Land Cruiser.

Ana Maria was in the parking lot. "*Carlos*, tell me again you'll be okay." He could see she was frantic. There was time to calm her nerves one last time. But he couldn't allow himself to embrace her in front of the others.

"It's okay, *cariña*. I'm thrilled to have you as a teammate this time… We need you out there."

"I am very proud of you, *Carlos*. Make sure you come back in one piece." Unexpectedly, a smile graced her face. "Then we can get married."

Carl was stunned. "In that case, I'll be extra careful!" All of a sudden, he knew this would be his last mission.

* * *

Carl and his men met at the ISOFAC at 0700 to finalize the plan. One hour later, they fanned out to prepare their tools. Jerry and Billy Joe took the rifles and fast ropes to the Blackhawk, now sitting on the tarmac at Howard. Jose drove Juan and Rosa to the wharf downtown so they could race the go-fast boat out to Flat Top rock. Carl went to Jordy Fletcher's compound to ready the Zodiac that would take his team to the rendezvous. He then called the commanding officer of the *Servicio Maritimo* patrol boat and delivered instructions for vectoring them to the target ship. If he'd had more time, he would have fast-roped onto the vessel to meet with the skipper personally.

But there was no time.

Everything was happening suddenly again…and it was all happening at once. There would be no room for mistakes. Relentless focus all the way. Time for their training to kick in. The orchestra was playing the overture. Carl was the conductor. The first movement was coming up—like a freight train.

They came back together on Fletcher's dock at Rodman. Wearing unmarked jungle fatigues, black watch caps, body armor, and high-top sneakers, they piled into the rubber boat and motored out past Fort Amador into the Gulf of Panama. The MP-5 submachine guns were stored in a dry box between their feet on the aluminum deck. They wore SIG Sauers in thigh holsters and squad radios to communicate with Rosa. The timing of the assault was locked in. Four o'clock in the afternoon was a lousy time to do this.

Juan and Rosa were waiting for them at Flat Top with the bow of the go-fast resting gently on the shingle beach. The shooters unloaded the Zodiac and pulled it above the high-water line. They performed a final equipment check and blackened their faces. Jerry pushed the assault boat into the sea as they all climbed aboard. Juan and Rosa had learned to drive the high-performance ocean racer on the way to Flat Top. They sped off on the compass course given to them by the patrol boat. Rosa was at the wheel, and she would stay there.

As they bounced over the waves at forty knots, Carl thought about the angle of the sun. The target ship was on a course of 060 degrees, traveling at fifteen knots. The sun would be low in the sky by the time they closed with the target, but the blinding light would come from the starboard quarter. No help there. Coming up the wake, they would be exposed and visible to anyone on deck or the bridge wing. If this turned out to be the suicide ship, the assault team would be compromised before they could get within range. Carl decided to call an audible.

"*Chiriquí*, this is *Fuente*. What is your position?"

CHAPTER 31

CARL WAITED ONLY a few seconds for the response.

"*Fuente*, this is *Chiriquí*. We are due east of your position, headed west-southwest at twenty-one knots. At this course and speed, we will cross your present track in fifty-six minutes."

"*Chiriquí*, this is *Fuente*. Maintain course and speed for rendezvous with me. Repeat, rendezvous with *Fuente* and wait for further instructions."

"*Chiriquí*, roger, out."

Carl had almost an hour to think about the next play. He needed a diversion to mask his six o'clock approach to the target. Something to capture the attention of the ship's bridge watch.

The contact plodded on, making the turn into the Gulf, now steering for the canal entrance. The American and the Panamanian crews met at a point along the rogue ship's expected track. The easterly trade winds blew harder, kicking up more ocean spray. A good thing, Carl thought, as he climbed aboard the *Chiriquí*. Rosa held the go-fast just off the starboard quarter while Carl briefed the Panamanian skipper in rapid Spanish.

"Here is the plan, Lieutenant," began Carl. "This is the first of two merchant ships, perhaps loaded with explosives, we think might be planning to ram into the canal locks. You will place your vessel in the path of the oncoming ship, maneuvering back and forth as he closes. I want to have the master and his crew looking at *you* during the ten minutes it will take my assault boat to come up his wake."

The young commanding officer nodded vigorously—excitedly but professionally. Carl could see that he was not used to this kind of operation. But Carl was a good judge of seamanship. He quickly surveyed the shipshape vessel and decided the Panamanian and his crew were up to the task.

"Okay, sir, we will get his attention and give you visual cover. At the same time, we will continue to vector you."

"First, I will make a wide circle around the target, outside visual range, hidden from radar in the sea return. We will be running at top speed—in this sea state, about fifty knots—all the way to his starboard side. At that point, five of my team will climb onto the deck and take control of the ship. Keep station directly in front of him until we take him down. We will notify you at that point with further instructions. If this is the threat ship, we will sail it to a safe location, away from the canal."

"¡Sí…claro, señor!"

"My name is *Carlos*…if this is *not* the threat ship," he continued, "you can board it and find out why it is underway without broadcasting AIS. We will have six hours to assault the second ship… if that becomes necessary."

Before there was time for any more talk, Carl was over the side of the patrol boat and standing on Rosa's go-fast. The team sped over and through cresting waves, like a sailfish chasing bait, tracing a long semicircle into the low sun.

A kidney-pounding hour later, the go-fast made a slow starboard turn. With the help of the patrol boat's radar, Rosa positioned the team ten miles out, directly behind the target ship. She took the ocean racer off step, matching the speed of the quarry. A cat, waiting to pounce on a mouse.

Carl waited for the signal that *Chiriquí* was in position.

Fifteen minutes later, he got the signal.

"This is *Fuente*… We are increasing speed." Rosa was now the radio operator. The others were preparing to climb aboard a moving ship.

The assault boat rose from the sea and quickly planed, accelerating to fifty knots. Twelve minutes later, Rosa maneuvered the craft to parallel the course and speed of the target. Avoiding contact with the ship, she closed in. Billy Joe extended the aluminum caving ladder and hooked it onto the vessel's lifelines, a dozen feet above their heads. Going in blind, the team would have to react quickly.

Observe, orient, decide, act!

Speed without haste.

The ship was bigger than they thought it would be. Rusty and filthy, it smelled of fish.

Led by Billy Joe, they climbed aboard one by one. Once assembled on the deck, they fanned out. Carl, Jerry, and Juan ran up two wet ladders to the bridge. Billy Joe and Jose ran the opposite way, to the engine room. Rosa backed off and, using the enormous power of the boat's three engines, kept station in the ship's aerated wake.

Jerry opened the watertight door and burst into the pilothouse. Carl was right behind him. Prodding with MP-5s, they gathered the master, the helmsman, and the navigator into a tight circle behind the chart table. Juan ran in to take the wheel and keep the ship on course while Carl and Jerry flex-cuffed the sailors.

They were bearing down on the *Chiriquí*, now sitting dead in the water, a few miles ahead.

Billy Joe and Jose crashed into the engine room and leveled their weapons at two men, standing in front of a very loud diesel power plant, wearing headphones. Four hands shot quickly into the hot, stale air. Billy Joe ran to the control panel and pulled back on the main engine throttles. Jose pushed the Chinese sailors into a corner. He got on the squad radio, hanging from his vest.

"Carlos, Tinker, engine room secure. Engines shut down."

"Tinker, Carlos, bridge secure. Bring the prisoners to me."

Billy Joe and Jose cuffed the engine watch and dragged them to the bridge. Now they had a cluster of five crew under control. Carl shouted at the man he presumed to be in charge.

"Do you speak English or Spanish?"

"English," responded the timid voice in a heavy Asian accent.

"How many more in your crew?" demanded Carl. "And where?"

The intimidated mariner tried to calm himself. Carl and Jerry waited impatiently, training their weapons at the gaggle of prisoners.

"Four more… Three in berthing. One in galley."

Jerry and Jose were off like a shot. Five minutes later, they dragged four more Chinese sailors onto the bridge. Out came four more sets of cuffs. As the ship's speed bled off, Juan had difficulty holding a steady course. They felt the ship start to rock violently as it slid into the trough.

Billy Joe turned to Carl and spoke in a sarcastic tone. "Carlos, I don't think this is the threat ship."

Carl saw the rest of his team nodding. "I think you guys are right, but we have to check the hold. Tinker, you go down there with Bosco and tell me what you find."

Billy Joe and Jose ran from the bridge. About ten minutes later, Carl got a report.

"Carlos, Tinker, All we can find is dead fish…and they don't smell very good!"

"Tinker, send Bosco back to the bridge. You go to the engine room and restart the engines. Juan will maintain enough speed to keep us on a heading toward the *Chiriquí*. They have a case of illegal fishing on their hands…for later. For now, they have to help us find the second ship."

"Got it, Carlos. Out here."

Carl called Stewart in the Blackhawk. "Robinson, this is *Fuente*. Ship number one is a Chinese vessel, almost certainly fishing illegally in Panamanian waters. Recommend you return to Howard and wait there until we're ready for ship number two."

Stewart came right back. "*Fuente*, this is Robinson. Wilco. Roger, out."

Carl left Juan at the wheel and Billy Joe in the engine room. He kept Jerry on the bridge, in charge. He ran down to the main deck and signaled Rosa to pick him up for the ride over to brief the skipper of *Chiriquí*. He could see that she'd honed her go-fast coxswain's chops, waiting for him behind the ship. *No better high-pucker training*! Rosa was going to need that skill set. Before she pulled away from the slowly moving ship, Carl unhooked the caving ladder. They would need it again in a little more than five hours.

Carl and his team turned over control of the Chinese fishing vessel to the *Chiriquí*. They loaded the whole team back onto Rosa's boat and raced back to Flat Top Rock. The skipper of the 110-foot Panamanian vessel had agreed to stay within a box, centered on the first ship's track, searching for the second. Carl's team, crammed into a small boat, needed dry ground for the next few hours. The sun was down. Rosa was getting some essential night training on the way back to the layup point.

Once on the rock, Carl would take reports from *Chiriquí* as they waited for the second ship. Colonel Stewart and Ana Maria would be airborne again in a few hours. He was confident that CIA, NRO, and regional intelligence partners would track the target ship all the way to its surprise rendezvous with *Fuente*.

All his team had to do was stop the ship. At sea. Underway. At night.

* * *

Guided by the vertical array of lights, three sleek ocean racers converged at the shore in front of the shack on Bluefields lagoon. Darkness had come just in time, and they were not seen by the peasants, sheltered in their own shacks along the coastline. Even if they had noticed, the locals were too busy dealing with their own poverty and disease. They would not confront the intruders. Even if they heard the boats, they would not report them to an untrustworthy government. For all they knew, this *was* the government, sneaking around at night, up to no good. Each driver beached his craft on the bank and shut down the engines. They were met by three dark-skinned men in grubby clothes and long beards. No one shook hands. No one talked. There was much work to do, and the Colombians wanted to get back to sea as fast as possible. They were being paid to train the foreigners then turn over the boats at San Andrés.

They didn't have to like it.

The six men filed into the shack and began carrying the long boxes to the boats. They deposited three crates in each boat before taking off the covers to inspect their rockets. The dark-skinned men had been trained to fire the weapon; all they needed was a method of getting within two hundred meters of the target—preferably closer. The go-fast boats would take them there.

They did not plan on coming back.

When the boxes were loaded and all the weapons inspected, the six men climbed into the boats and slowly withdrew from the filthy lagoon beach. The foreigners had left nothing in the shack to indicate who they were or what they were planning to do. Even their Colombian partners did not know what they planned to do with the American AT-4s. They only knew that the attackers would have to drive the boats over rough seas to Panama. Not an easy thing to do, even in the daytime. Indeed, they thought, someone would have to be crazy to do it with so little training.

Even suicidal.

The Colombians pushed their throttles forward, and the boats leapt from the glassy smooth water. With minimal Spanish, the bearded men began to learn how to navigate at night. Once outside the bay, their Colombian instructors let them drive all the way. The run to San Andrés would take them a little more than three hours. The island was not home, but it was Colombian soil. The flight back to Barranquilla would be a lot more comfortable than the wet and wild ride to Bluefields.

* * *

As soon as they got all their gear cleaned and ready for another ship assault, the team managed to find some places to lie down on the gravel and get some rest. Just as Carl was ready to join them, his radio chirped.

"*Fuente*, this is Robinson. I have an update on the second ship. Stand by to receive details, over."

Carl adjusted his headlamp, taking out a notebook and pencil. He went over and got Jerry before responding to Stewart. "Robinson, this is *Fuente*. Go ahead, over."

"*Fuente*, Robinson, Ned passes the following update. New imagery places the second ship on track, now three hours from your current location." Carl looked at his watch: 2150. "My Panama liaison is relaying the exact position to *Chiriquí*, who will contact all of us once it has acquired the ship on radar. How copy so far?"

"Robinson, *Fuente*, copy all, five-by-five. What else do you have?"

"*Fuente*, Robinson, regional intelligence partners have identified the ship as a mini-bulk carrier, 118 meters in length and 10,500 metric tons. It has four cargo holds and low freeboard. You should be able to climb aboard without the ladder. Name of the ship is *Sixaola*, last seen at the Nicaraguan port of Corinto. The ship is registered in Panama, crewed by eight Nicaraguan and Philippine sailors. Ship's owner is Greek. How copy, over?"

"Robinson, *Fuente*, copy all. Guess we don't need permission from the flag state to board. We will stop the ship and defuse any ordnance found. Expect hostile actors to be controlling the vessel. They will be taken out. Will try to avoid hurting the crew. The government of Panama can sort out all the legal ramifications later, over."

"*Fuente*, Robinson, sounds good. Will pass to Ned and Pablo. Waiting for your signal to take station again in high orbit. Call me for whatever you need. Robinson, out."

Carl put down the headset and rounded up his team. He passed them all the details he'd just been given.

"Eat something, hydrate, and get ready to go!" shouted Carlos over the wind. "We're underway in one hour."

CHAPTER 32

IT WAS 2300 when Rosa backed the go-fast boat off the gravel beach. As before, the team sped into the sea separating them from the Panamanian patrol boat. Once underway, Carl got a call.

"*Fuente*, this is *Chiriquí*… We have the second ship on radar, forty-three miles from your position, heading 010 degrees at fourteen knots. I am loitering in front of him, twenty-two miles out. Waiting for your instructions, over."

Carl checked his watch: 2340. He would not need the *Chiriquí* to provide a diversion in the dark, but he needed the patrol boat close by. He *really* needed the Blackhawk overhead by midnight—for communications and maybe for something else.

He made two calls.

"*Chiriquí*, this is *Fuente*… Stay in front of the target at the same distance you are now. Steam a parallel course until we take down the ship. How copy, over?"

"*Fuente*, this is *Chiriquí*… I copy, five-by-five. Will stay on this station, relative to the target, out."

"Robinson, this is *Fuente*… Launch now and orbit Flat Top, over."

"*Fuente*, this is Robinson… Roger, out."

Carl would have both support platforms in position before making the same wide turn Rosa had made just a few hours before.

The approach to—and takedown of—the Chinese vessel had been a fortuitous dress rehearsal for what was to come.

Twenty minutes later, they were running south-southwest at just fifteen knots—a holding pattern. Carl waited not so patiently for confirmation that both the patrol boat and the Blackhawk were on station. Both transmissions came to him seconds apart. Hanging up the headset, he directed Rosa to begin a wide semicircle on the east side of the target ship. *Chiriqui* passed them regular updates on the ship's target angle, course, and speed as they traced the long arc that began their chase. The ghost ship was not wavering its course or changing its speed. It was clear to Carl that the target was locked in, now headed directly for the canal entrance, less than fifty miles away.

There were only two ways this would end, thought Carl. Either he and his team would stop the ship or the vessel would crash into *Miraflores* lock, possibly exploding on impact. He didn't want to think about what might happen after that. He was nearly certain this was the suicide ship attack they feared. But near certainty was the best he could do. Given the stakes, that was more than enough to use every tool in his tool kit. This was to be a life and death struggle. Carl wanted to come out alive, but that didn't matter anymore—as long as the attackers died first.

Nothing is simple. Nothing is certain.

Rosa had a smile on her face as she pushed the throttles forward. They were *all* smiling in the dark as the go-fast went faster. Seconds later, when the assault boat was on step, all the smiles disappeared, replaced by a calming focus. The minutes ticked by in their heads as Rosa continued to receive tracking information from the *Chiriqui*. They were all belted in, standing up. Carl and his men wore body armor over green fatigues, still without insignia. The sneakers had worked well on the fishing vessel, so they hadn't changed back to jungle boots. Each had a squad radio attached to his web gear. MP-5s were slung around shoulders. As before, SIG Sauer pistols rested securely in thigh holsters in case they needed secondary weapons. There was no requirement for handcuffs. Without saying it, the four of them understood that none of the terrorists would make it off the ship alive. They would try to save the crew, but that was considered a bonus.

They bounced violently through the darkness on the back end of the approach.

"*Fuente*, this is Robinson… Suggest I keep my orbit at three thousand feet."

"Robinson, this is *Fuente*… Roger three thousand… Go ahead. Break, break… Can you have M-21 ready to provide limited, on-call sniper support, over?" Carl was beginning to think he'd made a mistake by not insisting on mini-guns. But he'd been in a hurry. *Hindsight is always twenty-twenty*! Perhaps, a single rifle shot could make the difference. Colonel Stewart had not operated in the field for a long time, but he still knew how to shoot.

"*Fuente*, Robinson… I will prepare to close and take out individuals topside if needed. Tell me when to descend from high orbit, over."

"Robinson, *Fuente*… I will board the ship, then advise…out."

The spray flew higher as Rosa adjusted course closer to the wind. Suddenly, they were directly behind the target, catching up fast. Carl checked his watch again: 0120. They would be going in blind with no idea how many hijackers—and how many innocent crew members—were actually riding the ship. Carl had learned that a mini-bulk carrier of the size they were about to board normally carried a crew of eight to ten. He knew that the crew would be a mix of Nicaraguans and Filipinos. He did *not* know where the terrorists would be…or what they would be wearing. He assumed they would be armed…but with what?

This is going to be messy.

Billy Joe, riding nearest the bow, noticed it first. Bioluminescence, strung out in a line, leading them to the target. There was no stern light on which to focus. In fact, there were no lights at all. The *Sixaola* was churning through the relentless sea at "darken ship." A sign, but not a good sign. Soon they could *feel* the ship's wake. Foaming salt water, blazing a smoother trail to the objective. Rosa applied more power. The sound, they hoped, would be muffled to some extent by the ship's machinery. A single shooter on the stern could foil their approach…and alert the attackers. Jerry and Jose drew their pistols. Billy Joe readied the caving ladder…in case they had to climb. Juan, a quartermaster by training, stood next to his wife, wearing body armor and packing only a pistol. He would take control of the ship—after Carl and his men took it away from the men who wanted to use it as a weapon.

"Robinson, *Chiriquí*, this is *Fuente*. Commencing final approach, over."

"Robinson, roger, out."

"*Chiriquí*, roger, out."

Rosa closed the last two hundred yards between the assault team and the black shadow in front of them. Billy Joe could see that the starboard quarter of *Sixaola* would require a long climb. They could do it, he thought, but getting five men on the main deck would take too long. He knew that most small "bulkers" had a low waist amidships. Less freeboard. Faster transition. Better odds. Tinker turned and shouted at Rosa to take them one hundred feet farther ahead. She responded immediately by adding still more power. In a few seconds, the team was even with the ship's waist, and Rosa slowed abruptly to match the speed of the target. Everyone but the pilot unbelted themselves and waited for Billy Joe.

Now off-step, the assault boat bounced violently next to the ghost ship as Rosa somehow managed to avoid crashing into the hull. Without hesitation, Billy Joe, a virtual human fly, reached for the gunwale above his head and vaulted onto the main deck. Helping each other, the rest of the team quickly followed, forming a tight perimeter on the steel walkway.

Rosa veered away from the ship's hull but kept station just fifty feet off the drop point. The only thing trickier than delivering the team would be getting them back—or not. Rosa wore the same body armor as the others, but for now, she was the most exposed.

The team huddled for only a few seconds, unslinging their MP-5s and checking their gear. Jerry and Jose reholstered their pistols.

"Tinker and Bosco, go to the engine room and stop the ship," ordered Carl.

"Got it, boss," replied Billy Joe. And they were gone, searching for the ladder beneath the ship's bridge.

Carl looked at Jerry and then at Juan. He could barely make out their faces in the starlight. "You guys follow me!" And he ran to the ladder leading up to the bridge.

Rosa circled back and restationed the assault boat directly behind the target, one hundred yards away. Hidden by the night. Out of pistol range. Ready for the pickup, should it happen. Waiting for the ship to slide to a stop.

So far, there was nothing to indicate they had been detected. Carl stopped at the watertight door on the starboard bridge wing and glanced behind him to make sure his teammates were ready. As rehearsed, he thrust the door handle aside and burst into the dimly lit space, submachine gun shouldered. Jerry and Juan ran in right behind him.

Carl's worst nightmare rocked his consciousness.

The man at the helm had a long gun stuck in his back. The bearded man behind him saw Carl and immediately unlatched a hand grenade from his vest! Then he shouted at the top of his lungs.

"Do not move! Drop your guns, or I will shoot the captain!"

Neither Carl nor Jerry saw an angle they could use to shoot the hijacker...without losing the ship's master. Carl briefly considered shooting both of them...but hesitated. He did not have enough information yet to deal with the worst possible outcome. He needed to keep the captain alive...at least for now. *Shit*!

Carl and Jerry slowly laid their submachine guns on the deck. Juan, without an assault weapon, did nothing. The terrorist smiled as he regained control of the bridge. Standing up, Carl scanned the space again and found a second man lurking in the shadow of a bulkhead, pointing an assault rifle at him.

The man behind the captain confirmed that he was in charge.

"Put your hands in the air!"

Jerry and Carl stood next to each other, in front of Juan. Both of them were doing what they'd been trained to do: de-escalate the situation but plan for carnage. Carl maintained eye contact with the leader while Jerry shifted his focus between the other two men on the bridge—one innocent and one condemned. Juan, hidden from view by his teammates, peeled off the Velcro strap on his thigh holster.

"We are going to strike a blow against the infidels who occupy the sacred land of the Prophet Muhammad… Peace be upon him. There is nothing you can do about it!"

Carl sensed an opening. Rational argument was a form of de-escalation—and a method of finding things out. Maybe it would give him enough time to orient, decide, and act. Enough, he hoped, to give Billy Joe and Jose time to stop the ship…and to make sure it could not be started again. Time was now the only weapon available to him. Was there a rational argument to be had?

"And just *how* do you plan to do that?"

The zealot took the bait. *They want to talk…to justify what they're about to do.* Fanatics, thought Carl, just kill people and break things; zealots explain first.

Especially suicide attackers.

"We are going to ram this ship into the Panama Canal…that is how."

"But the canal locks are too strong… You will not make a dent in those steel gates." The argument was gaining steam.

"The ship is rigged with explosives… We intend to make more than a dent."

Fuck!

"But why target the Panama Canal? What have the Panamanians ever done to you and your land?"

"Panama is another American colony…just like Saudi Arabia. We hate them for supporting the world's biggest infidel."

Carl had no clever response for that one. "But why kill men from Nicaragua and the Philippines? They've done nothing to deserve that."

The seconds ticked by. Valuable seconds. But Carl needed *minutes.*

"We have already killed the crew…except for the master. We prefer to keep Captain Sandoval alive in case we decide to communicate with the authorities." The leader jabbed the barrel of his weapon into the master's back.

Carl was learning here. The killing of the crew would mean that terrorists were in the engine room. Billy Joe and Jose would have to kill them in order to stop the ship. Carl didn't know how much time they'd need to do that, but he continued to stall.

Sandoval, still on the helm, became agitated. He was no longer frozen in fear. He began shouting in broken English. "They killed my sailors but spared me! They forced me to load fertilizer into the forward hold! They will kill hundreds more innocent people!"

The Arab man behind him smashed the back of the master's head with the butt of his AK. "Shut up, infidel! We do not need you after all."

The master slumped to the deck. His captor stood firm.

Carl's nightmare got worse as the man brought the grenade to his beard and pulled the pin with his teeth!

Carl, Jerry, and Juan froze. The grenade pin bounced off the deck, next to the limp body of the Nicaraguan.

"*Now* who will steer this ship?" demanded Carl, eyeing the spoon of the grenade, still inside the man's palm.

The terrorist leader looked at him with hate Carl had not seen before—not in Grenada, not in Panama, not in Colombia. The man then pointed his weapon at Jerry Tompkins.

"*You* will…big man!"

Jerry stepped to the helm and stood next to the master, now writhing in pain at his feet. He took the wheel and brought the ship back a few degrees to starboard. Back to the track that was taking it right to the Panama Canal!

Carl tried to reason one more time with the evil man in control. "You will not get close to the canal, you know… I have men in the engine room. They will stop the ship."

The wild eyes opened wider against a forest of facial hair. Holding the weapon in his right hand, the man abruptly swung the barrel and aimed it at Carl's head. The grenade—still without a pin—threatened from his left fist.

Jerry moved with lightning speed. He grabbed the man's fist with his enormous right hand and drove his left elbow into the exposed temple. The man went down hard, but Jerry could not maintain his grip.

The live grenade bounced onto the deck!

Carl dived behind the chart table, drew his pistol, and came up shooting.

Jerry turned instinctively to fall on the grenade at his feet. Before he could smother it with his bulk, the master rolled over and absorbed the explosion with his own body.

Jerry landed on top of the Nicaraguan and felt the man's heroic life suddenly end.

In the same instant, Carl put two rounds into the second gun-man's chest…then spun around to find Jerry punching the life out of the lead hijacker. Captain Sandoval's blood gushed onto the rolling deck, mixing with rivulets of terrorist blood.

Carl then shouted the orders that would save the canal.

"Juan, take the wheel and execute a Williamson turn."

"Aye-aye, sir." The quartermaster ran to the helm and spun the wheel hard to port. The deck—with bodies sliding in their own blood—heeled heavily to starboard.

The ship was still making fourteen knots. There was a bomb rigged to explode in the forward hold.

What now?

CHAPTER 33

CARL'S SQUAD RADIO came to life. "Carlos, Bosco, we're in a firefight down here, boss. Tinker can't get to the control panel."

"You need reinforcements?"

"Maybe…these guys are shooting at us from the other side of the engine room. Plenty of cover for us…but also for them. It's a Mexican standoff."

"How many tangos in the engine room?"

"Two…we think."

"Got it, Bosco. Give me a few minutes to get Jerry down there. Juan now has the wheel, and the ship is turning away from the canal, but we need to get control of that engine room!"

"Yeah, Carlos. I got that. Tell Jerry to call me from the top of the ladder."

"Roger that… Carlos out."

Carl was continually assessing the situation. He now had control of the bridge. He did not have control of anything else. Two terrorists were dead, and there were at least two more shooting at his men in the engine room. Carl knew nothing beyond that. He needed to find out, but he only had four guys. He would have to use them individually as well as collectively.

Jerry was ready to go—despite having just tried to fall on a grenade! Carl would have to stay with Juan in case additional gunmen stormed the bridge. Whatever else happened, the team could not afford to lose control of the helm. The ship was now headed back along the wake it had laid down. Carl wanted to keep it that way.

"Butkus, you heard Bosco on the radio. Get down there and help him win that fight. Tell me what you need to do that."

Juan turned to both of them. "I don't see a way to override the control room. We'll just have to ride this bronco until one of you cuts off the power at the source."

Jerry ran to the starboard watertight door and down the first ladder. Carl ran to the port bridgewing and scanned fore and aft. No activity. Coming back into the pilothouse, he found a dogging wrench and wedged it into the door handle.

Juan was looking at the radar scope. "At this speed, we have clear sailing on present course for another hour or so, Carlos. I recommend we just keep what we have."

"Concur," said Carl, trying to calm himself. The flurry of action just concluded had shaken him more than he would ever admit. "By that time, our guys will have thrown the right switches down below."

Carl checked in with the assault boat. "Rosa, Carlos, tell me where you are now."

"Carlos, Rosa, right behind you at one hundred yards, over."

"Stay there and monitor. We're still trying to stop this beast. Carlos out."

He took the radio handset. "Robinson, *Fuente*, *Sixaola* now proceeding away from the canal. Repeat, away from the canal at fourteen knots. Still trying to stop the vessel. Big explosive charge in the forward hold. Will report when rendered safe. Pass update to Ned, over."

"*Fuente*, Robinson, roger, out."

Things were moving too fast…and too slow. Strategy worked slowly; tactics exploded like fireworks, again and again in different forms. Carl was trying to think two or three moves ahead, but this was not a game of speed chess. There were too many things he still did not know. He needed to get a fire team up to the forward hold. They would have to figure out quickly what the hijackers had done with the fertilizer. And what about the firing mechanism? Was it rigged for command detonation? If so, was it time fuse or electric? Or…was it somehow connected to a plunging device?

Those were the options. None of them were good. As a saboteur, Carl would have chosen the plunging device. He knew the "Tamil Tigers" of Sri Lanka were using suicide boats to sink naval and merchant ships in their terrorism campaign against the Sinhalese government. The Tamil boats were rigged to explode on impact; there was almost nothing the target crews could do to defend themselves. Now that he had diverted the ship's course, Carl was *hoping* the saboteurs had chosen the plunger. They had planned to ram the locks, after all. Carl would just have to make sure the ship didn't ram into something else.

But there was still a large explosive charge waiting for them in the forward hold.

"Bosco, Butkus, I'm at the top of the engine room ladder."

"Butkus, Bosco, wait for my signal then climb down. You'll see the control panel in the middle of the space. Tinker and I will draw fire away from you."

"Got it, Bosco. Waiting here." Jerry was staring straight down to the greasy deck plates of the engine room, listening to his teammates battle at least two gunmen. The space was better illuminated than the pilothouse had been. The large diesel engines continued to apply power to the ship's propeller. Jerry wasn't worried about his teammates losing the firefight. He was worried about making it to the deck plates, ready to help them win it. The ladder was vertical. Ship's crew would back down safely. Jerry would have to descend facing forward. Then he would have to find the emergency cutoff switch on the control panel. If there was one.

"Butkus, come down now!"

Jerry, already sitting on top of the scuttle with his MP-5 at the ready, took two steps down the ladder then jumped a dozen feet to the bottom. He landed on his feet in a deep squat and stayed there. Scanning for targets with the barrel of his weapon, it was clear to him that Tinker and Bosco had drawn enemy fire away from the control panel. Jerry could tell the difference between the enemy's louder AK ricochets and his teammates' lighter 9mm rounds. With an abundance of cover and concealment, the shorter 9mm barrels were better. But the tangos would have more ammunition! The big man knew that no one could hear him over the screaming machinery. But he didn't have a lot of time.

He ran to the control panel like a predator on the chase.

"Tinker, Butkus, I'm in front of the control panel and can't find an emergency stop lever! I can shoot the controls, but I don't have much ammo and don't know where to aim, over."

It took almost a minute for Billy Joe to come back. Jerry took cover as best he could and listened for the heavier ricochets. "Butkus, the emergency stop lever should be right in front of you. It will be in Spanish. Bosco says to look for *Parada de Emergencia*. Can you find that? Do *not* shoot up the controls... Repeat, do not shoot the controls! We'll need power again to get out of this situation."

"Okay, Tinker. Looking now, over."

Jerry looked up, down, and sideways on the panel. He found it. The switch almost came off in his iron grip. The diesels, suddenly deprived of fuel, began to die.

"Tinker, I got it. Now let's wax these guys."

"Butkus, work your way over toward Bosco and me. The bad guys are trying to kill *us*. I don't think they realize you're there... We'll keep 'em looking this way."

Enemy confusion is your friend.

Jerry crept along the control panel and down the outside walkway, port engine to his right, bilges below. Carefully, in a low crouch, he made his way to a concealed position at the far edge of the machinery. The firefight proceeded in slow motion, a single shot here, a single shot there. Jerry whispered into his radio in the temporarily quiet engine room.

"Tinker, Butkus, now directly across your position. Recommend you press with three-round bursts to flush them out. Recon by fire. If they move at all, I should be able to see them, over."

"Roger, Butkus, stay covered."

Jerry saw the results of their plan almost immediately. The requested bursting fire came from over and around the starboard engine assembly. He kept his head down...but only for a few seconds. As the friendly fire waned, he detected movement at the back of the space, behind the lube oil pumps. Then one of the tangos started running.

Right toward him!

Jerry leaned to his left and cut the man down with two shots in the chest. The second man shifted his fire as Jerry ducked back into his cover position. The heavy round slammed into the engine block just above the big man's head. Jerry leaned out again and sent a back a three-round burst toward the man now facing him.

Jose stood up and drilled two 9mm slugs into the exposed terrorist's back.

Four down...not sure how many to go.

"Good shooting, Bosco," radioed Jerry. "Did we get everyone down here?"

"Yeah, man," responded the medic, amped up more than usual. "Now what?"

"Tinker and Bosco, fall in on my position. I'll find out what Carlos wants to do with the forward hold."

Billy Joe and Jose ran to Jerry, and the three of them moved to the control panel. Jerry called Carl.

"Carlos, Butkus, two dead tangos in the engine room. Engines offline. Ready to go forward. Please advise, over."

"Butkus, without the engines, we've started to drift. All navigation and running lights are now back on, but the ship cannot maneuver to avoid collision. Before we restart the engines, the forward hold will have to be secured. We do not know how many tangos there are up there, but my guess would be only two, maybe three. Tell me if you need backup, over."

"Carlos, Butkus, recommend you stay put. We can deal with the hold, but it would help to have some fire support topside. If we can't wax them all, we'll try and flush the rest into the open. We gotta get rid o' these guys before we can tackle the explosive, over."

"Butkus, you should be looking for a main charge, connected to a plunging device at the bow. Remember the Tamil Tigers. I think this ship is rigged to explode on impact, over."

"Got it, boss. Will report when we know what we have up there, out."

Carl made a second call.

"Robinson, this is *Fuente*... Are you tracking us, over?"

Colonel Stewart came right back. "*Fuente*, Robinson, we see you on the FLIR scope, almost dead in the water."

"Robinson, we still gotta deal with the forward hold. They have a main charge rigged, we think, to explode on impact. My men will try and flush tangos topside. Request you move to my position and hover above the fo'c'sle. Can you get low enough to pick them off with the M-21, over?"

There was silence on the line as Stewart consulted the pilots. Carl knew it would be a tricky maneuver, but he trusted all of them. He needed to put the enemy in a sandwich, killing them wherever they tried to run.

Stay focused!

"*Fuente*, Robinson, descending now. Will hover as low as we can, ready to provide sniper support, over."

"Robinson, *Fuente*, your sidekick is also a crack shot. Request the major take aim as well, over."

"Will do, Carlos. Out." In his mind's eye, Carl could see Reginald Stewart smiling at Ana Maria as he handed her a rifle."

Carl made a third call—this time in Spanish.

"*Chiriquí*, this is *Fuente*... Confirm you are tracking target ship. We are moving forward to defuse the explosive device. Will advise when we have total control and the ship is no longer a threat, over."

"Fuente, this is *Chiriquí*... We have target ship DIW. Thank you for that. Standing by for your orders as soon as you have full control, over."

"*Chiriquí*, this is *Fuente*. Roger, out."

Jerry led Billy Joe and Jose along the outside catwalk and down the ladder to Hold No. 1. They stopped at the watertight door and prepared their weapons. Without a breaching charge, they would lose the element of surprise. So be it, thought Jerry. Just get it done.

Speed without haste.

Jerry wasn't sure the enemy even knew they were there. Jose had inspected the bodies in the engine room and found they did not have squad radios. That was a good sign. But the hand grenades they'd found on the bodies were not at all a good sign. Suicide terrorists, wading into a pile of explosive mixture, ready to blow themselves to kingdom come! He had tried to fall on a grenade to save his teammates on the bridge, but there would be no way to save any of them if the whole front end of the ship went up.

Billy Joe had an idea. "Butkus, let me go back up the ladder and try to access the hold from the top."

"Can you do that, Tinker?" Jose was nodding vigorously.

"Yeah, I can do that. There should be a scuttle I can open then a ladder I can climb down. We need to hit them from two sides at the same time...okay?"

"Okay, Tinker, but let me check with Carlos first."

Jerry lowered his face to the squad radio and spoke softly, "Carlos, Butkus, we're at the door to the forward hold. Tinker wants to go in from topside while Bosco and I enter from here. Any problem with that approach?"

"Butkus, Carlos, wait, out." The Blackhawk was slowly lowering itself to a stable position fifty feet above the bow of the ship.

"Robinson, *Fuente*, I have one man going into the hold from topside. Do not engage until I give you clearance, over."

"*Fuente*, Robinson, understood. Will wait for your signal, out." The Blackhawk held its hover...with two M-21 rifles trained at the top of Hold No. 1.

Billy Joe scrambled up the ladder to the main deck. The helicopter's deafening downwash almost blew him off the fo'c'sle. He reached the scuttle and called Jerry.

"Butkus, Tinker, ready to go in, over."

"Tinker, Butkus, go now!"

Billy Joe threw open the scuttle and hurried awkwardly down the ladder, aiming his MP-5 with one hand. In the same moment, Jerry and Jose opened the door to the hold and burst in. There were two terrorists in the far corner, taking aim at Billy Joe. Tinker's teammates cut them down with four shots. Untouched, Billy Joe thudded to the floor of the hold.

"Carlos, Butkus, Tinker is in the hold. Anyone on the fo'c'sle is now a target, out."

Carl passed the word to Stewart and Castaneda.

"Fall in on me!" shouted Jerry. Billy Joe ran to join the others. The three of them stood in front of the explosive pile of fertilizer and diesel fuel. Two black wires led from underneath the pile in the direction of the bow lazarette. Billy Joe and Jose moved carefully around the pile, tracing the wires—without disturbing the main charge. Jerry covered them, glancing up through the open scuttle to where the night sky should have been.

The Blackhawk was low enough to block his view of the stars.

Billy Joe and Jose followed the wires to the door of the lazarette. They knew the wires would be connected to booster charges, buried in the fertilizer pile. Probably, small blocks of TNT, wired together in series. The firing mechanism would have to be a plunging device, located somewhere forward of the storage locker. Maybe just a pressure switch.

But where?

"Butkus, Bosco, the wires lead through the lazarette. We're going in to find the switch."

"Roger, Bosco, do it. I'll be here if you need me." Jerry had to make sure no one followed his teammates into the lazarette—or escaped by climbing the ladder to the main deck. As a team, they had killed six tangos. They had to find out if there were any more.

Billy Joe and Jose burst into the lazarette…just in time to see the hatch above them closing!

"Butkus, there's another tango escaping the lazarette to the fo'c'sle!"

Carl heard the transmission and passed the word to the Blackhawk.

Colonel Stewart leaned out the starboard side of the hovering Blackhawk. Major Castaneda manned the portside door. Both were belted to leashes, with M-21s shouldered, scanning for targets.

The escapee ran into Ana Maria's crosshairs first. Without hesitation, she fired one 7.62 NATO round into his chest. The man fell in his tracks. As she lowered the weapon and surveyed the scene, there was no movement. Calmly (and surprised by that), she looked up at Reginald Stewart. The colonel gave her a thumbs up.

"*Fuente*, Robinson, one tango dead topside, over."

"Robinson, *Fuente*, well done, sir! I think we got all of 'em, over."

"*Fuente*, Robinson, you'll have to thank the major for that one, over."

Carl's love for Ana Maria surged. He took a quick glimpse of his new life and permitted himself a smile. Juan, still at the helm, did not notice. Carl looked at his watch: 0330.

Then he was back. "Tell the major I'll give her my personal thanks later. First, we have to defuse this bomb and figure out what to do with the ship. Please return to high orbit and stand by for further instructions. *Fuente*, out."

CHAPTER 34

THE RACING BOATS arrived at the island of San Andrés in the early morning, *La Madrugada*. The wet and tired crews had made the crossing from Bluefields in a little more than three hours. The Colombians had allowed their Arab students to drive most of the way, learning how to leap over the waves without burying themselves in salt water. Having delivered the boats and prepared their surrogates, the three men stepped up onto the dock and carried their duffel bags to a waiting taxi. They would enjoy the island for a few days before flying back to Barranquilla and then to Pasto. Jorge Mena Velasquez would be proud of them.

At least he wouldn't have them killed.

The Arabs (one of whom looked South Asian) took turns walking off the cramping effects of a high-speed run over moderate seas. There would be a longer leg to endure, beginning in less than one hour, six o'clock in the morning. Roughly six hours at sea...if they managed to find the target. And they would have to perform their duty at the other end. That would require them to stand up long enough to fire the anti-tank rockets.

The residents of the marina, having been awakened early by the sound of the boats, asked themselves what was going on. But they said nothing. Fast boats came into their marina all the time. The island was part of Colombia, after all, and it lay right in the path of *narcotraficantes*, ferrying drugs to the United States.

But these boats were not headed for the United States.

The silent bearded men, still in Western dress, ate their last meals and prayed surreptitiously in the boats. Just before dawn, the three craft cleared the marina breakwater, each driven by a single pilot. Each with three long boxes lashed to the deck. They fell into a parade file and slowly came up to speed. As they rounded the point, ocean waves began to build. The lead boat turned south-southeast with the others following at two-hundred-yard intervals. A formation shaped like a long sword. The same kind of sword used by the Prophet and his companions. *Inshallah*, they would make it all the way to the *Rio Chagres*. The three pious Muslims would go out in a blaze of glory. Thereafter, they would swiftly join their heroes in paradise.

* * *

Carl had two more calls to make. The canal may have been saved, but the ship was still very much in jeopardy. Juan remained at the wheel, but he couldn't steer as the ship wallowed in the trough. They weren't going anywhere, but they needed a stable platform to secure the forward hold.

"Butkus, Carlos, send Tinker to the engine room. We need the engines restarted and connected to the helm. As soon as I get Tinker's report, Juan will maintain bare steerageway downwind. That will give you a stable platform to work on. How copy, over?"

The squad radio was a party line. Billy Joe was on his way before Jerry responded.

"Carlos, Butkus, Tinker just left my position. I will wait until we have a smooth ride before attempting to defuse this thing, over."

"Butkus, do you need me up there?"

"No, sir, we're okay for now, over."

"Carlos out." As soon as he signed off, Carl grabbed the VHF handset.

"*Chiriquí, Fuente*, what is your position?"

"*Fuente, Chiriquí*, I am eighteen miles southeast of you. Where do you want me, and what can we do?"

"*Chiriquí, Fuente*, make my position soonest. Stand by five hundred yards south while we disarm the forward hold. Request you prepare to take control of this vessel after that. You know better than I do what can be done with a ship full of explosives, over."

"*Fuente, Chiriquí*, roger all that. We will move in and board on your command. Once we have control, you can withdraw. You are welcome to ride home with us…but it may be a while, over."

"*Chiriquí*, good copy. Thanks for the offer…but we have a faster way home. *Fuente* out."

Rosa, monitoring VHF from her station behind the *Sixaola*, mirrored Carl's optimism and gave herself a sigh of relief. She would see her husband again. Indeed, she would be giving him a ride back to the *Luisa*! This was not over yet, but things were looking up. All she had to do was wait until Carlos called her back in for the pickup.

Tinker made it to the engine room in just over three minutes. As a veteran mechanic, it didn't take him long to figure out how to restart the engines and reconnect them to the bridge. The inert bodies of dead terrorists and Filipino crew members lay behind him on the deck plates. On his way out, he drew his pistol and put one round into each terrorist head. Just in case.

"Carlos, Butkus, this is Tinker. Engine room back to normal. Be advised there will be no watch section down here until we finish work up forward. On my way there now to help Butkus, over."

"Tinker, Carlos, coming to new course at bare steerageway, over."

"Carlos, Butkus, will report as soon as we render safe the forward hold, out."

Jerry and Jose waited for Billy Joe. Three minutes later, they huddled next to the pile of fertilizer. "Carlos said to look for a plunging device forward of this space. That could be a pressure switch, attached to the bow." He looked at both his teammates in the dim light of the hold. "It's still dark out there, but one of us needs to trace the wires onto the main deck until we find the trigger."

"Can't we just cut the wires here and pull the boosters out of the pile?" asked Jose. "I don't think these guys are sophisticated enough to rig a second electric source to go off when the wires are cut."

"It would be great to have an EOD guy," added Billy Joe. "But we don't. I think Jose is right… We should just cut the wires."

Jerry thought about this for a few seconds. "You're right… We can find the plunger later to add detail to the after-action report. The sooner we cut those wires, the better."

Billy Joe, who never went anywhere without his Leatherman, walked calmly to the forward bulkhead of the hold, bent down, and snipped the two wires leading to the fo'c'sle.

Nothing happened.

Jerry and Jose slowly pulled the booster charges out of the pile. Then the three of them wrapped the eight TNT blocks in wire and carried them up the ladder to the main deck. Without any hesitation, they dumped the explosives over the side.

"Carlos, Butkus, forward hold defused and secure, over."

Carl took a deep breath, held it, then let it go until his lungs were empty. He did it again. Then he turned to Juan.

"Now we have to rendezvous with *Chiriquí* and transfer a prize crew to *Sixaola*. What's the best course and speed for doing that?"

Juan responded right away, "We should be steering into the wind at five knots. The patrol boat should come alongside from astern. Starboard side would be better than port. You and your team can stand by at the gunwale, same point where we boarded, to help them up. I think they'll need a total of six sailors. Two for the bridge, two for the engine room, and two deckhands."

"Thanks, Juan. I'll pass that to the skipper." Carl finally smiled. "You're coming with us in Rosa's boat."

Carl looked at his watch again: 0645. The sun was rising behind the *Serranía*. He could already feel the heat that came with it.

"Butkus, you and Bosco join me on the bridge. Send Tinker to the engine room to stand watch. *Chiriquí* will come alongside and transfer six crew to take control of this vessel. Tinker will stay below until relieved. How copy, over?"

"Got it, boss. On our way, out."

The transfer of the six-man prize crew went smoothly. Carl and Jose had to do some interpretation but by 0900, all the Panamanians were at their stations. Carl and his men shook hands with their reliefs then moved to the starboard waist. Rosa's pickup run was flawless. The men were feeling the afterglow of a critical mission accomplished. Flat Top was a half hour away, over the waves at close to fifty knots. Once there, they could start to relax, after twenty-four hours of nonstop action. Carl allowed himself to think about Ana Maria. He had accomplished his last mission. It had been, by far, the most memorable.

Before they got to Flat Top, Carl received a radio transmission that almost knocked him down.

"*Fuente*, Robinson, we just got an alert from the Caribbean side. The Panamanian patrol boat *Bocas del Toro* has reported three high-speed surface contacts, apparently coming from San Andrés, headed toward Colón. Multiple attempts to raise the contacts on Channel 16 have failed. *Bocas del Toro* is on course to intercept the boats. We must assume hostile intent, over."

Carl's perfect world suddenly exploded in front of him. He knew immediately that he had made a mistake. Perhaps a fatal mistake. He'd been taught that the best way to take out a linear target was to attack both ends at the same time. The Panama Canal was the ultimate linear target. He and his men had foiled the enemy at one end…but not at the other!

Never underestimate the enemy, you dumb shit.

Time to move!

"Robinson, *Fuente*, request you land at Flat Top and pick us up. Also, prepare to mount miniguns, both sides, on arrival at Howard. No time to lose. See you at the LZ, over."

"*Fuente*, Robinson, Wilco. Inbound Flat Top now. Will wait for your arrival, out."

Twenty minutes later, Rosa slowed the go-fast in front of the gravel beach at Flat Top. The Blackhawk was sitting on a level pitch in the middle of the tiny island, engines on. Carl, Jerry, Billy Joe, and Jose—with full kit—jumped in the water and swam to the beach. Juan stayed with Rosa, loitering off the island on standby.

Carl and his men ran up the steep backshore to the Blackhawk, now turning its rotor blades. Colonel Stewart and Major Castaneda ushered them into the bird. Carl sat next to Stewart as they all donned headsets in order to hear each other. Everyone belted into their seats. He reached for Ana Maria's gloved hand and squeezed it. She wore a worried face, but her eyes were filled with tears of relief. He smiled. Then he looked away.

Focus!

He heard Stewart's booming voice in his ear. "The ordnance people will meet us on the tarmac, Carl, but there's no time to mount miniguns. You'll have to do with M-60s."

Carl didn't have much time to think about that. "Yes, sir, make sure they give us at least eight hundred rounds per gun."

"Got it, Carl. Will do."

The situation was materializing in Carl's head. He spoke to himself…and to everyone on the aircraft. "We have to assume the worst-case scenario. That would be a standoff attack on the *Gatún* dam. The go-fast boats coming out of San Andrés are not heavy enough to damage the structure, even if they could get to it. The spillway will prevent them from driving the boats all the way in. The only way to breach the dam would be to fire missiles or rockets from the boats. We didn't consider this kind of attack a possibility." Carl looked around the crowded passenger compartment. "And that is my fault."

"We *all* underestimated these guys," responded Stewart, quickly. "Thanks to the *Bocas del Toro*, we have a chance to stop them." The colonel turned to Ana Maria. "Major Castaneda has been key to this whole operation…from liaison officer to sharpshooter."

"That's not a surprise to me," replied Carl, nodding. He locked eyes with Ana Maria. "Thank you, Major. We could not have done any of this without you."

Ana Maria knew how to count heads. The mad dash to the Caribbean would take Carl and his three men, along with fast ropes and rifles for four. Mounting the machine guns on each side would reduce the amount of space even further. At least some of the team would need extra room to fast-rope onto the objective. Either she or Colonel Stewart would have to stay at Howard.

"Thank you, Commander…but we're not finished yet. I want to go with you to the other side." It was a statement. Carl looked at her and recognized the determination on her face. He was not sure yet exactly what they would do at the objective; he was *very* sure it would be dangerous. He wanted to protect her. But he could not leave her off the bird.

Carl looked at his mentor. "Colonel, it's either you or the major. We can't fit you both in."

Stewart really wanted to go forward with the team. He was feeling the pull of the field again, after so many years behind a desk. They were about to conduct the most important operation of his professional life. But he realized that his presence would not be critical. He trusted Carl completely.

"Then take Major Castaneda. God is with you…and He doesn't need a seat."

Carl smiled at his boss. A preacher in the making. Then he looked into Ana Maria's fiery eyes. "Okay…just sit tight while we mount the M-60s. Carl grinned at her. You may end up with hot shell casings on your lap." He didn't need to tell her how easily they could all be killed.

"You'll be too busy to talk to the patrol boat," added Ana Maria.

"Of course, Major. I want to know as soon as they intercept the hostiles." Formality was the only way he could focus on the tactical situation. For the next two hours, he would need superhuman powers of concentration.

Carl took a quick glance at this watch: 1015 already! The distance from San Andrés to the mouth of the Chagres River was about three hundred nautical miles. The attacking boats were capable of fifty knots in the open ocean. He did the math. Carl's team would have to be there before noon.

Better, well *before* noon.

Minutes after leaving Flat Top, the Blackhawk flared to a fast landing at Howard. The ordnance specialists and their machine guns were waiting. Olive-drab cans of 7.62 belted ammunition were lying on the asphalt in front of them. The pilots kept rotors turning, engines at full power. Nobody moved as the machine guns were mounted on either side of them. Once the M-60s were in place and loaded, Jose checked the coiled, heavy-braid fast ropes. All four SEALs laid down their MP-5s and picked up scoped M-21s. Whatever they were about to do, it would be done with heavier ammunition at longer range. They slung the rifles around their shoulders and prepared for action. Again.

The Blackhawk lifted off and pointed its nose toward the Caribbean entrance to the Panama Canal. Carl noted the time again: 1105. It would take the Blackhawk thirty minutes to reach the Caribbean Sea. In his head, Carl was still working out the actions they would take when they got there.

This is going to be close.

CHAPTER 35

THE BLACKHAWK RACED across the isthmus of Panama at more than one hundred miles per hour. Low-level flight over the rainforest adjacent to the canal made it feel even faster.

For Carl, it was not fast enough. They would be there before the go-fast boats...but not by much. He used the flight time to decide how to use his small team in the most effective way. They'd have only one chance to stop the attack; they needed to get it right. Carl spoke into his headset.

"Major, can you get us an update from the *Bocas del Toro*? We need to make a better estimate of when the boats will get to the river mouth."

"Got it, sir. Wait one."

Two minutes later, Ana Maria was back on the line with a startling report. "Sir, *Bocas del Toro* says they just tried to intercept the boats. The lead boat abruptly slowed down and fired something at the patrol boat." Her voice betrayed a deep sense of fear—even doom. "The captain called it a standoff weapon, but he doesn't know what kind. He said the shot missed them...but not by much. The attack boats came back up to full speed, and *Bocas* can't catch them." She paused. "What are you going to do, *Carlos*?"

Carl had less than one minute to decide. The only course of action burst into his head.

"Butkus, we're going to rope you and Tinker onto the *Gatún* Dam. Bosco will drop the ropes and give you the signal to jump. You and Tinker will set up with M-21s in the best positions to take out the boat drivers, if they make it that far. You'll be the last line of defense. The fact that they planned this for broad daylight means to me they're not very experienced in firing whatever it is they're going to fire at the dam. The daylight will help you kill them before they do that."

"Got it, boss… Good to go," responded Jerry. "Whether it's TOW missiles or AT-4s, these guys will have to stop the boats and stand still long enough to get off a series of accurate shots."

"They made a mistake trying to take out the *Bocas del Toro* at sea," added Carl. "But the dam is an easy shot."

"Butkus and me'll be waitin' for 'em," added Billy Joe, flashing a grin.

Carl nodded visibly. "Bosco and I will man the M-60s while the Blackhawk searches for the boats. I'd rather find them in the open ocean, but we may have to take them out in the river. You and Tinker should plan worst-case…for three boats, each with at least one crew member. We'll try and wax 'em all before they get to you."

"Carlos…the *Bocas del Toro* reports that the boats are twenty miles off Fort San Lorenzo, headed for the mouth of the Chagres at fifty knots."

"Thanks, Major… We might not be able to beat them to the river. I need another update before we get there."

"Roger that, *Carlos*." Ana Maria felt the same unexpected exhilaration she'd experienced hovering above the rogue ship, aiming a rifle. This time, the feeling was magnified by her love for Carl. She had never seen him so animated.

He's giving this up just for me.

The Blackhawk was now streaking across Lake *Gatún*, straight for the critical node in the whole canal system. Billy Joe had dismissed the threat to the dam by saying that someone would need a missile to breach it. Now someone was about to do exactly that! Speeding toward the dam with multiple standoff weapons. Missiles or maybe rockets. Carl and his team had stopped the hijacked ship at the Pacific end, but that had not been the main attack. Ramming the *Miraflores* lock would have done major damage to the canal; taking out the *Gatún* dam would destroy it.

"Bosco, get ready to rope these guys down. Butkus and Tinker, take your positions." The pair, now wearing heavy gloves, stood across from each other in front of open doors.

Carl directed the pilot to do a rapid flare and hover just fifty feet above the dam. As soon as forward motion ceased, Jose threw out the thick ropes on both sides. Carl's snipers grabbed the heavy braid at eye level and disappeared beneath the chopper.

Jose watched them go.

"Butkus and Tinker on the deck!" His teammates hit the ground running. Jose unclipped the ropes and watched them fall behind the shooters. Without slowing down, Jerry and Billy Joe ran right past the surprised Panamanian police who had the good sense not to shoot them.

"Get us downriver as fast as you can fly!" said Carl to the pilots in his command voice. "Maintain this altitude." The thick jungle rushed by them as the Blackhawk raced along the smooth surface of the river. The Chagres would not be smooth much longer, thought Carl, if the attackers delivered their ordnance on the dam. What had been a wild river before the canal was built would again become a destructive torrent…draining the lake.

The canal would be no more. The holy warriors would be martyred. Jorge Mena would have his money. Panama would be in chaos. The United States would lose a strategic waterway. Manuel Noriega would have his revenge.

Carl and Jose took their positions behind the belt-fed machine guns and strapped into safety harnesses. Carl spoke to Ana Maria without turning his head. They needed one more update.

"Where are the boats now?"

Ana Maria came back to him after just a few seconds. "Boats are adjacent to *San Lorenzo*!"

San Lorenzo, a fort with pirate history, marked the entrance to the Chagres River. They would have to take out the attackers inside the river's banks. This is better, Carl rationalized, as he switched off the safety on his M-60. The river was only a couple of hundred feet wide.

"There they are!" shouted Ana Maria into her headset, pointing ahead. Carl leaned out the door and saw one of the three boats—but not the others. Another nasty surprise.

Not fish in a barrel!

"Bosco, how many do you see?"

"Just one, boss. You want me to take him?"

"Yeah, kill that one while I look for the others."

The Blackhawk made a low-level run-in to the target. Jose opened up on the racing boat, raking it with automatic fire from well within the weapon's effective range. Even running at fifty knots, the target was an easy kill. Suddenly dead in the water, the boat's gas tanks exploded in a yellow fireball as the Blackhawk passed overhead. Jose could feel the heat from the wreckage.

Carl was searching frantically for the other two targets. "How many in the boat, Bosco?"

"Just one...just one."

The riverbanks went by at sixty miles per hour. Carl—joined by Jose and Ana Maria—looked left and right into the blurred lines of trees on either side of the Blackhawk. A lot of foliage for a small craft to hide behind and underneath. *These guys have some training.* The attackers had obviously seen or heard them coming. Now it was a game of cat and mouse.

One down, two to go.

Carl was getting very nervous. He directed the pilot to reverse course and fly back down the middle of the river at slow speed. Fingers on triggers, Carl and Jose scanned for targets. They could reasonably assume that each boat had only one operator...but Jose's kill had told them nothing about the armaments the attackers had brought to the scene.

They were about to find out.

Without warning, a comet came streaking out of the trees on Jose's side and sheared off the helicopter's tail! The aircraft yawed right and rolled left. Too low to autorotate and cushion the impact, the pilot managed to fly his crippled machine to a crash landing at the edge of the river. The chopper lay on its left side, half in and half out of the water.

Jose regained his senses before the others. Everyone else was underwater! He unstrapped himself, took a deep breath, and submerged. Reaching for Carl's harness, he released the buckle and dragged him to the right door, open to the sky. Jose laid Carl on the outside skin of the aircraft and began administering CPR. Within seconds, Carl was conscious and breathing on this own. He had not been underwater long enough to drown.

Carl sat up like a rocket. Jose had to move quickly to avoid being knocked out. Carl shot glances fore and aft as he recovered his situational awareness. They were sitting on top of what looked like a beached whale.

Ana!

Carl suddenly rolled over and dived into the flooded carcass of the aircraft. He was thinking like a fighter pilot in a dogfight—acting without thinking—to pull Ana Maria from the wreckage. He did not hear Jerry's call.

"Carlos, Butkus, Tinker and I are set up and waiting at the dam. How copy, over?"

Nothing.

"Carlos, we're at the dam, ready to fire. How many boats can we expect? How many men per boat? Over."

Nothing.

Jerry soon got the answer to his question…but not from Carl. Two go-fast boats came roaring right at them from around the shallow bend in the river. He and Billy Joe were perched some twenty feet over the water on either side of the massive structure, just above the spillway. Through binoculars, they could see that both approaching craft had only one occupant. The drivers would have to stop the boats and pick up whatever standoff weapons they had. The *kind* of weapons didn't matter anymore. Surely, someone had done the research. At less than one hundred meters, a high explosive charge could be fired accurately. One well-placed round might weaken the dam to the point of failure. There was room for multiple projectiles in each boat but only one shooter.

One for each of us.

Jerry and Billy Joe shouldered their M-21s and followed the attackers through scopes. The targets, now framed in each shooter's reticle, grew larger with steady bearing and decreasing range—decreasing very fast! Jerry was tempted to start shooting before the boats came to a stop, but he had the discipline to wait. He and Billy Joe were lying prone, about seventy-five meters apart. The geometry worked. They would each have a good angle on both targets…and the enemy would not be able to kill them both with a single shot.

Just a little farther, you son of a bitch!

Three hundred meters out, the boats danced into a line abreast without slowing down. *Who trained these guys?* Billy Joe's trigger finger itched. The boats kept coming. *They don't know we're here!* He leaned into his right shoulder and spoke.

"Butkus, as soon as the guy on the right stops, I'll take him out."

"Okay, Tinker, I got the guy on the left."

Both targets started to slow around 150 meters from the dam. It took another 50 meters for the drivers to reverse engines and bleed off the speed. Less than a minute later, the boats sat dead in the water, rocking gently back and forth.

The calm before the storm.

Billy Joe squeezed the trigger…just as the bearded figure bent over to pick up his weapon! A loud crack came from the supersonic bullet as it zinged over the man's back. Now the attacker knew that Jerry and Billy Joe were there. Both drivers knew.

Shit!

The attacker in Billy Joe's target took cover behind the gunwale. Even a 7.62 mm round could not easily penetrate multiple layers of fiberglass and foam, built to withstand the stresses of open-ocean racing. Billy Joe kept the crosshairs right where the man had disappeared, waiting for him to pop his head up. Instead of the man's head, Tinker's scope found the business end of an AT-4 rocket launcher!

Billy Joe's nervous system instantly processed the muzzle flash. Reflexively, he ducked behind an iron strut. The high explosive shaped charge flew over his head…then over the dam behind him.

That was close!

Shouldering the rifle again, Billy Joe regained his sight picture. The backblast from the weapon had burned through the other side of the boat, leaving a jagged, smoking hole. The shooter had survived the fiery ricochet, but not by much. Severely shaken, he broke cover for a battle damage assessment. Billy Joe put one round through the man's head.

"Got him, Butkus!"

From his own perch, Jerry trained his weapon on the other boat. Alerted to their presence, his victim had also taken cover. Jerry waited a few seconds…then decided to change tactics. *Take advantage of the angle*! Knowing now what they were up against—and having witnessed a wild rocket flying by—the big man shifted his crosshairs to the extra gas tanks sitting just forward of the engines. He fired three times in rapid succession.

The boat exploded in a yellow ball of fire. Both shooters were dead. The dam was intact. The canal would not be destroyed.

But there was nothing to celebrate.

Two questions rushed into Jerry's overloaded brain. *What happened to Carlos? How do we get back to the Blackhawk?*

"Tinker, we're done here. Still nothing from Carlos. We need to get back to the chopper…fast."

"Butkus, we'll have to swim out to the go-fast that's still afloat. I think the engines are okay."

"Got it, man. No time to lose!"

Jerry climbed down, around the spillway and into the water. Billy Joe did the same on the other side. They met halfway to the smoldering hull and swam together. Even with all their gear and no fins, they made it to the wreck in under five minutes. Billy Joe tossed his rifle over the side and jumped in behind it.

He landed on the terrorist corpse.

Sliding all over the bloody deck, Billy Joe pushed the body into the water then turned and reached for Jerry's weapon. Billy Joe pulled the big man into the boat and scrambled to the controls. He hit the ignition and was greeted immediately by the music of internal combustion. His music. He rammed the throttles forward and felt the elation that comes with speed.

Downriver—the faster they went, the higher the crippled craft came out of the smooth water. Only the keel and three very large propellers skimmed the surface. Three minutes later, just beyond the last bend, Billy Joe's elation came to an abrupt halt.

Jerry stopped breathing.

Before them lay the downed Blackhawk, lying on its side in the shallow water. The tail was gone, the main rotor shattered. It was the ugliest sight they had ever witnessed. Death hung in the still air.

"Carlos! Bosco!" screamed Billy Joe as he pulled the racing boat alongside the wreckage.

Jerry saw them first. Jose was in the water with the surviving pilot, having buoyed the man with his own inflatable life jacket. The other pilot was obviously still belted into his seat near the bottom of the river. Carl was on the riverbank giving CPR to Major Castaneda. Even from thirty yards away, Jerry could see that she was not responding.

"Tinker, leave me with Carlos. Then go help Bosco!"

Billy Joe landed Jerry next to Carl on the bank then motored slowly to the front of the Blackhawk. Jose brought the pilot to him in a cross-chest carry. Billy Joe pulled the young warrant officer into his boat while Jose submerged again for the other pilot. After his second dive, Jose swam the dead copilot's body to Billy Joe's outstretched hands then jumped into the boat.

Jerry watched Carl with anguish as he worked furiously to bring Ana Maria back to life. He knew before Carl did that she would never come back. His boss—and his friend—was suddenly without the woman he loved. Jerry reached out with one hand and patted him gently on the shoulder.

"She's gone, Carl. You've done everything you can."

Carl stopped pumping Ana Maria's chest and looked into her lifeless eyes. The eyes that had always captivated him would never see again. Her death was the death of his very future. He didn't want to live. He wanted to be with her.

Staring straight ahead, Carl gave Jerry what he thought would be his final words. "I heard you and Tinker coming. I knew right away that you had completed your part of the mission. Well done."

In a monotone Jerry had never heard, Carl had one more thing to say. "I should have killed them all before they got that far. I should have known the main attack would be on the dam. Ana's death is my fault. Our job is done…but there's nothing left for me here."

Carl removed his hand from Ana Maria's face and reached for the secondary weapon in his thigh holster.

Jerry grabbed him by the wrist before Carl could get his fingers around the handgrip and trigger guard. He would not let this happen!

"She'll be up there when your time comes, boss." The big man looked at the sky. "We have work to do here. She helped us save the canal. And remember, she warned us about all the bad people in Panama. She can't stop them now…but we can. You and I owe that to Ana Maria."

Carl looked at Jerry for the first time. There were tears in his eyes. He bent slowly to kiss Ana Maria on the forehead. Then he stood up and turned around. A different face looked back at Jerry. Carl's game face. "You're right, Butkus. We have work to do."

Jerry could see that his boss would never be the same. Carl had already buried the sadness, but Jerry knew it would linger beneath the warrior's mien. Carl's humor would come back eventually, he thought, but the man Jerry so revered would have a hard time figuring out how to turn this tragedy into something productive. Jerry didn't know exactly what Carl would do…only that he wanted to be there to help him do it.

A loud, low-frequency whopping sound came from beyond the trees. Carl and his men looked up to see a double-bladed Chinook helicopter preparing to land in the field behind the riverbank. Even before the tail ramp came down, they all knew that Colonel Stewart had come to take them home.

EPILOGUE

January 1994

THE PASSENGER IN seat 29B stared out his window at the blue emptiness of the Caribbean Sea. Carl Malinowski, LCDR, USN (retired) had dealt with the one-two punch of losing his future wife and leaving the Navy career that had sustained him for twenty years. Now he was simply depressed, a long-term condition that he did not expect to abate any time soon. The ocean view from thirty-five thousand feet centered him, but it did nothing to dent his sullen mood.

Half Italian, Carl had always laughed easily. He'd always tried to see the bright side of things, even as the world around him seemed to be falling apart. Unexpectedly, his own life had fallen apart, and there was no bright side to pretend to see. The honor of military service, combined with the long thrill ride of special operations, had given Carl a life jacket to deploy when most of those around him were drowning in despair. The day he saved the Panama Canal—but lost Ana Maria—was the day he'd plunged into sorrow deeper than the sea. He dwelled there now as the plane began its descent into Miami International Airport.

The longest and saddest day of his life should have been a cause for celebration rather than a gut punch. His men had performed brilliantly, moving with speed (but not haste) from one tactical problem to a second, completely different one. The stakes—and the pressure—could not have been higher. Juan and Rosa had been a surprising but indispensable gift. He had gone out of his way to get the husband and wife team rewarded for their bravery. Carl had never been religious, but he believed there was something at work beyond the clouds that he did not understand. The series of missions they'd just completed could not have been successful without at least some divine fire support.

Carl, the former agnostic, had prayed for Ana Maria's soul and thanked the Lord for sparing his teammates. He had never known Father Castillo, but it comforted him to know that Ana and he were in the same place for eternity. If he could deal with his own demons, perhaps one day he would join them. Carl's life was at a tipping point. His mother was dead. His father was a drunk. He had no brothers or sisters. Only his teammates would miss him when he was gone. Ana Maria would reside comfortably in his memory. He would never say her name out loud again.

Freddy Alegre had made a full recovery and had returned to guiding large ships through the Panama Canal. Strengthened security at both ends of the waterway would continue, and the *Servicio Maritimo* would strengthen its surveillance regime in the Pacific and Caribbean approaches. With young professionals like Captain Alegre and the crews of *Chiriquí* and *Bocas del Toro* leading the way, the future of the canal—and Panama itself—was bright.

The six cartel prisoners awaited extradition to Colombia. They were happy not to have died from thirst on the island where Carl had left them (and continued to believe their rescue was a miracle). No one ever found out what happened to the Colombians marooned at *Bahía de Santa Cruz*. The government of Panama had learned the Pakistani citizens were wanted for insurgent activities in Kashmir. Their capture in *Darién* had resulted in extradition to India—and justice—rather than terrorism. Having seen firsthand the threat, and the power, of terrorists bent on suicide, Carl had begun to study more seriously the emergence of a mysterious group of Muslim zealots, calling themselves *Al Qaeda*.

The future, he believed, did not look good for the West.

The Chinese fishermen had provided an almost comical inter-lude for Carl's team. But the government of Panama—with its his-tory of pirates and plunder—had taken their crimes very seriously indeed (the very word *Panamá* translated as "abundance of fish"). Carl had insisted that *Chiriquí* take full credit for protecting the country's marine resources. The illegal fishing vessel would remain impounded until the Chinese government paid a million-dollar fine.

The *Chiriquí* had taken custody of the mini-bulk carrier *Sixaola*. With assistance from the Panama Canal Commission, the vessel's crew had off-loaded the five-ton mixture of fertilizer and diesel fuel, dumping it far out to sea. The ship had been returned to its Greek owner and continued to transport grain throughout the region. Carl's account of Ernesto Sandoval's heroism on the bridge had led to the award of a posthumous medal of honor by the Nicaraguan president...and to warmer relations between the governments of Nicaragua and Panama.

On the strong recommendation of Pablo Céspedes, Carl and his team had received Panama's highest civilian award, presented by the president of the republic in a secret ceremony. Reginald Stewart and his commanding general, along with Ned and his station chief, had been the only US government attendees. Stewart had just learned he would be promoted to the rank of brigadier general and assume com-mand of SOCSOUTH. Carl wished he could continue to serve the man who'd mentored him and supported his team so professionally.

Ana Maria Castaneda was given a stone memorial, prominently located at Fort Amador. The inscription read:

Major Ana Maria Castaneda, Public Forces, Panama
For acts of extraordinary bravery in the service of the republic

With supreme irony known only to the departed, Ana Maria's small monument would stand for generations right next to the statue of Omar Torrijos.

Carl was on his way to Washington, DC. The CIA station chief had recommended that he be interviewed by the deputy director of operations for a "contract" position with the agency. Carl's exploits were already well-known at Langley; the interview was just a formality. It had been explained to him that, as a contract employee without a "non-compete" agreement, he was obliged to make himself available for field operations when the CIA needed him…but that he could also pursue professional opportunities elsewhere.

He was about to become, for all intents and purposes, a mercenary.

The agency had made it known that Carl would be able to use his own team. He knew, better than anyone, how much work waited for them downrange. The prospect of performing dangerous but critical missions for the US government—using CIA's rules—softened the personal blows he had just sustained. He was, for now, a broken man. But he would still have three of the things he valued the most: violent exercise, tropical birds, and fieldwork. He would gladly have traded all of them for Ana Maria. With effort, he would try to enjoy what he had left.

But there was something he needed to do first.

He drove his rental car to the Miami Federal Correctional Institution and parked in the same lot as Father Castillo and Ana Maria before him. He concentrated for a few minutes on her image then brought up the pockmarked face of Manuel Noriega. He forced himself to temper the fury welling up inside him. *Anger without rage!* Carl was not looking forward to meeting with the man who'd started all this, but he owed it Ana Maria—also, to himself. He'd played a small role in taking down the dictator—and a much bigger role in stopping Noriega's spiteful act of revenge. Carl needed to sit across from the prisoner and tell him he had wasted a lot of money. When he felt his anger under control, Carl got out of the car and walked quickly into the prison lobby.

"*Buenos días, señora*. I have a ten o'clock meeting with the prisoner Noriega," said the visitor.

"Good morning, sir. Please sit down. I will call you when the general is ready."

Carl thought it odd that prison staff would refer to the prisoner as "general" but then remembered Ana Maria telling him that Noriega always wore his old uniform when meeting with visitors (his lawyers had argued that, as a "prisoner of war," Noriega could be given this privilege). Carl had taken the time to pin the Panamanian Medal of Honor to the pocket of his white guayabera. Noriega would know that Carl had received the medal from the justly elected leader of Panama—a country the former strongman would never see again. Noriega would not be intimidated, but Carl wanted to send him a message.

"The general will see you now, sir."

Carl passed through the metal detector without having to forfeit his medal. He walked into the office of the deputy administrator to see Manuel Noriega remain sitting on one of the two chairs in the room. Carl overlooked the slight and sat down across a desk from the man in uniform. He caught a momentary glimpse of Noriega's insecurity as the prisoner noticed the gold hanging from Carl's chest. A good start to the very short conversation he intended to have with the man who'd made him both a hero and a victim (Carl hated both words).

"Good morning, Commander," said the prisoner in Spanish.

How did he know I was a naval officer?

"I am no longer a commander, sir…and you are no longer a general," replied Carl in English, a language he knew Noriega understood.

Noriega's pineapple face lit up as he found an opening. "But I am still in uniform, and you are not. I suppose 'Mr. Malinowski' will do."

"You can call me whatever you like," said Carl dismissively. "But I am free to go wherever I want…and you are stuck *here*."

Noriega's smugness disappeared. "I am a prisoner of *war*…still serving my country! I am proud to render that service inside this imperialist fortification."

Carl cut to the chase. He didn't want to debate the prisoner… even if Noriega had been a real POW. Carl began speaking precise Spanish; he wanted the prisoner to understand everything perfectly. "I came here to tell you in person that your plan to destroy the canal has failed."

"I read about it in the paper, Mr. Malinowski."

Carl had expected that response and had prepared his own. "Ah, yes…but you don't know *everything* about it. That, I am sure, has caused you great anxiety."

Noriega had regained some of his cockiness. "Yes, I admit that not knowing everything is painful to me…as an intelligence officer."

Carl pounced, "Then you will be interested to know that your friend, Jorge Mena Velasquez, elaborated a scheme far beyond your own imagination. You asked him to destroy the canal, but you did not tell him how to do it. He devised a brilliant plan…using very little of your money. And now the government of Panama has seized the rest of your numbered bank account. It is Mena, not you, who gets the credit for nearly taking down the canal. He is a billionaire, living in a villa. You have lost fifty million dollars and still live in this prison."

Carl stopped long enough to see Noriega's chest heaving with extra adrenaline. "So now you know some of the details… You want more?"

"Yes," responded Noriega, barely controlled. "I always want more information."

Carl's eyes narrowed as he delivered it. "Father Castillo was gunned down on the street by a Colombian hit man."

"That was a tragedy."

"That was your buddy Mena. He murdered your childhood friend just for taking a letter, from you, to Pasto. Then one of his *sicarios* tried to kill Major Castaneda!"

"I do not believe you!" shouted Noriega. "Panama City is full of murderers, especially now that I am no longer in power."

Carl went on, "Mena contracted FARC dead-enders to kidnap a canal pilot in order to discover the canal's vulnerabilities. Then the kingpin provided an opportunity for his Middle Eastern contacts to order suicide attacks on both ends of the canal… You knew he was smuggling Muslim extremists into Central and North America, did you not?"

"¡*Si…por supuesto*!" came the reply. Carl could see on Noriega's face that he had not known about the terrorists.

"I don't believe you," said Carl evenly. "You did not know everything *then*…and you will never know everything ever again."

Noriega shot him a more confident look. "I know that you were Ana Maria Castaneda's partner in espionage." To Carl, hearing Ana's name from Noriega's lips was like being stabbed in the gut. The dictator twisted the knife. "She had been passing secret information to *you*, her lovesick American spy, before the invasion to take me down." Noriega sat back. "She was just a common whore."

It was Carl's turn to be surprised. After a brief pause, he said what he had always believed. "We are *all* Americans…Latin or otherwise! My country gave birth to yours, and we have long wished for your success. You could have become the great elected leader Panama has always needed…a democratic Torrijos. But you became a monster, just like your cartel friends. It was always about information… the money and the power it could bring. Ana Maria died a hero. She gave her life for something larger than herself. For Panama. You never believed in anything but yourself! You will die a villain…in this place." Carl swept his arm at the bare room, emphasizing the point.

Manuel Noriega said nothing. Carl struggled to keep his growing rage where it belonged. He almost spit in Noriega's cratered face. Leaning forward, he had one more thing to add. "Sooner or later, justice comes for everyone who plays by the rules of the jungle. Morality is all that stands between us and the animals."

Carl stood up abruptly and walked out of the room. He did not turn around as Noriega began screaming at him. He had an appointment at CIA to keep.

There was a lot more work to do in the jungle.

ABOUT THE AUTHOR

PAUL SHEMELLA LIVES in California with his wife, finally settled after more than forty years of traveling on behalf of the United States government. He was a Navy SEAL for more than half that time then taught government responses to national security threats all over the world. He has written important textbooks on terrorism, maritime security, and African governance. Now in retirement, he writes thriller fiction. *The Dictator's Revenge* is a prequel to *Jungle Rules*, published in 2018, and the final book in *The Jungle Rules Trilogy*.